The Adventure of
The Bloody Tower

Dr. John H. Watson's first case

by
Donald MacLachlan

First published in 2013 by
The Irregular Special Press
for Baker Street Studios Ltd
Endeavour House
170 Woodland Road, Sawston
Cambridge, CB22 3DX, UK

ISBN: 1-901091-59-7 (10 digit)
ISBN: 978-1-901091-59-5 (13 digit)

Cover Concept: Antony J. Richards

Cover Illustration:

Typeset in 8/11/20pt Palatino

To the father I never knew, Alastair Robert Anderson MacLachlan, DFC, Path Finder Force pilot in the RAF, shot down by a night-fighter over Munich, Germany, on September 6, 1943. He managed to hold his damaged Lancaster bomber steady enough so that the crew could bail out, but he could not escape himself. I was 10 months old at the time.

About the Author

Sheffield-born Donald MacLachlan's interests in Sherlock Holmes and Dr. John H. Watson came after a ride on a London Underground train in 1955, when he was 13 and his family lived in Earl's Court.

The eastbound District Line train from Earl's Court went through what was then an open triangle of land bounded by the Earl's Court, Gloucester Road and High Street Kensington stations. (Later, the triangle was covered from 1957-84 by the BEA West London Air Terminal, and the site now houses a Sainsburys shop.)

This triangle, Donald thought, must be where foreign spy Hugo Oberstein supposedly heaved the body of Arthur Cadogan West onto the roof of a briefly stationary Circle Line train. This in the Sherlockian tale *The Adventure of the Bruce-Partington Plans.*

Donald found that 'Caulfield Gardens', Oberstein's street, did not exist under that name. But there were indeed houses with rear windows that overlooked the Underground tracks (although the story confuses the issue of exactly *which* track.) Happily ignoring all the *No Trespassing* and *Danger* signs, and carefully crossing the live rails, Donald explored the area. Only to determine that it would take a man of superhuman strength to toss a body onto the roof of a train anywhere there.

That led to further and deeper interest into the Holmesian stories. Then, later, he heard how Jeremy Potter, chairman of the Richard III Society from 1971-89, had invited a senior member of the Sherlock Holmes Society of London to a Richard III Society dinner. That, in turn, led Donald to a study of Richard III, and the thought that Richard's *alleged* murder of The Two Little Princes in the Tower was a mystery worthy of Mr. Holmes (or, indeed, of Dr. Watson.)

A move to Canada in 1962, and a journalism career that ended in 1993, interfered with further research. During a subsequent career in public relations (the last stop as director of public affairs and media relations for Canada's Simon Fraser University) he gathered boxes of books and research material, and in 2007 began bit by bit to write this book.

Now retired, Donald and wife Cailleach (who is herself working on a historical novel about the Glencoe Massacre of 1692) live in White Rock, British Columbia, with 19 large bookcases – and more of them in mind. He is a member of the Sherlock Holmes Society of London and of several Richard III societies.

Donald also has plans to write another adventure of Mr. Sherlock Holmes, involving him in a famous real-life murder case, and for three historical novels to follow that.

Chapter One

Eagerly I sprang to my feet in the crowded, sweltering and gassy Shoreditch Music-hall, in response to an impassioned and urgent cry that rang from the stage. "Is there a doctor in the house?"

"I am a doctor," I shouted hastily, raising a proud and prominent hand on high. The actors stopped, confused, glancing in puzzlement at me and at each other. Only then did I understand, mortified, that theirs was not an authentic appeal; it was merely a supposedly comic line in the remarkably vulgar act.

I can look back now with a wry smile at my blushing humiliation before scores of cackling, finger-pointing Londoners. And, worse, before a roaring dozen of my fellow medical students, who had chosen this low venue to celebrate our final examination results and to launch our new careers in an atmosphere thick with smoke, sweat, beer and onions.

The incident comes wistfully to mind whenever I have occasion to tell my friend Mr. Sherlock Holmes that he is lucky to have a doctor in the house at 221B, Baker Street; a doctor who can, and does, keep a watchful eye on his health, and is ready, no matter how brusquely treated, firmly to order him to rest and to recuperate from his constant overwork.

It was my own health, however, that was the more troubled in the summer of 1883. Holmes had kept me exceedingly busy on a skein of trying cases in the preceding months. The consulting detective, who was now working on a difficult case of embezzlement, was dog-tired, irritable and snappish. I, depressed also by a deep disappointment in my personal affairs, was truly brought low.

I had sought to divert myself from my depression by compiling notes on a most *outré* case of murder and attempted murder upon which Mr. Holmes (with me and my revolver in support) had been engaged early in the spring. The murderer's foul *modus operandi*, and his horrible choice of a poisonous snake as his weapon, were truly bizarre, fantastic, even lunatic; yet a young woman had died, almost on the eve of her marriage. Her twin sister had been saved only by the skill and determination of Mr. Holmes; and justice had been visited upon the cruel and choleric murderer by his own serpent. It had struck me that if I had Mr. Holmes's permission, and that if names, dates and circumstances were suitably disguised, I might submit this story to a magazine for publication as fiction. Thus I might increase my limited income and rely somewhat less on the unremitting generosity of my good friend. However, depression soon returned, and on this particular July day, despite the advanced morning hour, I had declined breakfast, and lay spiritless and despondent in my rumpled bed.

I had received a long letter from my old friend Stevenson, in France, reporting upon his own health, which, happily, was somewhat improved since the winter. He expressed his gratitude, once again, both for my professional advice and for my past praises of his adventure story of the one-legged sea cook and the tropical island of pirate treasure. Stevenson told me that yet another tale of adventure for boys by "Captain George North", his *nom de plume*, was beginning its appearance as a serial story in *Young Folks*. I had sent out for the edition of June 30th of this juvenile magazine, and finally began dejectedly to read Stevenson's historical tale of *The Black Arrow* when Holmes bounded up the stairs and erupted loudly into my hitherto silent room. He announced that I must immediately accompany him on yet another expedition that promised more long and wearing hours. I regret to say that I simply blew up at him.

"Holmes, blast it, I cannot. You have worn me out. I am done in. I must have a rest; no, a proper holiday. You may go out on your own, and you are welcome to it. I shall finish my reading on Jon Amend-All and his Black Arrow, and then, this very day, I shall pack a bag and take a train to the seaside somewhere. I shall see you in two weeks time."

"Oxford," said Holmes, blandly.

"Oxford?" I returned, puzzled, and somewhat nettled at the offhand manner in which he greeted my unusual emotional outburst. "What has Oxford to do with it? Oxford is nowhere near the sea."

"True, my dear Watson, but it is where I recommend that you and I begin this little holiday of yours."

"You and I?" I exclaimed, rolling reluctantly out of bed and aiming my feet at my comfortable old slippers. "We? Well, I should be delighted if you would accompany me, most delighted. You most certainly need a holiday, too; but what of your cases, your work? And why Oxford, may I ask?"

"Because we have an intriguing invitation to visit there," replied Holmes, with a sudden twinkle in his eye.

He went to the ornate Sheffield-plate letter tray as we entered our living room, and passed to me an opened cream envelope. "It is from my old sparring partner in Oxford, Masterman-Pugh, who has proposed a brief visit, and has included you, my dear and very tired friend, in his invitation. Work can wait; I seem to have mislaid my few skills anyway."

"Sparring partner?"

"Edward Masterman-Pugh and I were intellectual sparring partners at the University," said Holmes. "We were not close friends – I had but one, a chap called Trevor – but we did form our own private debating society, as it were, and fought many a strenuous battle of words and ideas with each other. I found his cerebral company both stimulating and challenging, and he mine. He is, *pro tem.*, a Fellow at Magdalen. I imagine everybody there detests him."

"Detests him?"

"Oh, indeed, Watson. He is quite the most arrogant and infuriatingly superior man I have ever known; outside myself, that is." Holmes smiled easily. "He is also, outside my own family, quite the most naturally intelligent man I have ever met."

Holmes began to fiddle with the ugly bronze ink well on his cluttered desk. I winced, awaiting the inevitable spill. My friend is a tireless fiddler, constantly picking objects up and putting them down again in the wrong place; he cannot stay still for a minute. Except when he is transported by good music, his hands, eyes and brain are constantly on the move.

"Holmes, do put the blessed ink well down," I commanded him, wearily.

Holmes obeyed, hastily apologizing. His lofty brow knitted. "On second thought, Watson, perhaps a visit to the abrasive Masterman-Pugh would be far from a holiday for you. Better the seaside, although, in July, it would surely be far too crowded."

"Holmes, I am intrigued, I admit it. Someone who draws from you such high praise, and high criticism, must be a man worth meeting. Oxford it shall be, then; but I shall be most careful to pack my swimming suit, and to flee at once for the seaside if he is one half as unbearable as you suggest."

Holmes and I laughed together. "Good old Watson," cried Holmes, clapping me on my pajama-clad shoulder. "Why, you are in better health already. We can go on to the seaside after Oxford, if you wish. I shall send a wire to Masterman-Pugh at once. Shall I call down for a late breakfast for you? Or is it an early luncheon?"

Masterman-Pugh's reply stated that he would hope to see both of us on the 24th of the month. Magdalen's hospitality then would extend, he added, to what he described as a special and unusual dinner in Magdalen's Hall.

Then his beautifully scripted letter offered an intriguing challenge:–

> "Your professional services may be called upon to resolve a most puzzling criminal case: the mysterious disappearance of two young brothers, some time ago, and perhaps their foul murder by their own uncle."

Mr. Holmes laughed in delight.

"The question is: Is Masterman-Pugh playing games? Or does he mean it? I can think of no such disappearance in the area of Oxford, and certainly of no such murder. I shall examine my records, but surely I should be aware of such an unsolved mystery. Aha, Watson, perhaps we face another challenge."

"Holiday," I replied, wearily. "A holiday, not work; not a challenge, and not another case."

"Very well, Watson," said my companion. "You win. But you never know –" his voice trailed off. "It might be –"

"Holmes, you are incorrigible."

The detective looked up apologetically from the puzzling letter.

"You know, Masterman-Pugh would have made an excellent consulting detective if he had chosen so to apply himself. Alas, I regret to say, while he has his good points and can be most generous, he is a living caricature of supercilious academic snobbery. What he thinks of Army physicians, I hesitate to imagine. What little he thinks of consulting detectives, I am afraid that I already know."

The ominous thought began to restore my dejection. Holmes then kindly and manfully tried to cheer me up, fussing over me like a solicitous mother hen, and playing for me his own most spirited and uplifting solo version of the third movement from Mendelssohn's lovely violin concerto.

Magdalen College was all that Holmes had spoken of, and everything that an Oxford college should be, with its fine

Founder's Tower, its echoing and beautiful chapel, and the soothing play of light through the arched openings of the flagged cloisters. Its dignified Perpendicular Gothic architecture was engaging. Its lichened, crenellated walls were studded with fantastic gargoyles and grotesques, of abbots and apes, of bishops and beasts, of mitres and monsters. It was a quiet, soothing world, and upon entering it I felt strangely at peace, if a little nervous at the prospect of encountering the daunting Masterman-Pugh.

I found that Masterman-Pugh was also all that Holmes had described. I have encountered some exceedingly strange customers in my time, and many of them have been inflicted upon me by the detective and his cases. Masterman-Pugh eminently so qualified. He was remarkably tall, taller than Holmes by two full inches, gangling, jerky in his movements, never still. Like Holmes, he was always moving and fiddling, his eyes constantly roving, and his mind, clearly, always at full gallop. No wonder, I thought, that he and Holmes had gravitated together; two rushing rivers of nervous energy clashing together in an intellectual whirlpool of argument and debate. And his voice! A sneering voice of pretentious accent, more offensively "cultured" than that of any starched young society snob. It was a voice that dominated conversation, made it clear that its owner suffered not fools gladly; and implied that, in Masterman-Pugh's world, everybody but Masterman-Pugh was by definition a fool. He spoke, even to one person, as if addressing a large and slow-witted audience, and with painfully pedantic exactitude.

He greeted us cordially enough, however. His small but comfortable rooms were fastidiously tidy. While Holmes's part of our Baker Street quarters was a hopeless mess of books and papers, strewn at random as if by a tempest, Masterman-Pugh's immaculate mahogany desk and table bore precise pyramids of books; the largest book at the bottom, the smallest at the top. His bookshelves were not sorted by author or by subject, but uniformly had the tallest books at the left, the shortest at the right. Masterman-Pugh even used his pocket-handkerchief, needlessly, to dust our chairs as he showed us to them.

Mr. Holmes and Masterman-Pugh touched verbal foils, and fenced with each other over names and arguments from the past, and more created on the spur of the moment. Musing over Masterman-Pugh's *fino* for almost an hour, I could see why they suited each other so well as intellectual sparring partners. As they tussled, Masterman-Pugh's acid voice soon became less urgent, and Holmes's more relaxed, too. I could even follow some of their inductive flights, but carefully stayed neutral on the touch line, watching and listening and occasionally nodding.

"Time for dinner," Masterman-Pugh declared at last, consulting his watch and meticulously polishing it with his handkerchief before returning it to its pocket. "President Bulley is a brilliant man. But he is a devil for punctuality, and reprimanded me for supposed tardiness upon one occasion. I disliked his tone, and, in consequence, I make it a practice to be precisely one minute late for engagements with him; but for your sakes, gentlemen, we shall be on time tonight. We are, after all, honouring a royal visitor."

I was about to inquire as to the visitor's identity, when Masterman-Pugh continued.

"I cannot imagine why Magdalen would want to honour a reputed murderer, but so be it."

I gasped. "A reputed murderer? We are to entertain a murderer? A royal murderer, you say? A royal murderer, really? Here? On the loose?"

"Oh, a murderer several times over. And I think he will entertain *us*, rather than we entertain *him*. We must go. Follow me."

Chapter Two

Masterman-Pugh's promise of a special and unusual dinner was duly delivered.

We dined in the lofty Hall, empty and echoing in this time of the long vacation. I had what was, I confess, an especial thrill of delight at being escorted to the High Table. This brought back the most nostalgic memory of my first elevation, in school, to the offices of Prefect and, coincidentally, to Captain of the First XV. I do not know which position afforded the greater sense of honour; perhaps the captaincy of the rugby team, for as a slogger rather than a natural athlete, I had not at all expected it. I remember well my first dinner at Head Table in school. I was seated in the least prestigious of the scarred old chairs, true, and in the draughtiest position by the servants' door, as befitting the most junior and raw prefect; but I felt nonetheless extraordinarily elevated as, from the däis, I surveyed the ranks of chattering boys below us in Hall. It was there that Watson, John, school number 31, began to learn something of leadership, and of the values of honour, tradition, and patriotism. I took those lessons seriously (more seriously, perhaps, than the lessons in class, for I was there, too, a slogger rather than a natural "brain") and they have stood me in good stead to this day.

I was seated towards a corner of Magdalen's deeply polished High Table. John Rigaud, the Dean of Divinity, an accomplished humourist with an infectious laugh, was at my left. Henry Wilson, the gentle junior bursar and librarian, and son of the Bishop of Glasgow, was beyond him. Masterman-Pugh was at my right, and at his right was Holmes, looking dapper and handsome indeed.

While I have seen Holmes in every imaginable disguise, from the foul rags of an ale-swilling tramp to the silver-buttoned plum jacket of a prim porter at a gentlemen's club, I must proclaim that he looked entirely comfortable and "in the right place" in evening dress. So do I, I believe, if with some vanity. I certainly enjoy the leisurely formality of dressing for dinner. We occasionally dress for dinner in our own simple bachelor diggings in Baker Street; at least, we do so when we know that we will be able to dine together at an agreed time. I particularly take pleasure in dressing for the theatre or a concert, although at a full guinea for a seat in the stalls, it was then a luxury in which I could all too seldom indulge. My medical practice was still largely limited to sporadic positions as a *locum tenens*, my wound-pension was small, and my share of the rent left but little change out of two pounds a week.

Our dinner companions at Magdalen that night, a dozen at the High Table and more below, were a most engaging, amusing and liberal company. It was now possible for a layman to be a fellow, but five of the first eight Magdalen men introduced to me were clerics and a sixth, Yule, the senior dean of arts, told me of his own private pursuit of religious studies.

"Venison!" I exclaimed, when Dean Rigaud advised me of what was on the menu. "Masterman-Pugh promised us a special dinner, but venison I did not expect."

The dean of divinity laughed warmly. "It is not merely venison; it is our own Magdalen venison, from our own college park, with our own traditional *sauce chasseur*. Perhaps a few weeks early for it, some would say, but there is an historical reason for enjoying venison tonight.

"Tonight, Doctor Watson, is indeed something of a royal occasion for Magdalen. We were founded, you see, in 1458, and it was four hundred years ago today, on July 24th, 1483, that Magdalen was paid a royal visit, by the king himself, Richard the Third. This dinner will mark the anniversary of King Richard's visit. We are proud that every ruler since Richard has visited Magdalen. Indeed, Magdalen is required by statute to entertain the reigning monarch and the Prince of Wales."

Now, at last, I understood what Masterman-Pugh had meant by his tantalizing preface to dinner: Richard the Third, the medieval king who had murdered, among others, his own nephews, the poor Little Princes in the Tower, so that he could seize the kingdom, and had so earned a cruel and bloody place of horror and shame in our island's history.

Mr. Holmes, who had been naturally and visibly most eager to hear more from Masterman-Pugh, also caught on to his meaning, and as visibly lost interest. He looked bored, as he so often did at large, formal dinners, while Dean Rigaud continued.

"King Richard the Third came here with a bevy of dukes and barons and lords on his first royal progress after his coronation on July 6th, 1483. He stayed here in Magdalen for two days, on July 24th and 25th, and left Oxford for Woodstock on the 26th. Here at Magdalen, he was entertained by debates staged by the leading scholars of the day. He presented the speakers with gifts of money, and with royal venison; hence tonight's menu. And we also have a commemorative reason for dining in Hall tonight, even if there are so few of us here. King Richard ate in this very hall, although its appearance has naturally changed in the four hundred years since then."

I felt a little overawed by the dean, but was able to reply easily.

"Oddly enough, I once dined in King Richard's old home in London. A friend of my father's took me there; to Crosby Place, in Bishopsgate; it was Richard's London residence at one point, I understand. It has been used for many things over the years, and when we visited the hall it was serving as a restaurant and dining room. I must confess that I was far more interested in its food and in its cellar than in its historical associations or in its wonderful medieval ceiling.

"You have a very fine ceiling of your own here," I added.

Rigaud coughed nervously. "Yes, but not yet one hundred years old. It is a more modern plaster ceiling, replacing the old wooden medieval one. Indeed, much of what you see in Hall now is from the sixteenth and seventeenth centuries."

"I still find it most interesting to think of a medieval king in this very hall," I replied, "in full panoply, the High Table set with Magdalen's best linen and your best bowls and vessels. Perhaps a special chair, like a throne, for Richard. Why, I can see it all now. A veritable invasion of the nobility and the bishops. Nervous servants scurrying with food from the kitchens, and wine from your buttery. I wonder what else the royal party ate. Venison, as we shall? Swan? Peacock?"

Dean Rigaud smiled at my childish enthusiasm. "You must be aware, Doctor Watson, that Richard the Third has a somewhat tarnished reputation. I shall therefore not say that tonight we are celebrating his visit, but the President and I thought it at least worthy of being marked at a little dinner in Hall.

"Yes, indeed," I threw out. "Richard Crookback, the hunchback king. He murdered his nephews, the Two Little Princes in the Tower. I remember reading of him in school. I also remember being forced, as a penalty for poor work, to sacrifice a whole Saturday afternoon of play to copy out endless passages about him from Shakespeare."

"He was not, though, I believe," said Rigaud.

"Not what, Dean?" I asked, falling easily into the titular form of address used there.

"Not a crookback, not a hunchback," said the dean, punctuating his statement with a generous wave of a silver butter knife. "He had no humpback. It is a myth. Richard was of normal build, or so I understand. It is also argued by some historians, and quite persuasively, that in fact he did not murder your two princes."

Richard the Third became lost for the moment in the gentle clatter of cutlery, the ebb and flow of good conversation, and an '80 Margaux that was a pleasant improvement upon the modest Beaune that Holmes and I normally order from

Dolamore's. We spoke of the death of the Duke of Marlborough; of the shooting matches, a few days earlier, in which Oxford had once more defeated Cambridge; of the merits of the second Suez Canal proposal and its enormous cost of eight millions of pounds; of the bloody outrages of the extreme Fenians; and of the new plans to form the Oxford Historical Society. Even Masterman-Pugh, surprisingly, contributed with increasingly cordiality to the easy *bonhomie* of a dinner that I found the most pleasant and relaxing that I had enjoyed in many a month.

For Magdalen's famed port, we repaired to the ancient, tapestry-lined State Room, where, I was told, Richard the Third had lodged during his visit to Magdalen. I soon watched our cigar smoke climb thickly to the ceiling, and smiled as Holmes again and again blew perfect rings of smoke. Magdalen's imposing and patrician president, Frederic Bulley, soon rose to his feet.

"Consider our world here at Magdalen," he invited. "How settled we are, how comfortable, how secure. Our afflictions are few, our satisfactions and rewards many. We can count upon each other. We can count upon the University. We can count upon Magdalen. We have our skills, our learning. We have our positions. We are safe in our situations. We are gentlemen. We are exposed to few dangers. Our futures are largely known to us, and settled, and satisfactory.

"Beyond Magdalen's walls, we Englishmen have an established monarchy, we have Parliament; we have reliable and honest processes of government. We have the Army, the Navy, civil police forces, honest courts.

"When Richard the Third was born, however, life in the England of the fifteenth century was far more precarious. There was a monarchy, indeed; but the kings of that era often ruled by might as much as by right. There were always powerful and wealthy rivals who might claim a greater blood-right to the throne, or simply seize it by force. Many nobles were so rich and so strong that they were almost kings on their own vast estates. Many could raise private armies quite big enough to challenge the king.

"Richard the Third's father, Richard Duke of York, was the richest and most powerful of the nobles of his time. He *did* challenge the king, Henry the Sixth, and *did* claim the throne. There are many, indeed, who contend to this day that York's claim to the throne was more legitimate than that of Henry."

While speaking, Bulley had walked slowly to one of the ancient tapestries hanging on the wall. He fell silent for a moment, lost in thought, and ran a finger lightly over the smoke-darkened cloth. How bright and proud those colours must once have been; how dingy and lifeless they were now.

Bulley turned back to us, and began an absorbing lecture. Henry the Sixth, Bulley told us, was never a strong ruler, and was clearly uncomfortable with the naked exercise of power that was necessary in that era. Gentle, peaceable, deeply religious, he seemed more like a simple monk than an English monarch. Worse, Henry was afflicted by hereditary insanity, and was at least once rendered incapable. His court was riddled with corruption and greed, and intrigues were carried on behind his trusting and innocent back. There was civil strife, aggravated by England's inability to maintain the lands that we had won by costly conquest in France in the Hundred Years War.

Parliament named the Duke of York as Protector, to act for the king while Henry was in a period of mental alienation. There followed a move to establish York as the childless Henry's heir to the throne. Indeed, York had some legitimate claim to the crown himself, by reason of his own descent from the line of King Edward the Third.

If York had hopes of simply succeeding Henry the Sixth, however, they were soon dashed. Henry's strong-willed French queen, Margaret of Anjou, at last bore a son, Prince Edward. Henry, recovering from his alienation, recognised Prince Edward as his heir, and York was ousted from power and from favour by Margaret and her allies. Soon, inevitably, York rose against Henry, and pressed his own claim to the throne.

There followed an irregular series of battles, and reversals of political and military fortune for both sides, the Yorkists and Henry's Lancastrians, in the years from 1459 until 1471. The Duke of York himself died in one early skirmish in what we now know as the Wars of the Roses. So did his second son, Edmund. Henry the Sixth's only son and heir, Prince Edward, died after another battle. Eventually, York's eldest son, Edward Earl of March, routed the Lancastrians in 1471 and became King Edward the Fourth. He succeeded Henry the Sixth, as President Bulley put it, by conquest, by Parliamentary law, and by public acceptance.

"The unfortunate Henry the Sixth was quickly put to death in the Tower of London," Bulley continued. "So too, later, was the elder of Edward's surviving brothers, George, Duke of Clarence, who had joined a rebellion against Edward. Edward himself was passably effective as a king, but disgracefully licentious. He visited Magdalen in September of 1481, by the way. He stayed here overnight, attended and took part in a debate, and subsequently founded a lectureship in divinity.

"Edward the Fourth died of natural causes, that are often attributed to his carousing and debauchery, in 1483. He left two sons, Edward the Fifth and Richard, popularly known to posterity as the Two Little Princes in the Tower.

"Young Edward the Fifth was never crowned, however, for King Edward the Fourth had another brother, Richard, Duke of Gloucester. This Richard placed his two little nephews in the Tower of London, and took the throne himself – should I say, rather, usurped the throne? – as King Richard the Third. Richard was thirty years of age. The young brothers in the Tower soon disappeared, and were never seen again. It is widely assumed that Richard had them murdered, to clear his path to the throne. He was crowned on July 6th, 1483, and soon set off on the royal progress that brought him here to Magdalen and to this room, this very room, four hundred years ago today. There were then forty Fellows and thirty demies. Now, of course, we have four and twenty Fellows, thirty demies and ninety-two commoners. The scholars came here then at the age of fourteen –"

"As did you, President," interjected Henry Bramley, Magdalen's vice-president, with a smile.

Bulley grinned. "The lectures in 1483 began at six o'clock in the morning. Perhaps, gentlemen, you would wish to return to that invigorating precedent?"

His audience laughed comfortably.

"A number of our buildings were in existence in 1483," the president continued, "although the Bell Tower had not yet been begun. Still, if King Richard were to appear tonight, I am sure that he would easily recognise Magdalen."

Since my boyhood, I have always thrilled to stories of the Age of Chivalry, of knighthood and honour and jousting and heraldry. Even now, I love to dip into my father's old *Chronicles of Sir John Froissart*, of a winter's evening before our coals at 221B, Baker Street. As the President spoke, I painted a picture in my mind of the huge, colourful, noisy medieval caravan that brought Richard to Oxford within days of his coronation. Magdalen was newly built, and its revered founder, William Waynflete, the Bishop of Winchester and former Chancellor of England, was there in person to greet the new king. At that time, there were perhaps fewer than one thousand scholars in all of Oxford.

President Bulley paused, and picked up a document from a side table. "Wilson was kind enough to translate and transcribe the following from our archives here:–

"The twenty-fourth day of this month, the most illustrious King Richard the Third was honourably received, firstly outside the university by the chancellor of the university and by the regents and non regents; then he was received honourably and in procession at the College of the Blessed Mary Magdalene by a speech by the lord founder, and by the president and scholars thereof; and he lodged there overnight. And on the morrow, which was St. James the Apostle's day and the feast of St. Anne the mother of Mary, he stayed until after dinner with as many of his lords spiritual and temporal and other nobles as follows: The same day there came to the college with the lord King, the Lord Bishop of Durham, the Lord Bishop of Worcester, the

Lord Bishop of St. Asaph's, and Master Thomas Langton, the bishop elect of St. David's, the Earl of Lincoln, the Lord Steward the Earl of Surrey, the Lord Chamberlain Lord Lovel, Lord Stanley, Lord Audeley, Lord Becham, Lord Richard Radclyff, knight, and many other nobles, who all stayed overnight in the college.'

"The University gave to the dignitaries the traditional gifts of wine and gloves," added Bulley.

Masterman-Pugh, sprawled in his chair, broke in loudly. "Wine for me, please, President." I noticed that Bulley, without even a glance, carefully ignored him, and continued:–

"'Twenty-fifth day of this at the command and desire of the lord king two solemn disputations were performed in the great hall of the college, the first being in moral philosophy by Master Thomas Kerver, and, replying, a certain bachelor of the same college. Next was held another solemn theological debate, also in the presence of the King, by Master John Taylor, Doctor of Sacred Theology, opponent, and Master William Grocyn, respondent, all of whom the lord King magnificently and honourably rewarded, to wit: the Doctor of Sacred Theology a buck and 100 shillings, and his disputant with a buck and five marks, and the bachelor disputant with a buck and forty shillings. Moreover, the great King gave to the president of the college and the scholars two bucks, with five marks for wine.'"

"Hence the venison tonight," whispered Rigaud, "in memory of the bucks from the royal forests, you see."

It was in the hall of Magdalen, where we had just dined, that Richard listened to the "disputations". William Grocyn was a reader in theology, a noted student of Greek, and the future patron of the famed scholars Desiderius Erasmus and John Colet. He was also to become the friend and preceptor of the lionised Thomas More, with whose history I was soon to grow more familiar.

I found it incongruous that Richard, now so widely condemned as an arch-villain and cold-blooded murderer, should be so interested in learning and debate as to express his "command and desire" for these academic debates. My interest was strangely aroused, particularly as my friend Stevenson had mentioned in his letter that this same Richard would appear in his new story of *The Black Arrow*. Stevenson told me that he would paint Richard as a brave warrior, but also as calculating, cruel and "stained with crime."

I made the painful mistake of mentioning Stevenson's story, after the President's speech, in the hearing of Masterman-Pugh, and suffered in return an incredulous glare and a sour sneer. "*Young Folks' Paper*, indeed."

President Bulley went on to tell us how Richard's rival, Henry Tudor, brought down Richard. Richard died at the Battle of Bosworth in 1485, and Henry took his crown as Henry the Seventh. As king, Henry visited Magdalen twice, and his son, Prince Arthur, three times. Indeed, the tapestries that faced us were from Arthur's time, commemorating his betrothal to Catherine of Aragon. It was she who, after Arthur's death, became the first wife of his brother, King Henry the Eighth.

President Bulley declared that much of what we commonly know and believe of Richard the Third today comes from Shakespeare.

"'A horse! A horse! My kingdom for a horse!'" I interjected ringingly, a little emboldened by the memorable port and with a flash of recollection of Shakespeare's play about Richard the Third.

Bulley smiled in an avuncular manner.

"Exactly, Doctor Watson, exactly. Yet Shakespeare, as an historian, should, I believe, be taken with more than a few grains of salt. Dean Rigaud and I read the play together, in preparation for my remarks tonight, and I commend it to you. In the most dramatic language, Shakespeare describes Richard as an evil usurper and bloody murderer; yet this treatment of Richard has been much challenged. In particular, in the matter of the deaths of the young Edward the Fifth and his little brother, King Richard the Third has partisans who declare him entirely innocent of their murder.

"Further, as I mentioned in my address, there was some good in the man. Our college records were perhaps premature in recording the politic message, '*Vivat rex in aeternum.*' However, Richard deserves full credit for many benefits to the common man; good government, good laws and fair courts among them."

Wilson, the Magdalen librarian, broke in.

"Oh, indeed, President. As a dramatist, Shakespeare may have no peer, but as an historian he leaves very much to be desired. His English historical plays are well known to be full of errors, and it is clear, I think, that he valued his audience first and his facts second.

"You spoke of 'usurpation', yet the partisans of Richard make a very effective argument that Edward the Fourth's marriage to the mother of the Two Little Princes was not a legal marriage. That, therefore, the boys were illegitimate and, as such, had no legal right to the throne. The treason of George of Clarence, the brother of Edward the Fourth and of Richard, had disinherited his heirs. So Richard was truly the legal heir to the throne, and thus became king in his own right, rather than through usurpation.

"As for the murders of the Two Little Princes, it is said today that no court could possibly convict Richard on the flimsy circumstantial evidence of the case."

Masterman-Pugh had been silent for some time, and appeared morose. A slight film of perspiration covered his forehead, and the thought occurred to me that, were I his physician, I should sternly recommend markedly less wine and port in the course of his evenings. He now broke brusquely into the conversation.

"You are a consulting detective, Holmes. I hear the words 'circumstantial evidence'. Evidence in murder cases is supposedly your professional field. What say you?"

Holmes gave a quick diplomatic smile. "Alas, I *have* no evidence. It might be a most interesting case, true, to track down and examine the historical evidence, circumstantial or otherwise. The trail, however, is four hundred years old; and, besides, even if King Richard has been wrongly accused of murder, it is hardly a task for a modern consulting detective."

I chided him, although in friendly fashion. "What, Holmes? You of all people, actually ducking a murder case? Would you not care to apply your skills to determining if Richard was indeed a murderous villain?"

My friend chuckled. "Perhaps if I were in practice in 1483, Watson. But in 1883 I can find little prospect of profit in it."

We laughed with him, but Masterman-Pugh spoke up sharply. "Oh, profit," said he, with a derisory sneer. "So profit is your motivation, is it? Then we are not to see your craft, unless you are paid a town journeyman's wage? I am sadly disappointed in you."

Unruffled, Holmes shrugged loosely. "No, indeed, a documentary investigation after four centuries is surely work for an historian, rather than for a practical consulting detective whose cases are of more immediate importance. This is surely a case for one of you gentlemen of the University. Is there an historian among us tonight? Wilson, you clearly know some of the history." Wilson shook his head modestly.

Masterman-Pugh looked directly at Mr. Holmes, with no trace of a smile on his narrow, sour features.

"You suggest, I take it, that the learned are not practical? Come: You are on holiday, are you not, Holmes? Will you not accept my poor, simple challenge? It is, after all, an opportunity to show that your university years will not be entirely squandered upon such practical cases as determining which ungrateful servant has stolen the household spoons."

"With regret, I must decline," said Holmes, still pleasantly, and refusing to rise to Masterman-Pugh's clumsy casts. "It is well after ten o'clock.

"Perhaps Doctor Watson will assist you, if he is staying up," continued Holmes, carelessly. "He knows something of my methods. Indeed, he has often been of invaluable assistance to me in my work."

"Oh, really?" remarked Masterman-Pugh, and this time the sarcastic tone was hostile, biting and unmistakable. The Magdalen men looked uncomfortably away in embarrassment. President Bulley flushed heavily, and swung his white-whiskered face severely towards Masterman-Pugh as the latter continued. "An army commission is not, I am given to understand, an academic credential of notable value."

If Masterman-Pugh was setting a trap, I promptly plunged into it, feet first, black patent shoes and all.

I lectured him, stiffly. "The skills used in medical diagnosis, in Mr. Holmes's detective work, in police work, and in your own academic work, are not at all dissimilar, surely. One gathers pieces of evidence, assembles them, analyzes them with a trained mind, and reaches a conclusion or conclusions.

"As a doctor, I read patients and their symptoms. As a detective, Holmes reads footprints and bloodstains. Your doctor of history reads books and papers. It is much the same, is it not?

"Mr. Holmes has been kind enough to call me a promising pupil. I would not claim that honour myself, but he has certainly tried hard and patiently to teach me well. He has quoted to me over and over again a warning from *Great Expectations*, in which Pip said:– 'The Constable and the Bow Street men from London ... persisted in trying to fit the circumstances to the ideas, instead of trying to extract ideas from the circumstances'.

"Thus the single most important lesson that Mr. Holmes has taught to me is that it is a mistake to give life to theories before one has sufficient facts and knowledge. That biases the judgement. I have learned from him and others also, sir, to maintain a healthy professional silence unless I have something fruitful or constructive to say."

I stopped, embarrassed at my impetuous incivility, but Masterman-Pugh had me on the point of his foil.

"Ah, you fancy yourself as both a detective and as a professor of history?" said he, silkily. "Perhaps *you* would take on this challenge, then? It is, if I recall your words correctly, merely a matter of reading books and papers. You, too, are on holiday, I gather. Perhaps you will spend it reading? Wilson, our librarian, will no doubt assist you, although I much doubt that he can easily provide you with copies of your beloved *Young Folks*. Wilson, perhaps you will give Doctor Watson an appointment in the library in the morning; unless, of course, he wishes to back out?"

I was about to reject a challenge that I considered offensive and mean-spirited, when Holmes himself unwittingly pulled the rug from beneath my feet.

"I am sure that Doctor Watson could solve the mystery most capably, but –"

Masterman-Pugh ignored the word "but", and buried it for ever beneath a ringing declaration delivered in impatient and pompous tones. "Then that is agreed. Doctor Watson, I shall look forward to receiving the findings of your attempts at research, no matter how amateur they may prove to be. I am sure that we all shall. Let us set no date upon the matter; I would not wish to press a deadline upon you lest you should be forced to give life to theories before you have sufficient facts and knowledge."

"Oh, I am no consulting detective –" I began, weakly, glancing nervously for support at the Magdalen men, who, uncomfortable and puzzled, watched us blankly. They seemed at a loss for words, as was I.

"Holmes seems to disagree," retorted Masterman-Pugh. "I shall of course, as your client, be responsible for your fees as a detective. What are they? As a physician, do you charge by the day, or by the case? As we ask our cabbies, 'Are you engaged by time or distance?' Assuming that you *have* patients, that is."

"I say," broke in President Bulley, firmly. "Hold on. Enough. Come now, Masterman-Pugh, Doctor Watson did not –"

"I shall do it nonetheless," said I, firmly, with sudden resolve.

I could not begin to explain to you, the reader, why I did so. I knew, though, that the insufferable Masterman-Pugh had deliberately tried, in public, to make fools of Mr. Holmes and me. A century earlier, and no doubt Masterman-Pugh's second (if he could somehow find a friend to serve as one) would be solemnly making the formal arrangements with mine for a daybreak exchange with sword or pistol in the quiet green fields by the river. Now we are more advanced, and I have ever been slow to anger; even so I would have no more of it.

At that point, committing myself irrevocably to the unknown, I delivered to Masterman-Pugh a cutting statement that Holmes oft recalls with an unholy delight, and has since appropriated to himself.

"As a doctor, Masterman-Pugh, my professional charges are on a fixed scale. I do not vary them, save when I remit them altogether in the interests of charity. Of course, I, as a gentleman" – I added, with coldly deliberate emphasis on the words 'I' and 'gentleman' – "shall trouble you for no fee, I assure you."

Masterman-Pugh nodded curtly. "I accept. I insist that you must hold me to account in full for your expenses, however. Then it is agreed. Good night." He turned instantly on his heel before I could answer, and bolted with a suspicion of a stagger from the hushed room.

"I say, Doctor Watson –" began Dean Rigaud and President Bulley, in apologetic chorus. I cut them off with a determined wave of my hand.

"No, really, President, Dean. Some hours beneath the dome of the reading room at the Museum would be just as much a holiday for me as going down to Derbyshire. I must say, too, that you have genuinely stirred my interest. *Was* Richard a hunchback? *Was* he a murderer? *Was* he Shakespeare's bloody villain, or a good king, or both? I would indeed like to learn a little about his life. I must confess, to boot, that it would be something of a pleasure to show Masterman-Pugh that even a simple army doctor can well use the brains God gave to him, just as well as can a doctor of history, or even an accomplished doctor of law such as he.

"No, my mind is quite made up, and Mr. Holmes will tell you how hard it is to dislodge me when that is so.

"Besides," I added, with a broad smile that I genuinely felt, and that instantly dispersed the tension and embarrassment in the atmosphere, "Masterman-Pugh has agreed to pay my expenses, has he not? I rather think that I shall enjoy that. I would not take undue advantage of him, of course, but there may be one or two little surprises for him in my accounting.

"For one thing, I shall certainly not walk to the Museum when Masterman-Pugh's money is so generously, and so very politely, made available to pay for my cab fare. Nor shall I take a paper of sandwiches, when I may quite properly submit to him my expenses for a considerably more satisfying luncheon at an excellent restaurant with a reputation for the very best in roast beef and claret."

The company burst out laughing.

"Good for you, Doctor Watson," applauded Dean Rigaud. "My cloth, of course, requires that I must preach against petty revenge, but I must confess that, if there is some prospect of you making Masterman-Pugh pay for this evening's rudeness, I, for one, should not be averse to seeing it happen. As he has sown, so should he reap; forgive me."

We broke up our gathering with cheery, if nervous, good-byes, and Holmes and I walked slowly and reflectively through the deserted city of learning to our temporary hotel rooms.

"Masterman-*Pig*," I said, with bitter emphasis, as I entered my own tiny chamber.

"Good heavens, Watson," said Holmes, from the door. "Now, that is exactly what we called him, although not to his face, in my time here."

"Masterman-*Pig*," I repeated, as I forcefully deposited my dinner jacket on my bed and viciously stripped off my bow tie.

"The trouble is, Holmes," I confided, "that I seem now to have painted myself into a very awkward corner, and, short

30

of grovelling before Masterman-Pugh, which I am simply not prepared to do, I have absolutely no idea how I can get myself out of it."

Then, for the very first time since I had met him, Mr. Sherlock Holmes let me down.

"Nor have I," said he.

Chapter Three

I was angered by Masterman-Pugh and his infuriating challenge, and at my stupidity for accepting it. "So much for my holiday," I snapped at Mr. Holmes, unfairly, as if here were to blame. My friend, seeking to please and placate me, enthusiastically proposed a more distant destination to succeed Oxford.

"You shall have your holiday, Watson. May I suggest the Peak District?"

"Like Oxford," I returned with a conciliatory smile, "it is nowhere near the sea."

"True, Watson," began Holmes, steepling his fingers together in the familiar pose that he unconsciously adopts when lecturing. "However, in the marine fossils of the limestone crags and outcroppings of the White Peak, I can show you geological proof that Derbyshire, while indeed nowhere near the sea now, was in some past era actually beneath it."

My friend leaned forward suddenly, his grey eyes bright.

"I think I can promise you a memorable holiday. There are few sights in England sweeter than that gained by walking slowly through Cave Dale and scrambling up the height behind Peverel's castle, to watch the summer sun set deep red over Mam Tor. There are few experiences sweeter than strolling down silent Winnat's Pass into old Castleton at dawn. There are the fine caverns at Castleton, Watson, and old villages nearby, full of history; Hathersage, and the plague village of Eyam. Oh, and we must walk along the Lathkil; such a short river, but so crystal clear that you can count the scales upon the Brown trout in it. It is such wonderful area for long, restful walks. It is still the season for Derbyshire's traditional well-dressing ceremonies, too; perhaps we shall attend one."

Holmes, who had never before spoken of such interests, waxed so unusually eloquent that I was easily persuaded to visit a quarter of England that would be new to me. We made plans for a journey to Derbyshire to follow our foray to Oxford. That we did not go on to Derbyshire, nor yet to the seaside, is now, if you will pardon a little joke that will soon become clear, a matter of history. Indeed, much murky water flowed under the grimy bridges of populous London before I was able to take my much-needed holiday.

In the end, I could not shake Masterman-Pugh's challenge from my head, and so, by mutual consent, Mr. Holmes and I abandoned our plans to go on to Derbyshire, and we returned to Baker Street on the following Monday morning. On the Tuesday, I was listless all morning, and composed resignedly in my head a letter of surrender and apologies to Masterman-Pugh

I was seated at our dining table, finishing a solitary and unusually early luncheon, when Holmes entered breezily, and tossed two books onto the Nottingham lace table cloth.

"Here from the box-room is Shakespeare's play, *King Richard the Third*. As for the other book, I am afraid that our dear landlady's library is somewhat bereft of serious works historical," said he, with a wink. "The best that she seems to be able to provide is this, Charles Dickens's *A Child's History of England*."

I managed a weak laugh. "Masterman-Pugh would not be surprised after *Young Folks*," I replied.

Holmes then produced a new, expensive note book with a fine morocco cover.

"A small gift," he explained, with a warm smile. "You seemed to be somewhat low in spirits again this morning, and

I thought that you might like at last to set a hand to your mission, as a diversion."

"But, Holmes," I protested, "beyond President Bulley's speech at Magdalen, I know absolutely nothing about Richard the Third."

"Excellent, Watson," replied Mr. Holmes. "Your mind is therefore unmarred and unprejudiced by prior knowledge. *Tabula rasa.* That is the very best frame of mind for a consulting detective; and doubtless for a consulting historian. It is something for which I have to strive at the beginning of each new case. You have a natural advantage, Watson. Indeed, I believe that you also have a natural ability to excel in this undertaking. You have a rare flair for understanding what character is inside people, and also for retaining in your memory the written word."

Disarmed, and rather flattered, I opened the play. "Listen to this, Holmes." I began to recite:–

"'But I, that am not shaped for sportive tricks,
Nor made to court an amorous looking-glass;
I, that am rudely stamped and want love's majesty
To strut before a wanton ambling nymph;
I, that am curtail'd of this fair proportion,
Cheated of feature by dissembling nature,
Deform'd, unfinish't, sent before my time
Into this breathing world, scarce half made up,
And that so lamely and unfashionable
That dogs bark at me as I halt by them; –
Why, I, in this weak piping time of peace,
Have no delight to pass away the time,
Unless to spy my shadow in the sun,
And descant on mine own deformity:
And therefore, since I cannot prove a lover,
To entertain these fair well-spoken days,
I am determined to prove a villain,
And hate the idle pleasure of these days'."

I looked up. "Our wicked Richard, it seems."

"Shakespeare's wicked Richard, anyway," returned Holmes, with a shrug. "Now, I must be away again; I shall hope to return at dinner time."

I opened the tattered Dickens book, and leafed through its dog-eared pages to find those concerning Richard the Third. I learned that, if Charles Dickens was to be believed, Richard, Duke of Gloucester, was "avaricious and ambitious" and an "usurper and murderer." He was "one of the boldest, most crafty and most dreaded noblemen in England", and was "dreaded and hated by all classes of his subjects." He was also, wrote Dickens, a brave soldier, "as fierce and savage as a wild boar." No evidence was presented to support these characterizations, and I recognised that Mr. Dickens was writing in a style and depth most highly simplified and dramatic, for his eager young audience.

I learned that the Two Little Princes, Edward and Richard, were aged thirteen and eleven, respectively, when, after the death of their father, their uncle Richard put them into the Tower of London, and took the young Edward the Fifth's throne for himself.

I noted these items carefully in my new red note book. I recorded also for the benefit of Masterman-Pugh that Mr. Dickens made no explicit mention of a crookback, stating only that Richard was "not ill-looking, in spite of one of his shoulders being something higher than the other." Dickens also wrote, however, that Richard had, from birth, a withered or shrunken arm.

I leafed back and forth through the book, with growing interest, and found, too, that Dickens suspected Richard of having had a hand in the execution of his ill-starred brother, George, Duke of Clarence. Dickens also reported that Richard had ordered the executions of two nobles, Lord Hastings and the Duke of Buckingham. He also suggested that Richard had arranged the death of his own wife, Queen Anne.

The passage I found most absorbing, and most disturbing, was that describing the deaths of the Two Little Princes, and I copied it in its entirety into my new journal:–

"He sent instructions home for one of the wickedest murders that was ever done – the murder of the two young princes, his nephews, who were shut up in the Tower of London.

Sir Robert Brackenbury was at that time Governor of the Tower. To him, by the hands of a messenger named JOHN GREEN, did King Richard send a letter, ordering him by some means to put the two young princes to death. But Sir Robert – I hope because he had children of his own, and loved them – sent John Green back again, riding and spurring along the dusty roads, with the answer that he could not do so horrible a piece of work. The king, having frowningly considered a little, called to him SIR JAMES TYRREL, his master of the horse, and to him gave authority to take command of the Tower, whenever he would, for twenty-four hours, and to keep all the keys of the Tower during that time. Tyrrel, well knowing what was wanted, looked about him for two hardened ruffians, and chose JOHN DIGHTON, one of his own grooms, and MILES FOREST, who was a murderer by trade. Having secured these two assistants, he went, upon a day in August, to the Tower, showed his authority from the king, took command for four-and-twenty hours, and obtained possession of the keys. And when the black night came, he went creeping, creeping, like a guilty villain as he was, up the dark stone winding stairs, and along the dark stone passages, until he came to the door of the room where the two young princes, having said their prayers, were fast asleep, clasped in each other's arms. And while he watched and listened at the door, he sent in those evil demons, John Dighton and Miles Forest, who smothered the two princes with the bed and pillows, and carried their bodies down the stairs, and buried them under a great heap of stones at the staircase foot. And when the day came, he gave up the command of the Tower, and hurried away without once looking behind him; and Sir Robert Brackenbury went with fear and sadness to the princes' room, and found the princes gone for ever."

Dickens's account was substantially the same as that I now remembered from my turgid school history lessons. But was it true? How did Dickens know about Green and Tyrrel, Dighton and Forest? How did he know that the princes had said their prayers? How did he know that they were asleep in each other's arms? Had Dickens consulted records? *Were* there records? Who had made them? And when? Had one or more of the guilty made a confession? Had there perhaps been a fourth witness, in addition to Tyrrel, Dighton and Forest? There were, however, no answers to hand.

My mind kept turning to the dark passages of the fabled Tower of London, and the horrible deed that had supposedly been carried out there. I went to my unmade bed, and, lying on my back, forced a pillow against my face, cutting off my breath for some moments. I tried to imagine what cruel terror must have visited those innocent, struggling children as they died.

Reading my borrowed Shakespeare later, I was interrupted by a clipped Cockney voice from directly behind me.

"Halloa, sir. Are you reading for pleasure or for profit, then?"

Without moving a muscle in reaction, I gave a haughty reply. "For purpose, of course. Were you selling matches for pleasure, or for profit?"

"Oh, well bowled, Watson," Holmes laughed in true delight.

With a satisfied laugh, I spun around. "Yes, middle stump, I think. I could see you and your match-seller's tray reflected in the glass of the clock as you entered."

"You gave no sign at all of having seen me, Watson, let alone of having studied me," said he, still smiling. "Your talents as assistant consulting detective are improving daily."

"Why, thank you, Holmes, thank you. If I have displayed any small skills, I owe them all to you, my revered teacher. I believe that I shall have need of them, too; I have in one short afternoon compiled many more questions than I have answers. I shall have to bear carefully in mind your *dictum* that 'It is a capital mistake to theorise before you have all the evidence.' Would you care for a sherry, Holmes? The time has quite flown."

"Yes, thank you. Tell me about your reading."

I restored the old crystal decanter to the dark oak tantalus, licked a spilled dribble of sherry from my fingers, and, as we settled comfortably into our accustomed chairs, began with Shakespeare.

"You will remember, Holmes, that President Bulley said that Richard had been an usurper, murderer and regicide. If Shakespeare is to be believed, Richard was all those things; an usurper, who took the throne of the young King Edward the Fifth; a murderer more than ten times over, and twice a regicide."

"Twice?" prompted Holmes, as I paused.

"Richard's eldest brother, Edward the Fourth, seized the throne of Henry the Sixth, by force. Henry's son and heir, also named Edward, the Prince of Wales, was taken prisoner. According to Shakespeare, Richard murdered the young Edward on the spot. Then, or so says Shakespeare, Richard went on to kill Henry the Sixth himself, stabbing him while in the Tower of London. Richard also, according to Shakespeare, had his older brother George, Duke of Clarence, murdered in the Tower."

"Three murders, thus far," said Holmes, "and one a regicide."

"Right, Holmes, although at this stage I must be far from satisfied that Richard committed any of the three.

"Then King Edward the Fourth himself died. His young prince Edward was the heir, and should have been crowned as King Edward the Fifth. Richard, however, seized little Edward and his younger brother and put them away in the Tower; those two, of course, are our Two Little Princes in the Tower. Shakespeare's story is that Richard the Third first had three of their supporters killed, to wit: Earl Rivers, Sir Richard Grey and Sir Thomas Vaughan –"

"Six murders," tallied Holmes.

"Richard also had Lord Hastings murdered, and the Duke of Buckingham."

"Eight."

"Shakespeare also implies that Richard killed his own wife, Queen Anne."

"Nine."

"And, of course, Richard had the Two Little Princes killed."

"And since the young Edward was the legal heir to the throne that I take to be the second regicide," said Holmes. "And a toll of eleven murders."

"Right, Holmes. Eleven murders, and a great deal of dastardly plotting. Why, Richard publicly accused his own mother of adultery, so that he could declare his brother Edward the Fourth a bastard, and thus never the true king. Then Richard declared the Two Little Princes as bastards, as well, and therefore unable to inherit the throne. He promptly proceeded to take the throne for himself. Mind you, Holmes, this is all according to Shakespeare, and I have not yet had opportunity to examine his accuracy."

Holmes frowned. "There is also the question of the crookback. Shakespeare takes it as fact?"

"Yes, indeed, and he also says that Richard had a withered arm. I have sent a telegram to ask if I may call upon my father's old friend, Mr. Marmaduke Hornidge, who is a great student of Shakespeare's works. First, however, I think I shall visit the Tower of London to inspect the scene of the crimes."

"With Masterman-Pugh paying your expenses," observed Holmes with a happy laugh. "There I can help you, Watson. The Resident Governor of the Tower is in my debt, and I shall send him a telegram asking him to assist you."

Holmes chuckled, rose, and began to set cutlery meticulously upon the tablecloth.

"Well, Watson, what a marked change has come over you. This morning, I swear, you were actively seeking a way of escape from this troublesome assignment; yet now you seem to be quite caught up in it."

"I am indeed, Holmes," I returned, as our landlady's distinctive quadruple knock on the door heralded the arrival of a welcome dinner. "My distant Highland ancestors had the motto *Fortis et Fidus,* Strong and Trusty. I shall not give up now."

Holmes's appeal to the governor of the Tower brought the speedy offer of an appointment at two o'clock on the following day. My first official charge upon the account of Masterman-Pugh was, therefore, not for a cab to the Museum and its reading room, but for a hansom from Baker Street to the Tower of London. Like my friend Holmes, I am still reluctant to ride upon the sulphurous underground "Railway of the Rats", even though it now is somewhat cleaner than in years past. We both prefer to walk, or to take a cab. I recorded, for Masterman-Pugh, my cabby's fare and tip, and the fee I paid for admission to the wonders of the notorious Tower.

It had been many years since I last visited the Tower. It was as majestic and as imposing as I remembered, although more begrimed with soot. I waved to one of the uniformed Yeomen Warders at the Byward Tower, and asked for his assistance. Would he, I requested, show me where Richard the Third and the Two Little Princes had lived in the Tower? And then take me to the Resident Governor's office?

He politely declined my proffered coin. "Thank you, sir, but that won't be necessary. We're all old soldiers, sir. I was Troop Serjeant-Major with the 7th Dragoon Guards. I am Yeoman Warder Watson, sir."

"Good heavens. My name is also Watson," I replied with a smile.

"Now, sir," continued Yeoman Warder Watson. "You are interested in Richard the Third? To tell you the truth, he did not really live here, sir. There were royal apartments in the Tower, that is true, but he did not live here himself. But he did send the Two Little Princes here, his two young nephews, and this is where he had them murdered, sir. Right there in the Bloody Tower, that square tower over the portcullis gate, sir.

"A real bloody villain was Richard, by all accounts, sir. Did you know he was two whole years in his mother's womb before he was born, sir? It is absolutely true, sir; a fact, sir."

My bemused brain was still reeling at this startling piece of medical novelty as Yeoman Warder Watson marched me through the vaulted gateway beneath the Bloody Tower and thence to the timber-framed Queen's House, and the office of Major-General Sir Bryan Milman, Major and Resident Governor of Her Majesty's Tower of London.

I half expected Milman's office to be full of suits of armour, cannon and bloodied instruments of torture, but it was much like any other office. A large ceremonial axe, which I learned was the staff of office of the Yeoman Gaoler, stood against one wall. A young lady with bright blue eyes, wearing a buttoned walking dress of hunter green, rose from a chair beside Milman's desk.

"Dr. Watson, allow me to introduce Miss Callie Rivas," said Milman, as I presented my letter of introduction from Holmes. "She is a family friend who is visiting from York, and has some interest in Richard the Third. I took the liberty of explaining your mission to her, and she expressed an interest in meeting you."

I bowed, and Miss Rivas's face lit up with a delicious smile. "I am a school teacher in York, a city with a long and proud association with Richard the Third. However unpopular he was with the nobility in the South, he was much loved in his time by the people of the North, and of York in particular."

Milman waved me to a chair. "Now, Dr. Watson, I have arranged for one of our Yeomen Warders to escort you through those areas of the Tower that are associated with Richard the Third. He is Yeoman Warder Henry Baker, and we call him the unofficial historian of the Tower. It is quite a hobby with him. He will be here in a few minutes. Perhaps Miss Rivas would like to accompany you? May she?"

She nodded enthusiastically, her jewel-blue eyes flashing with interest. I signalled whole-hearted agreement, of course.

While waiting, the governor told us that the accounts of historians of Richard's ascent to the throne were substantially the same. The authors differed, however, on whether Richard had long intrigued to usurp the crown, or whether he had reluctantly come to see his accession as both legal and necessary for the good of the troubled country.

The early death of Edward the Fourth had left the court and nobility bitterly divided. Edward's haughty queen, Elizabeth Woodville, had caused Edward to grant high positions and generous favours to her many rapacious relatives, giving rise to much jealousy and hostility. "A greedy and grasping lot, the Woodvilles, if you ask me," said Milman.

I laughed. "Woodvillains, perhaps?"

Edward's leading Yorkist supporters had felt particularly cheated. On his death bed, Edward the Fourth had tried to end their quarrels with the Woodville brigade. He succeeded merely in patching them over, and then only briefly.

In his will, Edward had named our Richard, his brother, to be Protector. He was to assist the young Edward the Fifth to rule if Edward the Fourth died while his heir was still a child. On Edward the Fourth's premature death in 1483, however, the Woodvilles moved first. With an armed escort, they began to bring the young prince to London, without so much as a by-your-leave to Richard, who was away in the North. They began issuing state orders and planning Edward's coronation, and through their high offices they had control of the Tower of London, its royal treasure, and the navy.

Richard soon caught wind of all this, thanks to the powerful Duke of Buckingham, who was at that time his ally. Richard brought his own men from York, and intercepted the Woodville escort in Northamptonshire. Before they knew it, the quick-thinking Richard and his force had taken over the duty of accompanying Prince Edward to London. The leaders of the Woodville escort were arrested. They were Earl Rivers (Anthony Woodville, Queen Elizabeth Woodville's brother); Sir Richard Grey, her son from her first marriage; and Sir Thomas Vaughan, who had long been Prince Edward's chamberlain. Richard brought the child Edward to London, and on to the Tower, ostensibly in preparation for his coronation.

That coronation never took place, however. Richard soon produced evidence that Edward the Fourth's marriage to Elizabeth Woodville was bigamous, and had never been legal. Thus Prince Edward was illegitimate, and was not entitled to the throne. Richard of Gloucester was himself, then, the legal heir, and he assumed the crown as Richard the Third in 1483.

Milman said that some historians held the belief that Richard had never intended that young Edward the Fifth should be crowned. Others, however, believed that he truly did, but came to change his mind because of the prospect that the country would fall into chaos, and possibly civil war, if a child were upon the throne.

"A realistic fear, I may add," said Milman. "During the minority of Henry the Sixth, when he was an infant king, England did indeed experience much civil chaos.

"In the end, Richard was chosen as king by the Parliament. His claim was recognised as legal, and he became king legally. The Two Little Princes disappeared, of course, and are presumed to have been murdered and buried here in the Tower. We know not where, although some bones discovered here in 1647 may be theirs. They were then assumed so to be, and they are buried now in Westminster Abbey.

"The opposition to Richard, the Lancastrian supporters of Henry the Sixth, soon began to unite behind one Henry Tudor, who had a remote and even spurious claim to the throne.

"One Owen Tydder, or Tudor, a mere Welsh clerk, was a member of the household staff of Katherine of Valois, the widow of King Henry the Fifth. Tudor and she had a *liaison*. The outcome, if I may so put it, was Edmund Tudor, father of our Henry Tudor. Henry Tudor's mother was the redoubtable Margaret Beaufort, who was well trained in the politics of power herself. Owen Tudor claimed that he and Katherine were secretly married, by the way. There is no proof of that, but perhaps it was true; they had four children, and they were all apparently accepted as legitimate.

"Edmund was a half-brother to Henry the Sixth, but that, of course, gave Edmund's son Henry Tudor no proper claim to the throne. He had some Lancastrian blood, true, but his lineage was flawed by bastard blood in the past, both paternal and maternal. There were a good dozen or more people with a better claim to the crown than Henry, including his mother, and including the king of Portugal."

"What about Edward the Fourth's daughters?" I asked,

"They were eligible, at least in theory, to inherit the throne. As Queen Elizabeth would after the death of Henry the Eighth. However, no woman had yet occupied the throne; unless you count Henry the First's daughter, Matilda. In a period of civil war in the mid-twelfth century, both she and her cousin Stephen claimed to be the ruler, and there were, in effect, *two* courts. If you include the fair sex in the times we are discussing, Doctor Watson, then there were probably *two* dozen people with a better claim to the throne than Henry Tudor.

"Be that as it may, Henry Tudor brought an army from France, and his men killed Richard the Third at the Battle of Bosworth Field in Leicestershire in 1485. Richard was two and thirty years old, and had been on the throne not quite twenty-six months. Henry Tudor was crowned, as King Henry the Seventh."

I looked at Miss Rivas. "York," I said. "I have it now. The Yorkists, the House of York, had the white rose as their symbol. The House of Lancaster chose the red rose. The Wars of the Roses indeed."

"Top marks, Doctor Watson," said Milman with a laugh. "Although the red rose was, more properly, I think, the symbol of the Tudors; and the campaigns were not called the Wars of the Roses until many, many years later. In the end,

Henry Tudor, as King Henry the Seventh, married Edward the Fourth's eldest daughter Elizabeth, uniting both houses and extinguishing the Yorkist claim to the throne. He was followed by their son Henry the Eighth, of course, but that is getting well away from Richard's time.

"As for Richard, the more I know, the less I judge him. All in all, I would say that his reign was simply too short to succeed. He had too little time to build the necessary foundations of power and support. As well, he simply could not, as was the usual royal practice, pay enough to his foes to buy their loyalty. He inherited from Edward the Fourth a terribly depleted treasury; and it seems he stretched the remains too far in hastily rewarding loyal supporters. He was unable to be generous to those whose support was lukewarm. He certainly could not secure the tolerance of those who were hostile.

"I think things might have been very different if the Battle of Bosworth had taken place at the start of his rule, rather than two years later. I wonder what the outcome would have been if he had lived and ruled longer."

A sharp double knock came at the door and Yeoman Warder Henry Baker entered. Broad-shouldered and brisk, his grey beard freshly and neatly trimmed, he gave us a deferential but appealing smile. I felt an instinctive friendliness and respect for this fine-cut man, strong, hale and still on the right side of sixty. He wore the Distinguished Conduct Medal on his blue and red working uniform, but neither then nor later would he answer my questions about it. It was only from his colleagues that I eventually learned of his bravery in the mutiny at Delhi in 1857. He had been a serjeant-major in the 61st Regiment and had served in India for almost twenty years. He had fought in some famous engagements.

"You will be in good hands with Yeoman Warder Baker," said Milman, with a kindly glance at Baker. "He has a way of challenging the traditional views of history. You must ask him about Thomas More."

Baker snorted. "Ah, yes, Sir Thomas More, sir," he said, with dripping sarcasm. "Almost all the stories about Richard the Third originate with Thomas More. Shakespeare's plays, sir, miss, are very much based on More's *History of King Richard III.* A lot of books since then have just picked up what More wrote, and taken it as the truth. He is the one that says Richard was a hunchback, and a murdering villain, and he is the one who accuses Richard of murdering his two nephews, them we call the Two Little Princes in the Tower."

Baker paused for effect. "Sir Thomas More. He was a lawyer and a judge and a famous author, a chancellor of England, and a Roman Catholic martyr and hero. I do not believe he had yet been knighted when he wrote his famous *History* – he was just one of the under-sheriffs of London – so we should really call him Master More. But I always think of him as 'Master More-Fiction-than-Fact'."

"Why so?" inquired Miss Rivas, softly.

"Well, miss, for one thing, he is always giving the exact words of long conversations that he was not there to hear himself. He could not have been, could he? After all, he was only five years old."

I almost dropped my tea cup.

"He was what, Baker?"

"Only five years old, sir. When Richard the Third came to the throne, Thomas More was only five years old. When Richard died, More was still only seven years old.

"On top of that, sir, Master More gets his history very badly wrong in his very first sentence. Right off the bat, he says that King Edward the Fourth was fifty-three years old when he died. Wrong, dead wrong. Edward was only forty, sir, when he died; not yet one-and-forty. That is a fact.

"If Master More was wrong in something as simple and as well known as that in his very first sentence, sir, why on earth should we believe that he was right about the other things that he says happened? So why should we believe anybody who bases his history on More's book?

47

"Not only that, sir. Master More was not only a child when the Two Little Princes were in the Tower, but he grew up himself in the household of Cardinal Morton.

"And Cardinal Morton, sir; well, he was a long-serving Lancastrian, and one of Richard's most bitter, bitter enemies. No fair shake for Richard there, sir."

Chapter Four

Yeoman Warder Baker proved to be a most intelligent, well read and articulate guide, whose hobby of Tower history was clearly a consuming passion. He led Miss Rivas and me to Water Lane and, placing us with our backs to the notorious Traitor's Gate, he pointed first to the gloomy, rectangular Bloody Tower. He began a clear and confident monologue, delivered with the distinctive rise-and-fall cadence of the parade-square serjeant-major.

"The story is told, sir, miss, that it was right there in the Bloody Tower that the Two Little Princes were kept prisoner. It is not open to the public, but I have permission to show you where it is claimed that they were murdered. You notice that I say 'claimed'. There is a good reason for using that word, because there is no proof that they were, in fact, murdered. And if they were, sir, I am sure that it was not in the Bloody Tower. On top of that, there is very strong doubt as to whether Richard the Third was the man responsible, or even that they died during his reign."

I listened intently, rapidly scribbling notes with my father's old silver pencil, as Baker paused and pointed to a tower to our left.

"That is the Bell Tower. Sir Thomas More was held prisoner there, before King Henry the Eighth finally beheaded him. But I must not get started on Master More and his mistakes again."

"Shakespeare was sometimes wrong, too, they say," I replied.

"Oh, yes, sir, constantly," said Baker, with a wondering shake of the head and a pitying smile. "Shakespeare actually wrote that Julius Caesar built the Tower, sir. Now, we know that is not so. There was a Roman city wall here, that came down to the river; but it was William the Conqueror who started the Tower. William began to build the White Tower in the year 1078, and his son Rufus completed it about twenty years later.

"Then Henry the Third built a royal palace in the Tower grounds, and made a real job of expanding the defences. In 1240 or 1241, he gave the White Tower its first coats of whitewash; and that appears to have given rise to the name.

"From 1275 to 1285, King Edward the First, the great castle builder, did an enormous amount of work here, sir, miss. By the time he had finished, most of the Tower and the fortifications, as we see them today, were in place. There was a lot of demolition and building and rebuilding, on and off, during the next centuries. But Julius Caesar, sir? Rubbish."

I threw in a comment as a question. "Yeoman Warder Watson told me that Richard the Third never actually lived at the Tower."

"Right, sir," replied Baker. "I looked up my notes for you this morning. Richard's first visit to the Tower that we know was in June of 1465, when he was made a Knight of the Bath, at the age of twelve. The surviving records mention perhaps a dozen visits to the Tower by Richard, but the records are few. He must have been here much more often than that, as a guest at King Edward the Fourth's quarters, sir. King Edward used the Tower constantly. It was never really Richard's home, but he did follow his brother Edward's example of staying in the royal apartments in the Tower on the eve of his coronation. We know that during his reign King Richard commissioned some building and repair work here at the Tower. We also know that he built up an arsenal of artillery in the Tower, in early 1484. Some of the cannon were made right here at the Tower, and others were brought from the Continent. I am afraid that is pretty well all that we know about Richard's life at the Tower, sir."

Miss Rivas and I stood gazing in silent awe at the Tower buildings. What a formidable place, a walled fortress, covering some 18 acres. Castle, palace, arsenal, barracks, treasury, armoury, royal mint, astronomical observatory, public records office, zoo, prison and place of torture and execution; it has been and contained all of these things.

Baker brought us back to earth with a polite cough. He pointed. "As I say, this gate with the big portcullis is the Bloody Tower. It is joined to the Wakefield Tower there on the right. Along over there, farther on to the right, is the Lanthorn Tower, where you can see the repair work going on. The Bloody Tower entrance used to be the main water gate to enter the Tower, with the Wakefield Tower overlooking and guarding it. That iron ring (he pointed) is what the boats tied up to at the water gate. Where we are standing, Water Lane, was where the river actually ran, until St. Thomas's Tower and the new water gate behind us were built. Traitor's Gate was a name that came later.

"The Bloody Tower has not always been called that, you know. When the Two Little Princes were here, and for a long, long time after them, it was actually known as the Garden Tower. The Lieutenant of the Tower used to have a garden next to it. That old portcullis still works, Doctor Watson; we still lower and raise it every once in a while, and we keep it in good working condition."

We followed him through the vaulted Bloody Tower gateway. Baker pointed out the place where the Lieutenant's garden used to be located. He turned back to face the Bloody Tower again.

"They say that the Two Little Princes were held prisoner in this tower. Up there" – he pointed a muscular, uniformed arm –"in the upper room, they were supposedly murdered by King Richard's assassins.

"I said that I do not believe that, and I will tell you why. There are two reasons. First, sir, miss, in that time, the Garden

Tower was the main gate and guardhouse of the Tower. The royal residence itself was not in this area.

"There have been a lot of changes to the Tower over the centuries, with buildings rising and falling. The Bloody Tower itself has been altered several times. If you look at the archway, you can see that it looks a bit out of proportion. The original roadway must have been somewhat lower, and then was raised at some point. The uses of many of the buildings changed frequently, and there are very few records preserved. We do know, however, that the royal residence at the time of King Edward the Fourth and King Richard the Third was in the Lanthorn Tower, and in a number of adjacent buildings that no longer exist. They were in the inside area of the Tower, known as the Inmost Ward, and were between the Wakefield and the Lanthorn Towers. These royal buildings later fell into disuse, and were eventually demolished in the 1670s.

"The two little boys were not just ordinary nobility, as you know, sir. One of them was really the new king, Edward the Fifth, and his little brother Richard was the Duke of York. Their uncle Richard might have sent them here so that they were not in the way of his taking the throne, but I do not think that they would have been treated as prisoners in the criminal line. We know that many prisoners, even if they were not royalty, were allowed to have their families and servants with them, and they were not so badly treated at all. They were kept in some comfort, and they were certainly not all chained up in dungeons, by any means.

"So I think that it is much more likely that the two princes were kept in the royal residence, sir, in the Inmost Ward, and probably in proper royal luxury, not just locked up here in the Garden Tower. After all, they were aged only nine and twelve, and were of royal blood.

"Besides, they say now that the Bloody Tower got its name because the princes were murdered there, but the truth is that it was still being called the Garden Tower fifty years *after* the princes disappeared. The name was not recorded as the Bloody Tower until at least 1597, more than a hundred years after the princes."

I nodded. "Do go on, Baker. You're being most helpful, and I am taking many notes."

Baker nodded back, proudly, and resumed an enthusiastic oration that wove English history and the techniques of castle building into an unpredictable and fascinating chain. Miss Rivas was clearly as interested as I, her eager blue eyes darting from building to building as Baker related the intriguing history of the Tower.

"Right, sir; thank you, sir. By the way, a few people also say that it was here in the Bloody Tower that King Richard's own brother George, the Duke of Clarence, was executed. The old tradition is that he was up-ended and drowned in a barrel of malmsey wine. Some people have tried to blame Richard for that, too, but I think most authorities agree that it was not he. It was Edward the Fourth who had Clarence killed, for plotting against Edward with the Earl of Warwick."

"Charles Dickens suspects Richard of having had a hand in George's death," I observed.

"Yes, sir. *A Child's History of England?* I have read it, sir. Mr. Dickens seems to have taken his story straight from Thomas More for the most part. I am absolutely sure that, whatever happened to Clarence, it was not here at all, sir. Most people say that he was held in the Bowyer Tower, away up at the north side, and that has become the tradition; but I think that is wrong, too, sir."

Baker led us to the gloomy floor above the Bloody Tower entrance, and, opposite the great portcullis, we entered a tidy but cold, spartan, and ill furnished chamber. It exuded age and mustiness, and served as a combined bed room and sitting room. I determined that it was being used as a Yeoman Warder's private residence.

"Now," continued Baker, "here is my second reason for doubting the tale about the Little Princes being murdered here in the Bloody Tower, sir. The traditional story is that they were smothered in their bed in the upper room above us. That simply cannot be. You see, the upper room was not built until the early 1600s, when Sir Walter Raleigh was held prisoner here. The tower was raised in height a little to accommodate

53

him and his family and servants, who were allowed to be with him. The upper room did not exist when the Little Princes were here in 1483. There was only the one room above the gateway, this room, when they were here."

"Thomas More says that they were killed in the upper room?" I asked.

"No, sir, neither More nor any of the early writers says exactly where they were murdered," returned Baker, forthrightly. "It is, though, the common story."

"Which just goes to show," broke in Miss Rivas, "that the common story is not necessarily the true story." With a smile, she continued. "I have rather a preference for the uncommon story, myself."

Baker's head bobbed, respectfully. "One much later historian, Francis Sandford, wrote in 1707 that the princes were held, and killed, in the Bloody Tower, and were buried at the foot of the stairs that come down into the duty-guard's post, or porter's lodge, in the gate. But Sandford did not say how he knew that. I am willing to bet that this tower was used just for the men who guarded the water gate. General Milman disagrees on that point. He feels that a room of this size, with a fireplace and a *garderobe* – that is a medieval privy, miss – was a bit too good for us ordinary soldiers. He thinks that it was more likely to have been used as an office by the Constable or Lieutenant of the Tower. It was, indeed, used in later years as a state prison, sir, but neither the governor nor I believe that this was a royal prison when the princes were here."

Baker paused, and shook his grizzled head.

"Now," he continued, "the way that Master More tells the story, the princes were buried at the foot of the stairs and a heap of stone was piled on top. I do not see how anyone could have been buried under the stairs, sir. You could not get under them. Even if you could, in a busy area like this, with men always coming and going on and off duty, surely people would notice any fresh digging, or a new pile of stones. And they would surely notice that the Two Little Princes had vanished. They would ask questions, and gossip, and word would get out. I do not see how you could suddenly bury two bodies here one night, and hope to get away with it.

"And then Master More asks us to believe that King Richard decided that it was not a proper place to bury the sons of a king, so a Tower priest secretly dug them up again, and then re-buried them somewhere else, but died before he could tell anyone where the new grave was. Again, sir, how could all that happen without people seeing something, or knowing?"

As my pencil raced across the pages, Baker, at a fast clip, led us through a well guarded door into the Wakefield Tower, and past a group of visitors waiting to see the fantastic riches of the Crown Jewels in their locked cage. We descended into the dank lower floor of this tower, and Baker took down and lit a lantern. We saw a dark clutter of wood and coal and pieces of masonry and detritus, pierced by a huge central column that supported the weight of the impregnable jewel cage above.

"Has either of you any Scottish blood?" inquired Baker.

"Yes, if distant," I replied.

Baker nodded. "I ask because some of the Jacobite prisoners were held in here after the rising of 1745, sir. Anyway, some say that this is really where the bodies of the Two Little Princes were taken, and buried, under this stair there. Perhaps; but a bit unlikely. The original floor is somewhat below us. Given the lie of the land, I am sure that it often would have flooded in rainy weather and on a good high tide.

"Still, sir, there is one thing to be carried in mind. It is quite possible that the Princes were held prisoner above us, in the Wakefield Tower. It was a royal apartment, all right, and we know that it was used as a royal prison, too, to hold King Henry the Sixth. He was murdered right above us."

Baker returned the extinguished lantern to its hook, and rushed us back to the vaulted upper floor of the Wakefield Tower. We forced our way past the awed visitors who were listening to a tall Yeoman Warder reciting a droning description of the Crown Jewels.

"What you might find interesting here is the murder of Henry the Sixth," said Baker. "This recess over here in the wall was a little chapel, the Oratory. It was here, they say, that Henry was murdered, in 1471. Some writers say that Richard the Third himself stabbed the king to death, sir."

We left the octagonal chamber, and Baker's steady voice and military rhythm drummed on.

"Of course, there is no good evidence that Richard the Third killed Henry the Sixth at all, sir. Thomas More reports this charge, and so does Shakespeare, following More's lead. Funny thing, though: Shakespeare says that Richard also killed Henry's only son, Prince Edward, but Master More does not mention it at all. More was powerful hard on Richard, but he never accused him of young Prince Edward's murder. Shakespeare does, but not More. Peculiar, sir, is it not?"

I finally got some words out. "Peculiar, or significant. I shall have to read More's account in full. I remember only that we had to do an essay in school on his *Utopia*, and the teacher told us that he was a Roman Catholic martyr."

"Perhaps one day he will be made a saint, sir. I still call him Thomas More-fiction-than-fact, though," said Baker, with a smile.

"You see, sir, More's story about the murder of the princes is all a bit too simple for my liking.

"According to Master More, Richard decides to kill the princes, so he sends a messenger to Sir Robert Brackenbury, who was the Constable here at the Tower. Sir Robert, though, refuses to go along with it. He refuses to commit a royal murder. He disobeys and defies King Richard. The next thing is, he gets an order from this chap sent by Richard, Sir James Tyrrel, to hand over his keys. And Sir Robert now just hands them over? Without a peep, just like that? And then the King somehow forgets about Sir Robert's refusal of the first order, and allows Sir Robert to keep his job here for the next two years? And then Sir Robert, despite knowing what villainy has happened, joins Richard's army at Bosworth Field and dies for him, in his service?

"It could have happened that way, I suppose, sir. Sir Robert might have just changed his mind. Threatened by Tyrrel, maybe. There might be explanations. Maybe the princes were moved especially into the Garden Tower for the occasion, sir. It could all be true. But I have a bit of trouble making it all hang together, I really do, sir.

"Of course, there is a lot more in the books that I have read, that I have not time to mention. I am just giving you a lick of the stirring spoon, sir, to give you an idea of the taste of the stew.

"But I do find Thomas More very hard to believe. He says that Sir James Tyrrel was knighted as a reward for killing the Two Little Princes. That is just sheer rubbish, sir. Sir James had been knighted a good twelve years earlier, in 1471. Master More says that Tyrrel confessed to the murders before he was executed for treason against Henry the Seventh. To begin with, that was in 1502, some nineteen years after the murders are supposed to have taken place, and seventeen after Henry took the crown. And Tyrrel was not publicly accused of the murders; nor was he ever tried for them. He was executed for some *other* crime of treason, *and* his confession was never made public. Why would not Henry the Seventh have accused him of the murders? If King Henry had his hands on such a confession, why would he not want to publish it up and down the land, to blacken Richard's name and to bolster his own claim to the throne? Even more important: Long before that, if Henry had found the princes dead or missing when he took the throne, why did he not say so then? Why did he not blame Richard then, sir?"

The questions echoed with heavy significance as we emerged into the daylight and fresh air again, and began to walk uphill towards the White Tower.

"There are serious doubts, sir, miss, as to whether any such confession was ever made," Baker continued. "It was certainly never seen or heard of again. Again I ask: If Henry the Seventh had his hands on such a confession, why would he not want to publish and post it up and down the land, to make sure that everybody saw the proof of Richard's

57

murders? Tyrrel's accomplice, John Dighton, is also supposed to have confessed to the murder, but Dighton was apparently never even arrested, and nobody has ever seen his confession, either. You have to wonder if there ever were any confessions at all.

"From what I have read," Baker continued, "Shakespeare got most of his history at second-hand from Thomas More; so if Master More was wrong they were both wrong, and the untruths just got carried on, and became the common story.

"As a Yeoman Warder, I have to know the official history of the Tower inside and out. Worst day of my life, having to stand there and tell it to the Governor and to the Yeoman Porter and the Yeoman Gaoler, sir. Just the three of them testing me, real experts, and me quaking in my boots. Worse than the first time I had to talk to my old serjeant-major; my voice just went all tight and squeaky on me, sir."

I laughed with happy reminiscence. "We must have run into the same serjeant-major, Baker. Ours was a fine chap called Slack. 'Slack is my name, but not my nature!' He never let us forget it, either."

"Right, sir. Well, I passed my test, but then I started doing a bit of reading on my own, and I kept finding things wrong with the official history, or, at least, things that do not add up, sir.

"I got in a bit of trouble for asking too many questions, but in the end the Governor said that it is all right to question even the official history, as long as we do so fairly, and point out both sides of the coin.

"If you will come this way, now, I will show you where they say the princes' bodies were buried, or re-buried, and then I shall tell you about another death in the Tower that Richard definitely ordered, sir."

"Ah, Lord Hastings?" said I. "Will you will point out both sides of that coin, too?"

"Not much doubt about that particular coin, sir. Richard ordered his execution, all right. From the time I came here to the Tower in '66, though, I have found that some of the coins in the official history have so many sides that they would be a dead loss for our games over at The Tiger tavern."

I looked hard at Baker.

"Baker, I am sorry that you got into some trouble, but it is hardly surprising. You seem to be saying that More and Shakespeare and Dickens are wrong, and that the official history of the Tower is wrong, and that my schoolbooks and my teachers were all wrong."

"Well, sir," replied Baker, as he led us briskly to the south side of the imposing White Tower, "all I am saying is that a lot of things just do not add up. It could be that Master More and Mr. Shakespeare and Mr. Dickens are right. I do not deny that, sir; but a lot of things that they wrote do not add up."

I served Baker with a frown intended to leave a cautionary impression on him.

"Baker, we must not be too quick to reach conclusions. My friend Mr. Sherlock Holmes, the consulting detective, has often shown me how dangerous it is to reason from insufficient data. In my commission from Oxford, I must be very much on my guard against falling into that trap."

Baker signalled understanding.

"Now, sir, this is the famous White Tower, the Norman keep." Miss Rivas and I looked up, in silent awe, at this celebrated castle and symbol of Britain.

"The Normans' first stone keep in England," continued Baker. "Ninety feet from ground to battlements. The walls are fifteen feet thick at the bottom, and eleven feet at the top. It looks square, but all four sides are actually of different lengths. A typical Norman castle, with that single entrance" – Baker pointed to a round-arched doorway, some fifteen feet above the ground –"up there, approached by wooden stairs that would be easy to defend; you could lock yourself in and set fire to the stairs if you needed to.

"In Richard's time, that door took you into the Constable's Hall. Behind that was the Constable's chamber, and, in the opposite corner to the door, in the round tower at the northeast corner, there was a spiral staircase. Up that was the king's council chamber. Nowadays there are three floors in the White Tower. The third floor, though, was not built until early in the 1600s. In Richard's time, there were actually only two floors. The council chamber rose all the way to the roof, at that time, and had an upper gallery around it. Richard the Third attended a number of meetings in the council chamber, and it was from there that William, Lord Hastings, was taken down to his death.

"Now, Doctor Watson, Miss Rivas, you will remember the story that the murderers buried the Two Little Princes under some stairs. Master More-fiction-than-fact says that a priest then re-buried them in some secret place. Some say that they were dropped in the river or the sea, but others say that they were buried again here in the Tower.

"The reason that I have brought you to this spot is that right at this place, there used to be a stone fore-building that contained a stair up to the main entrance up there. It was in 1674 that workmen tore it all down, and discovered a wooden chest with two skeletons in it, buried some ten feet deep, in the ground under the stair.

"They were the skeletons, sir, of two youngsters."

Miss Rivas gasped. "The Two Little Princes, found at last."

"That was the common belief, Miss Rivas, yes. The king, Charles the Second, and his authorities, said that they must be the bones of the Two Little Princes. The king had them properly buried in Westminster. You can see their tomb in the abbey."

"Baker," said I, "could this mean that More was right all along? I mean, it seems too much of a coincidence. More says that the princes were buried under a staircase, as these were.

"But hold on. More says the boys were re-buried by a priest. Then you have these bones found under a staircase. Why would the priest, having been instructed that Richard III wanted them given a proper burial, simply bury them again under yet *another* staircase? Indeed, *could* a priest, secretly and on his own, bury anybody ten feet deep under a staircase, let alone two bodies?

"Perhaps Thomas More got it wrong, or made up the story about the priest. Perhaps the boys were in reality buried only once, right here, under the stairs in your fore-building. I wonder, then, could the princes have actually been held prisoner in the White Tower itself?"

"Yes, sir, that is quite possible. The truth is, there are no proper records at all of where they were actually held in the Tower."

Despite Mr. Holmes's solemn warnings against theorizing without data, I was leaning somewhat favourably towards Sir Thomas More's account, when Yeoman Warder Baker interrupted my train of thought with yet another stunning piece of information.

"On the other hand, sir, it has also been said that the Princes were not smothered in their bed at all, but were just walled up and left to starve and die. That is the story given by a French writer, Jean Molinet. And, sir, there is a record that, long before 1674, the skeletons of two children *were* found walled up in a small room at the Tower. They say they were the skeletons of two little boys, sir."

"Baker," I burst out, "I am afraid that nobody could determine from the skeletons alone, at the ages of the Two Little Princes, whether they were male or female. Nor could they determine their ages from the skeletons, be they the walled-up ones or the ones from under the stairs.

"So, in truth, Charles the Second and his authorities were merely guessing when they identified the bones found under the staircase in 1674 as those of the princes.

"Nor, by examining the bones, could anybody say *when* they died.

"Indeed, the best that anyone could say is that your bones found under the stairs in 1674 were of two smallish people, genders unknown, ages unknown, names unknown, who died of unknown causes at an unknown time prior to their discovery. And that is about all that one can make of it."

I shook my head in heavy disapproval.

"What became of the earlier skeletons, Baker, the ones that were found walled up in the small room? Do I take it that they were not sent to Westminster Abbey?"

61

"No idea, sir. They were found quite early in the seventeenth century, but there is no further record of them, I am afraid."

I looked Baker in the eye. "Then we seem to be back to that strange coincidence of the burial under the staircase by the White Tower. As I say, I must read Thomas More's account for myself."

"Well," said Miss Rivas, confidently, "if they were the skeletons of the Two Little Princes they were obviously murdered by *somebody*."

"How do you know that?" I asked.

"Because of the care taken to put them into a chest and bury them ten feet deep in the ground. Is that not extraordinarily deep for a grave?"

"They might have died of a plague," I suggested. "But you make a very good point. Mr. Holmes should offer you a situation as a detective."

"If so," she returned, "I can not for the life of me deduce why the bodies would be buried underneath a staircase, then dug up and re-buried under another staircase. It sounds highly improbable, to put it mildly."

A thought came to me. "Hum! Baker, you said that the Two Little Princes were aged nine and twelve. Mr. Dickens said – I am sure of this – that they were eleven and thirteen."

"Master More said the same, sir, but they were in fact nine and twelve. Little Richard was not yet ten and Edward was just a little older than twelve when their father died.

"Now, sir," Baker added, carefully, measuring his words, "I suppose the question of their ages all depends on exactly *when* they were murdered.

"Was it in the summer of 1483, after Richard took the throne? The summer when one was twelve and the other not yet ten? Or did they live past that? Into the reign of Henry the Seventh, when they indeed *were* eleven and thirteen?

"Even Thomas More admits that some people believed they were in fact not killed during Richard's reign."

"Sir Thomas says that?" Miss Rivas asked in surprise.

"Oh, yes, miss. Odd, is it not, after all his efforts to accuse King Richard of murdering them?"

The broad-shouldered Yeoman Warder turned to me.

"Doctor Watson, if you have not already become aware of it, I should tell you that some people believe that it was really Henry the Seventh who killed them, to get them out of his way as he put on Richard's crown. Some believe that another suspect was the Duke of Buckingham. He was one of Richard's allies, at first, but rebelled against him, and may have aimed to claim the throne himself. Some say he might have killed the boys, either to further his own aims or those of Henry."

This was the first intimation to me that history had identified other suspects. Why had not this been mentioned in my school books?

I was naturally eager to know more, but Baker broke in.

"Right, sir, miss. My time is getting on, I am afraid, and I had promised to tell you about the other murders in the Tower in which Richard the Third is accused. Lord Hastings I have already mentioned. He was a very, very powerful noble, and a member of Edward the Fourth's royal council. When Richard began to make his own claim to the throne, Hastings turned against him, and began to plot against him with the Woodvilles, the family of Edward the Fourth's queen, Elizabeth Woodville. If you do read Master More-fiction-than-fact, he will tell you how Richard had Hastings dragged out of the council chamber in the White Tower and had his head chopped off on a length of wood over there on the Green, sir. As I say, I do not think anyone has ever not accused Richard of that one."

I was staring towards the place of Hastings's summary execution when Baker tapped me politely on the shoulder.

"Now, Doctor Watson, we spoke a bit earlier about Richard's brother George, the Duke of Clarence. Nasty bit of work, sir, greedy and ambitious, and a traitor. I side with those who say that King Edward the Fourth had him done in, rather than Richard being to blame. But I have an idea about his death that does not go along with the usual thinking. Some say that Clarence was killed in the Bloody Tower, but most people, and the history books, say that it was in the Bowyer Tower, up north over there behind the Waterloo Block, the barracks.

"That could be true, but I keep wondering why Clarence would be shoved all the way over there in the Bowyer Tower, so far away from the royal apartments. Did Edward the Fourth really want him that far out of sight? If he did, well, you would certainly not see Clarence from the royal apartments. However, as far as we know, at that time the Bowyer Tower was still a manufactory and stores and residence for the royal bowyer and his men. The Bowyer Tower that you see today was rebuilt after a terrible fire in 1841.

"Now, where we stand, Doctor Watson, Miss Rivas, at the south-west corner of the White Tower, was the old Coldharbour Gate, the entrance to the Inmost Ward where the royal apartments were. Above the gate were chambers that were first used as a royal apartment, and later as a prison. Do you know what its popular name was? The Nun's Bower.

"My idea is that Clarence was really locked up there. Not in the Bowyer Tower, but in the Nun's Bower above the Coldharbour Gate. And the word 'Bower' got passed down to history, by mistake, as 'Bowyer'. Maybe I have come upon the answer, sir, to an old, old mystery; me, sir, an old soldier of the 61st Regiment of Foot."

Baker was visibly excited, and I pumped his firm hand warmly in congratulation, although my mind kept wandering back to that story of Sir Thomas More's about the staircase, the burial, and the bones. I shook my head back into the present. Baker was leading us once more to General Milman's office.

"Please remember to ask the governor about Mr. Clements Markham and Mr. James Gairdner, sir."

"Who are they?"

"Well, sir, Mr. Markham is an explorer. A real one, sir; the North Pole, and places like that. Big in the Royal Geographical Society, sir. You must have heard of him; he has often been in the newspapers.

"He is a friend of the Governor, sir, and the Governor once sent him to ask me some questions. Mr. Markham holds that Richard the Third has been slandered, and I believe that he is going to write a book to restore his reputation. I am sure that the governor would give you an introduction to him, sir."

"And Gairdner?"

"He is an antiquarian, sir, and a senior man in the Public Record Office. He has written a book about Richard the Third. Now, he has written to the Governor with questions a few times, and we have tried to help him with his studies. I thought, sir, that you might also ask the Governor for a letter of introduction to him, too, if you wished to speak to him. I would think that he owes the Governor the courtesy of seeing you, sir."

We bade a most grateful farewell to Baker. What a fine example he was of the gallant British soldier. Oh, how we value and honour too little such men, to whom we all owe so much.

Milman greeted us heartily once again. "Baker insists, Doctor Watson, that I must give you letters of introduction to two fellows who should be able to help you. I am happy to do so. James Gairdner you will find more than a little reserved, but I think that nobody knows more about Richard the Third than he. Clements Markham you will like, I know. Everybody does. Did Baker mention Markham's Tudor Conspiracy?"

"Tudor Conspiracy?"

"Markham argues that the history of Richard the Third, as we know it today, was largely written by writers who were in the pay of the Tudors who succeeded Richard, or had very good reason not to offend them by being kind towards Richard. Sir Thomas More, for example, or Polydore Virgil. Virgil was an Italian historian who was actually in the pay of Henry Tudor, the man who took Richard's throne. Markham will tell you that the Tudors and their hired writers deliberately created a black legend of Richard that has lasted until today. Gairdner vehemently disagrees. Markham tells me that he and Gairdner have exchanged strong letters on the subject."

As we parted, I found that the kindly governor had already prepared my two letters of introduction, and he now gave them to me with a flourish.

Miss Rivas's bright smile flashed again as I bade farewell to her.

"Doctor Watson," said she, "I should be most happy to assist you with your investigations, should you have need of information from York. I should much enjoy the challenge." I stammered my thanks, and found myself eagerly exchanging addresses with this charming young lady.

Milman looked impishly at us, with a light smile playing at the corners of his mouth and framed by his white whiskers.

"I would not wish to spoil Markham's surprise, Doctor Watson, but you do know that Thomas More was but an infant when Richard came to the throne?"

"So I understand. Five years old."

"Well, you will hear from Clements Markham an interesting proposition. That is, that Sir Thomas More did not write the book so widely attributed to him." Milman paused.

"You must ask Markham who *did* write it."

Chapter Five

As my dusty cab rattled noisily from the Tower towards Baker Street, again at Masterman-Pugh's expense, I reviewed some of the scrawled jottings that all but filled my new note book.

Puzzle piled upon historical puzzle. In particular, I chuckled as I read "2y n t wm" in the condensed note-hand that I had taught to myself. Mr. Holmes was a champion in shorthand, but I did not take to it naturally. Like David Copperfield, I should have been quite triumphant if I had the least idea what my notes were about. This scrawled notation, however, I could read as "two years in the womb." How on earth could Yeoman Warder Watson insist, with apparent sincerity of belief, that Richard the Third had been two years in his mother's womb? I wondered if Thomas More had recorded this medical miracle.

I stopped at Salmon and Gluckstein's to stock up on ship's tobacco. I also purchased in Oxford Street a new, larger, and cheaper note book and carefully stowed away the receipt for Masterman-Pugh's benefit.

I found on our letter tray a brief note from Holmes. "Back at seven o'clock, if all well. Dinner ordered for half past. S.H."

I began to read the copy that I had borrowed from General Milman of Sir Thomas More's short history, and encountered immediately More's extraordinary error, of which Baker had spoken so strongly, concerning the age of Edward the Fourth.

More wrote in his very first sentence that Edward the Fourth died "after he had lived fifty and three years, seven months, and six days". Yet, according to Milman and Baker, he was in fact aged only forty years, eleven months and twelve days. It was very, very odd, I thought. More must have known better, surely. Further, I was to find, More erroneously gave the Christian name of William Lord Hastings as Richard, and that of Henry Duke of Buckingham as Edward.

I found, also, those long speeches and quotations that seemed to have been recorded *verbatim*, as by an eye-witness; but I knew that More, a little child, could not have been such a witness. From where, then, did More get all this fine detail? From John Morton, perhaps, the man described by Yeoman Warder Baker as one of Richard's most bitter enemies?

I soon found, too, another oddity in Master More's account. He explicitly accused Richard of the cruel murder of the two unfortunate princes, and he provided much detail that lent some verisimilitude to his tale. Yet, at the same time, like a village gossip (or the lawyer that he was), More went to some trouble to stand at a safe distance from these claims. With pursed lips, I read such quibbling *caveats* as "it is for truth reported that" and "as the fame runs", and such careful qualifications as "as men constantly say" and "as men deemed".

More gave a detailed account of the murder of the princes by Richard's agents, in substantially the same form as did Dickens. Yet Sir Thomas carefully hedged it all about by saying that it was a story that "I have so heard by such men and such means as methinks it were hard but it should be true." At that, I shook my head; and I did so with even greater vigour when More openly admitted that there was doubt about whether the Two Little Princes died in Richard the Third's time at all. More conceded that "some remain yet in doubt whether they were in his days destroyed or no."

This was undoubtedly the peculiar and significant passage to which Baker had referred. So the Two Little Princes might in fact have survived Richard? They might actually have died in Henry the Seventh's reign?

Yet, I noticed, the cautious stipulations disappeared as More wrote on. Despite his many *caveats*, More left no doubt as to his belief that Richard was a malicious and murderous villain:–

> "He was close and secret, a deep dissembler, lowly of countenance, arrogant of heart, outwardly companionable where he inwardly hated, not hesitating to kiss whom he thought to kill, pitiless and cruel, not for evil will always but oftener for ambition and either for the surety or the increase of his position. 'Friend' and 'foe' were to him indifferent: where his advantage stood, he spared no man's death whose life was contrary to his purpose."

More also spoke of the crookback of which I had read in Shakespeare, saying that Richard was "little of stature, ill-featured of limbs, crook-backed, his left shoulder much higher than his right."

My list of eleven murders was in front of me, and I began in my second note book to record what Sir Thomas said about each of them. I found his archaic writing and spelling awkward, and so, where necessary, I have transcribed his words into somewhat more current English, while most carefully preserving their meaning and flavour.

First on my list was the murder of the young Edward, Prince of Wales, son and heir to Henry the Sixth. Shakespeare wrote that Richard stabbed Edward. Strangely, however, as Baker noted, Thomas More simply did not mention this murder. "Now that is most peculiar," said I to myself. "Why would Sir Thomas not play that card against Richard? Did he not know of the accusation? Surely he must have done. Or did he, rather, reject it as untrue?"

Second, I had on my list the murder of Henry the Sixth. Shakespeare accused Richard of stabbing Henry, also. Here, More wrote:–

> "He slew with his own hands – as men constantly say – King Henry the Sixth, being prisoner in the Tower, and

that without commandment or knowledge of the King, who would undoubtedly, if he had intended that thing, have appointed that butcherly office to some other than his own born brother."

I underlined in my note book the careful words "as men constantly say".

Third was the murder of Richard's own brother George, the Duke of Clarence, who had plotted and rebelled against Edward the Fourth. Shakespeare said that Richard betrayed George and brought about his death. Sir Thomas More wrote of Richard:—

"Some wise men also think that his drift, covertly conveyed, lacked not in helping forth his brother of Clarence to his death, which he resisted openly, howbeit somewhat (as men deemed) more faintly than he that were heartily minded to his welfare. And they that thus deem, think that he long time in King Edward's life forethought to be king in case that the King his brother (whose life he looked that evil diet should shorten) should happen to decease (as indeed he did) while his children were young. And they deem that for this intent he was glad of the death of his brother the Duke of Clarence, whose life must needs have hindered him whether the same Duke of Clarence had kept him true to his nephew, the young King, or enterprised to be king himself. But of all this point there is no certainty, and whoso divines upon conjectures may as well shoot too far as too short."

Again, I noted the trained lawyer's careful words, such as "some wise men also think" and "as men deemed" and "of all this point there is no certainty".

Fourth, fifth, and sixth upon my Newgate Calendar were the deaths of Earl Rivers, Lord Grey and Sir Thomas Vaughan, leaders in the Woodville plot to keep young Edward the Fifth under their control. Shakespeare said that Richard had them executed. Master More had it that they were beheaded at Pontefract. He said that they had had no trial.

Lord Hastings, seventh in my index, had no trial, either, it would seem. More painted a dramatic picture of Richard, in front of an audience of Lords in Council at the Tower of London, charging Hastings with treason. First, according to More, Richard asked the Bishop of Ely, the famed John Morton, to send to his garden for strawberries:–

"My Lord, you have very good strawberries at your garden in Holborn; I request you, let us have a mess of them."

"Gladly, my Lord," quoth he. "Would God I had some better thing as ready to your pleasure than that."

Then Richard supposedly made the amazing charge that Edward the Fourth's queen had, "by sorcery and witchcraft", recently shrivelled his left arm. Thomas More bluntly stated, however, that the arm "was never otherwise". If so, however, More had not mentioned this withered arm in his own earlier description of Richard's appearance.

There followed the sudden accusation against Hastings of treason, and his speedy execution, beheaded upon a baulk of timber at the Tower. "For by St. Paul," said Richard, "I will not to dinner until I see thy head off." Or so said Thomas More, who had, of course, not been there himself to witness any of this.

Eighth upon my bloody register of death was Henry Stafford, the Duke of Buckingham. Here was the spectre of Morton again. At first, Buckingham was Richard's ally, but later turned against him. It was Bishop Morton who artfully moved Buckingham against Richard. More said that this led to Buckingham's destruction, but More's story broke off short at this point, and gave no account of Buckingham's end.

Ninth on the roll was the death of Anne Nevill, Richard's queen. Shakespeare hinted that Richard was responsible for her death. There was, however, no mention of this death in More's tale; just as there had been no mention of the murder of the Prince of Wales. Odd, again.

The two most important deaths were, of course, the murders of the two Little Princes, and it was to More's account of these that I paid close attention. Wrote More:–

> "I shall rehearse you the dolorous end of those babes, not after every way that I have heard, but after that way that I have so heard by such men and by such means as methinks it were hard but it should be true."

Once more, even my poorly developed detective skills trumpeted a strident alarum. So Sir Thomas More had heard *other* stories and other versions of the Two Little Princes' deaths, had he? What were those stories? Why were they not in his account? Who were the men from whom, and the means by which, he had heard the particular story that he had selected to relate?

More went on to declare that, after his coronation, Richard went to visit Gloucester. As he rode, he made plans to kill the princes because, if they lived, his claim to the throne could be challenged. "He thought therefore without delay to be rid of them."

> "Whereupon [More continued] he sent one John Green, whom he specially trusted, unto Sir Robert Brakenbury, Constable of the Tower, with a letter and credentials also that the same Sir Robert should in any wise put the two children to death. This John Green did his errand unto Brakenbury, kneeling before Our Lady in the Tower, who plainly answered that he would never put them to death, though he should die therefor; with which answer John Green returning, recounted the same to King Richard at Warwick, yet on his progress.
>
> "Wherewith he took such displeasure and thought, that the same night he said unto a secret page of his, 'Ah, whom shall a man trust? Those that I have brought up myself, those that I thought

would most surely serve me, even those fail me, and at my commandment will do nothing for me.'

"'Sir,' quoth his page, 'there lies one on your pallet without that, I dare well say, to do your Grace pleasure, the thing would be right hard that he would refuse' – meaning by this Sir James Tyrrell, who was a man of right goodly personage and, for nature's gifts, worthy to have served a much better Prince, if he well served God and by grace obtained as much truth and good will as he had strength and wit.

"The man had a high heart and sore longed upward, not rising yet so fast as he had hoped, being hindered and kept under by the means of Sir Richard Ratcliffe and Sir William Catesby, who, longing for no more partners of the Prince's favour, and especially not for him, whose pride, they knew, would bear no peer, kept him by secret drifts out of all secret trust. Which thing this page had well marked and known. Wherefor, this occasion offered of very special friendship, he took the opportunity to put him forward and by such wise to do him good – such that all the enemies he had, except the devil, could never have done him so much hurt.

"For upon this page's words King Richard arose (for this communication had he sitting on the stool – a fitting carpet for such a counsel) and came out into the pallet-chamber, on which he found in bed Sir James and Sir Thomas Tyrrell, of person like and brethren of blood but nothing of kin in qualities. Then said the King merrily to them, 'What, sirs, be ye in bed so soon?' and calling up Sir James, broke to him secretly his mind in this mischievous manner. In which he found him nothing unwilling. Wherefor on the morrow he sent him to Brakenbury with a letter, by which he was commanded to deliver Sir James all the keys of the Tower for one night, to the end he might there accomplish the King's pleasure in such thing as he had given him commandment. After which letter delivered and the keys received, Sir James appointed the next night ensuing to destroy them, devising before and preparing the means.

"The Prince [by which More meant the uncrowned Edward the Fifth], as soon as the Protector had left that name and took himself as King, had it showed unto him that he should not reign but his uncle should have the crown. At which word the Prince, sore abashed, began to sigh and said, 'Alas, I would my uncle would let me have my life yet, though I lose my kingdom.' Then he that told him the tale, used him with good words and put him in the best comfort he could. But forthwith were the Prince and his brother both shut up and all others removed from them; only one, called Black Will or William Slaughter, was set to serve them and see them sure. After which time the Prince never tied his laces nor in any way cared for himself, but with that young babe his brother lingered in thought and heaviness till this traitorous death delivered them of that wretchedness.

"For Sir James Tyrrell devised that they should be murdered in their beds. To the execution whereof he appointed Miles Forest, one of the four that kept them, a fellow fleshed in murder before time. To him he joined one John Dighton, his own horsekeeper, a big broad strong knave."

Thus did More write of the preparations for the murder of the Two Little Princes. It was more detailed than the tale of Mr. Dickens, but it left in even my simple mind a long list of questions.

Who was John Green, also mentioned by Dickens? When did Green see the Tower's commander, Sir Robert Brackenbury (the more usual spelling, I was to find)? Dickens, I noted, had said this was "upon a day in August", and I knew that must be in 1483; but More gave no date. Was Richard really so rash as to put such dangerous secret instructions in writing? If Richard was intent upon murder, would he not have sounded out Brackenbury before leaving London? Who was this ambitious Sir James Tyrrell (whose name, I later found, was more properly spelled Tyrrel)? Who was the aptly named Slaughter, by the sound of him both servant and gaoler? Why did More call Slaughter the "only one" to guard the boys, but immediately go on to say that *four* people kept them? Who was Miles Forest, described by Dickens as a "murderer by trade", and whom had he killed before in this trade? Who was John Dighton?

Above all, how did Sir Thomas More come to know of all these events and conversations and dark secrets, being only five years of age at the time?

I wrote these questions and others down in my journal, and returned to Master More's tale. It continued:–

"Then all the others being removed from them, this Miles Forest and John Dighton about midnight (the innocent children lying in their beds) came into the chamber and suddenly lapped them up among the bedclothes – so bewrapped and entangled them, keeping down by force the featherbed and pillows hard unto their mouths, that within a while, smothered and stifled, their breath failing, they gave up to God their innocent souls into the joys of heaven, leaving to the tormentors their bodies dead in the bed.

"After the wretches perceived them – first by the struggling with the pains of death and after, long lying still – to be thoroughly dead, they laid their bodies naked out upon the bed and fetched Sir James to see them. Who, upon the sight of them, caused those murderers to bury them at the stair-foot, meetly deep in the ground under a great heap of stones.

"Then rode Sir James in great haste to King Richard and showed him all the manner of the murder, who gave him great thanks and, as some say, there made him a knight.

"But he [here, More meant Richard] allowed not, as I have heard, the burying in so vile a corner, saying that he would have them buried in a better place because they were a King's sons. Lo, the honourable heart of a King!

"Whereupon they say that a priest of Sir Robert Brakenbury took up the bodies again and secretly interred them in such a place as, by the occasion of his death – for he alone knew it – could never since come to light.

"Very truth is it and well known that at such time as Sir James Tyrrell was in the Tower, for treason committed against the most famous Prince, King Henry the Seventh, both Dighton and he were examined, and confessed the murder in the manner above written, but whither the bodies were removed they nothing could tell.

"And thus, as I have learned of them that much knew and little cause had to lie, were these two noble princes, these innocent tender children – born of most royal blood, brought up in great prosperity, likely long to live to reign and rule in the realm – by traitorous tyranny taken, deprived of their state, shortly shut up in prison, and privily slain and murdered, their bodies cast God knows where, by the cruel ambition of their unnatural uncle and his pitiless tormentors.

"Which things on every part well pondered, God never gave this world a more notable example, neither in what unsurety stands this worldly state, or what mischief works the proud enterprise of a high heart, or finally what wretched end ensues from such pitiless cruelty. For, first to begin with the agents – Miles Forest at St. Martin's piecemeal rotted away. Dighton indeed yet walks alive, in good possibility to be hanged ere he die. But Sir James Tyrrell died at Tower Hill, beheaded for treason. King Richard himself – as ye shall hereafter hear – slain in the field, hacked and hewed by his enemies' hands, haled on horseback dead, his hair contemptuously torn and pulled like a cur dog. And this mischief he took within less than three years of the mischief that he did."

Hold hard! I cried. Did not Yeoman Warder Baker say that Tyrrel had confessed, and had been executed, some nineteen years after the supposed murder of the Little Princes, in 1502? Yet Dighton, who had also supposedly confessed, was still walking free when More wrote his story, in or about 1513. How, and why? Had Dighton been pardoned by Henry the Seventh? Or turned King's Evidence? Above all, why, as Baker asked, was Tyrrel executed for treason rather than for the murder of the Two Little Princes?

More directed no hint of suspicion of the murders at either Henry Tudor or the Duke of Buckingham, although Baker had named both as possible suspects. More said only that Buckingham fell out with Richard because Richard rejected his claim to the lands of the Duke of Hereford. Then the wily Bishop Morton planted the thought that Buckingham was well suited to be king himself, and precipitated Buckingham's revolt against Richard the Third. That ended in Buckingham's capture and execution.

I heard heavy footsteps on the stairs, and the door to our chambers smacked sharply into the door-stop as it was flung violently open.

An ill-clad and ill-shaven Sherlock Holmes, his match-seller's tray under his arm, glowered darkly at me.

"I am a complete and utter fool, Watson. Two solid days of work, two whole days of my life, utterly wasted. I am, as you know, investigating the embezzlement of considerable sums from a company in the City. My chief suspect is one of the partners in the company. He has covered his trail well enough, but I have discovered that he has secret rooms not far from Victoria Station, where he stays on occasion. I have been using my trusty match-seller's disguise to observe these rooms, while unobserved myself.

"I saw nothing useful, literally nothing, for the past two days. I finally sought information in a public house, at the cost of a small fortune in libations for some of the regular patrons. There I learned that for the whole two days the entire street has been fully aware of my role as an impostor and watchman. It seems that the selling of Bryant and May's Vesuvians in that neighbourhood is more commonly done by children. I should have known. I should have taken the knife-grinding wheel. They had also seen through all of my agents who maintained the vigil for me through the nights. Some wag christened me the 'Vesta Virgin', and they have to a man been laughing up their sleeves. Warning word has surely been passed to my suspect, and he must know that somebody is on his trail. I am mortified, Watson, mortified."

I regret that I could not resist. "You have met your *match*," I quipped.

Poor Mr. Holmes winced. He looked so thoroughly crestfallen, and so remarkably like a miserably bedraggled heron, that I put a comforting hand on his shoulder.

"Watson, pour me a stiff whisky, if you will, and tell me that I have your sympathy."

I hastened to comply with both appeals, and sought to divert him by reporting hastily on my own researches.

"Well done," said he, at length, somewhat more relaxed than when he entered. "I applaud your methodical approach, of making a guiding list of all the many questions and issues that you must address. Were I not feeling so thorough a dunce today, I would say to you that you have done exactly what I would have done in the case. I am not sure that you would take that as a compliment, given my miserable failure."

I reassured him that I was both moved and encouraged by his praise.

"Thank you." He paused. "Well, Watson, I think that in my own case I shall be reduced to engaging new and more effective agents to watch further for my quarry, and to determine where and how he spends his money. Few thieves can resist the temptation to spend promptly their ill-gotten gains. Many a man has gone to prison after it was observed that his care-free spending far exceeded his known and legitimate income. But what of your own case? What is your next move?"

"I think, Holmes, that I must look for the writings of contemporaries of Richard. First, however, I will further examine Shakespeare. Mr. Marmaduke Hornidge has responded with an invitation to see him. He is an old friend of my family and almost a godfather to me. He is something of an expert on Shakespeare. I have a vague memory, too, that Mr. Hornidge's house in Barnes has some connection with Richard the Third.

"Now, Holmes, we have a little time until dinner. Would you care for a brief walk?"

"Indeed, Watson, I would much love a walk, if you can put up with such a desperate amateur for company."

Holmes's good spirits returned during our short ramble. Despite the setback in his current case, he gave me a most interesting lecture on the art of secretly following a suspect. "Shadowing," he called it. He demonstrated his techniques on unsuspecting pedestrians, and then made me attempt them, with some success under his tutelage, as we walked.

After our dinner of curried mutton, as I fell asleep, I thought again of More and Morton. Who on earth were More's sources, who "much knew and little cause had to lie"?

Morton had been arrested at Richard's council meeting, after sending for his serving of strawberries, and had then been imprisoned by Richard at Buckingham's chief castle in Wales.

Morton therefore had much, rather than little, cause to lie; and he might indeed be a hostile source, or *the* hostile source, from which More and then Shakespeare had drawn their history. Yeoman Warder Baker clearly thought so.

And what of the intriguing question raised by General Milman? If More had not written his account, who had?

Chapter Six

Mr. Sherlock Holmes had a number of eccentric habits. One was that of haphazardly stuffing all his bills, money and accounts into an old opera hat upon his desk. Another, one of his more destructive, was that of pinning his unanswered letters to the centre of the mantelpiece with an old jack-knife. I discovered to my horror in the morning a new assault on that well scarred wood. A note was speared to the very front of the mantel with the blade of a Scottish *sgian dubh*. "No more matches. Gone to look up Wiggins. Good luck to us both. *Fortis et Fidus!* S.H."

Wiggins was the Artful Dodger and serjeant-major of a corps of unruly street urchins who assisted Holmes from time to time. I deduced that Holmes, the frustrated Vesta Virgin, was now going to unleash his ill-washed Baker Street Irregulars against his elusive embezzler.

There was also a letter for me from Thomas Warren, the bright-eyed dean of arts and senior tutor at Magdalen. Holmes's pencil had scrawled another note on the unopened envelope. "The game is afoot!"

I hastily opened the letter.

"My dear Doctor Watson [it began], Wilson and I were talking on Saturday night about the historical accuracy or inaccuracy of Shakespeare's *King Richard the Third*, and we decided to read it in full together in my rooms. This we did after Chapel on Sunday, going without our usual walk. On Monday, we did the same with scenes from Shakespeare's *Henry the Sixth, Parts II and III*, since it was there that Richard was first introduced to theatre audiences as a deadly villain. After our readings, we reminded ourselves that you must be hard at work on the chase in London. With our apologies for any trespass upon your field, we offer some simple observations, in the hopes that they may be of assistance to you.

"As far as we can determine, *Richard the Third* was composed and first presented between 1592 and 1593 or 1594, some one hundred and seven years or more after Richard's death. It seems fairly quickly to have followed Shakespeare's *Henry the Sixth, Part III*, which we believe was written in 1591 or 1592.

"While we cannot vouch for the accuracy or otherwise of Shakespeare's physical or moral portrayal of Richard, we do note that he takes certain theatrical liberties with dates. We, naturally, after our conversation here, wondered if Shakespeare has also taken melodramatic liberties with fact. You will recall Wilson suggesting that William Shakespeare valued his audience first and his facts second. No doubt you will address such matters in your research.

"One of our scouts here, Sawkins, has a talent (if one may so call it) for impromptu rhymes and light doggerel. With his popular example in mind, Wilson and I (normally poets of more classical instinct; Greek verse being a particular love of mine) composed together the following verse, using the descriptions of Richard the Third that were given by Shakespeare's characters in the plays:–

    'O indigested and deforméd lump,
    Crookback prodigy (with birthright a hump);
    Loathéd issue, and minister of Hell,
    The devil's butcher; bloody boar, as well;

Execution'r, and guilty homicide,
Villain, tyrant, and bloody wretch, beside;
Damnéd son, foul swine, hellhound, carnal cur,
Hedgehog, and hell's black intelligencer;
Defuséd infection of mortal man,
Cockatrice; also murderous villain;
Cacodemon, and, more, bottled spider;
Of God's own handiwork foul defacer;
Elvish markéd abortive rooting hog,
O rag of honour, toad, and bloody dog.'

"While we composed it lightly [Warren continued], it paints a dark and dramatically violent picture of Richard. This fits, of course, with President Bulley's description, at our dinner, of Richard as a regicide, usurper, and murderer. Shakespeare, however, gives Richard no credit whatsoever for those other legacies that our President mentioned, of benevolent laws, fair courts, good government and the like. It struck us that Shakespeare has nothing but the most damning evil to say of Richard, yet, in the view of President Bulley, there was some good in the man.

"According to our library notations here, Shakespeare's sources for his history were Edward Hall's *The Union of the Noble and Illustre Famelies of Lancastre and York*, published in 1548, and Raphael Holinshed's *The Chronicles of England, Scotland and Ireland*, of 1587. Holinshed follows Hall closely in his story of Richard the Third, and Hall has quite clearly taken his lead from Sir Thomas More's *History of King Richard III* and, for the period following Richard's accession to the throne, from the *Anglica Historia* by a foreigner, Polydore Virgil. Indeed, Hall simply reproduces much of More's account in his own volumes.

"As an interjection, we may mention that it is sometimes reported that More was a scholar here at Magdalen. There is, we note, no record of that; and his own great-grandson recorded that More in fact attended

Canterbury College, a Benedictine institution, which was demolished in the last century.

"If Shakespeare's dark picture stems, as our brief researches suggest, from Sir Thomas More, an interesting question is raised: From where did Sir Thomas More obtain *his* picture? He was not born until 1478. He was therefore only five years old when Richard took the throne, and only seven when Richard died. More did not write his *History of King Richard III* until 1513 or thereabouts, almost thirty years after Richard's death.

"We wonder, Doctor Watson, if More drew his water from a poisoned well? If so, where – or, rather, who – was that well?"

Warren ended his letter with cordial wishes, but the urgent question that he and Baker and Milman raised rang relentlessly in my head. More was only a child when Richard ruled. How did More the adult writer know of what he wrote? Did he draw his water from a poisoned well? And was that well Richard's sworn enemy, Bishop John Morton?

I sent out for *Henry the Sixth, Parts II* and *III*, and set myself to reading the Shakespeare plays, carefully and in full, in preparation for my visit to Marmaduke Hornidge, the old friend of my late father.

I re-read the last ringing verses of Shakespeare's *Richard the Third* as my cab rattled through the Tuscan arches of Hammersmith Bridge and down Upper Bridge Road towards Barnes.

The elderly Mr. Hornidge, churchwarden and Justice of the Peace, was often in low spirits. Consumption had claimed the lives of several of his children, and their premature deaths preyed often upon his mind. He greeted me, however, with energetic enthusiasm, and his fingers twisted in his whiskers with unusual excitement.

"I have my notes on Shakespeare's *Richard the Third* all ready for you, John," said he, with pride.

"I must point out that our house here, Milbourne House, has some connection with Richard, at least indirectly. I am not sure who possessed it in Richard's time; there are no records for that period. However, in 1517 or so, it was owned by Sir Henry Wyatt. Long before that, he had been opposed to Richard's usurpation of the throne, and was imprisoned in the Tower. Why, it is said that he was tortured and racked, and in Richard's presence, too. The story is told that Wyatt so tamed and trained a cat that it would catch pigeons for him, and bring them to his cell, so that he might eat better fare than that given to him by his gaolers."

Milbourne House truly reeked of history. After Sir Henry Wyatt, the house had passed to his son Sir Thomas, the poet and lover of the ill-fated Anne Boleyn. From him it went to Sir Thomas's son, who was executed for treason by Queen Mary, Bloody Mary. Robert Beale was a later tenant; he was one of the official Elizabethan party sent to advise Mary Queen of Scots of her imminent execution, at the castle of Fotheringhay where Richard was born. The novelist Henry Fielding lived at Milbourne House, and may have written *Amelia* here.

After an early dinner, Mr. Hornidge and I retreated to deep cane chairs in his elegant first-floor study looking out over the pond. Mr. Hornidge read Warren's letter from Oxford carefully, and began to squint at his notes on Shakespeare's writings on Richard the Third.

"*The Tragedy of Richard the Third: with the Landing of Earle Richmond and the Battell at Bosworth Field,*" intoned my host, ringingly. "The full title, John, from the *First Folio* edition, as published in 1623, some seven years after Shakespeare's death. Alas, I have only a more modern version in my library.

He paused, then spoke slowly. "I must first remark that your friends in Oxford are perfectly right. We should most certainly look upon Shakespeare as a dramatist and not as an historian. He was not an historian as we understand the term today, and he did indeed severely distort the record of history to make his dramatic points. His *Macbeth*, for example, is but a travesty of Scottish history, and his characters in that melodrama bear little resemblance to reality.

85

"Still, a fine play *Richard the Third* is," he continued, with enthusiasm. "The last performance I saw myself was in 'seventy-seven, Henry Irving's version. Somewhat closer to Shakespeare's original version than usual, by the way. But the question we address is one of Shakespeare's accuracy and reliability.

"Shakespeare's treatment of Richard the Third does indeed take numerous liberties with the truth. For example, we first meet Richard in *Henry the Sixth, Part II,* and Shakespeare most clearly has it in for him from the start.

"Richard is clearly portrayed as an adult, at the time of the execution of the rebel, Jack Cade. That was in 1450; but the fact is that Richard was not even born until 1452.

"Shakespeare has Richard as a hardened warrior at the Battle of St. Alban's. Shakespeare has him saying:– 'Priests pray for enemies, but princes kill.' Indeed, in the play Richard kills the Duke of Somerset. But, again, this cannot be so. Richard was only a little over two years old at the time of that conflict.

"At the Battle of Wakefield, in 1460, Shakespeare places Richard at his unfortunate father's castle of Sandal, and has him already, it would seem, casting a covetous eye towards the Crown. 'And father, do but think how sweet a thing it is to wear a Crown.'

"Yet Richard was at that time only eight years old, and, we know, in the care of his mother in London.

"We go on to see Richard plotting his own quest for the crown:–

> "'I'll make my heaven to dream upon the crown
> And, while I live, t'account this world but hell,
> Until my mis-shaped trunk that bears this head
> Be round impaled with a glorious crown.'

Richard goes on, in the play, to remark that many persons and their lives stand between him and the throne. But no matter:–

> "'Why, I can smile, and murther whiles I smile.'

"All this when, in truth, Richard was but a small boy.

"Shakespeare has Richard as a warrior at the side of Edward the Fourth at every battle in Edward's forceful ascent to the throne. Yet Richard was still a child when Edward became King, and there is no record showing Richard acting in any military *rôle* at all until a full ten years later. Thus Shakespeare has Richard present at the battles of Mortimer's Cross and Towton, in the winter of 1461. In fact, Richard was still but a lad, and, to boot, was at that time on the Continent."

I sniffed. "I suppose that the same gross inaccuracies are to be found in his play *Richard the Third*?"

Mr. Hornidge raised a bushy eyebrow. "Oh dear, yes. Your friends' letter from Oxford mentions only the half of it

"Shakespeare has his chronology in that play hopelessly wrong. He presents an unbroken *continuum* of time, with no retrospective scenes. To do so, he strings together historical events in any old order, and makes a marvellous jumble of them.

"Right off the bat, in Act One, Scene One, we have the arrest of George, Duke of Clarence, followed by the death of Henry the Sixth. Yet Clarence's imprisonment took place in 1477, and Henry died six years earlier, in 1471. Shakespeare also has Clarence's arrest in 1477 precede Richard's marriage to Anne Nevill. Yet Richard married Anne in 1472. The Bard has Clarence arrested and imprisoned by Sir Robert Brackenbury, yet Sir Robert did not become Constable of the Tower until 1483, six years later. He was not in charge when Clarence was sent there, and was never Clarence's 'gentle keeper' as described in the play. We go on in this same scene to hear that Edward the Fourth is ill and close to death. Yet Edward's fatal illness struck in 1483, not in 1477.

"Another very fine example: Shakespeare has Henry Tudor and his army landing in Wales and marching to victory at Bosworth in November 1483; but those events, of course, took place in August 1485."

I nodded, politely. "I see that my friends at Magdalen indeed do not mention half of it in their letter."

Hornidge chuckled. "Oh, there is much, much more. The Bard blatantly alters people's ages and the dates of their deaths. He has George of Clarence's wife alive at the time of George's death. In fact, she died before him. Shakespeare has Queen Margaret of Anjou, the wife of Henry the Sixth, alive in England in 1483. Yet we know that she left England for ever in 1475, and died in France in 1482.

"Clarence's son Edward was but two or three when his father died, but Shakespeare presents him as an older and eloquent child. Shakespeare goes on to have Richard imprisoning Clarence's boy. 'The son of Clarence have I pent up close.' It was not Richard who imprisoned the boy, however; it was Henry the Seventh, and Henry went on to have him executed. Shakespeare also has Richard deliberately arranging a poor marriage for Clarence's daughter. That is simply not true; and, further, she was not married until some ten years later. Incidentally, Henry the Eighth eventually had her killed, to eradicate the Plantagenet line.

"There are other errors and misrepresentations, in addition to these. In Act Two, Scene Two, Shakespeare has the deaths of Clarence and King Edward coincident. Obviously that is rubbish. Clarence was executed in 1478; Edward died in 1483. The bard telescopes geography, too. In that same scene he has on stage together a number of characters including Richard, the Earl Rivers and the Duke of Buckingham. But we know that Richard was, at the time of the supposed scene, up in the North; Buckingham was in Wales, and Rivers was at Ludlow Castle.

"I note also that both Richard and Margaret of Anjou speak of her having been banished under pain of death. Yet she was not banished; the French ransomed her. Shakespeare calls Lord Stanley 'Lord Derby', yet Stanley did not assume the title of Earl of Derby until after Henry the Seventh took the crown. In Act Two, a messenger announces that Rivers and Grey have been imprisoned at Pontefract. In fact, Rivers was imprisoned at Sheriff Hutton castle in Yorkshire, and Grey at Middleham, Richard's own castle in Yorkshire. They were not moved to Pontefract until shortly before their execution. In a later scene, Lord Hastings is told that Rivers and Grey are to be executed on 'this same very day'. In reality, Hastings was himself beheaded twelve days before Rivers and Grey.

"I could go on, John, as there are other demonstrable inaccuracies and anachronisms in the play. But I believe I have made the point. The Bard was more than willing to alter history to make his play a dramatic success."

I spoke up, bitterly. "It is a case of fraud from beginning to end."

"Do not be too harsh on that account," replied Mr. Hornidge. "The telescoping of sequences and the re-arrangement of events was a common enough device in the theatre, and it still is. As Chorus says in *Henry the Fifth*:–

"'For 'tis your thoughts that now must deck our kings,
Carry them here and there, jumping o'er times,
Turning th'accomplishments of many years
Into an hour-glass.'

"Quite acceptable from the point of view of writing a play, John. Indeed, it was a hallmark of Shakespeare's historical plays. He used such tricks to build tension and drama, and to make it easy for the audience to follow the plot and its various threads."

I snorted in disdain. "Should I take it that the famous scene of Richard's seduction of the Lady Anne is equally as fraudulent?"

Mr. Hornidge chuckled.

"Ah, well, when you get into the matter of Shakespeare's historical verdicts, rather merely than his times and dates, that is perhaps a different matter.

"Act One, Scene Two, is indeed famous, or perhaps I should say infamous. Shakespeare, as you know, has Anne Nevill meeting Richard *en route* to the burial of her father-in-law, Henry the Sixth, whom Richard has supposedly murdered. He has also supposedly murdered Anne's husband, Henry's son Edward, the Prince of Wales, after the Battle of Tewkesbury. As you have read, she calls Richard every foul name under the sun, and invites him to hang himself. Richard openly confesses to both murders – but then successfully woos her, literally over Henry's dead body.

"Let us look at what they say over Henry's corpse."

He began to read, dramatically, his eyes twinkling as he read Richard's lines in a booming male voice, and Anne Nevill's in a more feminine pitch that made us both chuckle.

Lady Anne: [recited Mr. Hornidge]:
    Avaunt, thou dreadful minister of hell!
    Thou hadst but power over his mortal body, –
    His soul thou canst not have; therefore, be gone.
Richard:
    Sweet saint, for charity, be not so curst.
Lady Anne:
    Foul devil, for God's sake, hence, and trouble us not;
    For thou hast made the happy earth thy hell,
    Fill'd it with cursing cries and deep exclaims.
    If thou delight to view thy heinous deeds,
    Behold this pattern of thy butcheries.
    O, gentlemen, see, see! Dead Henry's wounds
    Open their congeal'd mouths and bleed afresh!
    Blush, blush, thou lump of foul deformity;
    For 'tis thy presence that exhales this blood
    From cold and empty veins, where no blood dwells;
    Thy deed, inhuman and unnatural,
    Provokes this deluge most unnatural.

I broke in. "I take that to reflect the old wives' tale that the corpse of a murder victim bleeds in the presence of his murderer."

"Shakespeare obviously so intended it, yes," replied Mr. Hornidge. "It is clearly meant to demonstrate to the Elizabethan audience Richard's guilt as a murderer. The Lady Anne roundly damns Richard as an assassin, and then alludes to the death of her husband Edward, Henry's son."

Richard:
    Fairer than tongue can name thee, let me have
    Some patient leisure to excuse myself.

Anne:

Fouler than heart can think thee, thou canst make
No excuse current, but to hang thyself.

Richard:

By such despair, I should accuse myself.

Anne:

And, by despairing, shouldst thou stand excused
For doing unworthy vengeance on thyself
That didst unworthy slaughter upon others.

Richard:

Say that I slew them not?

Anne:

Why, then, they are not dead;
But dead they are, and, devilish slave, by thee.

Richard:

I did not kill your husband.

Anne:

Why, then, he is alive.

Richard:

Nay, he is dead; and slain by Edward's hand.

Anne:

In thy foul throat thou liest; Queen Margaret saw
Thy murderous falchion smoking in his blood.

Mr. Hornidge looked up. "In reality, Queen Margaret of Anjou did not witness the death of her son Prince Edward. She was not there at all. She did not see Richard's smoking sword, or that of anybody else. Listen, as Anne continues; listen to Richard's smooth tongue."

Anne:

Didst not thou kill this king?

Richard:

I grant ye.

Anne:

Dost grant me, hedgehog? Then, God grant me too
Thou mayst be damned for that wicked deed!
O, he was gentle, mild and virtuous!

Richard:
    The fitter for the King of heaven, that hath him.
Anne:
    He is in heaven, where thou shalt never come.
Richard:
    Let him thank me, that holp to send him thither;
    For he was fitter for that place than earth.
Anne:
    And thou unfit for any place but hell.
Richard:
    Yes, one place else, if you will hear me name it.
Anne:
    Some dungeon.
Richard:
    Your bed-chamber.

"Well, I shall not read on. You have read the play yourself, John. Richard goes on to confess that he did indeed kill her Edward. She spits at him, and tells him she wishes her spittle were mortal poison. In the end, though, she accepts his ring and his suit.

"Is it not wonderful drama? In Shakespeare's Richard, I recognise Iago, of course, the soft-spoken villain. The wooing of Anne recalls Lycus's wooing of Megara in Seneca's *Hercules furens*. Shakespeare's play is indeed an absorbing drama.

"But what of Shakespeare's historical accuracy? That is the question that you are addressing.

"First, Shakespeare implies that Henry's coffin went by road to Chertsey. In fact, it went by barge, up the river. But let us be charitable to the bard, and suppose that his scene is set on a street between the Tower and St. Paul's, where the corpse was taken to lie in state, or, later, between St. Paul's and the river at Blackfriars.

"Second, Richard was almost certainly in Kent at the time. And Anne Nevill had been taken into custody some time earlier, after the Battle of Tewkesbury, and was almost certainly still held in safe keeping. Shakespeare's entire scene of their meeting is fictitious.

"Third, Shakespeare has Richard killing Prince Edward, but in reality there is really no historical evidence that Richard was in any way involved in his death. Certainly, no contemporary writer so alleges. Later in the play, Richard's brother George pleads guilty to this stabbing, although there is no evidence for that, either.

"Fourth, Richard speaks of Prince Edward's death as having taken place some three months earlier. But Edward died at Tewkesbury, less than three *weeks* earlier.

"Fifth, Richard did not kill Anne's father, the Earl of Warwick, at the Battle of Barnet, as Richard's character relates in the play. Nobody knows who killed Warwick, and nobody but Shakespeare has ever credited Richard with it.

"Sixth, Shakespeare then goes on to imply that Richard brought about Anne's death; and, at that, some two years earlier than the actual date of her death. There is no historical evidence, however, to suggest that Richard killed her, or had her killed. Richard had been a ward of Anne's father. I understand that Richard and Anne had been childhood friends, that their marriage was normal and a good one. They were certainly both deeply affected, together, when their young son died. Anne died young, indeed, but there is no evidence at all for Shakespeare's suggestion that Richard murdered her.

"In all this, Shakespeare has gone beyond telescoping dates. He now is simply and blatantly making up history. There is no evidence that Richard killed Warwick, no evidence that Richard killed Henry the Sixth, no evidence that he killed Prince Edward, and no evidence that he murdered his wife. Shakespeare's history is nonsense.

"As for the two princes, Shakespeare has Richard, of course, instructing Sir James Tyrrel to kill 'two deep enemies … those bastards in the Tower.' I do not have to tell you that this is Thomas More's story, and that in reality we do not know if the children were murdered; nor, if they were, do we know who did it, where, or when, or how.

"One more example: Shakespeare holds Richard responsible for plotting and bringing about the death of his brother George. In the play, Richard sends two hired murderers to kill George, bearing a warrant from King Edward the Fourth that Richard knows has since been countermanded. Again: Excellent drama, but the story was simply fabricated by Shakespeare."

"It is dishonest," I burst out. "Fraudulent."

Mr. Hornidge shook his head, patiently.

"Look on the play, rather, as a sermon on good and evil, with Richard's villainy, and probably his physical defects also, exaggerated for dramatic effect, the better to drive home the theme of the sermon: 'Crime does not pay.' In addition, since it was written for the common audience, for the popular Elizabethan theatre, it is all leavened with a tremendously entertaining dose of pageantry."

"A medieval morality play, in short?"

"Oh, yes, very much so. Remember, too, that Shakespeare's historical sources were severely limited. There were then few historians and textbooks and libraries as we know them today."

Mr. Hornidge looked down at his notes.

"Sir Thomas More's account was written, we believe, in 1513, although it did not come to light until after Henry the Eighth executed More in 1535. It was so full of errors, and had so many blanks left for names, that one doubts that it was ever intended for publication. Some have wondered, indeed, if it was but an academic exercise, borrowing writing techniques from some of the ancient classical authors.

"In the event, it did not appear in print until 1543, in a prose continuation of John Hardyng's *Chronicle* in verse, published by Richard Grafton. More's story was then absorbed into the book mentioned by your friends, Edward Hall's *The Union of the Noble and Illustre Famelies of Lancastre and York*. That was published in 1548, also by Grafton. It is abundantly clear that Hall also drew from the *Anglica Historia* by an Italian, Polydore Virgil, which had been published in 1534.

"In 1557, William Rastell, More's nephew, published what he described as a true version of More's *History*. Rastell declared that the versions relied upon by Grafton and Hall were 'very muche corrupte in many places.' Grafton, however, went on to reproduce the old Thomas More story, complete with Hall's embellishments, in his own *Chronicle* in 1568. Holinshed lifted *that* story for his *Chronicles of England, Scotland and Ireland* in 1587, and Shakespeare subsequently drew from Holinshed, as you know.

"Thus Shakespeare really got his history from Sir Thomas More, by way of Hall and Holinshed. He drew on Polydore Virgil, too, as your friends note. Virgil's *Anglica Historia* may, like More's little book, bear the title of a history, but it is as much a moral thesis on good and evil, on man's sins and divine retribution. Virgil was a cleric as well as an historian. I must note also that his book was commissioned by Henry the Seventh. Edward Hall drew his material from More and Virgil, and let us not forget that Hall was a fervid supporter of Henry the Eighth, son of Henry the Seventh.

"So there is the dramatic chain: Hall drew from More and Virgil, Holinshed drew from Hall, and Shakespeare drew from Holinshed.

"Thus the picture that most people today have of Richard is one that was painted with the brush of hearsay by More, was touched up by Virgil, was embellished by Hall and Holinshed, and was finally theatrically framed and staged as public entertainment by Shakespeare.

"I would hope, however, that the *modern* reader does not look upon More's work, or that of the others, as true recorded history. You see, John, Tudor historians conceived of written history not simply as an objective matter of record, as we now prefer to do, but as, rather, moral lectures, establishing values and codes of conduct for man to follow."

"You are saying they distorted the truth to serve this end?"

"Oh, indeed. Your question, though, surely confirms that you see and expect a clinical distinction between recorded history and propaganda. That would have been something of a foreign concept to Shakespeare and More.

"*Richard the Third* is as fine a piece of classical drama as Shakespeare ever produced, although it was clearly written quite early in his career. It is a great, traditional Senecan tragedy, in which one sees also clever elements of comedy. It took advantage of every theatrical device of its time. It has been extraordinarily popular for almost three hundred years, and deservedly so."

I exploded again. "But it is a lie. People do look upon Shakespeare's plays as a record of history. They believe him."

"That is to be regretted," said Mr. Hornidge, simply. "One commentator on Shakespeare, Peregrine Courtenay, wrote, if I recall the words correctly:–

"'The youth of England have been said to take their religion from Milton and their history from Shakespeare.'

"And, of course, the Duke of Marlborough is often quoted as saying that Shakespeare was the only English history that *he* ever read.

"Of course, that should not be so. Shakespeare, however, surely did not *invent* the stories that he told about Richard. He drew upon the historians and popular beliefs that were available to him. They may indeed have been partisan. They may indeed have been grievously wrong. They may indeed have foully slandered Richard. By the time Shakespeare wrote his play, however, their accounts were the accepted history of the day.

"Today, in our own time, do not the common people regard Richard the Third as a cruel and murderous villain, and Henry the Eighth as a bluff and jolly hero? That is the vulgar view of our time, is it not? Yet Henry the Eighth was a far, far bloodier and more vicious and more vengeful man than Richard.

"In Shakespeare's time, I am sure, the common people believed that Richard had murdered your Two Little Princes and usurped the throne. We can hardly blame Shakespeare the dramatist for, as we would now say, writing to suit his audience."

Hornidge looked down at his crabbed notes once more.

"Sir Walter Scott subscribed to the popular thesis of Richard the Third as a villain. However, in *Rob Roy*, Scott has Diana Vernon rating Shakespeare as 'a sad fellow called Will Shakespear, whose Lancastrian partialities, and a certain knack of embodying them, has turned history upside down, or, rather, inside out'. Perhaps that is the case in Shakespeare's treatment of Richard, but you must also bear in mind the times, John.

"Remember that Shakespeare was writing in the time of Queen Elizabeth. Her grandfather, of course, was King Henry the Seventh, the man who overthrew Richard. Shakespeare would have been foolhardy to produce a play that insulted the family of the ruling Queen. He wrote one that, following popular thinking – popular prejudice, if you will – cast her grandfather as the hero and Richard as the villain. Queen Elizabeth much favoured the play.

"Polydore Virgil was, as I say, a writer commissioned by Henry the Seventh. He, too, would surely have been foolhardy to bite the hand of the king that fed him."

I gulped down the last of my cognac, almost choking with anger at the duplicity of these famed and trusted writers.

"I have heard of a theory that More did not write his book himself," said I.

"Really?" returned Mr. Hornidge. "Then who did? Henry the Seventh?" He laughed uproariously, obviously trying to lighten the moment.

Still irked, I reached for my copy of *Richard the Third* and found the erroneous reference to Julius Caesar as builder of the Tower of London, at which Yeoman Warder Baker had laughed so sarcastically.

The young prince, the little Edward the Fifth, asked the Duke of Buckingham who had built the Tower.

"I do not like the Tower, of any place –
Did Julius Caesar build that place, my lord?"

There followed Buckingham's reply:–

"He did, my gracious lord, begin that place;

97

Which, since, succeeding ages have re-edified."

Little Edward had another question:–

"Is it upon record, or else reported
Successively from age to age, he built it?"

Buckingham replied:–

"Upon record, my gracious lord."

The Prince spoke again:–

"But say, my Lord, it were not register'd;
Methinks the truth should live from age to age,
As 'twere retailed to all posterity,
Even to the general all-ending day."

I looked askance at Mr. Hornidge. "How appropriate," said I, with heavy sarcasm, "that Shakespeare should so speak of the truth."

Mr. Hornidge looked back at me kindly. "I wonder, rather, if Shakespeare meant that passage as a signal to us to take his own recorded history with a pinch or two of salt?"

I snorted in disbelief. "Are we to believe, then, that Thomas More was sending such a signal when he made such an egregious error about the age of Edward the Fourth in his opening paragraph? I am not convinced."

Mr. Hornidge rose slowly from his chair, peering at his enormous gold watch.

"Voltaire said that ancient histories are but 'fables that have been agreed upon'. In other words, only God makes true history. Man makes history up. Shakespeare most certainly made it up.

"As for other historians of Richard's era, John, even in our own time and in our own experience, is not history written by those who *win* the battles?"

98

Chapter Seven

To my letter of request for an appointment, James Gairdner replied stiffly, and recommended me first to study carefully his book, *History of the Life and Reign of Richard III*, and then to reapply for an appointment. The word "study" was heavily underlined. Clements Markham's prompt reply, in contrast, was a warm and pressing invitation to visit him.

I walked briskly across Hyde Park to the headquarters of the Royal Geographical Society, of which Markham was the honourary secretary. A beaming Markham greeted me as if we had known each other all our lives, and the explorer-geographer chattered away at a fast trot.

"Come in, Doctor Watson, come in. A happy Monday to you. Shall I send for coffee? Good. I must say, I am extraordinarily glad that you are able to call. Richard the Third. Hum! A Yorkshireman, really, by nature and upbringing, if not by birth. I am a Yorkshireman by birth, myself. From Stillingfleet. Must be what stirred my interest. I tell you, Doctor Watson, I have believed since a very early age that the record regarding Richard the Third has been grossly falsified. I was a bit precocious, I am afraid, and I can remember things that happened when I was only two. Actually wrote a little history of England when I was ten.

"You have written to Gairdner? Infuriating man. I have sent him a number of letters; all polite, questioning his accuracy and interpretations. He has replied to only three, and those rather brusquely. Been thinking of doing a book myself; I have a box full of notes. Ah, coffee; and sugar buns, too. Excellent, excellent. Just back from Holland, I am; forgive me if I and my things are not quite in order."

Over our first cup of extraordinarily strong coffee, Markham chatted, albeit modestly, about his life and explorations. He was in his early fifties now, and he had packed much travel and adventure into those years. He had sailed in the Pacific with the navy, had travelled to South America and India and had been, several times, on Arctic expeditions. It was the story of Peru and India that, given my time in India and my profession, I found most fascinating. It was Markham who, at considerable risk, had smuggled the jealously guarded cinchona and its seeds out of Peru, and had successfully introduced it to India. The Dutch had tried and failed in a similar venture to cultivate their own source of quinine. Markham succeeded, and the Empire – indeed, the world – owed to this exciting but unassuming hero an enormous debt.

I discovered, too, that I had previously met his daughter May, an active participant in the work of her church among the poor. I had been introduced to her in the course of my own weekly afternoon of charitable practice in the East End.

"Wonderful," declared Markham, his strong but sensitive features wreathed in a huge smile. "You must come to dinner. Minna would love to have you, and we shall insist that May be there. Yes, yes, now, you were asking about Richard the Third."

Markham's room was a bewildering clutter of books, papers, maps, equipment and mementos of his travels. He dragged a large, heavy wooden box over to his chair and threw back the lid with enthusiasm. "My Yorkist treasure-chest. Notes on Richard. Thoughts and documents that I have assembled. Really should write that book, should I not? Let us dig in. Good exercise for the old brain."

Keeping up with Markham's rapid-fire discussion of Richard the Third was not easy, since he constantly scrambled away to other subjects, interrupted himself, and kept repeating that "I am *most* worried about the Leigh Smith expedition. Oh, *when* will we get news?"

Nonetheless, he skillfully stitched into a clear and fascinating tapestry all the historical threads and loose ends that I had so far gathered on my mission. My pencil raced, and I was grateful for my note-taking hand, with its systematic abbreviations. In the account that follows, I have omitted Markham's many distractions and diversions.

Markham told me of his childhood conviction that the vilification of Richard was a plot by Southerners to defame a feared and resented Northerner. The way that Markham explained it, Richard had as king favoured his strong and silent Yorkshire and Northern friends over the more *effete* Southerners at court, and had thus bred an army of jealous Southern enemies.

"They plotted against him. The Tudors who destroyed him and took his crown were master plotters. They have quite destroyed Richard's reputation, and their calumny is still widely believed today. A Tudor conspiracy, and still taught as gospel in our best schools. Incredible. If Richard performs a generous act, they vilify him as seeking to purchase friendship. If he puts down a treasonous rebellion, he is called a bloodthirsty and cruel tyrant. Take Sir Thomas More, for example. Brought up in the household of Cardinal Morton. Thoroughly untrustworthy. I say that Morton himself – oh, but I must not put my thumb upon your scales like this. I must present the evidence as fairly and factually as I can."

"Thank you," I replied. "I am instructed by General Milman to ask you, first, if I may, who wrote More's *History*. You have a theory, he tells me."

"I do indeed; and it was certainly not More. But perhaps you will forgive me if I address that issue later. You are here to investigate the life and reign of Richard the Third. Where shall we begin?"

"At the beginning?" I returned. "Tell me, if you would, about Richard as a child."

"Right. Born on Monday, October 2nd, 1452, eleventh of the twelve children of Richard Plantagenet, third Duke of York, and Lady Cicely Nevill. She was the youngest daughter of Ralph Nevill, Earl of Westmoreland. Five of the children died in infancy. As I say, Richard was not actually born in Yorkshire, but at the castle of Fotheringhay, in Northamptonshire. Same place where Mary Queen of Scots was executed in 1587. The castle has gone now; Mary's son, James the First, had it razed.

"Richard was the youngest son. Nobody knows very much about Richard as a young child. Few written records, you see. Anyway, they grew up pretty fast in those days. Think of Richard as quickly becoming a capable young man, all right? Well trained in the arts of power and war and law and political survival at an early age."

Two others of the children I knew of. One was the oldest, Edward, Earl of March, he who became King Edward the Fourth, and the other George, the ninth child, the ambitious, greedy and treacherous Duke of Clarence. Both of their parents were from enormously wealthy families, held vast estates in more than twenty counties, and had the bluest of blood. Richard's father was probably the richest magnate in England, as President Bulley had suggested at Magdalen.

"I have heard that young Richard was two years in his mother's womb," I said, with a smile.

"Oh, Heavens, Rous," replied Markham, with a patient sigh. "That fable comes from one John Rous, a chaplain and an antiquarian of sorts. In a work dedicated explicitly to Henry the Seventh, who dethroned Richard. Not much use, Rous. In Richard's time, Rous writes of him as 'a mighty prince and especial good lord'. Rous says that Richard enjoyed the 'great thanks of God and love of all his subjects, rich and poor'. Then Henry comes to the throne. Rous hastily revises his gospel. Richard suddenly becomes a 'monster and tyrant', a murderer, and the poisoner of his wife; and we get this silly tale about Richard being two years in the womb. John Rous? John Rubbish.

"Please allow me, though, to start well before then," Markham continued, after a pensive pause. "You have a choice, you see: Richard was either a murderous and treacherous criminal who let nothing and nobody stand in the way of seizing kingship and power; that is Gairdner's thesis. Or Richard was a pretty decent sort of fellow who was forced by circumstance and lineage to wear a crown he neither sought nor wanted; was a pretty good king, and left us an inheritance of fair laws. That is my thesis.

"I think it important, therefore, to set the medieval stage for you. If Richard was a bloodthirsty monster, what made him so? Some personal perversion? Or the harsh times in which he lived? If he was, rather, a reluctant king, what were the circumstances under which he came to be crowned against his desire? And if he was indeed a pretty decent sort of king, was it *despite* his times?

"Let me take you back, Dr. Watson, to the time of King Edward the Third. You have read *Froissart's Chronicles*? Froissart said of Edward, "His like has not been seen since the days of King Arthur.' Edward ruled for fifty years, and, by claiming the French throne in 1338, began the Hundred Years War. He and his dates are not important to your quest. What *is* important is what happened next, because it was to forge and temper the lives of Richard and everyone around him.

"Edward's eldest son and heir is the famous Black Prince, but the Black Prince dies in 1376, a year *before* his father. When Edward the Third himself dies, the English crown, properly, then goes to the Black Prince's son, King Richard the Second, who is ten years old, and is at first guided by councillors.

"But as an adult Richard becomes an erratic, self-centred and extravagant king, and in 1399 he is deposed by his own cousin, Henry Bolingbroke, a man he had banished. Bolingbroke now takes the throne, with Parliamentary approval, as Henry the Fourth. He can trace his lineage back to Henry the Third. He is also the son of Edward the Third's *fourth* son, John of Gaunt, the first Duke of Lancaster. The House of Lancaster, you see. Richard the Second not only loses his crown, he then loses his life; he is murdered.

"Now, Richard the Second had no children. Edward the Third's second son, William, had died young and heirless. By precedent, if not by written law, the throne now properly belongs to the line of Edward's *third* son, Lionel. But Bolingbroke and the House of Lancaster are firmly entrenched in power, and when Henry the Fourth dies, in 1413, the crown goes, however improperly, to his son, Henry the Fifth. He is the fellow who conquers northern France. Battle of Agincourt, you know."

I smiled, and quoted with some confidence from the one, stirring, Shakespeare play that I knew well enough:–

"Once more unto the breach, dear friends, once more;
Or close the wall up with our English dead!"

"Ah, the Taking of Harfleur," said Markham. "Just before Agincourt. That is he, Henry the Fifth. 'The signs of war advance; no King of England if not King of France.'

"In 1415, a descendant of Lionel's line, one Richard Plantagenet, Earl of Cambridge, is caught red-handed in a plot to depose Henry the Fifth, and to restore the line of Lionel. It costs him his head, and the enmity between the House of York and the House of Lancaster is forged in the strongest of steel. The important fact for you to note is that this Earl of Cambridge has a young son, and that son is Richard Duke of York.

"The one who was to be the father of our Richard the Third?" I asked.

"Just so, but not for many years yet. Richard Duke of York is only three or four years old when his Plantagenet father is executed. It is not until 1425 or so, after Henry the Fifth's death, that he finally comes into his titles and estates as Duke of York. He was then thirteen or fourteen years of age.

"So, I ask you, what lessons has young Duke Richard learned from all this, and what lessons will he pass on to his own children, including our Richard the Third."

I answered hesitantly. "That possession of the crown was nine points of the law?"

Markham smiled wryly. "That possession of the crown was *ten* points of the law. That might is right. That medieval government was a bare-knuckled blood-fight, with no rules.

And the family of York will learn those lessons again and again.

"Henry the Fifth dies young, in 1422. He is succeeded by his own son, Henry the Sixth, but little Henry is only eight months old, and we now start on the longest and most unstable minority rule in our country's history.

"Times are terribly troubled. The long war with France has been horribly expensive and still is, because it is still going on. Little Henry is, in theory, the king of France, as well. By an old treaty, that is; the French, of course, repudiate it. The crown is heavily in debt. Factions and feuds flourish among the nobles. The infant Henry's court circles are full of corruption, and greedy nobles plunder the treasury. The rule of law is weak. The people are restless.

"Henry the Sixth's court are divided. Some want peace with France; some want to continue the war. The chief peace-seekers are the king's great-uncle, Henry Cardinal Beaufort, a rich and shrewd man if ever there was one, and his follower, the Duke of Suffolk. They have King Henry's ear. The war party are led by Henry the Sixth's uncle, Humphrey, Duke of Gloucester. By the way, you must tell your friends at Oxford that it was this same Humphrey whose generous gift of books began their Bodleian Library. In Humphrey's camp is Richard Duke of York, the future father of our Richard the Third.

"Soon, we have the devil of a job holding on to our lands in France. Joan of Arc gives the French some backbone. Our main ally, the Duke of Burgundy, deserts us, and the tide of war begins to turn inexorably against us. In 1436, the French take back Paris.

"At this time, Richard of York has just been appointed Lieutenant and Governor of France. He is only seventeen years of age, but with Lord Talbot as an exemplary general, he at least manages to hold onto our remaining territory. However, York returns to England a year later. He is sorely frustrated. The Crown has never sent him the men and money that he really needed. He has paid thousands upon thousands of pounds out of his own pocket to conduct the war in France, and the Crown never does repay him all that it owes.

"Humphrey and Cardinal Beaufort quarrel, all the time, and openly, over the French issue. The King's council of lords and bishops become deeply split. The country is paralysed. The Crown is almost bankrupt.

"As for Henry, he is not his strong and powerful father. He is deeply religious, he is honest, he is chaste, he is pious, he is truly virtuous, he is humble, he is sweet and gentle, he is literally saintly. He has no interest in being a king, and no idea of *how* to be a king. Competing nobles and squabbling courtiers run the realm, and run it in their own interests. Henry is but a pawn.

"Cardinal Beaufort is aging, and soon all but retires. His campaign for peace with France is carried on by Dukes of Suffolk and Somerset. Henry the Sixth is by his very nature a lover of peace. In the end, Suffolk wins his case for the peace, and goes on a mission to France on Henry's behalf in 1444. He arranges for a two-year truce with the French, and also arranges for Henry the Sixth, who now is in his twenty-third year, to marry Margaret of Anjou. She is fifteen, and is the niece, by marriage, of the French king, Charles the Seventh.

"A two-year truce? More like a surrender. Only two years of guaranteed peace, and Henry has to marry a French woman, Margaret of Anjou. A penniless French woman, at that."

I broke in. "Good heavens; marry a poor French woman? All those years of war, and that is all that England had to show for it?"

"You do not know the half of it," returned Markham, heavily. "The English people have been taxed onerously to pay for the long war, and they *do* see it as a surrender. Unrest grows in the country. And there is worse news yet to come out: We go on to return our territories of Maine and Anjou to the French.

"Margaret of Anjou is a most beautiful woman, by all accounts, but she is an ambitious she-wolf, while gentle Henry is nothing but a mouse. Putty in her hands, he is. As queen, Margaret immediately becomes thick with the Duke of Suffolk and his cronies. They are the ones who brought about the peace with France, and her royal marriage. Margaret and Suffolk simply rule the roost. Henry has little or no interest in governing, and, for all practical purposes, Margaret is the ruler.

"In 1447, Suffolk and his followers summon their rival Humphrey of Gloucester to answer charges of treason. A few days later they announce that he has been found dead. Very convenient, I must say."

Markham sprang to his feet and began to pace the room, navigating rapidly and confidently around the piles of boxes and papers and maps on the floor.

"With Humphrey of Gloucester gone, Richard Duke of York inherits his mantle as leader of those opposed to Margaret and Suffolk. At the same time, Doctor Watson, we must recognise another vital fact. Henry the Sixth is still childless. His uncle Humphrey was his legal heir, and now Humphrey is dead himself. So *now* who has the best legal claim to be Henry's heir, and to succeed to the throne if he remains childless?"

"Let me tell you who," declared Markham, wide-eyed and dancing with glee, as if he were producing a surprise birthday gift for a child. "The new heir apparent, the heir presumptive, is" – he paused dramatically – "Richard Duke of York.

"Not to put too fine a point on it, York's claim to the throne, if pressed, is better than Henry's own. Again, Richard is descended, through his mother, from Lionel, the *third* son of Edward the Third; Henry the Sixth, of course, derives his position from John of Gaunt, the *fourth* son of Edward. For what it is worth, by the way, Richard was also descended from Edward's fifth son. But will Henry, Margaret and the Lancastrians recognise York's claim? Not likely."

"Possession of the crown was ten points of the law," said I, with a grimace.

"Possession of the crown was *eleven* points of the law," returned Markham, with a fleeting smile, as he took his seat again. "And, indeed, the House of Lancaster now hold the crown for the third generation, with the acceptance of the prelates, the peers and the people.

"Richard of York is supplanted as the king's lieutenant in France; first by John Beaufort, the cardinal's nephew, and then by John Beaufort's brother, Edmund, who is Suffolk's chief crony and another favourite of Queen Margaret. Edmund soon becomes the new Duke of Somerset. Duke Richard is shipped off instead to a rebellious Ireland, as lieutenant of Ireland."

"Sent to exile," I suggested.

"Certainly out of the way," replied Markham. "So now, after Humphrey of Gloucester's death, we have Richard of York stewing in what amounts to exile in Ireland, and still not being repaid by the Crown for his costs in France or, now, his costs in Ireland. And all the while, of course, he is seething as Margaret and Suffolk and Somerset and their followers rule the royal roost at home.

"To add insult to injury, Somerset has some claim to the throne himself. He is the king's nearest Lancastrian relative. He is head of the Beaufort family, and he is a truly powerful man at court. He is indeed a rival to Richard of York."

"And while York is stuck in Ireland, Somerset is free to build up his power and position," I ventured.

"Exactly, although Somerset and Suffolk turn out to be utter failures, while Richard does a superb job of governance in Ireland.

"In 1449, one of Suffolk's lieutenants decides to take and sack the town of Fougères in Brittany. That pushes the Bretons firmly into the French camp. The King of France, Charles the Seventh, then invades Normandy. His troops simply roll all over us. They take town after town, and drive us out of Normandy.

"The people of England are outraged. There are disturbances and riots. Things finally get so hot that, in January 1450, Parliament denounce Suffolk for treason and corruption, for selling out to the French. To save him, Margaret and Henry tell him to flee to Calais. Calais is about all that we have left in France at this point, and it is where Somerset is stationed. While Suffolk is on the way there, however, rebels seize him and they summarily execute him.

Parts of England, particularly Kent, are in chaos and open rebellion, and in the early summer of 1450 a rebel army led by one Jack Cade actually threaten London."

Markham scrabbled furiously in his deep wooden box of notes.

"Here we are. Listen to this. From Cade's manifesto attacking Henry the Sixth's advisers, and demanding sweeping legal and tax reforms:–

> "'Also we say our sovereign lord may understand that his false council hath lost his law, his merchandise is lost, his common people is destroyed, the sea is lost, France is lost, the King himself is so beset that he may not pay for his meat and drink, and he oweth more than ever any King of England ought, for daily his traitors about him, when anything should come to him by his laws, at once ask it from him, or else they take bribes of others … to get it for them.'

"That is but part of Cade's complaint. The rebellion collapses, however, and Cade is soon captured and killed. But the unrest continues, and, a few months later, Richard Duke of York suddenly turns up in England. He has left his post in Ireland, without notice or permission, saying that the state of emergency requires him here. He first takes to his earth at Ludlow Castle, in Shropshire, by the Welsh border. Then he comes to London and demands his place at the royal council table. This is granted, and King Henry agrees to summon Parliament.

"What comes now is an open clash for supremacy at court between York and Somerset, who has also returned to England.

"Parliament demand several reforms. Somerset is popularly held responsible for the loss of Normandy. Parliament demand that York be recognised as head of the king's council. York is much favoured by the Commons, as he is demanding reforms, just as they are. He does not openly claim any right to be named Henry the Sixth's heir; not himself, not at this time. One of his supporters, however, one

Thomas Young of Bristol, sits in Parliament, and he publicly calls for York to be recognised as Henry the Sixth's successor.

"Queen Margaret and Somerset quickly pull their puppet Henry's strings. Thomas Young is sent to the Tower for his rashness. The Parliamentarians are soon sent home. The Duke of York is isolated once more, and he retreats to Ludlow again.

"We now have a perilous peace, with Queen Margaret of Anjou and Somerset still controlling the crown. Then, in 1452, Richard Duke of York has had enough. He accuses Somerset of plotting to destroy him. York raises an army and marches for London. On the brink of civil war, Henry opens negotiations with York. York demands that Somerset be put on trial. Henry agrees. So York promptly disbands his army.

"Henry does arrest Somerset, but Margaret quickly orders him released, and he is set free." Markham's fist slammed onto his oak desk, making our empty coffee cups dance and clatter. "York now has no soldiers with him, and is as good as a prisoner himself. He is forced to swear a public oath to obey the king, to keep the peace, and to raise no more troops. York is thus publicly humiliated once more, and retreats to Ludlow again, in bitter disgrace. Somerset and Margaret hold all the trumps."

"And then little Richard the Third is born, in October 1452," I mused.

Markham suddenly smiled, boyishly, and winked at me.

"Some of the best twists in the plot are still to come. In 1453 we were soundly beaten in the Battle of Castillon in France. We lost Bordeaux. We lost Guienne. All we had left in France was Calais, and the Channel Islands. England is truly enraged. As one chronicler wrote:– 'The hearts of the people were turned away from them that had the land in governance, and their blessing was turned to cursing.'

"Then comes the first twist: In the summer of 1453, Henry goes mad. Loses his mind. *Non compos mentis*. A mental alienation no doubt inherited, through his mother, from her father, Charles the Sixth, the Valois king of France."

"Yes," I interjected, nodding. "I have heard of Henry's unfortunate illness."

"Oh, there is another twist on top of that," crowed Markham happily. "In October 1453, while Henry is still helpless in his imbecility, his Queen Margaret of Anjou gives birth to a son and heir, Prince Edward. There is considerable popular doubt as to who is actually the father. Is it really hapless Henry? Or is it actually Somerset? Regardless, Edward is the official heir, and any hope that York might have had of succeeding to the throne himself some day is gone. Queen Margaret, the ruthless she-wolf, now has her own little cub to fight for, and she knows who the cub's natural enemy is: Richard Duke of York.

"Henry is entirely disabled by his sad lunacy. The council therefore exercise the royal powers, of course. Now, Somerset may have Queen Margaret's especial favour, but he does not control the council. York wins the vital support of Richard Nevill, Earl of Warwick, and of Warwick's father, the Earl of Salisbury, who is York's own brother-in-law; quite a family business.

"We come now to the spring of 1454. Henry is still disabled. Parliament appoint Richard of York as 'Protector and Defenser' of the realm and chief of the king's council. As such, York sends Somerset to the Tower, and replaces some Lancastrian loyalists at court. It is made quite clear by Parliament that York's appointment as Protector does not in any way alter Prince Edward's position or rights as heir. There are still disturbances in the country, you see, and Parliament expect York to deal with them as Protector. This he does, quite ably, and he begins to bring about some of his reforms of government.

"However, during the Christmas season of 1454, Henry recovers his sanity. He formally recognises Prince Edward as his heir. Mind you, many, as I say, still insist that Somerset is the boy's real *pater*. In any event, Queen Margaret wins from Henry the release of Somerset from the Tower, and York's protectorship is formally ended. Yorkist councillors are replaced by Lancastrians again, and Parliament are dissolved."

I leaned forward in my chair. "So we are back at the beginning of the game? In other words, Somerset is back at the head table, and York is seated somewhere well below the salt again."

"Indeed," returned Markham, dexterously tossing me another sugared bun from the silver basket beside him.

"York is kept out of the royal council. He goes back to his estates yet again, with his pride once more sorely hurt. Somerset and Margaret steadily increase their dominance over poor Henry and his court. In May of 1455, Somerset calls a Great Council to take place at Leicester. Its stated purpose is to safeguard the king against his enemies. But some important Yorkists are simply not invited. The great Duke of York should properly be among the very first of the nobles to be invited; but he is not *invited* at all. Instead, he is *summoned*, along with his allies the Earl of Salisbury and the Earl of Warwick."

"It would be obvious to York," I proposed, "that the three of them are the 'enemies' in question."

"Exactly," replied Markham. "York concludes that he and his allies are to be accused of treason. Or at best forced to take another humiliating oath of allegiance. He urgently seeks an audience with Henry, so that he may neuter Somerset; but how can he break through the barriers that Margaret and Somerset have erected around the king? Once more, York resorts to arms, with assistance from Warwick and Salisbury. He marches to St. Alban's and on May 22nd, 1455, sends a demand to Henry that he hand over Somerset. Henry refuses. Fighting breaks out. A skirmish, really, rather than a battle. Somerset is killed, and poor Henry suffers a flesh wound himself, nicked by an arrow. York is triumphant."

"This is the battle of St. Alban's at which Shakespeare says the future Richard the Third was present," I broke in, "although Richard was in fact only two years old."

"Correct," returned Markham.

"Richard's father, the Duke of York, now obtains a pardon from Henry, and is at your head table again, dominating the council. There is trouble in the West Country, where the Earl of Devonshire, Somerset's cousin, is creating mayhem. Late in the year, it seems that Henry the Sixth suffers another, if shorter, mental collapse. The council need leadership and action. Once more, Parliament appoint York as protector. York deals successfully with the Devonshire problem. And, once more, he begins to reform the government,

"Margaret, however, has taken up with a convenient new ally, Somerset's son. Her new favourite becomes the new Duke of Somerset. Margaret and he soon have Henry firmly under their control again. And so in February 1456, Henry comes to Parliament and relieves York of his protectorship once more.

"We now have another three years of troubled, precarious peace. The nobility are divided. Some support Henry as their rightful king; some jockey with Margaret and the new Duke of Somerset; some support York. Queen Margaret soon causes the court to move out of London, to the Lancastrian Midlands. There, she steadily reinforces her influence over poor Henry the Sixth and the state, and strengthens her support among the Lancastrian nobility."

Markham plucked a document from his treasure-chest.

"A letter of the era says this:– 'The Queen, with such as were of her affinity, ruled the realm, gathering riches innumerable.'

"In 1459, everything boils over again. The Lancastrians call another Great Council, at Coventry, and, once again, York and his friends are the targets. York's allies, Salisbury and Warwick, publish a manifesto accusing their enemies of trying to destroy them and seize their property. They proclaim their loyalty to Henry. The Yorkists then take up arms, and apparently hope once more to force a meeting with the king to air their grievances.

"However, Margaret's royal army face them near Ludlow, and, in the name of King Henry, a free pardon is offered to anybody who deserts York. This ploy works all too well, and many Yorkist soldiers do indeed desert. So does an important lieutenant who knows all of York's battle plans. Facing certain

113

defeat, therefore, York flees to Ireland. Salisbury and Warwick run to Calais, which Warwick controls.

"York's wife Cicely and three of their children, Margaret, George, and Richard, our future Richard the Third, are captured and put into safe-keeping. Richard was seven years old."

Markham paused, anxiously. "Am I going on too long, Doctor Watson? I am constantly accused of talking too much, too often and too fast."

"Not at all," I replied. "My note-taking hand is tiring, but I am still able to keep up with you."

Markham nodded enthusiastically. "November 1459, and a Parliament packed with Lancastrians accuse York of treason. He and Warwick and Salisbury, and York's eldest son Edward, Earl of March, the one who will eventually be King Edward the Fourth, are declared 'traitors to their king, enemies to their country, and rebels to the crown'. They are attainted, and their lands are confiscated."

Markham began to pace the cluttered room again, his jerky movements adding intensity to his rapid-fire speech.

"Look back for a moment over the full picture, Doctor Watson. York has several times tried to use peaceable means to bring about much warranted reforms in Henry's corrupt and inept court. In that, York has considerable public support. There is no evidence that York has anything else in mind. He has not claimed the throne, even if he does have a fair and legal right to it. He has resorted to force only when there is no real alternative. But now that he has been declared a rebel, an outlaw, the gloves come off and are replaced by steel gauntlets.

"In June 1460, Warwick, Salisbury and York's eldest son, Edward of March, mount an invasion from Calais. They land at Sandwich, and march through Kent. They take control of London, although the Tower remains in Lancastrian hands, and they move on to Northampton. There, they meet Henry's army, and rout them. It is all over in half an hour. They capture poor Henry in his tent. Queen Margaret flees, and makes her way to Wales and finally to Scotland with her son Prince Edward."

"Where was Richard, the Duke of York?"

"Ah, he stayed in Ireland during this invasion. He does not come back to England until some two months later. When he does, he goes to Parliament, and finally plays his court card. He claims the crown. He literally walks into the Painted Chamber in Westminster, and puts his hand on the throne, to make his point. He is claiming it by right of superior descent. One can see why; it was either seize the crown, or spend his life at war with Margaret. Even James Gairdner concedes that York 'exhausted every form of peaceful remonstrance' before claiming the throne himself.

"Here, however, York is humbled once again. Parliament and the nobility resist his claim. After all, even if he is subject to lunacy, Henry is an anointed king, and that truly meant something in those days. To attack Henry was to attack the consecrated agent of God. Even York's allies are none too happy with him. York's promise had been to reform Henry's corrupt government, not to replace poor Henry. Eventually, the Lords reluctantly agree on a hopeless compromise. They declare that Henry the Sixth is to remain as king, but that when he dies Richard of York is to succeed him."

"Surely that would disinherit Prince Edward," I observed.

"Of course; and so Queen Margaret simply has to fight back. The enraged she-wolf, safe in Scotland, bares all her fangs. She sends for the new Duke of Somerset, who raises an army for her, with the Earl of Devon. At the same time, she has other important anti-Yorkist allies rallying under arms, the Duke of Exeter and the Earl of Northumberland among them, and some barons. She has a formidable force.

"Her army assemble in the North, in my Yorkshire. Richard of York takes his own army north, in December 1460, and goes to one of his castles, at Sandal, near Wakefield. At the end of December, York boldly sallies out of his stronghold, apparently to attack a corps of Lancastrians. But it seems there are many more Lancastrians concealed in the woods. York is

115

hopelessly outnumbered, and he has bitten off far more than he can chew.

"It is a fatal mistake. York is captured, humiliated, and beheaded. So is his second son Edmund, Earl of Rutland. Salisbury, too, is captured and executed. The heads of York and Rutland and Salisbury are stuck up on the gate of Micklegate Bar in the city of York. York's head is garlanded with some sort of mock crown. Other Yorkists' heads went up on the other gates.

"Our Richard the Third, the Duke's son, was eight years old,' I observed. "Shakespeare says that he was at Sandal Castle, but I gather that this was not so."

"Right, Richard was eight years old, and his brother George eleven. They were in fact in London with their mother.

"So now Queen Margaret's victorious army set off for London, pillaging and burning all the way. 'A whirlwind from the North,' one account says. A whirlwind that 'universally devoted themselves to spoil and rapine.' They sack and plunder Yorkist property in particular, but loot others' houses and shops and churches as well. And ravage many innocent women, I fear.

"So we come, for the second time, to St. Alban's. The Second Battle of St. Alban's, in February 1461. Warwick has brought a Yorkist army here, and they fall to. Margaret's men win, decisively, and they recapture poor Henry the Sixth from Warwick. Warwick himself escapes.

"Margaret's army, though, run short of supplies, and they are uncertain about trying to enter London. Margaret is not loved there. The gates are barred by the city, and her army face a hostile welcome, or at least an uncertain one. So they begin to march, and to plunder, back north again."

"Where was little Richard?" I asked.

"Oh, his mother packed him and brother George off to safety in Holland, in what was then Burgundy, under the protection of the Duke of Burgundy."

My pencil raced over my fast-diminishing note paper as Markham resumed his fascinating story.

"York may have been defeated. Warwick may have been defeated, but there is still another Yorkist army in the land. The Duke of York's eldest son Edward, our future Edward the Fourth, commands it. He is only eighteen years of age, but he has just defeated Jasper Tudor and his Lancastrians in the Battle of Mortimer's Cross. Jasper is the Earl of Pembroke, and is Henry the Sixth's half-brother. Warwick now manages to join up with Edward, and together they make their way to London. There, Edward is hailed as king by the Londoners. Then Edward and his troops march north in pursuit of Margaret's army.

"Margaret is brought to bay at Towton, near York. If Culloden was the last real battle fought on our British soil, the battle of Towton was, I think, the biggest. March 29th, 1461, and the two armies may have had as many as forty or fifty thousand men apiece, although such numbers are invariably exaggerated in the histories. There is a terrible snow storm, and a bloody battle. It must have been sheer hell. The outcome is a smashing victory for Edward and the Yorkists. Perhaps twenty-five thousand men are killed or wounded; some say more. The carnage on Bloody Meadow, as they call it, is unbelievable. Edward wins, but Margaret and poor Henry the Sixth and their son manage to escape to Scotland with some of their nobles.

"Edward goes on to York and removes the skulls of his father and brother and Salisbury from Micklegate Bar. Then he goes back south to Westminster, and is officially crowned as king, as Edward the Fourth. He is not yet nineteen years of age."

"Young Richard was still in Holland?"

"Yes. Safely away from it all. He and George were then brought back to England, of course. Edward has his coronation, and George is made Duke of Clarence. Richard becomes a Knight of the Bath, and, a few months later, on the first day of November 1461, he is raised to the dignity of Duke of Gloucester. He later becomes a Knight of the Garter, and Admiral of England, Ireland and Acquitaine. He is only 10 years old.

"At some point after that, Richard is sent away, to the household of his cousin, the Earl of Warwick. For his training as a knight, and his education, you see. That was the usual practice: Board your son out in another noble's household for a few years, to be raised in the arts of war and chivalry, the law, the arts, and the management of property. He went, no doubt, to several of Warwick's holdings, and certainly to Warwick's castle of Middleham, in the North Riding of Yorkshire. Lovely, wild country, Wensleydale and Coverdale, if terribly bleak in winter. You can still see the castle ruins; massive place. The Windsor of the North, somebody called it."

Markham's tone suddenly became heavy.

"I have related the history of the era at some length. I apologise again, if I have taken up too much of your time. I have done so because I urge you to consider what lessons our young Richard must have absorbed from it all. Brutal lessons of the age. That a noble's rights, even his legal birthrights, can be ignored and demeaned by rival nobles who have the ear of the king and queen. That if you cannot defeat these rivals by means diplomatic, then force, even civil insurrection, may be justified by the political end. That a weak king is a dangerous king for the welfare of the country. And, as important, the lesson that a child as a king is but a pawn in the hands of his closest nobles."

I nodded. "So Edward the Fourth is on the throne, and Margaret is defeated. Peace at last?" I proposed.

"Heavens, no," replied Markham. "Pockets of Lancastrian resistance flare up in a number of places. Margaret of Anjou still has strength in Wales and on the Scottish border, too. She goes to France, and wins assistance from King Louis the Eleventh. With the help of the French and the Scots – to whom she has ceded Berwick-upon-Tweed in exchange for support – Margaret rallies an army in Northumberland. In October 1462, Edward the Fourth and Warwick close in upon her, and she flees with Henry the Sixth.

"King Edward is soon able to arrange truces with the French and the Scots, and deprives her of their assistance. The Lancastrians then mount their last desperate campaign in the

North, and they lose their last battle, at Hexham, in 1464. Margaret flees once more, to France. Poor mad Henry is left behind in England. Loyal Lancastrians do manage to hide him, for more than a year, but he is eventually captured, in 1465, and he is taken to the Tower.

"So now Edward has taken all the tricks. The House of York are triumphant." Markham raised a make-believe trumpet and, pursing his lips, cleverly imitated a royal herald's fanfare.

"However, Doctor Watson," he continued, lowering the imaginary instrument with a flourish, "the Yorkists are not yet *established*. And Edward the Fourth begins his reign with a truly ghastly mistake."

Chapter Eight

We were interrupted by a crisp knock on the door, and, to my surprise, the stolid porter ushered in Mr. Sherlock Holmes. A glance told me that this Monday morning had not passed over him lightly. His embezzlement case, I concluded, was deeply troubling him.

Holmes, while a reserved and private man, was no reclusive misanthrope. He enjoyed the company of friends, although one or two at a time were enough for him; large and noisy gatherings soon had him repeatedly examining his watch and trying to find excuses to leave. His friendships were forged on the anvil of time, slowly, link by link, with Holmes only gradually revealing more and more of himself as his comfort and trust in the other grew. To my knowledge, he had only one close friend, myself. The moment his eyes met those of Clements Markham, however, I knew that another strong friendship was about to be born, and I rejoiced. The magnetism between them caused them almost to embrace as they shook hands warmly, each seizing the other's proffered hand with both of his own.

"I must apologise for the interruption –" began Holmes, glancing nervously at me.

"Your case troubles you," I ventured, as I slipped back into my chair.

"Indeed it does, Watson," returned Holmes, his long face dropping. "I am so glad to find you still here. It is a most difficult case of embezzlement at a company in the City," said he, turning back to Markham. "I am quite sure that the culprit is one of the partners in the company. Yet I have no proof, no evidence, and I have had so little success on his trail that I begin to doubt myself as well as sometimes to doubt his guilt."

Markham nudged Holmes to a chair, into which the lanky detective slumped dejectedly.

"You wish to employ me as a sounding board," I suggested, gently.

"True," replied Holmes, but with reluctance. "I am afraid that I do."

"How was the embezzlement conducted?" I inquired, knowing that if I could turn him to the details of the case, and could keep him talking, his embarrassment would be lessened.

"It is a shambles," replied Holmes, shaking his head. "The company have been in the habit of advancing sums of money, as a convenience, to a number of their clients, who are, by and large, successful small men of business. It now has become apparent that in the last few months numerous advances were made, fraudulently, to clients and companies who simply did not exist. But the records of them are missing. The ledger for this year has simply disappeared; stolen. A shambles, indeed. We do not yet know how much money has vanished, or when, or how; and I wonder if we ever shall.

"Who had the authority to make such loans?" I asked. "And who had access to the ledgers and records? Who could make free with them, undetected?"

"Excellent questions, Watson," returned my friend. "First, only four men had the ability to make loans upon their own initiative. They are the chairman, the secretary, the senior partner, and the accountant, who is also a partner. One of them must therefore be the embezzler. As for your second question, I fear that far too many people have had free access to records and ledgers. Only the wretched tea boy seems to have been denied licence in that regard, and I am not too confident about that limitation."

"You suspect one of the four," I observed. "You have been dogging his footsteps. Who is he? And what reasons do you have for suspecting your man, Holmes?"

Holmes coughed nervously in the direction of Markham. "I have often impressed upon Doctor Watson the need for tangible evidence. Yet, I must confess, and as he well knows, I do not always have to bustle about and examine things in person. Indeed, I just as often employ and rely upon – initially, at least – my intuition, my sixth sense. My suspect is the accountant, Mr. Somerset."

Markham burst out laughing. "Why, we have just been talking about the history of King Richard the Third and his father, and remarking upon the *rôles* of the nefarious Dukes of Somerset."

Holmes nodded distractedly, and addressed me again. "My investigations to this point show that all four men have been living within their means. None displays any spending or extravagance beyond his known income. I have not a shred of evidence against any one of them. All insist that some *employé* must somehow be the villain; anybody but one of their number. Yet Somerset has about him an air, a cockiness, that sets my sixth sense all on edge. He appears to be a respectable man of business, but he has secret rooms in Pimlico and enjoys low company in the public houses near them. He uses there an *alias*, the name Dorset."

"What does Somerset-Dorset use the rooms for?" I inquired. "A woman? Women?"

"Neither sign nor report of such, no," returned Holmes. "I have no evidence yet as to why he maintains these rooms."

I paused. "Do any of the clerks recall preparing loan documents for Somerset?"

"Of course. He must have approved hundreds of advances during his twelve years at the company. I have been looking into those loans of the recent past that are clearly remembered by the clerks, and for which we therefore do not need the ledger. Every one of them has proved proper. Those who borrowed the money all confirm the transactions, including some loans authorised by Somerset. Those who say that they have repaid the advances, as promised, can prove it. However, Somerset was certainly in a position to make a series of fraudulent advances to fictitious clients, to keep the money, and then to construct or falsify records to explain or conceal his actions."

"Yet if the ledger disappeared, it would quickly be noticed," I interjected. "I wonder if your man began to fear that his scheme was about to be exposed, and covered his trail by abstracting the records in one speedy move."

"You are quick today," returned my friend. "The first instance of a fictitious loan was uncovered by the chairman, fortuitously, on June 27th. The trusting soul mentioned it to his three colleagues, but no examination of the books was called for until the morning of the 28th. It was then discovered that this year's book had vanished. My theory is that, as soon as the first alarum was raised, my suspect came in surreptitiously that night and removed, then destroyed, all evidence of his improper loans."

"Hum. Did the night watchman see anything?"

"There is none. I have canvassed the neighbourhood, and the police, but have found nobody who remembers seeing Somerset, or anybody else, in or near the company's premises on the night of the 27th."

"Associates?" I asked. "Has Mr. Somerset any co-conspirators? Perhaps one of the clerks? Or a former clerk?"

"None that I can identify."

"You say that Somerset had been at the company for twelve years. How do you know that these fraudulent loans began only this year?"

"Because only this year's record has disappeared."

I rose and began silently to pace the room, frowning deeply, my arms folded across my chest, just as Holmes is wont to do in Baker Street. After a minute, I turned to Holmes.

"If you have found no positive evidence of his guilt, Holmes, have you found any evidence that would point to his innocence? What of his whereabouts on the 27th? Has he an *alibi*?"

Holmes smiled. 'Good, Watson, good. No, I have found no evidence of his innocence. As far as I can determine, he was at home in Richmond, but I can hardly barge in and interrogate his family or his servants. I remain convinced for the present, therefore, of his possible guilt. I have tried to catch him out by watching him, by tracing as much as I can of his spending and purchases. I have observed and learned nothing helpful. I have set my faithful Baker Street Irregulars on his trail, but he is almost certainly on his guard, and I fear that even those young hounds will come up with nothing. His spending seems, as I say, to be comfortably within his income. Yet I cannot escape the thought that, with these secret rooms and this taste for low public houses, there is something untoward going on. I have thought of vices such as women, gambling, and worse, but can yet find no evidence of such."

"Then what is your next step?"

Holmes winced. "I am at somewhat of a dead end, for the present."

Then I played my master stroke, with deliberate drama.

"Rubbish, Holmes," I intoned, loudly.

Holmes started in his seat, and looked, by turns, angry, shocked, nettled, and puzzled. Markham looked aghast.

"Rubbish, Watson?" said Holmes, his eyes flashing steely grey. "What is rubbish, may I ask?"

I roared with schoolboy laughter. "Rubbish, Holmes. I mean it, literally. Search his rubbish. Perhaps there are clues about his double life, or his sources of income, or his investments, or his banking. Or his vices. In particular, I should look for discarded documents in the names of Dorset, and other neighbouring counties: Devon, Cornwall, and so on."

Holmes actually began to clap. He applauded for several seconds, beaming at me. Markham smiled broadly as he caught on.

"Excellent, Watson," crowed Holmes. "Superb. Of course. I should have thought of it myself. Hah, hah. Yes, I shall become a dustman in Richmond. And Wiggins shall become an apprentice dustman serving Somerset's secret quarters in

Sutherland Street. Rubbish indeed, Watson; search his rubbish. Hah, hah."

Markham glanced at his watch and seized the moment. "Luncheon time. Hungry? Will you join us, Holmes?"

Without waiting for the answers, Markham quickly shepherded us from the room. In the four-wheeler that responded to the porter's double whistle, Markham explained concisely to Holmes how we had been talking of Edward the Fourth and his ascent to the throne.

At Simpson's, Markham once more held me spellbound. Even Holmes seemed to be interested, although I could tell that he was still fretting about his case as he silently attacked the delicious roast beef.

"Yes, Edward the Fourth makes a truly ghastly mistake," repeated Markham. "He is a terrible ladies' man, you know, and impetuous. Somehow, presumably to complete an amorous conquest, he goes through a secret marriage ceremony in May 1464. She is Elizabeth Grey, widow of a knight. Secret ceremony, very risky business. Medieval kings are supposed to marry for political reasons. They are expected to marry to make or strengthen powerful alliances, not to marry for love or lust. Edward is a king, and this is an entirely unsuitable match. A beauty, they say, but a mere commoner, and five years older than Edward, and with two sons. A Lancastrian widow, to boot. Her husband died fighting for Queen Margaret at the second Battle of St. Alban's. Yet Edward actually marries her, and secretly.

"There are two important things to note at this stage, Doctor Watson, Mr. Holmes. First, Elizabeth Grey is a Woodville. That is the spelling we use now, although the name was traditionally spelled Wydville or Wydeville, or in some similar way. Greedy, ambitious, and self-serving lot, the Woodville family. She herself is cold and calculating."

"I have christened them Woodvillains," I broke in, smiling.

"Villains? Richard would surely agree," returned Markham, seriously. "If not actually villains, they are a true plague of voracious locusts. With Elizabeth as Queen, Edward starts to give important positions and prominence to a whole

126

flock of upstart Woodvilles and their ilk. She has five brothers and seven sisters. They not only have his ear, they surround him. Nepotism is rampant. Edward is generous enough to others, the Nevills among them. But just as court favourites were established under Henry the Sixth, the Woodvilles are soon strutting like peacocks as court favourites under Edward the Fourth. The rest of the nobility do not like it at all; very, very jealous.

"Second, the Earl of Warwick, our Richard's guardian and tutor, slowly descends to treason.

"Warwick is the richest noble in England. He is a cousin of Edward the Fourth, and has supported him throughout. We now call him 'Warwick the King-maker', and he must have thought of himself as such. Indeed, I think that Warwick truly expected Edward the Fourth to be his grateful puppet. Edward richly rewarded him, with land and lucrative offices, and one writer described him as 'the conductor of the kingdom under King Edward.' But Edward would not be his puppet.

"At first, Warwick and the court are unaware of Edward's secret marriage to Elizabeth Woodville. Warwick has become, in effect, Edward's minister for Europe. As such, he has been making diplomatic peace overtures to the French, who have in the past firmly supported the Lancastrians. The idea, I take it, is to ensure that Margaret has no support there. King Louis the Eleventh responds favourably, and he and Warwick develop a very cozy relationship. What Louis wants is a peace treaty, and an alliance against Burgundy. There was also talk of a marriage bond: Edward the Fourth to marry Bona of Savoy, the sister of the French king's wife. The wily Louis, I am sure, holds out to Warwick some tempting personal rewards.

"So here you have Warwick working hard to bring about a French pact and perhaps a French marriage. Edward, with his Woodville marriage still kept secret, plays a theatrical part. He indicates that he does not entirely rule out a treaty with France, but points out that Burgundy is an old ally of England. It is obviously hard, too, to trust France, our traditional foe. The people of England still regard France as the enemy, certainly. The Woodvilles, too, have some connections with Burgundy. So, to Warwick's French proposition, Edward temporises, and carefully says neither yes nor no."

Markham signalled briskly to our lugubrious waiter for another slice of Simpson's perfect rare beef. Mr. Holmes and I took second helpings, too.

"Warwick presses hard his campaign for the French marriage and a French treaty," continued Markham, talking energetically between each mouthful. "There may also have been discussion with Spain of a marriage to Isabella of Castile, according to Thomas More; and there was even talk of a Scottish marriage and of a Burgundian marriage. Edward of England would certainly be a prize catch for any unmarried princess. Into the middle of all this, however, Edward finally sets off his bomb. He discloses that there can be no marriage, French, Spanish, Scottish or Burgundian, because he is *already* married, to Elizabeth Woodville, and has been for some four months.

"Warwick is outraged. His plans for the royal marriage with France are demolished. He does not openly sever relations with Edward, not yet, and Edward tries to keep Warwick on side. King Louis, a crafty devil, is very careful to maintain his friendly contacts with Warwick. So Warwick now keeps pressing Edward to treat with France, even if there can be no French marriage. And so, in 1467, Warwick is sent back to France to negotiate further with Louis.

"It soon becomes pretty clear, however, that Edward has simply shipped Warwick off to France to get him out of the way. In Warwick's absence, Edward ousts Warwick's brother George as Chancellor of England. Edward also signs an anti-French treaty with Brittany. Warwick returns to England, but Edward charges ahead on his own and negotiates a pact with Burgundy, France's sworn enemy. He also signs anti-French treaties with Castile and Aragon. And, on top of all that, Edward commits his sister Margaret to marry the Duke of Burgundy.

"It is all a disaster for Warwick. He has not only played second fiddle to Edward for years, he has been thoroughly duped, and, worse, made to look like a dupe before all the courts of Europe. He is an international laughing-stock.

"While all this is going on, too, your Woodvillains are getting their snouts ever more deeply into the royal trough.

"Edward arranges for rich marriages for a number of Elizabeth's *parvenu* siblings and relatives. He even marries one of her brothers, John Woodville, who is not yet twenty, to the dowager Duchess of Norfolk, who is thrice a widow and well into her sixties at the very least. Some say she was in her seventies or even eighties. And she, Doctor Watson, is Warwick's aunt."

I almost dropped the lid of the mustard pot. "How on earth could Edward be so short-sighted?"

"A *'mariagum diabolicum,'* one chronicler wrote," said Markham, with a sour grimace.

"And there is more. Warwick has no son to succeed him. He has, however, two very fine daughters, Isabella and Anne. They are, without doubt, the greatest heiresses in England. They must have suitable marriages, of course; but Edward has married off some of the best male prospects to Woodville women. So who are the two most eligible bachelors remaining in England? Why, Edward's brothers, George, Duke of Clarence, and our own Richard the Third to be, Duke of Gloucester and Admiral of the Sea. King Edward, though, flatly refuses to countenance the idea of them marrying Warwick's daughters. Between all this, and Edward's rejection of Warwick's overtures to and from France, the stage is well set for Warwick's treason."

I shook my head in honest wonderment.

"Extraordinary, is it not, how history repeats itself?" I mused. "Henry the Sixth was plagued with court favourites. They managed to exclude Richard Duke of York from his rightful place at court, and eventually drove him to treason. Now his son Edward the Fourth does exactly the same with the Woodvilles as his court favourites, driving Warwick to treason. Could Edward not see what he was doing?"

Markham shrugged. "Simply reluctant to give Warwick any more power, I would say. Shall we go back to my office?"

We returned to his headquarters in the garden seats atop an omnibus, with Markham almost shouting to be heard above the constant roar and clatter of a myriad London carriage wheels.

"Edward does try to keep Warwick in his camp, treating him generously. But it is too little, and too late. Warwick begins to foment trouble, and to court Lancastrian support. The French back the Lancastrians, too, and there are Lancastrian plots and disturbances all over the place.

"Warwick is pretending to be still loyal to Edward, but the king-maker begins to think of un-making that king, and making a new one. If King Edward will not play the puppet, perhaps King Somebody Else will. And if Edward is deposed, who has a claim to the throne? Why, Edward's nasty brother George, Duke of Clarence, whose selfish, fickle and unstable brain is no match for a crafty Warwick. Oh, yes, greedy little George would make a perfect puppet. So Warwick craftily suborns George, and then secretly marries his daughter Isabella to him, in Calais, in the summer of 1469, without Edward's knowledge and in defiance of Edward's orders. The ceremony is performed by the archbishop of York, who is Warwick's brother.

"At the same time, armed rebellion is stirring in the North. It is clear that Warwick fostered it. King Edward begins, if slowly, to move north. And now Warwick fully shows his true colours. As Edward heads north, Warwick and George cross to England from Calais, and move to join forces with the rebels. Near Banbury, at the Battle of Edgecote, Edward's troops fall quite apart, and Warwick triumphs. He captures Edward, and holds him prisoner. He captures and executes the father of Edward's queen, and executes her brother John, the one who had been married to Warwick's aged aunt.

"Warwick had wanted a puppet king. Now, with King Edward as his prisoner, Warwick begins to rule England in Edward's name. Warwick, however, does not win the vital support he needs from the leading nobles. There is chaos and unrest. A new Lancastrian uprising breaks out in the North, but while people may be willing to fight for King Edward, they are not prepared to fight for Warwick. Edward soon contrives to be visited in force by loyal friends, perhaps with Richard's assistance, and Warwick simply has to let Edward go.

"The rising is successfully quelled. Edward is free again, and back in power, but he can really do very little about Warwick and George. They are simply too powerful and too wealthy. But he does begin, we see, to place ever more responsibility on our young Richard."

"Richard remained loyal, I take it," said I.

"Oh, yes, absolutely. Richard entirely lives up to his motto, 'Loyaulté me lie', 'Loyalty Binds Me'. If he was asked to choose between Warwick and Edward, he unarguably chose Edward. He is at Edward's side, and never wavers for a moment. Edward creates him Constable of England, and sends him to Wales to deal with an outbreak of Lancastrian rebellion. This Richard does, and in short order, too.

"Edward tries to mend fences with Warwick, but the rift is too deep and permanent. Edward has shown that he will *never* be a puppet of Warwick's. So Warwick falls back on the idea of making George king. Warwick and George go on to foment another rebellion, in Lincolnshire, in the winter of 1470. Edward crushes it quickly and decisively, at the Battle of Lose-coat Field."

"Lose-coat?" inquired Holmes. "Literally?"

"Oh, yes," said Markham, with an exuberant smile. "The rebels threw off their jackets – they were made of boiled leather or padded canvas, which served as armour – and ran for their lives.

"Captured rebels confess that the rising was indeed sparked by Warwick and George. Edward now proclaims the pair as traitors, and they hastily flee to France.

"Next thing you know, Warwick is at the court of his old friend King Louis the Eleventh in France. He is taken in by Louis, in all senses of the words. For whom do you think Louis sends? Why, Margaret of Anjou. The tricky Louis persuades Margaret and Warwick to put aside their old enmity. I am sure that neither found it easy, but they do cook up a plot together. With French assistance, Warwick and George are to invade England, depose Edward, restore Henry the Sixth to the throne, and join France in declaring war on Burgundy.

"For Louis, of course, it would mean England off his back, and on his side against Burgundy. For Margaret, it would mean her son confirmed as heir to the throne. And for Warwick, it would mean a chance to regain power and prestige.

"The pact is sealed with a contract of betrothal between Warwick's younger daughter, Anne, and Prince Edward, the son of Henry the Sixth and Margaret of Anjou. Anne will thus become Princess of Wales and eventually the queen if Edward succeeds Henry the Sixth. But the plan is that they will not marry, and the marriage will not be consummated, until Warwick has first restored Henry's rule.

"All that stupid George gets is a worthless promise that, if young Edward and Anne have no heirs, George will succeed to the throne. Can you imagine?"

"Anne," said I. "That was Anne Nevill, who eventually did become Richard's wife."

"Exactly," returned Markham. "She was fourteen years of age, as I recall."

As we re-entered his headquarters, Markham resumed his stirring tale. "In September 1470, Warwick and George return to England with an army. They land in the West Country, and are joined by Lancastrian supporters from that region. They proclaim the restoration of Henry the Sixth.

"Edward has been decoyed to the North. Young Richard is with him; now aged almost eighteen. Edward is counting on Warwick's brother, John Nevill, the Marquis Montagu, to support him. John Nevill has been steadfastly loyal to Edward. But Edward had not long before restored Nevill's earldom of Northumberland to the Percy family, the previous holders. Seeking to placate Nevill, Edward named him as Marquis Montagu, gave him considerable land, and pledged to marry his daughter to Nevill's son. But this was not enough for Nevill. He felt slighted and betrayed, and now he goes over to Warwick's side.

"Edward thus is on the point of being caught between the armies of Montagu and Warwick. Many of Edward's men desert. Edward flees, taking with him Richard and two old friends and loyal supporters, Lord Hastings and Lord Howard. They have with them Queen Elizabeth Woodville's brother, Anthony, and they manage to sail to Burgundy; to Holland, we would now say. They escape from England on Richard's eighteenth birthday, October 2nd, 1470.

"Back in England, Warwick frees Henry the Sixth from the Tower and restores him to the throne, at least in name."

I shook my head. "So Margaret of Anjou won, and Henry the Sixth was back on the throne. Now may I say, 'Peace at last'?"

"Not yet,' continued Markham, chuckling happily. Holmes, however, interrupted his story. The fidgeting detective had been constantly glancing at his watch for the last ten minutes, and he could be distracted no more.

"Excuse me," said Holmes, hastily sidling towards the door. "I must get back to my case." He threw open the door, and literally ran. Markham and I laughed fondly as we watched our friend dash frantically from the building, fumbling for his cab whistle.

Markham grinned happily at me as we eased ourselves once more into our deep leather chairs.

"Now, Doctor Watson, you wished to say, 'Peace at last.' Not yet, I say, not yet. For one thing, Louis the Eleventh of France declares war on Burgundy. He demands that England follow suit, as agreed in the pact with Warwick and George. As an incentive, he promises to Warwick personally the provinces of Holland and Zeeland. Naturally, in turn, the Duke of Burgundy quietly provides Edward with money, ships and men."

"Of course," said I. "Duke Charles of Burgundy was married to Margaret, the sister of Edward and Richard."

Markham nodded. "Right. And Burgundy was England's favoured trading partner. Edward also secures support from the Hanseatic League, the rich German-Baltic traders. They help him to obtain more ships. Our Richard helps to fit out Edward's expedition himself, and in March 1471, Edward lands in Yorkshire. At Ravenspur, same place where Henry Bolingbroke landed, to end his exile and to become King Henry the Fourth. Up there, they tell a story that Edward set fire to his ship on landing; no retreat, you see; win back the crown or die trying.

"He has lost sight of his other vessels, including Richard's, in a storm. Richard and the others do land safely, however. They join forces. It takes a little time, but Edward is able to assemble an army of some five thousand men. Oh, how I would wish to have been there to see it. Only five thousand men against the might of Warwick and Margaret's armies, yet Edward foxes the lot.

"He bypasses Marquis Montagu's troops, then bottles up Warwick at Coventry. The only soldiers between Edward and London are those of his brother George, and George outnumbers him by two to one. So Edward sends our Richard to see George.

"What does Richard say? Let me speculate. 'Come on home, George. Edward forgives you. You have been tricked and betrayed by Warwick, by King Louis, and by the Anjou woman. They have chosen lunatic Henry as king rather than you. Warwick is marrying his daughter Anne to Henry's heir, and Warwick has given some of *your* lands to Margaret of Anjou. You have been swindled and cheated.'

"The appeal must have gone something like that. It is clever, and it works. It brings to fruition long efforts to re-convert George.

"And so our fickle friend George turns his coat again, rejoins Edward, and Edward enters London triumphantly. Waiting for Edward in London are his wife, Elizabeth Woodville, and the son she has borne him in sanctuary. That is Edward, the elder of your Two Little Princes in the Tower."

"What of Warwick?" I asked.

134

Markham jumped to his feet to ring the bell for coffee. "Warwick is desperate. Not only has Edward the Fourth taken London, and been re-crowned, but Warwick receives word that King Louis of France has signed a truce with Burgundy. Louis, it seems, has turned his back on Warwick.

"Warwick manages to get his forces reorganised for a final attempt to dethrone Edward. Easter Sunday, 1471, and the two armies meet at Barnet. Edward now has some nine thousand men. Warwick has perhaps twice as many

"You will remember the snow at the Battle of Towton? Here it was dense fog.

"Warwick's army finally break. It is a lovely story. The Lancastrian Earl of Oxford leads his men to attack the rear of Edward's army. In the thick mist, however, he runs by accident into Marquis Montagu's men. They see Oxford's de Vere emblem, a star with streaming rays, and mistake it for Edward's emblem, a sun with streaming rays. Montagu's archers open fire, sending volley after volley of arrows into Oxford's troops. There are cries of treachery and treason, and Oxford's men panic. They run in confusion, and Edward promptly drives hard into Warwick's line. Warwick himself is slain. So is his brother Montagu. Edward wins handsomely, and recaptures Henry the Sixth. Richard has been in the thick of the fighting. Two of his esquires fall beside him. He is a hero at the age of eighteen."

"Peace at last?" I suggested, once more.

Markham burst out laughing, in a kindly manner. "No, not quite. Same day as the Battle of Barnet, guess who lands in England with another army."

"Hum. Margaret of Anjou?"

"Right; top marks. Margaret lands at Weymouth. She is too late to reinforce Warwick, so she heads towards Wales, to join up with Jasper Tudor's Welsh Lancastrians and to form a new army. Edward anticipates this, and races fast to stop her crossing the Severn and joining Tudor. Margaret's men run out of steam before they get to the river, though, and they have to stop to rest at Tewkesbury.

"Edward drives his army relentlessly, and catches up to her. May 4th, 1471, and now we *do* have the final battle, the Battle of Tewkesbury.

"Young Richard commands the vanguard. Somerset falls on Richard's men, but Richard drives him off. Edward and Richard then rout Margaret's army. Margaret's Edward, Henry the Sixth's son, is killed. Some now say that Richard killed him, in cold blood, after the battle, but that is not what the contemporary writers report.

"*Our* Edward wins. The young Somerset and other rebel leaders are seized from Tewkesbury Abbey, tried, and executed. As Constable of England, Richard was part of the court that convicted them. Margaret is taken prisoner and goes to the Tower. Henry the Sixth was already a prisoner there, and he is quietly put to death.

"Some writers, hostile to Richard, say that Henry was murdered by Richard himself. Thomas More says so, for one. So does Polydore Virgil, Henry the Seventh's Italian historian."

"I have heard of Virgil from General Milman," I interjected. "The general says that Virgil was in the pay of Henry the Seventh."

"No argument about that," replied Markham, crisply. "Further, Virgil did not come to England until 1502 or thereabouts, so he knew, and wrote, only what he was told.

"Rous also says Richard murdered Henry the Sixth. So does the chronicle of Robert Fabyan, a London merchant and alderman, and a Lancastrian. But there is no evidence that Richard was the executioner. You can be certain that it was Edward who ordered Henry killed, anyway. You cannot really blame Edward, either; Henry had to go, in the interests of peace and order.

"There you have it: Edward on the throne, Richard a hero, Henry the Sixth dead, Henry's son dead, Margaret of Anjou a prisoner. In the end, she is ransomed back to France, but it is all over for her. The game and the kingdom go to Edward the Fourth."

"I should like, if we have time, to come back to the murder of Henry, and the death of his son, and the other murders attributed to Richard," said I. "I have a number of questions to ask, in my pursuit of evidence for and against Richard. But, first, may I now say 'Peace at last'? Or will you correct me once more?"

Markham chuckled, his eyes twinkling over yet another cup of strongly brewed coffee.

"Oh, there is military peace, yes. There is even peace at court, at least for a while. Edward wisely brings old enemies to court, pardons them, and gives them their lands back. But true peace? No. The problem is the perfidious George, Edward and Richard's own brother.

"George has already shown his worth. Thomas More called him 'a goodly noble prince' but, in truth, George is worth even less than stable-muck. Shakespeare was right for once: 'false, fleeting, perjur'd Clarence.' Warwick's huge estates are forfeit because of his treason, and greedy George has his eye on them. He is married to Warwick's elder daughter, Isabella, of course. You will also see her name given as Isabel, by the way. As her husband, George controls her half of the enormous Warwick inheritance. Seeking to gain control of the other half, George now claims the wardship of Isabella's younger sister, Anne Nevill.

"She, as you know, had been betrothed to Henry the Sixth's late son and heir. But now our Richard himself asks for Anne's hand in marriage. They have known each other since childhood; they must have been playfellows at Middleham, her father's castle where Richard was resident. I like to think that I was a love-match, but, she is a most eligible and most wealthy heiress, and that cannot have escaped Richard.

"So Richard wants to marry her, and George wants to keep her single and under his thumb, so that he can enjoy the benefits of the wealth of both sisters. The outcome is that Richard and George have a truly monumental row. The family battle lines are irrevocably drawn."

Markham erupted from his scarred leather chair once more, and pawed like an enthusiastic badger in his treasure trove of Yorkist papers. "Here is a rough translation that I have made of the *Croyland Chronicle*. It is a contemporary chronicle of Richard's time. Passed down to us, in Latin, by the monks of Croyland Abbey, in the Fen country, near Ely. Not always favourable towards Richard, by any means. The chronicler is clearly a Southerner, who speaks of Richard's North as a well-spring from which 'all evil spreads'. He is critical of Richard for rewarding Northerners with Southern estates. Nonetheless, while sometimes clearly biased, his account is most useful. And we should note that, although he finds Richard's coronation was outright usurpation, significantly, he does not accuse Richard of murdering the Two Little Princes. But I am getting ahead of myself; I was talking about Anne Nevill.

"Allow me to read an extract from the chronicle:–

"'Richard, Duke of Gloucester, sought to marry the said Anne himself. This proposal, however, did not suit the intentions of his brother, the Duke of Clarence, who had previously married the eldest daughter of the same earl. Therefore, he had the maiden hidden away, so that her whereabouts might not be known by his brother, as he feared a division of the inheritance, which he wished to come to himself alone, through the right of his wife, and not to have to share it with any other person'."

"Good heavens," I exclaimed. "George actually hid Anne from Richard?"

"Wait until you hear the details," responded Markham, chuckling cheerfully, and he began reading aloud once more:–

"'However, the intelligence of the Duke of Gloucester was superior, for he discovered the maiden in London disguised in the clothing of a kitchen maid; whereupon he had her taken to the sanctuary of St. Martin's. As a result of this, violent quarrels arose between the brothers'.

"You see?" said a beaming Markham. "George actually dresses Anne up in servant's clothing, and literally hides her away.

"Mind you, while I love the story, I have never had much faith in it. George may have been unstable, and perhaps even afflicted in his mind, but he had estates all over England, and in Ireland, where he could hide her, and plenty of staff and followers to keep her prisoner. There was no need for the mummery and disguise. Indeed, some think it more likely that *she* put on the disguise to escape from George, and was still wearing it when she got word to Richard of her escape and her whereabouts.

"In the end, Edward has to act as referee. He approves of Richard's marriage to Anne, in 1472, but greedy George still resists. He has no right in law to any of Anne's portion of Warwick's estates, but demands it all, as if by right. By precedent, Warwick's own lands should have gone to his nephew, the Duke of Bedford. Warwick's widow's property should have remained with her. Edward the Fourth and his Parliament, though, have different and, frankly, irregular ideas. Bedford is simply disinherited, and the countess's property is assigned to her daughters, as if she were, in the words of the bill, "naturally dead". That put her wealth under the control of the husbands of those daughters.

"All in all, Edward's decisions as referee, irregular or not, mean that Richard and Anne have to cede to George the lion's share of Anne's wealth. But Richard's portion, by way of Anne, does include Warwick's old castle at Middleham, and there he eventually makes his home with Anne. Richard is nineteen years of age, and Anne, I believe, just sixteen.

"Some say the marriage was simply and solely a means of securing more property and income for Richard. I prefer to believe that it was a good marriage, and a happy home at Middleham. Their own son, Edward, was born there the following year. And Richard becomes Edward's lieutenant and lord paramount in the North. It was in this role as viceroy that Richard showed that he had indeed the makings of a king."

To give my aching right hand a rest, I broke in. "I have read Shakespeare's tale, of Richard courting Anne while she is accusing him, most bitterly, of murdering Henry the Sixth and Prince Edward, her betrothed. I am given to understand that this is a case of dramatic licence."

"Oh, a fairy tale," replied Markham. "As is Shakespeare's proposition that Richard soon murdered her, too. Good drama, but in truth just a fairy tale."

We spent some welcome minutes discussing Shakespeare, while my weary right hand and wrist recovered. I signalled to the patient Markham to continue.

"Good, let me go back now to Edward the Fourth. He is firmly established as king, and he soon makes plans to attack France again. He has great difficulty in raising taxes for this, and puts pressure on the rich to give him huge donations, or 'benevolences'. In 1475, with the promise of help from Burgundy, he sets sail for France with his army. Richard comes from Middleham Castle, with more than a thousand armed men, to accompany him.

"However, the Duke of Burgundy fails to provide the troops he has promised. King Louis of France sends the message that he is interested in a truce, and so Edward begins to negotiate a peace with him.

"Louis literally buys a seven-year treaty from King Edward with French gold. He pays fifteen thousand pounds to Edward's treasury. He gives Edward himself an enormous annual pension of ten thousand pounds. I must say, Edward may have needed the money; by all accounts, his treasury was rather bare. Louis gives generous gifts to Edward's advisers and courtiers, and he agrees that his son, the Dauphin, shall in time marry Edward's eldest daughter Elizabeth of York, the Princess Royal.

"King Louis goes away crowing about the treaty. In his words, 'I have chased the English out of France more easily than my father ever did; for my father drove them out by force of arms, whereas I have driven them out by force of arms, whereas I have driven them out with venison pies and good wine.'

140

"The *Croyland Chronicle* calls the pact 'honourable'. Our Richard, though, sees it as quite the opposite. He opposes it, and does so openly. Even Lord Bacon, the Lord Chancellor, although he was no admirer of Richard, wrote in 1622 that 'as upon all occasions, Richard, Duke of Gloucester, stood upon the side of honour.'

"Richard finally does subscribe to the peace, however. Edward must have called upon him to do that. They return to England, and Richard goes off to Yorkshire. He may have objected to the French treaty, but he is loyal to Edward. He is Edward's right-hand man in the North, and he does an excellent job of it. In effect, he manages half the kingdom for Edward.

"Brother George, though, simply can not let well enough alone. Let us go back to the *Croyland Chronicle*. It tells us how Edward is trying to secure the finances of the crown, and is taking back some prior grants of royal property. Listen to this:–

"'There arose another dispute with his brother, the Duke of Clarence, which greatly tarnished the glory of this most prudent king. It was noticed that the duke by degrees was withdrawing himself from the king's presence, speaking scarcely a word in council, and eating and drinking at the palace with reluctance. Many were of the opinion that this reversal of his earlier friendship had arisen in the duke's heart because of the general taking back of grants that the king had lately enacted in Parliament. On this occasion, the duke lost the noble lordship of Tutbury and several other estates that he had previously obtained by royal grant.'

"Now George's wife, Isabella, dies," continued Markham. "George declares that one of her maids has poisoned her. He has not the slightest shred of evidence of this, but he has the maid seized and executed, and without trial. He even suggests that Edward's queen, Elizabeth Woodville, had cast spells on his wife.

"You would think that King Edward would take action, but, oddly, he does nothing. And that seems to encourage George even more. George is simply incorrigible. It is probable, for example, that he was plotting with the Lancastrian Earl of Oxford in 1473, when that gentleman invaded Cornwall, seized the fortress of St. Michael's Mount, and held it for many months.

"In early 1477, the Duke of Burgundy is killed at the Siege of Nancy. His only heir is a daughter, from a marriage prior to that with Margaret of York. As a widower, George promptly seeks to marry Burgundy's wealthy daughter, and asks his sister Margaret, the girl's stepmother, to support the idea. Edward the Fourth blocks the plan, however. England's relations with Burgundy are a little touchy, at this stage, and the last thing Edward needs is George, with his eyes on the English crown, heading a Burgundian army. Edward refuses to sanction the marriage, and George is infuriated.

"Soon, one of George's retainers is arrested by Edward's authorities and accused of witchcraft. He is executed, protesting his innocence to the very end. Perhaps he was indeed innocent, and Edward was using him to send a none-too-veiled warning to George. If so, it is far too subtle for George. Next thing, George rashly barges into to the royal council chamber, and publicly accuses the king of injustice. This is *lèse-majesté* on the grandest scale. The outcome is that Edward has George arrested, and sent to the Tower.

"Before Parliament, in January 1478, Edward formally accuses George of 'unnatural and loathly treason', fomenting rebellion, and seeking the throne himself. The king also charges George with spreading rumours that Edward is really a bastard and has no right to the throne. George was, in effect, thus claiming the crown for himself, as well as foully insulting his own mother. George is promptly found guilty, and is sentenced to death. He is sent to the Tower.

"As Thomas More put it:–

"'Heinous treason was laid to his charge, and finally, whether he be guilty or faultless, he was attainted by

Parliament and condemned to death, and thereupon was hastily drowned in a butt of Malmsey'."

I interrupted, creating another opportunity to rest my cramped right hand by telling Markham of Yeoman Warder Baker's theory of George's imprisonment in the Nun's Bower in the Tower's Coldharbour Gate.

"Interesting," said Markham. "The *Croyland Chronicle* does not mention where in the Tower George was held, but it does record George's death – not hastily at all, but some weeks later. Let me read it to you:–

"'The execution was delayed for some long time, until the Speaker of the Commons came with his colleagues to the Lords to make a new request to bring the matter to an end. As a result, whatever was the method of the execution, it was indeed brought to a conclusion within a few days – but would that this were the end of the troubles – in the Tower of London.'

"That was in February 1478. Drowned in a barrel of Malmsey wine, they say. More likely slipped some poisoned Malmsey, I would think, to avoid an embarrassing public execution.

"But why *did* the Commons insist that George be executed? Did their request originate with Edward, so that he could defend the execution on the grounds the people had demanded that their sentence be carried out? Or did it originate with the Woodvilles and well placed Woodville gold, to ensure that Clarence was truly disposed of? That would hardly surprise me. George had viciously slandered Queen Elizabeth. He had declared that her husband, Edward the Fourth, was a bastard, with no right to the throne. Warwick had executed her father and her brother after the Battle of Edgecote, and George was a vital part of the whole Warwick plot. The Woodvilles would naturally have had it in for George.

"They profited from his death, too. *Cui bono?* On George's execution, much of George's land went to the Woodville

143

queen's brother Anthony, the Earl Rivers; and the lucrative wardship of George's son and heir went to the Woodville queen's eldest son by her first marriage.

"What of the charge," I inquired, "that Richard was somehow behind Clarence's death? I intend, as I say, to examine the murder accusations against Richard one by one, in some detail, but can you answer this one now?"

"Even hostile writers, such as Edward Hall and Raphael Holinshed, say that Richard protested the sentence," replied Markham.

"It is the so-called Thomas More history that insinuates that Richard protested George's sentence 'somewhat more faintly' than he would if he were seriously interested in saving George. However, More does specify that it was Edward who commanded George's execution.

"Later on, in typical Tudor fashion, the story becomes thoroughly embellished, and distorted to the point where Richard is accused of taking part in the execution itself."

Markham dived into his box of papers again. "Here is what Francis Sandford's *History* says, in 1707:–

"'After he had offered his mass penny in the Tower of London, he was drowned in a butt of Malmsey, his brother the Duke of Gloucester assisting thereat with his own proper hands.'

"As you see, we have thus moved from Richard protesting George's sentence, to Richard not protesting the sentence strongly enough, and finally to Richard actually killing George with his own hands. Typical Tudor myth. But, oh, I have been trying to give you as objective an account as I can, and I must withdraw that remark."

"Thank you," I returned. "You have given me a wonderful account. I only wish that my school teachers had taught history your way. They just made us learn and recite all those horrible dates."

"Oh, no," said Markham, raising an eyebrow. "History is not *dates*. History is what happened *between* the dates."

I broke in. "My goodness, look at the clock. I am imposing on your time."

"No, no, Doctor Watson. I have time enough to put Edward in his grave and Richard upon the throne for you. Then I shall indeed have to leave, I am afraid, or my dear Minna will be chasing me. We dine rather early, and I am constantly late. I am a terrible trial upon her patience. If we cannot address all of your questions this afternoon, I do hope you that will return?"

I stretched and settled back into my chair. "Markham, why would Edward kill George, his own brother? Why not just lock him up in the Tower, and leave him there?"

Markham nodded heavily. "An excellent question. I will come back to it shortly, if I may."

Markham began his purposeful pacing of the room again, while I grasped my pencil with renewed vigour.

"Edward is secure enough on the throne, but not all is well. King Louis the Eleventh fails to make his agreed treaty payments, and breaks his promise to marry his son to Edward's daughter, Elizabeth of York. Jilts her, he does. Encouraged by Louis, the Scots now breach their truce with Edward, too. Richard commands the army that goes against them. He is successful. Edward broods mightily on France's duplicity, and finally calls for war. He has Richard's whole-hearted support in this.

"But then Edward becomes ill. We do not know the nature of his ailment. Polydore Virgil, the Italian historian, suggested that Edward may have been poisoned, but we have no evidence for that, nor any clue as to who might have done it.

"Edward is only forty years old, but dies in his bed on April 9th, 1483. His ranking son and heir, Prince Edward, is but twelve years old. On his deathbed at Westminster, Edward the Fourth tries to bring about peace between the two court factions, the *parvenu* Woodvilles and the old blue-blood Yorkists and Plantagenets. Their promises of friendship are short-lived, however.

"And now England is to pay once again the price of Edward the Fourth's favours to the Woodvilles."

Chapter Nine

Markham frowned severely as he continued.

"Richard takes on the *rôle* of Protector of the king and kingdom. Edward the Fourth's will named Richard as Protector during young Prince Edward's minority, and this office was later confirmed by Parliament. The Woodvilles, though, have other ideas.

"Richard is in the North. On hearing of Edward the Fourth's death, he goes to York. He attends funeral masses for his brother in the Minster. He publicly recognises Prince Edward as the new king, and publicly swears allegiance. Then, with a retinue of several hundred knights and esquires of the North, all dressed in mourning, he sets off for London, at an unhurried pace.

"Let us call the young Edward prince still, although he is truly King Edward the Fifth, awaiting only his coronation ceremony and anointing. He is living at Ludlow with his uncle, Anthony Earl Rivers, the Woodville queen's eldest brother. Rivers is his governor and guardian, and the prince's household is dominated by Woodvilles. Rivers assembles two thousand armed men, and sets off for London with Prince Edward. The size of his train was much smaller than the Woodvilles had first proposed, but the Council, and Lord Hastings, would not allow them to bring more. Even so, two thousand men constitute a significant force, and they apparently carry in their waggons extra arms and armour.

Meanwhile, Thomas Grey, Marquis of Dorset, Queen Elizabeth Woodville's eldest son by her first marriage, is acting as constable of the Tower, and loots the royal treasury there. The Woodvilles also assemble a squadron of warships in the Channel. The royal council, which is dominated by the Woodvilles, set May 4th as the coronation date.

"All of this is done without any consultation with Richard, the Protector.

"Some of the council make efforts to hold the Woodvilles back. Lord Hastings, for one; he was Edward the Fourth's Chamberlain and Captain of the Guard, and was also a staunch friend, and a partner in Edward's exile. It is clear that the Woodvilles are intent on holding Prince Edward in their power. They obviously intend to take control of the new king, and the kingdom, before Richard can reach London and take office as Protector. It is a Woodville *coup*, a Woodville regency, in the making.

"The Duke of Buckingham sends word to warn Richard of all this, and races to meet Richard at Northampton, with some three hundred soldiers. Buckingham is of Plantagenet stock himself, although his family had fought for the House of Lancaster. He was not at all an insider in Edward the Fourth's court, although he was married at a tender age to Catherine Woodville, a sister of Edward's queen. Now Buckingham quickly seeks a place under Richard's sun. Perhaps his motive was to press his claim to certain rich estates, a claim that Edward had rejected.

"Whatever Buckingham's motives, he and Richard catch up to Earl Rivers at Northampton, on April 29th, 1483. However, they find that Rivers has sent the prince on to Stony Stratford, another half-day's journey towards London. Richard arrests Rivers, along with Queen Elizabeth Woodville's second son by her first marriage, Sir Richard Grey; and Sir Richard Haute and Sir Thomas Vaughan. Haute is a cousin of Elizabeth Woodville, and is controller of Prince Edward's household. Vaughan is Prince Edward's chief chamberlain, and has been a devoted servant since the boy was a baby. Other members of the prince's party are also arrested, but are soon freed.

"As soon as she gets word that Richard has foiled the Woodvilles' plot, Elizabeth Woodville hastily takes sanctuary at Westminster with the other little prince and her daughters."

I interrupted. "Sanctuary? She had cause, then, to be scared of Richard?"

"I suppose that she had some right to be nervous," replied Markham. "Richard had just arrested her brother, her son and her cousin. As well, she and her kin had been plotting against Richard, and he knew it. Even John Rous reports that the Woodvilles had plotted Richard's death.

"But one could also argue that she sought sanctuary as a crafty public ploy, to discredit Richard and portray him as an ogre threatening women and children. Hard to tell, at this remove, but I would certainly not put it past her. It would also help to poison Prince Edward against his uncle Richard."

Markham shrugged again, sniffed, and then picked up his tale.

"Our Richard then catches up to the young Edward, and resumes with him the journey to London. They arrive on May 4th."

"Rivers, Grey and Vaughan are on my list of murders of which Richard is accused," I interjected.

"Quite so," returned Markham. "Add Haute to your list, too. I believe he was executed along with them."

I looked up from my notes. "It cannot have gone down too well with the prince; that his uncle Richard had his Woodville relatives seized, and also his faithful servant Vaughan."

Sadness showed in Markham's eyes. "When they were arrested, Thomas More certainly suggests that the boy wept. I can only assume that they had continued to intrigue with the other Woodvilles, and that the royal council approved their arrest and eventual execution. As I say, even John Rous reported that the Woodvilles had been aiming to kill Richard."

He shook his head woefully, and continued.

"All is soon in order, now that Richard is in London and the Woodvilles' machinations have been quashed. Their leaders have been arrested. Their fleet have been disbanded, although Sir Edward Woodville did escape to the Continent with two ships and, I believe, the bulk of Edward's treasury. The Woodville *coup* is over. Not one drop of blood has been shed.

"And I point out that Richard's *contre-coup* has been directed against the Woodvilles, and not against young Edward the Fifth. Acting as Protector, Richard once more publicly swears fealty to the new king, and appoints a new council, including some Woodville adherents. And under Richard's guidance, young Edward enters upon his new duties. Even Rous says this:–

> "'The laws were administered, money coined, and all things pertaining to the royal dignity were performed in the young king's name, he dwelling in the palace of the Bishop of London from his first coming to London.'

"And on May 19th, young King Edward the Fifth delivered a speech to the estates of Parliament, in which he asked Parliament to confirm formally his uncle Richard as 'Protector and Defensor' of the Realm. This they did. As the *Croyland Chronicle* said:–

> "'With the consent and good will of all the lords, the Duke of Gloucester was given the authority to order and forbid in everything, just like another king, and as the occasion should require.'

"A new coronation date is set for Edward, on Sunday June 22nd, and Richard gives Parliament notice to meet on June 25th. Coronation robes are ordered. On June 5th, some fifty esquires and gentlemen are summoned to become knighted, to mark the occasion. Nobles are invited to the coronation ceremony, and begin to make their way to London. Richard's own wife, Anne, comes to London, leaving their son at Middleham."

"In other words," I observed, "the plans for the coronation of young Edward are proceeding apace, with Richard's approval."

"At Richard's *command*," said Markham, emphatically.

"As the *Croyland Chronicle* held:– 'A reign of peace and prosperity seemed to have begun.'

"But then we begin what *Croyland* was to call 'seditious and disgraceful proceedings' – Richard's accession to the throne."

He paused, and looked earnestly at me. "Doctor Watson, I must tread carefully here, as I have firm opinions on Richard's accession. I have a lifelong bias towards Richard as a goodly man; others find him an evil monster. I shall do my best to keep the account straightforward.

"Amidst all the preparations for the coronation, the Bishop of Bath and Wells, Robert Stillington, comes to the royal council on June 8th or 9th, and tells them an extraordinary story. He declares that in 1461, three years before his secret marriage to Elizabeth Woodville, Edward the Fourth had made a binding marriage pre-contract or 'troth-plight'. With the Lady Eleanor Butler, a widow and a daughter of John Talbot, first Earl of Shrewsbury. To complete another conquest, perhaps?

"Stillington discloses that he had himself witnessed this clandestine contract, and had been ordered by the king to keep it secret.

"Now, according to the church law and the *mores* of the time, a pre-contract like this is as good as a legal marriage. Indeed, Parliament later condemned the Woodville marriage on the grounds that Edward already 'stood married and troth plight' to Eleanor Butler. This was a trump that Henry the Eighth was to play to rid himself of Anne Boleyn, as well.

"Eleanor Butler died in 1468, but that is irrelevant; she was alive at the time of Edward's marriage in 1464 to Elizabeth Woodville. Thus the pre-contract means that Edward's Woodville marriage was bigamous, and invalid. This means that the Two Little Princes are illegitimate; they are bastards.

And that, in turn, means that Prince Edward is not the legal heir to his father's throne.

"Brother George is dead, and George's heir, his eight-year-old son, has lost his right of inheritance because of his father's treason. George's boy is feeble-minded, too, by all accounts. So that leaves, as heir to the throne of England – well, who?"

"Our own Richard," I replied, slowly. "It must be. Richard Duke of Gloucester, the next oldest brother, our Richard the Third."

"Exactly. Richard is the lawful heir to the throne."

"If Stillington's claim stands up," I remarked.

"Oh, Stillington is no simple cleric," returned Markham. "He had been Lord Chancellor under Edward. That means he was on the level, roughly speaking, of the Prime Minister today. He resigned because of ill health in 1473. A Yorkist, yes, and an astute politician. But now he is elderly, infirm, and with nothing to gain by bringing this charge against Edward.

"Let me go back now to your very perceptive question about why Edward has executed Brother George. Why did Edward not just lock him up in the Tower and drop the keys into the river? Was there, in fact, a very good reason to have George permanently removed?

"Now, Doctor Watson, when was George sentenced on the charges brought against him by Edward?"

"Hum. Hold on. Ah, I know. In 1478, the winter of 1478."

"Exactly. And at just that time, Stillington himself is arrested and imprisoned by Edward for 'uttering words prejudicial to the King and his State.' There exists a letter, dated March 6th, 1478, that reports that Stillington has been brought into the Tower, some time before that date.

"So, suppose that Stillington has told *George* all about this pre-contract with Lady Butler. Suppose that George is threatening to tell the story, and threatening to use it. George had already publicly claimed that Edward was a bastard, which would give George the crown by right. Edward's charges against George, in Parliament, explicitly include the accusations that George was challenging Edward's right to the throne, and was suborning people to swear allegiance to George instead.

"That little campaign went nowhere, but is George now threatening, further, to establish that Edward's children are illegitimate? If they are, then who would be the heir to the throne? George, of course. So tell me, Doctor Watson, if George were indeed threatening to tell the world about the pre-contract, so that he could take the crown, what would Edward the Fourth do?"

"He would have George executed," I replied, confidently. "He could not trust George to keep quiet, ever, even in the Tower. And if the Woodvilles heard that George was going to expose the illegitimacy of the Two Little Princes, they would certainly press Edward to silence George permanently. George was far too volatile and irresponsible. He would blab to guards, servants, friends, visitors. George would see the throne as his by right. He would try to send messages to the French and the Scots seeking support. He would again foment rebellion and revolution."

"Precisely," continued Markham. "And that would explain why Edward would throw Stillington into the Tower, too, to remind him of the value of judicious silence. That is surely why Stillington was arrested. He was soon freed, but was heavily fined."

"You say, 'Suppose Stillington has told George'," I broke in. "Is there evidence that he did?"

"I must say that there is no proof," returned Markham, evenly. "I find the theory plausible enough, though. Even Gairdner supports it."

"I am puzzled," said I. "If Edward was prepared to have his own brother executed, why would he merely hold Stillington in the Tower? Why not execute him, also, to be on the safe side? If Stillington had blabbed to George, could he be trusted not to blab again to others? After all, Edward's right to the throne was at risk."

"Stillington had certainly held his tongue previously. Neither he nor Lady Butler spoke up prior to her death in 1468. Of course, he did not know of Edward's marriage to

153

Elizabeth Woodville until it was a *fait accompli*. If he had known of it in advance, as a churchman he would have had to speak out. But as a statesman, faced with that that *fait accompli*, he remained silent again."

"Hang on," I interjected. "You said Stillington was Lord Chancellor for Edward. Could that have been his reward for his silence?"

"That is not my impression," returned Markham. "Stillington was a capable and experienced administrator and well worthy of the office.

"You ask why Edward did not execute Stillington. Executing a bishop without papal authority would be a most risky business for any king. An oath of renewed silence would have to suffice. What we do know is that Stillington is turned loose, with a pardon, in June 1479. It seems that he does keep faith; he never mentions the subject of the pre-contract again until he brings it to the council four years later, after Edward the Fourth's death.

"You can imagine the thunder clap when he does so. Chaos, shock. Proof is demanded of Stillington, of course. He brings in a troop of lawyers, and depositions from witnesses. He himself was an eye-witness. The case is clearly not frivolous. Richard's right to the throne is obviously strong.

"I have said that Stillington presented his case to the council. But it is also clear that this was not the full council. A contemporary letter shows that there was no communication of this council to Elizabeth Woodville. And we have evidence that the Woodville supporters on the council were holding their own and separate meeting on June 9th, and tried to issue state orders in the name of Edward the Fifth, without Richard's knowledge or approval."

"There were, then, two separate, rival councils?" I asked.

"It seems so," returned Markham. "The Woodville band may not have heard from Stillington, but they do not trust Richard, and believe, or pretend to believe, that he is making moves to seize the throne for himself.

"And at this stage, there comes a disaster for Richard. He loses the vital support of William, Lord Hastings.

"Hastings is far from being a natural ally of the Woodvilles. According to More, Elizabeth Woodville detested Hastings because he had been a fellow-roisterer with Edward the Fourth in the king's wenching and debauches. The *Croyland Chronicle* also speaks of the mutual ill will between Hastings and the Woodvilles. And until now, indeed, Hastings helped to foil their plans. He has stood with Richard against them to ensure that Richard became the Protector. He had always been loyal to Edward, and shared Edward's exile in late 1470 and early 1471.

"But now Hastings will not stand still while Edward's heirs are disinherited. Perhaps, in addition, Hastings is infuriated by Richard's obvious favouritism and generosity towards the Duke of Buckingham. There are also others who do not want to see Richard on the throne, and one of them, of course, is our old friend" – Markham's sarcasm was thick – "the revered Bishop John Morton. Instantly, the Woodvilles, Morton and Hastings are off and plotting. One of their go-betweens is one Jane Shore, the favourite mistress of Edward the Fourth; she now is Hastings's paramour.

"Richard becomes alarmed, and sends an urgent letter to the Mayor of York for help." Once more, Markham burrowed into his box of Yorkist papers. "Here we are:–

> "'We heartily pray you to come unto us to London, in all the diligence ye can possible after the sight hereof, with as many as ye can make defensibly arrayed, there to aid and assist us against the Queen, her bloody adherents and affinity, who have intended, and daily do intend, to murder and utterly destroy us and our cousin the Duke of Buckingham and the old royal blood of this realm –'."

Markham broke off. "That is written on June 10th. We know of a similar letter to one Lord Nevill, which was sent on June 11th. Richard presumably sent such letters to others, as well."

I broke in sharply. "'Defensibly arrayed'. Does that reflect a purely defensive intent? As opposed to offensive?"

"A shrewd question," returned Markham. "But I do not know if there was such an expression as 'offensibly arrayed'," he added, with a smile. "The City of York decided to send two hundred men, by the way.

"The conspirators now make a fatal mistake. One of Hastings's men is one William Catesby. He sends word to Richard, exposing the plot. On June 13th, Richard breaks up the council session at the Tower, arrests Hastings and Morton, and smashes the conspiracy."

"Ah, I get it," I interjected. "The scene in Shakespeare's play, Morton and his strawberries, and the arrest and speedy execution of Hastings."

"Yes," said Markham. "One wonders if it was Buckingham who persuaded Richard to execute Hastings. The two were rivals for power under Richard. Buckingham would have been happy to see Hastings out of the way."

I broke in. "Could all this not be seen by the populace as a plot *by* Richard, rather than a plot *against* him? With the Woodvilles and Hastings as innocent victims?"

Markham shook his head. "The writers of the era are agreed that the Woodvilles made the first suspect moves. To the point that, when the Woodvilles proposed to bring a veritable army with the prince to London, Lord Hastings threatened to withdraw to Calais. He was the governor there, and commanded the garrison. He was, clearly, warning the Woodvilles that they were going too far. That if they pressed ahead with their plans, civil war might follow. The Woodvilles backed down, but they had made their game clear. They still tried to keep control of the prince. They seized the royal treasury from the Tower. They sent warships to sea. There is some evidence that, without a by-your-leave from Richard, they tried to send out orders cancelling the sitting of Parliament that Richard had called. Not too surprising, as Parliament obviously would confirm Richard as Protector.

"Now, after Richard's *contre-coup* of June 13th, the council lack dedicated Woodville partisans. Elizabeth Woodville is still in sanctuary with Prince Richard, the other little prince, as you know. And on June 16th, the council asks her to send little Richard to join his brother in residence at the Tower. She does so, willingly."

I coughed, politely. "I find that a little hard to believe, Markham, if I may say so. She must surely have feared Richard and what he might do to her sons. She knows that the Woodville plot has been smashed, that her relatives have been arrested, that Richard holds the uncrowned king, that Hastings has been executed, and that Morton has been seized. She surely must feel that she and her sons are in dire peril. And yet she would *willingly* release her other boy to Richard?"

"It is true that most people insist that Hastings was instantly executed on June 13th. I believe, however, that I can show that the execution was not until the 20th, and after a trial. If I am right, then Elizabeth Woodville did not know that Hastings was dead, for he was still alive; but she would certainly know that he had been placed under arrest. If I am wrong, then, yes, she would have known of Hastings's death. She would probably also know that Richard, as Protector, had seized the lands of Rivers and his party. Richard was to give them to his own followers."

"But she did not know on the 16th of Stillington's revelations about the pre-contract?"

"Correct. What went on at Richard's council meeting of June 8th or 9th was not made known to her, because her supporters were not at that meeting, and were off somewhere else holding their own gathering."

"Hum. I doubt that she would so easily have released her young son to Richard on the 16th if she had known," I observed. "I am surprised that she released him at all. Yet you insist that she did so willingly?"

"Willingly, I say. I accept that the *Croyland Chronicle* suggests that she was threatened at some stage, but it does not say who made the threats; it certainly does not name Richard. In the end, though, the *Chronicle* assures us that she 'graciously assented' to the child's removal. Indeed, that could also be translated as 'assented with gratitude'.

"I have cited the *Chronicle* before. It is an account, a diary, of public affairs, from the Abbey of Croyland or Crowland in Lincolnshire, a Benedictine abbey. As I say, it is often not favourable towards Richard, and slings mud at him. Indeed, it describes Henry the Seventh as some sort of angel:–

> "'(Henry) began to receive praise from everyone as though he was an angel sent from heaven, through whom God deigned to visit his people and free them from the evils which had hitherto afflicted them beyond measure.'

"Despite its biases and mud-slinging, it is a most useful document. It tells us, as I say, that Queen Elizabeth assented to releasing the young prince to his uncle."

I coughed once more. "Markham, forgive me, but I still find that hard to swallow. It would certainly be deeply embarrassing to Richard that his own brother's queen is still claiming sanctuary with Prince Richard. He would certainly want them to leave sanctuary. It would be natural, too, to want little Richard to attend his brother's coronation. I find it hard to believe, however, that she simply 'assented' to sending the boy from sanctuary, in the way I would use the word. Surely it is more likely that assent was wrung from her. How free was she to say no?"

Markham smiled. "There is nothing to forgive. I hope that you will continue to challenge my interpretations. That is essential to your mission. I hope, however, that, as you challenge me, you will also challenge More and the others. It is true that More says that she objected to young Richard going to the Tower, and that Westminster was ringed by soldiers. Polydore Virgil insists that 'the innocent child (was) pulled out of his mother's arms' with deceptive promises. But release young Richard she did, persuaded by Cardinal Bourchier, and *Croyland* says that she willingly assented."

"When did word come out of Stillington's disclosures?"

"On June 22nd, when a famed preacher, Ralph Shaw, unveiled them in a sermon at St. Paul's Cross in London. He took for his text 'Bastard slips shall not take deep root'. From the Book of Wisdom, is it not? I do not know if he named Stillington, but Shaw did present in public the case that Edward the Fourth's marriage to Elizabeth Woodville was invalid, and that the Two Little Princes were therefore bastards, and ineligible to succeed to the throne.

"The Duke of Buckingham presented the same case to the mayor – Shaw's brother, Sir Edmund Shaw – and to the leaders of the City. And on June 25th, the estates of Parliament met, and concurred in Richard's right to the crown.'

Markham seized yet another document from his collection. "I point out, then, that Richard did not *seize* the throne or usurp the Crown. As the Parliamentary record of the time notes:– 'Previously to his coronation, a roll containing certain articles was presented to him on behalf of the three estates of the realm, by many lords spiritual and temporal, and other nobles in great multitude ... whereunto he, for the public weal and tranquility of the land, benignly assented.'

"Richard was unanimously *elected* king by the three estates, which they had every right to do. As they had done in the case of Edward the Fourth and, earlier, for Edward the Third and Henry the Fourth. And when the full Parliament next met, it endorsed Richard as king and his son Edward as heir apparent.

"Richard did not seize the Crown; he was *given* it by the country."

I looked hard at Markham. "There must have been strong mistrust of Richard, I would think. People must have thought that this card played by Stillington and Richard was altogether far too convenient. Surely, many must have seen it as a grab for the throne by Richard."

Markham shrugged. "Richard's enemies would, yes, of course. But remember that the country suffered badly under the last minority rule, when Henry the Sixth was an infant king. Many would have legitimately feared another minority rule under Edward the Fifth. 'Woe to thee, O land, when thy king is a child.' That is from Ecclesiastes.

"Richard would have had some support, therefore. If some see Richard as reaching for the crown, as you suggest, others would obviously see the Woodvilles as grasping for control of the crown themselves. So Richard won acceptance because of dislike of the Woodvilles, fear of a minority rule, and acceptance of the bastardy of Edward the Fourth's heirs due to the pre-contracted marriage."

"People must have thought that the timing of the unveiling of Stillington's pre-contract story was suspiciously convenient," I persisted.

"But when and how else could it have come out?" responded Markham. "Edward the Fifth, a minor and a bastard, was going to be crowned king, within a matter of days. Stillington had to come forward then, or stay silent and live with the consequences."

"Stillington felt bound by conscience, you mean? But he had apparently lived well enough with his conscience during Edward's reign."

"Richard may have called on him to own up, I concede," said Markham. "Nobody knows when and how Richard first became aware of the pre-contract. Perhaps George had told him. Or the family of Lady Butler. Or Stillington. Or perhaps Richard had recently learned of it from Buckingham. Buckingham, you see, was Eleanor Butler's cousin, and Richard's cousin, too."

"Could Stillington's story have been a lie from the start?"

"If it had been, surely the Woodvilles would have loudly and publicly protested that it was a lie, but there is absolutely no record of them so doing. Did Elizabeth Woodville cry out? Did she insist she had been legitimately married? Did she appeal to the Church? No, no, and again no.

"Her silence, the Woodvilles' collective silence, can only mean that the story was true; that the marriage of Edward the Fourth and Elizabeth Woodville was indeed a sham, and that the Woodvilles knew it.

"Further, if Stillington had told a lie, Henry the Seventh would undoubtedly have forced him to withdraw it. He did imprison Stillington, but Henry was careful not to specify what the alleged crime was. And the story of the pre-contract was *not* withdrawn. Nor did Henry try positively to disprove it. Instead, Henry tried to seek out and destroy all copies of *Titulus Regius*, the *Title of the King*, the act that confirmed Richard's right to the throne, and disqualified the princes because of their illegitimacy. The act proclaimed their bastardy. That act, of course, meant that Elizabeth of York, Henry's own wife to be, was legally a bastard as well.

"Calling *Titulus Regius* 'false and seditious', Henry repealed it, and ordered the act destroyed, according to the records of his own Parliament, 'so that all things said and remembered in the said Bill and Act thereof may be for ever out of remembrance and also forgot'.

"Henry's insistence on actually destroying all copies of the act surely speaks to the truth of Stillington's story.

"Henry first pardoned Stillington, by the way, but it seems that he was not comfortable with Stillington at large. He then accused Stillington of being mixed up in a Yorkist plot, and, without laying any actual charge against him, re-arrested him and kept him a prisoner at Windsor." Markham shook his head.

"Even if the story were true," said I, "could not Edward and Elizabeth Woodville have gone through a proper marriage ceremony, after Miss Butler's death, to make all legal?"

"They could have, I suppose, assuming the church so permitted. But they did not. Even if they had, I understand that it would not have made the Two Little Princes legitimate."

"Was illegitimacy really a bar to the throne?"

"Bastard children had no legal rights of inheritance, although presumably Parliament could have decided otherwise for Edward the Fifth and named him as king. Later on, Queen Elizabeth was declared a bastard by Henry the Eighth, but succeeded to the throne without any formal reversal of her status. The same was so for her sister Mary.

"In the case at hand, *Titulus Regius* confirmed Edward's pre-contract with Eleanor Butler. Here is what it says:– 'It appears and follows evidently that the said King Edward during his life and the said Elizabeth' – that is Elizabeth Woodville, of course – 'lived together sinfully and damnably in adultery … Also it appears and follows that all the issue and children of the said King Edward being bastards and unable to claim or inherit anything, by the law and custom of England.'"

I broke in. "A question: Could not one argue that Edward the Fifth was already king? That he inherited the crown upon his father's death, and was recognized as king? So was not the issue of bastardy simply moot?"

"No, no," Markham responded. "Not at all. Little Edward was merely king-in-waiting. His coronation had not yet taken place, so he had not yet been anointed as king. That was essential. Without that, he was but king-to-be. And the three estates had the legal right, and precedent, to disqualify him as heir and to name another as king. Indeed, they could have deposed him even if he *had* been anointed and crowned."

Markham cast yet a nervous glance at the clock.

"On or about July 2nd, 1483, Richard's troops arrive from York and elsewhere. A real army, they are not. There are but four thousand of them, poorly equipped and unimpressive, to say the least. They make camp, and play no important *rôle* in what is going on.

"On July 4th, our Richard and Anne go to the royal lodgings in the Tower. That was the usual thing before a coronation. On Sunday, July 6th, 1483, Richard is crowned king, and Anne queen. Richard is not yet one-and-thirty years old. It is the most splendid and opulent coronation ever."

Silence prevailed for a moment. Then I broke in with another question.

"Markham, we have it from Thomas More that Richard declared that Edward the Fourth was a bastard. That impugns Richard's own mother. Why would Richard publicly accuse his own mother of adultery, when he already had Stillington's case against Edward's marriage? That case was strong enough to win in Parliament. So why would Richard need to claim that Edward was a bastard? Why impugn his own mother?"

Markham thumped the arm of his chair in glee.

"Exactly, Doctor Watson. Why on earth should he? Excellent question.

"Now, Robert Fabyan's *Chronicle* reports that, in his public sermon, Shaw attacked the legitimacy of Edward's marriage because of the pre-contract with Eleanor Butler. That is what Fabyan reports. It is *all* that Fabyan reports, despite the fact that he was a good Lancastrian. And as an alderman of London, Fabyan may very well have heard Shaw's address in person.

"Thomas More's account adds something new. It says that Shaw *further* declared, in addition, that Edward the Fourth was a bastard, and so was brother George.

"Polydore Virgil, the Italian historian in the employ of Henry the Seventh, then goes a significant step farther than that. Virgil's version is that Shaw spoke *only* of the bastardy of Edward the Fourth; no mention of the pre-contract. Virgil goes on to say that Richard's mother complained about the injustice that her son Richard had done her.

"That is the very point, Doctor Watson. Why should Richard impugn his own mother? And who says that he did? No contemporary writer says so. It is later writers, hostile to Richard, who say so; starting with More and Henry's man Polydore Virgil.

"Remember Edward the Fourth's charges in Parliament against his brother George? Including the accusation that George had declared that Edward was illegitimate? It was George, not Richard, who said that Edward was a bastard. It was George, not Richard, who thus slandered their mother as an adulteress."

I broke in. "The picture that you have painted is one in which Richard is entirely loyal to Edward the Fourth. *Loyaulté me lie.* And then loyal to Prince Edward. What, then, made him abandon that faith? What made him cross the line, and take the throne for himself?"

Markham replied confidently.

"Simple: Richard knew that Stillington was right. That Edward's children were indeed bastards, and that they had no right to the throne. George's son was legally and properly barred from the throne as a result of George's treason. Like it or not, Richard was then the lawful heir."

I spoke carefully, for I did not wish to offend the gracious Markham.

163

"What about fear as a motive? Richard had placed the Woodvilles in check, but for how long? Richard's protectorship would not last for ever. Would it not end when the boy came of age?"

"In less than two years, perhaps," said Markham. "There was no legally established age of majority for a king, as far as I know, but fourteen or fifteen years had been accepted in some other cases. James Gairdner, for one, holds that young Edward's minority would have ended at fourteen.

I nodded slowly. "If so, Richard had comparatively little time, only eighteen months or so, before Edward the Fifth would be king in full, with all the powers of a king, and a king trained from infancy by the Woodvilles.

"In addition, the boy must surely have not understood why Richard executed Rivers and the others. Probably the boy even hated Richard, as a young child might. Richard might hope in time to regain the boy's favour. But could he do so, in only eighteen months, with the Woodville faction having the boy's ear? Richard would have good cause to fear for his own life if the boy took the throne, and then the Woodvilles once more came to control him."

Markham nodded, in turn. "Yes, Richard would be but a duke again, and a marked man, at that. I grant you that Richard's critics have suggested such as motives. I say, though, that Richard *was* the legal heir, and that the spectre of another troubled minority rule must also have been in his mind."

I massaged my aching right wrist, and spoke even more carefully. "Excuse me, Markham, but let me be blunt. Could there not be other reasons? Richard's own ambition? Greed? A thirst for power?"

Markham looked at me with a frown.

"There is no doubt at all that Richard was proceeding with plans for the coronation of little Edward. Numerous state documents attest unmistakably to that. Richard also re-appointed to office many of Edward the Fourth's men. Not, I suggest, the actions of a man with his eyes upon the throne. All was being done and carried on normally. Coronation

164

robes were ordered, for example, and those fifty esquires and gentlemen were invited to come and take up knighthoods. Invitations to the coronation ceremony itself were sent out. Food was ordered for banquets. Pageants were planned. I think it is clear from the record that Richard did not change his plan until the last minute, and even then did so at the behest of Parliament.

"One can argue that Parliament had no jurisdiction to decree that Edward's marriage was invalidated by the pre-contract; that would properly have been a matter for an ecclesiastical court. Very well. But Parliament certainly had by precedent the authority to make and unmake kings."

"You insist that the idea of taking the throne for himself had not occurred to Richard until late in the proceedings?"

"Exactly so," returned Markham. "The problem is that if you choose to believe that Richard had his eyes on the throne from the very start, as some hostile writers claim, then every action that he took can be twisted to fit that thesis. For example, Polydore Virgil proposes that, as soon as Richard heard of Edward the Fourth's death, 'he began to be kindled with an ardent desire for sovereignty'. Virgil further claims that Richard told Buckingham of this goal at the end of April 1483. In that light, you would insist that Richard sent to York for troops in June so that he could take the throne by force.

"If you believe that Richard did *not* want the throne for himself, then his actions can be taken in quite another way. To wit, he sent for Northern troops only because he knew that he was going to have to declare Prince Edward a bastard; and that there might then be disturbances, or attacks by the Woodvilles, that would call for troops to put down. The Northern soldiers would reinforce those he already controlled, as protector, in London. And, also, because the Woodvilles were hard at work plotting against him."

I interrupted once more. "Thomas More suggests that there was a belief that Richard had long planned to take the throne in the event that Edward died while his heir was a child."

Markham smiled patiently. "Ah, yes, but the plot implied by More requires a very long stretch of imagination. If you accept More's tale, Richard had to plot, as his first step towards the throne, to put both brother George *and* George's son out of the race. But you cannot sensibly argue that Richard somehow led George into all those treasonous plots with Warwick, or that Richard thus sent George to his death. George was an incorrigible schemer and traitor on his own account. He put himself and his boy out of the running.

"Further, how could Richard, or anybody else, have anticipated that Edward the Fourth, strong and virile Edward, would die so young? No, More's story simply will not do."

The explorer cast one more anguished glance at the clock, and with profuse apologies rose to leave. "I am afraid that we shall not get beyond Richard's accession to the throne today. We shall not get to the deaths of your Two Little Princes. You must return; please tell me that you will."

Suddenly, Markham's ever-present smile turned to a scowl, and he crisply began to answer the question that I had first put to him, by way of General Milman.

"Everything hangs on this so-called *History of King Richard III* by Thomas More. A history it is not; it is full of rumours, hearsay, deceit and exaggeration.

"To begin with, the author clearly implies that he was present at the death of Edward the Fourth. More was not, and could not have been; he was only a little child, only five years old.

"In the same vein, many of the details of which the author writes could not possibly have been known to More at first hand. More was but a little boy, a youngster who was to find a home in John Morton's household.

"We are told that More was a man of truth and principle. Think upon this: He gave his life, as a martyr, for truth and principle under Henry the Eighth. This volume is not one of truth and principle. It is thoroughly dishonest.

"And More's account of Richard's accession to the throne ends abruptly. When does it end abruptly? When Morton fled from England; that is when. Furthermore, the Latin of the volume is simply not up to the standard of More's other writings.

"So there is no doubt in my mind, Doctor Watson: This *History* was not written by More. I believe that the copy known to be in More's handwriting was just that, a copy made by More. A copy of a pre-existing document written by somebody else, somebody who *was* present at Edward's deathbed, and who *did* know some details at first hand.

"That somebody must have been, can only have been, Richard's arch-enemy, John Morton himself."

Chapter Ten

Back in Baker Street, I shook my head, if with a smile, at the latest mess. The box-room door was wide open. So was a door of one of the imposing wardrobes that stored Mr. Holmes's costumes and disguises. A welter of worn clothes, old hats and dirty boots and shoes littered the floor. My friend had obviously donned suitable apparel for a dedicated searcher of *detritus* in Richmond.

I ate dinner alone and, in lieu of pudding, tucked into James Gairdner's book, *History of the Life and Reign of Richard the Third*. Markham had, I believed, tried manfully to present a neutral account, but his respect, and even tenderness, for Richard was occasionally visible. He had, too, given but a sparse account of Richard's ascension to the throne. I was determined to keep an open mind, and to let Gairdner's book speak in its own right.

My resolve was soon sorely tested. Gairdner spoke of his "minute study of the facts of Richard's life", but admitted the scantiness of the known facts, and of the evidence against Richard. Gairdner then proceeded to place heavy reliance upon "tradition", and roundly defended it.

He began by saying that he had once doubted that Richard was a murderous tyrant. I wrote the following excerpt from his book into my notes:–

"I more than doubted that principal crime of which he is so generally reputed guilty; and as for everything else laid to his charge, it was easy to show that the evidence was still more unsatisfactory. The slenderness and insufficiency of the original testimony could hardly be denied; and if it were only admitted that the prejudices of Lancastrian writers might have perverted facts, which the policy of the Tudors would not have allowed other writers to state fairly, a very plausible case might have been established for a more favourable reading of Richard's character."

But Gairdner later changed his mind, and leaned heavily upon tradition. I wrote down another sentence from his book:–

"The scantiness of contemporary evidences and the prejudices of original authorities may be admitted as reasons for doubting isolated facts, but can hardly be expected to weaken the conviction – derived from Shakespeare and tradition as much as from anything else – that Richard was indeed cruel and unnatural beyond the ordinary measure even of those violent times."

And again:–

"The old traditional view of Richard III has certainly not been set aside in a manner to satisfy the common sense of the world ... On the contrary, I must record my impression that a minute study of the facts of Richard's life has tended more and more to convince me of the general fidelity of the portrait with which we have been made familiar by Shakespeare and Sir Thomas More."

"Hearsay masquerades as history," thought I.

At this, I reminded myself forcefully of my resolution of objectivity, and read doggedly on. For a moment, I wondered idly why Gairdner persisted in spelling the name of King Louis of France as "Lewis". Perhaps that was his editor's fancy, however. I could tell you a thing or two about editors myself.

As I read on, my eyebrows (and my choler) rose on numerous occasions as I wrestled with Gairdner's contradictions and contortions, and his determined reliance upon Thomas More and Shakespeare.

Gairdner conceded that on occasion More drew from "prejudiced sources", and that More used a "writer's imagination". He admitted that More erred in dates, that his writing was "highly coloured", and that it was "perhaps not without a little exaggeration". Gairdner further wrote that on at least one occasion More "does all he can to extenuate the conduct of the Woodvilles"; that More introduced "for effect" a rumour that Richard helped his brother George to his death; and that More deliberately misidentified the woman of Edward the Fourth's pre-contract.

Despite all this, Gairdner held to More as a credible source, "true in the main".

As for Shakespeare, Gairdner conceded that his historical accuracy was open to question "especially in *minor* facts and details" (those being my italics); yet Gairdner declared that Shakespeare's judgments were, all in all, "certainly impossible to ignore".

I literally snorted as I read Gairdner's evaluation of the reliability of Richard's sworn enemy, Bishop Morton, as a fount of information. Gairdner cited More's account of the council meeting at which Hastings, Morton and others were seized, and added:–

"And, strange as the story is, we have every reason to believe that the facts are strictly true; for there can be no doubt that Sir Thomas More derived his knowledge of what took place from one who had been an eye-witness of the whole scene, and who, though he can scarcely be called an impartial spectator, was undoubtedly a statesman of high integrity. Still, it is only right to remember that in connection with this story we have the report of one side only – the account, that is to say, of

Cardinal Morton, at this time Bishop of Ely. The colouring, therefore, is that of a partisan, though the facts, no doubt, are those of a truthful reporter."

As an historian, Gairdner wanted both to eat his cake and have it, I thought.

Assistant Keeper of the Records, Gairdner was an erudite, energetic and prolific historian. He was much respected for his work as editor of the papers and letters of Henry the Eighth, and of the fascinating *Paston Letters* and other documentary collections. In the case of Richard the Third, however, the antiquarian's prejudices were clearly visible. For example, when brother George called Edward the Fourth a bastard, slandering their own mother, Gairdner called this "probably no more than a hasty explosion uttered in a moment of anger." Yet when Richard supposedly echoed the charge, Gairdner called it instead "a disgraceful political figment, devised by a son in utter disregard of his mother's reputation."

Further, Richard *must* have publicly slandered his mother, according to Gairdner, because Henry the Seventh's historian, Polydore Virgil, said that Richard had. On that most shaky pro-Tudor foundation, Gairdner felt free to draw an uncompromising conclusion against Richard. "The evidences of the fact leave scarcely any doubt that he really authorised the scandal."

"Do not be too quick to dismiss Virgil," Mr. Gairdner told me later. "While he was indeed employed by Henry the Seventh, he did not publish his work until 1534, long after the expiration of any obligation to Henry. If Markham dismisses him as a tame creature of Henry, that is too harsh. Virgil was an accomplished historian in his own right. Furthermore, he tells us himself that he spoke to everyone he could who had been a public figure."

Markham had an answer to that. "First, Virgil did not arrive in England until 1501 or 1502. He was spoon-fed his history by the Tudors. Second, as even Gairdner admits, Virgil was paid by Henry. Third, Virgil was accused by more than one contemporary of having burned invaluable historical documents by the waggon-load, so that his errors and mistruths would not be detected. Errors and mis-truths that came to him from Tudor partisans. Fourth, when he did publish his work, Henry the Eighth, the Tudor's son, was on the throne. The book was dedicated to Henry the Eighth. Naturally, Virgil upheld the Tudor side; you could not expect him to do otherwise."

The part of Gairdner's book that bothered me the most, perhaps, came as Gairdner wrote of the death of Edward, Prince of Wales, the son of Henry the Sixth and Margaret of Anjou, after the Battle of Tewkesbury:–

"It is a tradition of later times that Gloucester tarnished the glory he had won that day by butchering in cold blood after the battle Edward, Prince of Wales, the son of Henry VI ... The story may be doubted, as resting on very slender testimony, and that not strictly contemporary; nevertheless, it cannot safely be pronounced apocryphal."

Gairdner went on to say that it was not unlikely that Edward had been slaughtered, and that Richard had a motive for killing him – to dispose of another Lancastrian threat to Edward the Fourth. I myself could accept that Richard had, as Mr. Holmes oft chanted, "the motive, the opportunity and the means." But while one writer named Richard as present at the murder, not one authority (even Gairdner conceded this) actually identified Richard as the actual murderer. Indeed, one later account held that Richard refused to draw his sword, out of respect for Anne Neville.

For a man who was not prepared to declare the story apocryphal, Gairdner admitted that the theory that Richard alone had struck the fatal blow was "contrary to the statements of the best authorities."

But could Gairdner leave it at that? No; he could not:–

"But if the murder of Prince Edward was in any degree attributable to ... Richard, it was doubtless the first of a

173

long catalogue of crimes, each of which rests by itself on slender testimony enough, though any one of them, being admitted, lends greater credit to the others. From this point of view, I must frankly own that it strikes me as not at all improbable that Richard was a murderer at nineteen."

Carried to its conclusion, it seemed to me that Gairdner was making an extraordinary argument: that if Richard did murder Prince Edward, then he probably murdered the Two Little Princes as well. If you now accept that he did murder the princes, then obviously he murdered Prince Edward, too. You can use each unproven case as persuasive "evidence" in the other cases. Believe in one murder; believe in them all.

Further, to cut to the heart of my distress, Gairdner agreed that there was insufficient evidence to prove Richard guilty of his various crimes. But "tradition" said he was guilty. Therefore, we were to take it that Richard was indeed guilty; there apparently being insufficient tradition to prove him innocent.

What outrageous and un-English arguments they were!

A short walk, followed by a pot of strong Assam tea, put me back into a more even frame of mind. In the morning, Holmes still being absent, I picked up Gairdner's book again, and lectured myself severely once more on the need to remain objective. I resumed my reading, and came to have a little more respect for Gairdner. He did, in fact, make some effort, if sometimes rather grudgingly qualified, to acknowledge positive factors about Richard and his reign.

Indeed, well into his book, Gairdner wrote:–

"As king, he seems really to have studied his country's welfare, passed good laws, endeavoured to put an end to extortion, declined the free gifts offered to him by several towns, and declared that he would rather have the hearts of his subjects than their money. His munificence was especially shown in religious foundations."

174

But Gairdner then spent much of the remainder of the book ardently portraying Richard as a cruel, murderous and hypocritical tyrant, and suggesting that Richard's religious donations were really an attempt to "buy back the favour of God".

I duly obtained my appointment with the redoubtable Gairdner, taking with me, to his spotless but sombre house, my letter of introduction from General Milman. Seating me in a hard chair in his austere parlour, and transfixing me with a cool and narrowed eye, Gairdner subjected me to a rigorous *viva voce* examination on my knowledge of the history of Richard, of Gairdner's own book, and of Markham's account. Soon, Gairdner's stiff tone and mannerisms eased a little, and he motioned me to a more comfortable armchair.

The antiquarian coughed nervously. "Doctor Watson, I must apologise for my rather stern treatment of you. I admit that I had feared that your mission, as you call it, was frivolous, despite the assurances in General Milman's letter. I apologise sincerely for doubting you. You have clearly invested effort in your research and reading, and I laud you for it. When you informed me that you had seen Clements Markham, I am afraid that my worst fears were fanned. Markham seems determined to portray Richard as the finest king that England has ever known. He is an apologist for Richard to the point of zealotry.

"For all that," – Gairdner continued, after a begrudging pause – "I must admit that Markham does seem to have given to you a reasonably factual grounding. I shall challenge a number of his interpretations, however."

Gairdner rang for a servant, and ordered tea and ginger biscuits.

"You say that you are striving to keep an open mind, but I do detect doubt in you as to Richard's guilt." The historian spoke in rather patronizing manner, as if addressing a Third Form schoolboy. "I, too, once entertained doubts about Richard's guilt. Four things swayed me against him, however.

"First, I am not prepared to dismiss contemporary, or near-contemporary, tradition out of hand. It is to me a form of evidence."

I interrupted, rashly. "Where there is smoke, there is fire?"

"Your tone smacks of the sarcastic," shot back Gairdner. "I am afraid that we shall get nowhere if you close your mind so soon. Tradition can not simply be ignored; nor should it be. Discarding tradition in the exploration of history is like trying to learn a new language without a teacher. Tradition is a most valuable interpreter."

Into my mind popped a scene from Mr. Dickens's *The Posthumous Papers of the Pickwick Club*. At the clamourous Eatanswill election, you may remember, Mr. Pickwick advised his nervous colleagues to "do what the mob do". "But suppose there are two mobs?" asked Mr. Snodgrass. "Shout with the largest," replied Mr. Pickwick.

That certainly seemed to fit Mr. Gairdner and his reliance upon tradition.

Markham later snapped:– "Gairdner's tradition is simply Tudor tradition. How can you learn a new language with a teacher who deliberately distorts it?" To which Gairdner shot back:– "Markham has created his own tradition, and that very largely from stubborn refusal to accept well recorded facts."

I apologised diplomatically for my sarcasm. Gairdner accepted my professed regrets blandly, sipping his weak tea delicately, and nibbling on a biscuit. He continued to speak in measured and professorial tones, as if there had been no unpleasant interruption.

"Second, in the murder of the two young princes, reports of the boys' deaths by assassination circulated widely, very soon after Richard took the throne; and, of course, the boys *were* never seen again. Richard never showed them to be alive, even when it was in his interest to do so. None of the surviving documents of the era shows the boys to have been alive, or to have been seen alive, after they went into the Tower.

"Third, Richard clearly had a reason, a motive, to dispose of the boys. He had caused them to be declared illegitimate.

He had usurped their throne. There was but one card remaining to play: to dispose of them to secure his crown.

"Fourth, I can find, to put it simply, no persuasive case against anybody else. While that of itself is not a *prima facie* case against Richard, I admit, it is yet another weight in the scales."

I thought to give the scholarly Gairdner a brief reminder of the British Rules of Evidence. "My friend Mr. Sherlock Holmes –" I began, but my voice trailed off as the blank look on Gairdner's grey face told me that he had never heard of my colleague the consulting detective.

I was about to raise, instead, the question of whether the Two Little Princes might in fact have survived into the reign of Henry the Seventh, who certainly had a motive for disposing of them. Thomas More had reported that such a belief existed, and Yeoman Warder Baker had spoken of it. Gairdner mentioned the theory in his book, but dismissed it. I decided that I would be wasting my time. The High Court of James Gairdner had clearly convicted Richard, and no amateur dabbler in history could launch a successful appeal.

I took a more diplomatic and fruitful tack. "Markham's account to me of Richard's ascension to the throne after Edward the Fourth's death was cut somewhat short. We simply ran out of time. I fear that he may have glossed over pertinent details."

Gairdner smiled warmly, for the first time, and settled back into his drab brown chair, his fingertips pressed gently together in a judicial and patient manner. "Then I shall be most happy to set the record straight for you.

"I think it self-evident, to begin with, that the Queen Dowager, Elizabeth Woodville, and her family, sought to keep the young Edward the Fifth under their thumb from the moment of his father's death, and were clearly prepared to do so by force. The use of arms they abandoned, after objections from the council, and threats of retaliation from Lord Hastings. As the *Croyland Chronicle* observes:–

"'(Hastings) feared that if supreme power fell into the hands of the queen's relatives, they would then sharply avenge the alleged injuries done to them by that lord. Much ill-will, indeed, had long existed between Lord Hastings and them.'

"Still, the young king remained firmly under their control; no doubt of it. And I will grant you that the only way to deprive them of that control would be by the threat or use of force. Such was the age.

"Further, the planned coronation would not merely have anointed Edward the Fifth as king; it would have given him the right to choose his own circle of advisers. He undoubtedly would have selected the Woodvilles. He had grown up with them, and was no doubt steeped in Woodville values and prejudices. Rivers had been his guardian and mentor from infancy. Richard was but a stranger to the boy and, no doubt, constantly portrayed to him by the Woodvilles as a dark and menacing stranger. All in all, in the days after Edward the Fourth's death, Richard was protector in theory only, and it is clear that the Woodvilles intended to keep it that way."

I placed my empty tea cup carefully on a small brass table, and opened my newest note book. Gairdner sounded almost sympathetic towards Richard, so I essayed a question. "When the Woodvilles began to escort the young prince to London, in some force, that was an open challenge to Richard?"

"Certainly," replied Gairdner. "I am happy to concede that. Indeed, I shall go farther. After Richard arrested Earl Rivers, Richard Grey, and the others, and took Edward the Fifth under his own wing, Lord Hastings assured the council that the arrests were made because of a conspiracy against Richard and the Duke of Buckingham. He said that the Woodville party were to remain under arrest, pending an investigation of this conspiracy. Hastings insisted that there were no designs upon the new king or crown. Sir Thomas More – no friend of Richard, as you know – reported that there was a general belief that Rivers and Grey had indeed entertained treasonable designs. More was of the opinion that the public were on Richard's side, at least at this time.

"Richard's postponement of the coronation to June 22nd was both inevitable and reasonable. So, too, was his decision to lodge Edward the Fifth in the Tower. It was an accepted and oft-used royal residence. Although it had certainly long been used also as a prison, it was really only in the 1500s that the Tower acquired its sinister reputation as a place of detention and torture.

"At this point, all seemed calm, at least on the surface. On June 5th, for example, eligible esquires were invited to receive their knighthoods, to mark the coming coronation. The plans for the new coronation in June were proceeding properly. All seemed well with England.

"However, on June 10th, Richard wrote to York to ask for troops. What, then, happened between June 5th and June 10th? We may never know the answer, but Polydore Virgil – again, no friend to Richard – does state that a sudden act of violence was contemplated to wrest Edward the Fifth from Richard's control."

I looked up from my notes. "Violence? The Woodvilles were about to attack, to seize the prince?"

"One could so assume."

I was struck by a new question. "Mr. Gairdner, why do you suppose Richard wrote to York for troops? As Protector, could he not call on troops in London itself?"

Gairdner scratched the grizzled hair behind his right ear. "It would seem that he could not count on London. London was not behind him. He needed the men from his North."

I frowned. The Yorkshire troops, four thousand or so of them, did not arrive until shortly before Richard's coronation on July 6th. (And a down-at-heel, ill-equipped lot they were; they played no real part in the developments.) Yet Richard had armed men at his side at the Tower on June 13th. A contemporary letter noted that Westminster was full of warriors shortly thereafter, at the time that the young Prince Richard left sanctuary. It has been suggested that this was because of a plot to liberate one or more of Edward the

Fourth's daughters, to be smuggled abroad. The *Croyland Chronicle*, for one, reported that there was such a plan.

Regardless, Richard clearly did have some armed support in London, then.

"Or perhaps," I suggested, "Richard sent all the way to York for men because he sought to conceal from the Woodvilles for some further time that he was aware of their plotting?"

Gairdner tipped back his head, eyes closed, lips pursed, waiting silently for his unruly Third Form pupil to come to order. With an exaggerated sigh of patience, he continued.

"To this point, Richard had the Woodvilles in disarray. And it is at this point that Lord Hastings turned against Richard.

"Hastings had previously stood firm against the Woodvilles, threatening to withdraw to Calais if they attempted forcibly to control of young king and his kingdom. From Calais, where he was governor, he could wage war against them if necessary; and they knew it. His opposition was, in large part, why Rivers was limited to a force of two thousand men to accompany young Prince Edward to London.

"Now, however, Hastings obviously thought it necessary to curb Richard's power as protector. The reason, I speculate, must have been that Hastings became aware that Richard had his own designs on the throne. Hastings was a true loyalist, loyal to Edward the Fourth and then to the young Edward the Fifth. It is also possible that Hastings felt that Buckingham was supplanting him in importance and influence; Richard had certainly treated Buckingham with unprecedented generosity, and had given little to Hastings.

"Whatever the motive, Hastings went over to the Woodville camp. Then there were, in effect, two councils then meeting in parallel; one comprising Richard and his supporters, and the other Hastings and the Woodvilles."

I broke in. "And so we come to that royal council meeting at which Hastings was arrested?"

"Just so, Doctor Watson," replied Gairdner. "The crisis came on Friday, June 13th, 1483. Richard arrested Hastings, Lord Stanley, Bishop Morton, and the Archbishop of York. Richard told London that Hastings and the others had planned to assassinate him and Buckingham in the council chamber itself. He caused a public proclamation to that effect to be published. However, he did so with such remarkable speed that shrewd observers noted that the document must have been conveniently prepared beforehand. Indeed, some suggested that it must have been written by prophecy."

Gairdner laughed, with a brief, dry chuckle that turned into a coughing fit as he unwittingly inhaled crumbs from his biscuit.

I knew that this report of a previously prepared document came from Thomas More. Markham had a different proposition, namely that Hastings's betrayal of Richard became known to Richard a little earlier than suggested by Gairdner. That Richard wrote to York for assistance on June 10th because he had by then uncovered that piece of the Woodvilles' plot, too. This advance knowledge of Hastings's betrayal explained why Richard had prepared his written indictment before the council meeting of June 13th.

Gairdner, gasping for breath, his eyes watering, slowly recovered, and I raised a question.

"Markham suggests that Buckingham might have persuaded Richard to get rid of Hastings, as the two were jockeying for power under Richard."

"Rivals for power and influence they certainly were," said Gairdner, "but there is no evidence to support Markham's contention; nor to refute it, I suppose. Richard must bear the responsibility, of course; in the end, the decision to execute Hastings was his.

"With it, the council was swept clear of the Woodville faction. The Queen Dowager's friends were either dead or in prison. She was persuaded, presumably under duress, to give up her son Richard from sanctuary, and he was taken to the Tower to join his brother Edward the Fifth. Richard was in full command of the reins of power. He postponed the coronation once more, giving November 2nd, 1483, as the new date. There may have been good reason to postpone it, I concede. The arrests, and the execution of Hastings, would hardly create an atmosphere conducive to coronation and celebration."

I held up an inquiring hand again. "So Richard *was* still planning to have Edward the Fifth crowned, would you say?"

Gairdner looked at me wearily. "I think not. Hastings's arrest and execution took place on June 13th. Young Richard was taken from sanctuary on the 16th. The last known document signed by the new king Edward was dated the 17th. On the 21st, there is reference, in a surviving letter, to some sort of crisis in the city. On the 22nd, Doctor Shaw delivered his public sermon that argued Richard's right to the throne. On the 25th, Rivers, Grey, Vaughn and Haute (Gairdner spelled the name Hawte in his book) were executed. The sequence of events can only mean that by June 21st, or earlier, Richard of Gloucester had resolved upon the deposition of young Edward the Fifth. Polydore Virgil wrote that Richard told the Duke of Buckingham as early as April 30th of his intention to seize the throne.

"As Doctor Shaw spoke, Richard planned to appear upon the scene to bask in the applause of the crowd. According to Thomas More's account, the timing of the actors was off; Richard's staged entry was too late:–

"'The people were so far from crying, "King Richard!" that they stood as they had been turned into stones, for wonder of this shameful sermon.'"

"More's words," said I, careful, however, to keep any overt cynicism from my tone.

Gairdner frowned at me, apparently unsure as to whether I was challenging him or not. "If you please, Doctor Watson. Richard's ally, the Duke of Buckingham, on June 24th, reiterated Richard's claim to the throne at the Guildhall, to the mayor and to leading citizens. Once more, the reception was cold. The mayor had the city's recorder repeat the substance of Buckingham's speech. He then asked if the city would accept Richard as their king. It was only the servants of Buckingham and Richard, at the back of the hall, who cried out for Richard, and obediently threw their caps into the air."

I knew, again, that Gairdner was relying solely on Thomas More for this tale.

"On June 25th," the antiquarian continued, "the Lords and Commons condemned Edward the Fourth's marriage to Elizabeth Woodville as illegal, and prepared a petition to Richard, asking him to accept the crown. He initially feigned reluctance, but on the following day he took the royal oath."

I massaged the cramped fingers of my right hand, and posed another question. I had learned by now that the more diffident I was, and the more I addressed Gairdner as "sir", the smoother was my path. Somewhat to my shame, I played the required game.

"You say in your book, sir, that it was an usurpation."

"Indeed," returned Gairdner, primly. "It was so considered at the time, even by writers favourable to Richard. The *Croyland Chronicle* suggested that the petition had been 'got up in the North'. Yet I also describe it as an election, do I not? The council approved it. The Lords and the Clergy and Commons concurred in it. London concurred in it. The country tacitly concurred in it. The accession took place peacefully, and at the request of Parliament. Virtually all of the nobility attended Richard's coronation, including ones of the Woodville camp.

"The Earl of Surrey fought for Richard at Bosworth, the battle in which Henry Tudor defeated Richard, and took the crown as Henry the Seventh. Henry demanded an explanation of why Surrey had supported Richard. Surrey replied that the reason was simply that Richard was the king, legally crowned, and, in Surrey's words, crowned to 'universal applause'. Henry sent Surrey to the Tower, but Surrey was right: Richard *was* legally crowned.

"Yet Richard did not last long. The nobility may have attended his coronation *en masse*, but only a handful fought for him at Bosworth. However, as also I say in my book, Richard was no monster. He had taken up the sword, and 'all they that take the sword shall perish with the sword'. He was simply, I believe, the product of his upbringing and his times, the product of monstrous and horrible, bloody times. "

I was tempted to ask if he would say the same of Henry the Seventh, but once more thought the better of it.

As my interruptions continued to be neutral and diplomatic, Gairdner settled comfortably into his account.

"The Lancastrians no doubt felt and declared that the pre-contract was a lie concocted by Richard. Parliament, however, were summoned by Richard and passed a bill, *Titulus Regius*, that condemned the marriage of Edward the Fourth and Elizabeth Woodville, on the grounds that he already 'stood married and troth-plight' to Eleanor Butler.

"*Titulus Regius* began by excoriating the rule of Edward the Fourth as 'led by sensuality and concupiscence', and it said that England was 'ruled by self-will and pleasure'. The act also claimed that all this led to murder, extortion, oppression, and more. It did not give any evidence of this, and I note that there is no record of Richard objecting to this propaganda.

"He obviously would not have objected to the way in which the act went on to brand Edward's marriage to Elizabeth Woodville as 'pretensed', because of Edward's troth-plight to Eleanor Butler.

"According to the act, Edward and the Woodville woman, then, 'lived together sinfully and damnably in adultery'. The act explicitly declared that their children were 'bastards and unable to inherit or to claim anything by inheritance, by the law and custom of England.'

"Parliament thus confirmed that the crown belonged to Richard."

"You support the theory of the pre-contract?" I asked.

"I do, although I admit the case rests solely on the testimony of Bishop Stillington," returned Gairdner, cautiously. "Some historians do challenge it, indeed. While supporting evidence is lacking, I must mention Sir George Buck, an antiquary, and supporter of Richard's cause, who wrote in 1646. Buck in his manuscript insists that the Lady Eleanor had a child by Edward. Buck gives no authority for this, and we know nothing of what happened to this child, if there indeed was one. The point I wish to make is this: Buck contends that Stillington told the secret of the pre-contract to Richard and that, as a result, Edward put Stillington into the Tower."

I ventured another careful interruption. "Markham suggests that Stillington told the secret to George, and that George threatened Edward with exposure."

"It is by no means improbable," returned Gairdner. "The date of Stillington's imprisonment does coincide almost exactly with that of George's sentence. Certainly, if George was threatening to expose the secret, whether he had learned it from Stillington or from Richard, and was about to use it to claim the throne for himself, that would explain why Edward had his own brother put to death. Indeed, why *else* would Edward have executed George? He had spared him for any number of treasonous offences in the past."

"You say in your book, Mr. Gairdner, that there is another reason to believe in the pre-contract."

Gairdner smiled, nodding regally as if accepting tribute from an underling.

"Indeed. When Henry the Seventh married Elizabeth of York, the daughter of Edward the Fourth and Elizabeth Woodville, he ordered that all copies of *Titulus Regius* be rooted out and destroyed, as scandalous. He would not have his new wife be a bastard in law. So Henry tried to suppress and destroy the story of the illegitimacy of Edward's marriage and of his children. This may explain, also, why Thomas More, in his account, named not Eleanor Butler but a known courtesan, Elizabeth Lucy, as Edward the Fourth's pre-contracted partner. In the end, however, a copy of the bill did survive, and the true story came out."

Gairdner looked up, with a rare chuckle.

"A rather clumsy substitution that, putting the name of Elizabeth Lucy in place of that of Eleanor Butler. Lucy had two illegitimate children by Edward, a son and a daughter. If *she* was legally pre-contracted to Edward, and that was therefore his legitimate marriage, then *those* two children were the heirs to the throne, were they not? I do not think that More had that in mind! As it happens, Lucy denied any pre-contract or marriage in her case. I believe that she was already married to someone else, anyway. Some do say that she had but one child by Edward, but no matter."

Gairdner laughed again, more heartily. I seized the opportunity to walk onto thin ice, and to ask about Markham's theory that Morton, not More, was the author of More's account. Mr. Gairdner dismissed the idea as frivolous. "Would Morton really have described himself as crafty and the next best thing to a sycophant, as does the manuscript?"

Gairdner told me heatedly that not a single reputable historian did or would accept Markham's proposition. Gairdner thus dismissed not only Markham but also Buck, and Sir John Harrington, who in 1596 reported a belief that Morton was the author.

The historian returned to Henry's attempted destruction of *Titulus Regius* to raise an important question: "Henry in effect legitimated Elizabeth of York. That would, at the same time, reverse the bastardy of the Two Little Princes, and revive young Prince Edward's claim to the throne. Is it not clear then, that Henry knew that the boys were already dead?"

Absorbed once more in his tale, the elderly records-keeper spoke now at a rapid clip, and my stubby fingers ached as my pencil raced to keep up with him.

"In preparation for his own coronation, Richard moved into the Tower on July 4th. He released Lord Stanley, who had been arrested along with Hastings, and restored him to grace. In hindsight, that was a disastrous mistake. Stanley was married to the mother of Henry Tudor, you see; he was Henry's step-father. Stanley and his brother, Sir William Stanley, turned against Richard at the Battle of Bosworth, and that decided the battle. Richard also freed the Archbishop of York. He did not liberate Morton, but placed him in the custody of Richard's right-hand man, the Duke of Buckingham. That was another disastrous mis-step.

"Richard's coronation went ahead on July 6th. Lord Stanley carried the mace. Buckingham bore the king's train. Henry Tudor's mother was among Queen Anne's attendants.

"Soon, of course, Buckingham, the new king-maker, rebelled against Richard and took to arms against him.

"Exactly why, we do not know. One school of thought is that he felt Richard had not sufficiently recompensed him for his support. Richard had given Buckingham vast estates and power, but Buckingham had long claimed the lands of his ancestor, Humphrey de Bohun, Earl of Hereford, and had been refused by Edward the Fourth. Naturally, he put the claim to Richard. Richard indeed made over to him the requested riches, by royal letters patent, and permitted Buckingham to draw upon them; but the promise had not yet been formally approved by Parliament, and supposedly Buckingham somehow felt betrayed.

"A second school of thought is that Buckingham felt slighted by being asked to bear Richard's train at the coronation; Buckingham felt he should have been named Lord High Constable, and carried the mace. In fact he *was* named Constable a few days later, but too late for his liking. That seems to me to be little enough reason to rebel, but some do contend that it was.

"A third theory is that Buckingham had his own eyes on the throne. He, too, was of royal blood, being descended from Edward the Third's fourth and seventh sons, but in law he was a remote candidate. More tells us, however, that Morton did plant in Buckingham's head thoughts of assuming the kingship; and Polydore Virgil reported that people said that Buckingham 'aspired by all means possible' to the crown. Indeed, Virgil said that Buckingham intended to depose Richard and be 'called by the commons' to the throne himself.

"A fourth theory is that Buckingham had proposed to Richard that Richard's son should marry one of Buckingham's two daughters. Indeed, More says that they had agreed upon this. The theory is that Richard then rebuffed him, and that Buckingham was thus mortally insulted. As Steward of England, Buckingham had been the one formally to

187

pronounce the death sentence on Richard's brother George of Clarence. Buckingham's duty, of course; but perhaps Richard never quite forgave him for it, and rejected his suit as a result.

"A fifth theory is that Buckingham learned of, or suspected, the deaths of the two young princes at the hand of Richard, and realised that he had been deceived by Richard all along. It made him fertile ground for Morton's subornation. Some, however, to the contrary, have it that Buckingham murdered the princes himself, without Richard's knowledge or acquiescence, to further his own claim to the throne.

"And a further theory is simply that Buckingham sensed the popular tide turning against Richard, and wanted to be on the winning side."

I flexed my aching fingers, and broke in once more. "To which school of thought do you lean, sir?"

"The account I find the most persuasive," replied Gairdner, "is that of Sir Thomas More. We know that Morton was put into Buckingham's custody, at his castle at Brecknock. According to More, Morton eloquently seduced and suborned Buckingham, and persuaded him to abandon Richard. This must have been after Buckingham left Richard's royal progress at Gloucester in the first week of August 1483.

"Morton subtly suggested, to begin with, that Buckingham could be king himself. However, as I say, Buckingham had but a very distant claim to the throne. The claim of his cousin Henry Tudor was more likely to succeed. Morton and Henry's mother, Margaret Beaufort, Countess of Richmond, then persuaded Buckingham to join their cause, in which Henry would seize the throne, and marry Edward the Fourth's daughter Elizabeth. What reward Buckingham would receive, I do not know. Morton – and this we do know – went on to become Archbishop of Canterbury and Lord Chancellor under Henry and later, with Henry's help, a cardinal. He certainly received *his* rewards."

Something must have shown upon my face, for Gairdner gave a dismissive wave of his thin, be-veined right hand.

"I see, Doctor Watson, that you have reservations about Sir Thomas More. In this case, however, he surely got his story of the conversion of Buckingham directly from Morton, and we can accept it as accurate; it is neutral toward Richard himself. Further, we can not say that Morton was More's only source. There must have been others, even if we can not identify them by name. I have heard More dismissed as an apologist of the Tudors, but that is unfair. He may have served Henry the Eighth, but he certainly had no great love for Henry the Seventh."

According to John Stow, the London annalist in Elizabethan times, there was a plot to liberate the Two Little Princes, including the setting of a number of fires in London as diversions to facilitate the rescue. Stow is not clear on the timing of this plot, but seems to suggest that it was not long after Richard's coronation; perhaps while he was on the royal "progress' that took him to Magdalen and on to the North. At least some of the conspirators were loyal servants of Edward the Fourth. They were caught and executed.

We call the armed uprising in early October of 1483 'Buckingham's rebellion', but was it? Some argue that this was a rising to free the young Edward the Fifth and to restore him to the throne. Others, however, argue that Henry Tudor had been making his own plot for many, many months, first in Brittany and then in France, and that those who *thought* they were rebelling for Edward the Fifth were, unknown to them, actually campaigning for Tudor. Certainly Buckingham would have found it easier to raise support in the name of Edward the Fifth than in the name of a little known outsider such as Tudor.

However, Gairdner told me that in late September Buckingham had been in correspondence with Henry Tudor on the other side of the channel; that Buckingham had written to Tudor on September 24th, proposing that Tudor invade England. Exactly what he wrote, we do not know. But it is clear that by then there must have been considerable planning, and many exchanges of messages and messengers. The *Croyland Chronicle* suggests that Richard's agents had become aware of the machinations, and gave him some advance intelligence of the uprising. If so, and if Richard thus knew of Buckingham's role in it, he did nothing until after a band of rebels in Kent rose up, on or about October 8th.

James Gairdner was sure that Richard was taken by surprise.

In a letter to his chancellor on October 12th, Richard called Buckingham "the most untrue creature living" and added that "never was falser traitor purveyed". On the 23rd, in Lincoln, Richard issued a proclamation condemning Buckingham as a traitor. Richard put an enormous price on his head, of one thousand pounds, and a retainer soon betrayed the Duke. Strangely, the proclamation, while it named a number of rebels, did not mention Henry Tudor.

Rumours of the deaths of the Two Little Princes circulated in association with the uprisings. But when, I wondered, had such reports arisen? The *Croyland Chronicle* said that the aim of Buckingham's rebellion was to free the Two Little Princes from the Tower. They were alive, therefore, as the plotting blossomed.

The chronology of *Croyland* suggests that the rumours of their deaths did not circulate until October. Gairdner, however, proposed that the principal players in Buckingham's plot must have known of the demise of the princes earlier, else Tudor would then have had no supportable claim to the throne. Gairdner suggested, then, that perhaps it was true that reports of the boys' deaths did not circulate more widely until early October, sparking the uprising in Kent.

Regardless, Gairdner said, the evidence all pointed to the boys having been killed in August 1483.

But were these reports of the princes' deaths true, in that the princes really had been dispatched by then? Or did Buckingham and his confederates merely spread false rumours and lies, to further their rebellion? To secure support, it was necessary for people to believe that the boys were dead, and at Richard's hand. Why else would they rise in support of the little known Henry Tudor?

Markham saw the rumours of the boys' deaths in one way. "To begin pulling Richard down, they attacked him with rumours. Think of the damage they could do to him by fomenting ale-house slanders that the cruel, wicked uncle had murdered in cold blood his sweet, innocent little nephews."

Gairdner, impatiently, gave his weight to the opposing thesis, that the rumours were true.

"Contemporary records show that, within weeks of Richard's coronation, rumours began to circulate that the boys were dead, and dead at Richard's hand. People believed this. The boys were not seen again. Richard did not produce them. Why not? He had every reason so to do, as rebellion broke out on the grounds that they had been slaughtered, but he did not. No records of the time show that they were still alive. All this was not the invention of later writers under the Tudors. Richard *was* mistrusted, and suspected, at the time."

Markham laughed bitterly. "And how does Mr. Gairdner know all this? Virtually all of his information comes from later writers under the Tudors, writing retrospectively. And why are there few contemporary records? Because Henry Tudor's man Polydore Virgil destroyed them by the waggonload; that is why."

I was to find that the Latin of the *Croyland Chronicle* could fairly be translated as suggesting or implying that the rumours of the boys' deaths *were* false, spread to reinforce the rebellion. However, the *Chronicle* went on to say that the conspirators thought of Henry as a potential king only after the rumoured deaths of the Two Little Princes.

Gairdner noted, too, that Polydore Virgil had said that Richard himself "permitted the rumour of their death to go about" so that people would accept that he was the sole heir, and thus "with better mind and good will bear and sustain his government."

Still, I wondered, if there was so much certainty of the boys' deaths having occurred in August or September 1483, why would More and others countenance suggestions that they were still alive in Henry Tudor's time in 1485?

If Richard had wanted to remove them, I mused, why did he not suffocate or poison them, announce with feigned sadness that they had died natural deaths, display their corpses so that witnesses could see no wounds or injuries, hold a state funeral, and simply carry on?

If he did not produce them alive, it could be because he saw no merit in it, or because he could not; they had somehow been taken from the Tower by others, and Richard did not know where they were or what had happened to them. Regardless, his silence must surely have made people wonder, or assume that he was indeed guilty.

Buckingham's poorly co-ordinated Southern revolt went ahead in October 1483, with a rash of small uprisings breaking out over the next several months from Kent and Essex to Exeter.

"Unfortunately for Richard, and for Clements Markham, the rebels were not all Woodvilles or even Lancastrians," said Gairdner. "Among them were many of Edward the Fourth's old courtiers. That must say something about the degree of popular feeling about Richard."

I looked up from my note book. "I am given to understand that there was resentment among the Southern courtiers about Richard favouring Northerners with patronage, at their expense. Could that not have been a spur to rebellion amongst these people? Looking after their own Southern nests?"

Gairdner paused for several beats. He looked older than his four and fifty years. "Perhaps it was a factor for some," said he, finally. "It is true that the Croyland Chronicle complained that he gave confiscated estates to his Northern friends, 'whom he planted in every spot throughout his dominions, to the disgrace and lasting and loudly expressed grief of all people in the South.'"

Henry Tudor was supposed to land from France with a force of mercenaries, but a violent storm broke up his fleet. Regardless, he prepared to land near Poole, but found Richard's troops ready. They tried to trick him into believing that they were Buckingham's men, but he was not taken in, and withdrew to France again, free to continue his plotting.

Buckingham, his own forces hobbled by storms and unprecedented floods, was deserted by his Welsh troops, and fled for his life, but was betrayed by a follower, and captured. Richard had him executed at Salisbury in November. Richard pardoned many of Buckingham's followers, but some of those, in the end, later fought with Henry Tudor against Richard.

I saw no point in asking Gairdner more at this time about the murder of the Two Little Princes. In his book, he had noted that some of More's details were hardly credible, but insisted that More's version "must bear some resemblance to the truth."

I was glad, if a little ashamed, that I did not now ask any more questions; for my judicious silences, coupled with my profound thanks and expressions of respect for his eminence as an historian, led to further and most useful meetings with Gairdner.

At this point, I shall break off these accounts of Richard's life, and return to them later. At this juncture, my brain has travelled back to the grim Tower of London. My Newgate Calendar of Richard's alleged murders is on my desk, and I shall now address it. I must first explain to the reader that I made, in all, three visits to Gairdner, and three to Markham, although in this volume I have, rather like William Shakespeare, made them seem fewer. I have drawn upon them, and upon other authorities, and upon further discussion with Yeoman Warder Henry Baker, to give the following accounts of the numerous murders of which Richard is accused.

Chapter Eleven

I began the detailed examination of my calendar of Richard's reputed crimes with Yeoman Warder Baker. The valiant old soldier swallowed the last of his well stewed breakfast tea, and banged his cup down on a painted tea chest that served as one of the tables in his spartan Tower quarters. "Right, sir. Ready?"

A yard-high pile of books from the Tower library stood by his cheap rocking chair, numerous pages carefully marked with protruding scraps of paper. Baker had been hard at work on my behalf, I could see. My own fast multiplying note books were spread before me upon a larger deal table. And so, under a roiling cloud of powerful pipe smoke, Baker and I began to call the roll of murders of which Richard the Third has constantly been accused these 400 years and more.

The first death was that of Edward, Prince of Wales, the seventeen-year-old son and heir of Henry the Sixth and Margaret of Anjou. He was slain during or immediately after the Battle of Tewkesbury in May 1471. The questions are: Was it murder? And was Richard guilty?

"I shall start out, sir, with an account that is written to present the Yorkists in the best light," said Baker. "It is called the *Historie of the Arrivall of Edward IV in England and Finall Recoverage of his Kingdomes from Henry VI*. How do you like that for a title, sir? It is also known for short as *Fleetwood's Chronicle*. It was the official Yorkist history, and it was written very shortly after the battle. Here is what it says:–

"'In the winning of the field, those who suffered handstrokes were slain at once. Edward, called Prince, was taken, fleeing towards the town, and slain, in the field'."

Baker solemnly watched me write down this excerpt in my notehand.

"Now let me move to some further accounts that are not as favourable towards the Yorkists, sir. The *Annals of Tewkesbury Abbey*, for one:–

"'When King Edward arrived with his army, he slew Prince Edward in the field'."

"Again, in the field of battle," I proposed, "rather than murdered as a prisoner after the fray."

"Just so, sir. The *Annals* say so twice. They list Edward as 'Ded in the Feld'." Baker chuckled as he gave me the contemporary spelling.

"So does Philippe de Comines, a foreign historian, Flemish. He wrote his *Memoirs* somewhat later, sir. He says that 'the Prince of Wales was killed on the battlefield, and several other great lords.'

"However, Doctor Watson, there are accounts that suggest Prince Edward was not killed in combat.

"There is the *Warkworth Chronicle*. That is more properly called *A Chronicle of the First Thirteen Years of the Reign of Edward IV*, and it was written by Doctor John Warkworth. He was a Lancastrian who was the Master of St. Peter's College, in Cambridge. He died in 1500, and I am not sure when he wrote his account; perhaps in about 1480. He adds a new twist to the Edward story, sir. He says:–

"'And there was slain in the field Prince Edward, which cried for succour to his brother-in-law the Duke of Clarence'."

I frowned. "No mention of Richard, then. What of the famous *Croyland Chronicle*?"

Baker began with something of a surprise for me. From the translation that I had borrowed from Clements Markham, I had somehow formed an impression of an ordinary cloistered monk reporting the rumours and hearsay of the day. Baker, however, had studied the Tower's translation of the *Chronicle* more carefully.

"There was more than one author of the *Chronicle*, Doctor Watson. The one in whom we are interested was clearly not a plain country monk, but a man well versed in the politics of the day. We are not certain as to who he was, but he seems to have been a senior official of the royal court, and perhaps a councillor of Edward the Fourth, sir.

"I have heard it stated that the *Chronicle* records that Prince Edward was taken prisoner and murdered. However, allow me to read to you exactly what it says, sir:–

"'For some time it was not clear who would prevail. At last, however, King Edward won a signal victory. From among the Queen's forces, the Prince Edward himself, King Henry's only son, the defeated Duke of Somerset, the Earl of Devon, together with other lords well remembered everywhere, met their deaths either in the field or at the vengeful hands of certain people afterwards. Queen Margaret was captured and held prisoner, so that she might ride in a carriage in his triumphal procession in London'."

"That does not say explicitly that young Edward was taken prisoner and murdered afterwards," I pointed out. "Nor does it suggest that Richard was the murderer, or even that he was in any way involved."

"Precisely, sir," responded Baker, nodding. "*Fabyan's Chronicle* says this:–

"'But after the king had questioned with the said Sir Edward, and he had answered him contrary to his pleasure, he then struck him with his gauntlet upon the face; after which stroke so by him received, he was by the king's servants incontinently slain'."

I interrupted, my brow creased and my lips pursed. "If memory serves, Baker, Fabyan was quite explicit in his accusation that Richard the Third murdered Henry the Sixth. Yet here he does not accuse Richard, by name, of murdering Prince Edward? He stops short, even though he could seize the opportunity to accuse Richard?"

Baker nodded, as if proud of a bright young student.

"That is exactly right, sir. Fabyan does indeed relate the story that Richard stabbed Henry. But, even though Fabyan was a good Lancastrian, he does not accuse Richard of killing Prince Edward. Even John Rous says nothing. Bernard André, Henry the Seventh's official poet laureate, and his biographer, says nothing, either.

"But now, sir, we come to Polydore Virgil, Henry's historian. Not a lover of Richard, sir, as you know. He says that Richard was present at Prince Edward's death, and clearly implicates him in the murder. He is the first writer to do that. He says this:–

"'Edward the Prince, an excellent youth, being brought a little afterwards to the speech of King Edward, and demanded how he dare be so bold as to enter and make war in his realm, made answer, with brave mind, that he came to recover his ancient inheritance. To this, King Edward gave no reply, only thrusting the young man from him with his hand; whom forthwith those that were present, who were George Duke of Clarence, Richard Duke of Gloucester and William Lord Hastings, cruelly murdered.'

"Sir George Buck, a later writer, said that, according to a manuscript of the time, Richard was the only one present who did *not* draw his sword."

"But then we come to Raphael Holinshed, Mr. Shakespeare's prime source. A nasty little, oh, what is the word? When you steal somebody else's writing and present it as your own?"

"Plagiarist?"

198

"That is it, sir. Holinshed copied by the yard from More and Edward Hall, and was not above adding his own details, sir. In this case, Holinshed says that Richard struck the first blow."

I looked up from my notes, intently.

"So the only historian who actually names Richard in this murder, if there was a murder, is Polydore Virgil, the paid writer who was commissioned by Henry the Seventh. Warkworth names George as present, but says Edward was slain in the field. Croyland blames 'certain people' but does not name them. Fabyan accuses the king's servants. It is not until we get to the later Tudor account, from Virgil, that we have Richard himself named.

"And it is not until later still that Holinshed takes it upon himself to declare that Richard struck the first fatal blow."

"That is right, sir," returned Baker. "And Sir Thomas More, sir? Why, he never even mentions the death of Prince Edward at all. The one man who you might expect to accuse Richard of this murder, or to report accounts of it, if they named Richard, and yet he does not say a single word against Richard."

When I spoke later to Markham, at a long and pleasant dinner with his family, he confirmed the picture painted by Baker and his books.

"The implication of Richard indeed begins with Polydore Virgil," Markham continued. "Then other later writers, in Tudor times, Richard Grafton, Edward Hall, Thomas Habington and Raphael Holinshed, go on to embellish the story planted by Virgil. As your man Baker notes, Holinshed goes as far as to add that Richard struck the first blow. Hall and Holinshed were drawn upon by Shakespeare, as you already very well know, and so you finish up with Shakespeare's unwarranted and unsupported account of Richard as the murderer of Prince Edward."

I looked searchingly at Markham. "More – or Morton, in your theory of authorship – does not mention the killing of Prince Edward. Why not, do you suppose?"

Markham's voice rose with excitement. He rubbed his palms together rapidly in glee. We all leaned expectantly across the table.

"Morton was actually present at the Battle of Tewkesbury, Doctor Watson. If Prince Edward was murdered there, Morton must have known it. Whether as More's source, or as the actual writer, Morton *must* have known. Yet he says nothing. Not a hint. No word, either, from Bernard André or John Rous, both writers in Henry the Seventh's camp. Not even by innuendo. Clearly, the story of the murder by Richard was not believed by them, or was unknown to them. It does not even begin to appear until Polydore Virgil. Morton's silence, or More's silence, if you prefer, simply explodes the myth. Virgil fabricated the story."

Gairdner, when I questioned him, artfully came down on both sides at once.

First, he agreed that the testimony against Richard was both sparse and not truly contemporary. But then he went on to cite Virgil and Hall and Holinshed as creditable authorities. He suggested that they might be relying on a tradition that was not recorded elsewhere, but insisted that "they are not on that account to be held unworthy of credit." Gairdner thus declared it not at all improbable that Richard himself really had murdered Prince Edward.

To account for the lack of contemporary accusations, Gairdner proposed that the country had approved of the deed.

"The chroniclers would thus understandably overlook it. They would consider it, and treat it, as no crime at all. Why, they would not bother to name Richard, until, later, he committed many more and worse crimes. Then they would naturally bring out this murder."

Shaking my head at this imaginative theory, I made in conclusion my own note on my detailed Newgate Calendar.

"Death of Prince Edward: No contemporary accusation. No accusation against Richard from More (or Morton) or others who were hostile to Richard. No accusation at all until Polydore Virgil and, even later, Raphael Holinshed. More than reasonable doubt, therefore. Verdict on Richard: Not guilty."

I intend to move on to the murder of poor Henry the Sixth in the Tower of London. First, however, let me clear up the question of two more supposed crimes of murder in which Richard has oft been named.

I begin with the public beheading of thirteen or more Lancastrians after the battle of Tewkesbury. The Duke of Somerset and some dozen or so others escaped from the bloody battlefield, and took refuge in the abbey church. Edward the Fourth, it is said, promised them their lives, but then had them hauled out, tried, condemned as traitors, and beheaded in the market place at Tewkesbury on May 6th, 1471. Markham believed that some had violated previous pardons from Edward. Richard, as Constable of England, and the Duke of Norfolk, as Lord High Marshal, were the judges at their trial, which I think is best described as a medieval form of drum-head court martial. Some Lancastrian supporters have since sought to present these deaths as murders. My own conclusion is that these were royal executions brought about by a vindictive Edward the Fourth, and, as such, were not murders by Richard.

I therefore reached the following finding on Richard: "Execution of Lancastrians after Tewkesbury: Richard was acting in his official capacity as one of two judges in a legal process of the day. Verdict on Richard: Not guilty."

I made the same finding in an earlier case, in which Richard sat on Edward the Fourth's commission of *oyer and terminer* that dealt with charges of treason against Henry Courtenay and Thomas Hungerford in 1469. They were convicted and executed in Salisbury. Edward was there at the time.

Next, I address the execution of Thomas Nevill, a kinsman and supporter of the ill-fated Earl of Warwick. Thomas Nevill was the illegitimate son of Lord Fauconberg and is often called "the Bastard Fauconberg" rather than by his own name. A cousin of Warwick (and of King Edward and Richard), this Thomas Nevill was admiral of Warwick's fleet in the Channel.

After the Battle of Tewkesbury, he sailed up the Thames and attacked London, apparently with the goal of freeing the captive Henry the Sixth. He soon surrendered, and Edward the Fourth pardoned him. Warkworth's Lancastrian chronicle, however, gave a report of his ultimate fate, some four months later, in September 1471:–

> "For anon after, by the Duke of Gloucester in Yorkshire, the said Bastard was beheaded, notwithstanding he had a charter of pardon."

The accounts of this case are scant, and confusing. One ancient letter says that Nevill was not only pardoned, but also knighted and reappointed as vice-admiral. Markham insisted that Nevill had been sent to Richard's Yorkshire castle of Middleham, as a prisoner or on parole, and had escaped. He was recaptured, whereupon he was tried for his original treason. The letter suggests that Nevill committed some fresh crime, and was executed for that.

In the event, I could not believe that, without authority, Richard would arbitrarily execute a man whom his brother the king had pardoned. The most rational theory was that Edward had revoked the pardon, for cause, and handed Nevill over to Richard, as Constable, to execute.

I wrote my decision into my current notebook. "Execution of Thomas Nevill: Richard was presumably acting in official capacity and under the legal rules of the day. Verdict on Richard: Not guilty."

Confusing accounts also fogged the death of the deposed King Henry the Sixth. The official Yorkist account, from *the Historie of the Arrivall of Edward IV in England*, I simply had to dismiss with a cynical laugh. This account began by prematurely reporting the final extinction of the Lancastrian cause and Henry's party throughout the land:–

> "The certainty of all which came to the knowledge of the said Henry, lately called king, being in the Tower of London. Not having previously the knowledge of the said matters, he took it to such great hatred, ire and

indignation that, of pure displeasure and melancholy, he died the 23rd day of the month of May."

Now, I have myself had an aged patient die of, I believe, pure melancholy after the death of his beloved wife of almost seventy-five years; he simply had no will to live any longer without her. I could not believe, however, that Henry the Sixth, no matter how simple and infirm a man, shuffled off this mortal coil from pure disappointment and melancholy. Nor, clearly, did the other writers.

The *Croyland Chronicle* was cautious and circumspect:–

"I shall say nothing about the fact that, at this time, King Henry was found lifeless in the Tower of London; may God have mercy upon and grant time for repentance to him, whoever he might be, who thus dared to lay sacrilegious hands on the Lord's Anointed. And so let the doer justly deserve the title of tyrant and the victim that of a glorious martyr."

Was this 'tyrant' Edward the Fourth, or Richard the Third? I took it to mean Edward, who was the ruling king; but, I suppose, the author could have meant Richard.

The Lancastrian Doctor Warkworth seemed to point the first accusatory finger towards Richard:–

"And the same night that King Edward came to London, King Harry, being inward in prison in the Tower of London, was put to death, the 21st of May, on a Tuesday night, betwixt 11 and 12 of the clock, there being then at the Tower the Duke of Gloucester, brother of King Edward, and many other."

Gairdner took Warkworth's report as tantamount to a formal accusation against Richard, despite the fact that the report specified that many others were also there; Earl Rivers, for one. "Surely he named Richard because he was the chief suspect," said Gairdner. (I decided not to interrupt him with the thought that Warkworth simply named Richard because he was the most prominent of those present.)

Gairdner agreed, however, that it was probable that Edward had commissioned the murder, and that it would be unfair to hold Richard solely responsible for it.

I noted the difference in dates, with the *Arrivall* giving the 23rd of May as the date of Henry's murder, and Warkworth the 21st. Later, I was to find other dates in other records.

I asked Baker about other versions. He struck a match, one-handed, using a thumb nail, and drew heavily on his ancient pipe. He spat a shred of rank tobacco onto the floor.

"Oh, several other accounts," began Baker. "John Rous also names Richard, for one:–

"'He killed by others, or, as many believe, with his own hand, that most sacred man King Henry VI'."

"John Rous?" I remarked. "Markham calls him John Rubbish, because of his *volte face* regarding Richard after Henry the Seventh took the throne."

One after the other, Baker picked up and referred to more old volumes.

"Fabyan adds more detail again in his *Chronicle*:–

"'Of the death of the prince – he means King Henry, sir – diverse tales were told, but the most common fame went that he was stikked with a dagger by the handes of Richard of Gloucester'.

"Polydore Virgil echoes this, sir:–

"'The continual report is that Richard Duke of Gloucester killed him with a sword, whereby his brother might be delivered from all fear of hostility'.

"And De Comines mentions the charge, as well:–

"'King Henry was a very ignorant and almost simple man and, unless I have been deceived, immediately after the battle the Duke of Gloucester, Edward's brother, killed this good man with his own hand or at least had him killed in his presence in some secret place'."

I broke in. "When did you say that De Comines wrote his account?"

"About 1490, sir, roughly speaking," replied Baker.

"Well into Henry the Seventh's reign, then. Was De Comines in England?"

"No, sir, he never visited England, not ever."

"Written abroad, then. So De Comines might very well have 'been deceived'."

Baker nodded. "Edward Hall is another later writer who repeats the tale of Richard stabbing Henry with a dagger. A lawyer and judge, Hall was, sir, and a Member of Parliament under Henry the Eighth, but he just borrowed wholesale from Thomas More and Polydore Virgil.

"Bernard André made it clear that it was Edward who ordered Henry's death.

"Now, Doctor Watson, you asked what Sir Thomas More had to say. Here, read this." The old soldier handed me an open copy of More's small book, and pointed with a calloused finger to these words:–

"He slew with his own hands – as men constantly say – King Henry the Sixth, being prisoner in the Tower, and that without commandment or knowledge of the King, who would undoubtedly, if he had intended that thing, have appointed that butcherly office to some one other than his own born brother."

"Here we go again," I remarked. "'As men constantly say.' Hum. Does More really expect us to believe that Richard acted on his own, without the knowledge or consent of Edward the Fourth?"

I knitted my brow as an uncomfortable thought came suddenly to me.

"Still," I observed, "in all honesty, I suppose that I must note that Thomas à Becket was murdered after a king said:– 'Will no-one rid me of this troublesome priest?'"

"Yes, sir, that was King Henry the Second," returned Baker. "But I would certainly say that it was much more likely that, if Richard *did* dispatch Henry the Sixth, he was acting for his brother King Edward, and on his command."

Indeed, Thomas Habington, in his *Life of King Edward IV* in 1640, put the blame squarely on Edward:–

> "It was therefore resolved in King Edward's cabinet council that, to take away all title from future insurrections, King Henry should be sacrificed."

Baker smiled broadly. "Habington was not at all friendly towards Richard, Doctor Watson. Yet even he went to some length to make it clear that Richard would not have killed Henry without Edward's direct command:–

> "'For however some, either to clear the memory of the king, or by after cruelties, guessing at precedents, will have this murder to be the sole act of the Duke of Gloucester, I cannot believe a man so cunning in declining envy, and winning honour to his name, would have taken such business of his own counsel and executed it with his own hands; neither did this concern Gloucester so particularly as to engage him alone in the cruelty, nor was the king so scrupulous, having commanded more unnecessary slaughters, and from his youth been never any stranger to such executions'.

"And, Doctor Watson," continued Baker, "Habington goes on to say more:–

> "The death of King Henry was acted in the dark, so that it cannot be affirmed who was the executioner; only it is probable that it was a resolution of the state'."

A furious argument erupted among my volunteer solons over the date of Henry's death. Various writers, documents and interpreters, I found, gave the date as May 21st, 22nd, 23rd and 24th in the year 1471.

"This is damned important," an agitated Markham bellowed, while his sweet wife and daughter blushed in embarrassment across the family dining table.

"You see, there is solid evidence from Henry's household accounts that he did not die until May 24th, or perhaps the night of the 23rd. On the 23rd and 24th, we know that Richard was at Sandwich, seventy miles from the Tower. He has an undeniable *alibi*.

"The reason that Robert Fabyan chose the 21st as the date for his *Chronicle* is simply this: That is the only day upon which Richard was at the Tower. To fasten the blame upon him, Fabyan falsifies the date."

With a flourish, Markham later handed me his copy of the household account in question:–

"Accounts of the costs and expenses for the custody of King Henry, the Wednesday after the feast of Holy Trinity, June 12.

"To the same William Sayer for money to his own hand delivered for the expenses and diet of the said Henry, and ten persons attending within the Tower for the custody of the said Henry, namely, for fourteen days the first beginning on the 11th of May last past, vi.li. v.s." [In Markham's hand, this last was translated in a footnote as six pounds, five shillings.]

"There," said Markham, proudly and firmly. "The account was made up on June 12th. This fellow Sayer, an esquire of Henry, I believe, was repaid for Henry's expenses for fourteen days, of which the first was the May 11th, and the last, therefore, May 24th. Henry's board was also paid for the same period, the last day again being May 24th. Henry, then, without doubt, died on the 24th, or during the night of the 23rd. Richard then was at Sandwich, as I say, more than seventy miles away.

"In addition, a contemporary letter reported to the citizens of Bruges that Henry died on May 23rd. Richard was not in London on the 23rd. He is innocent."

Gairdner did not raise his dry voice, but was equally emphatic.

"Markham's interpretation of the document is merely that, an interpretation. The account – and there are several such accounts preserved – is not explicit. It does not state or prove that Henry was *alive*; it shows merely that payments were made on behalf of him or of his household in the Tower up until the 24th. There are also several other accounts and documents that report that Henry was dead on May 22nd. Therefore Richard is not in the clear at all."

Still, in the end, I made a confident entry in my book.

"Murder of King Henry the Sixth: Richard was implicated by Lancastrians and Tudors, but without evidence that would stand up in court. If Richard did supervise the murder of Henry, he almost certainly did so on Edward's orders. There is clearly reasonable doubt. Verdict on Richard: Not guilty."

Next on my calendar of murders was that of Richard's own brother George, the flighty, fickle, treacherous Duke of Clarence.

Edward the Fourth's accusations against George, in January 1478, had resulted in a death sentence. This was not immediately carried out; that I already knew. The Commons pressed for George's execution, however, and the *Croyland Chronicle* recorded his passing on February 18th:–

"The execution, whatever the mode of death, was carried out secretly within the Tower of London ... "

What *rôle*, if any, had Richard played in his death?

"Well, sir, it was not for many years that anybody accused Richard of having any *rôle*," said Yeoman Warder Baker. "All the early accounts put the death on Edward, and several say that Richard protested. It is Thomas More-fiction-than-fact who lays the train of gunpowder towards Richard, sir."

We went once more to More's account:–

"Some wise men also think that his drift, covertly conveyed, lacked not in helping along his brother of Clarence to his death, which he resisted openly, howbeit somewhat (as men deemed) more faintly than he that were heartily minded to his welfare ... But of all this

208

point there is no certainty, and whoso divines upon conjectures may as well shoot too far as too short."

"Yes, sir, Master More cooked Richard's bacon, all right." Baker suddenly, to my astonishment, burst into a raucous cackle of laughter, pounding his meaty right fist into his left hand with glee, tears pouring down as he roared with jollity. After some few seconds, he heaved to a stop.

"Sorry, sir, bit of a joke, sir; sorry. The gentleman who first accused Richard directly in George's death was a Lord Bacon. He was the Lord Chancellor, and he wrote a book in 1622. It was the *History of the Reign of King Henry the Seventh*, and in it Lord Bacon says that Richard was – where is my note? – 'the contriver of the death of the Duke of Clarence his brother'."

"But 1622," I noted, "is almost one hundred and fifty years after George's death."

"Right, sir. Of course, Shakespeare also has Richard involved in the murder, a bit earlier, as you have seen. But his play was published well over one hundred years after George's death.

"Before that, Philippe de Comines wrote that King Edward had George 'put to death in a pipe of malmsey, because, it is said, he wanted to make himself king.'

"Then we go on to Francis Sandford's famous book, *A Genealogical History of the Kings and Queens of England*. That is in 1707 or thereabouts, and he makes Richard one of the actual murderers:–

"'After he had offered his mass penny in the Tower of London, he was drowned in a butt of malmsey, his brother the Duke of Gloucester assisting thereat with his own proper hands'."

"So there was not a hint of any accusation against Richard, not even from his enemies, until much, much later," said I, slowly.

"Right, sir."

"Once more, Baker, I see the birthing of so-called history under the Tudors. It starts with innuendo, innuendo later becomes accepted as truth, and 'truth' then is later embellished with fictitious detail. The embellished fable then becomes official fact."

To my surprise, James Gairdner readily agreed.

"I have little doubt that Clarence was executed by Edward's order," said he, without hesitation. "You may fairly blame him. I am satisfied that Richard was guiltless. Shakespeare's accusation is quite obviously founded on More's proposition. More, however, so surrounded the charge with cautious qualifications – as you quite properly note, Doctor Watson – that I think that he did not have much faith in it himself. Shakespeare presented it as fact for a dramatic reason, to add strength to the ominous portrait he painted of Richard."

Strange, I thought, how Gairdner was willing to accept More's careful *caveats* in this case, but not in the others.

I presently wrote my finding. "Death of George, Duke of Clarence: No contemporary accusation against Richard, then, later, merely More's innuendo that he did not protest enough. No actual accusation until one hundred or one hundred and fifty years later. Verdict on Richard: Not guilty."

The first death with Richard established as the Protector of the realm was that of William Lord Hastings, the old friend of Edward the Fourth. As I had learned, Hastings stood against the Woodvilles to ensure that Richard became the Protector. He would not ride any farther with Richard, though, and, apparently to ensure the succession of young Edward the Fifth, he began to plot with the Woodvilles and Morton. The *dénouement* came at a council meeting in the Tower on June 13th 1483.

Baker, with dramatic relish, read to me from More's work:–

"'He clapped his fist upon the table a great rap. At which signal given, one cried out 'Treason!' within the chamber. Therewith a door clapped, and in came rushing men in armour, as many as the chamber might hold. And at once the Protector said to the Lord Hastings, 'I arrest thee, traitor'.'"

"Right, Baker," said I, "and all that was preceded by More's tale about Richard asking Morton to send for strawberries from his garden. And More says that Richard also preceded the arrest of Hastings by accusing Edward's Woodville queen of using sorcery and witchcraft to shrivel his left arm."

"Yes, sir," said Baker, picking up the ball, "but why would Richard accuse the queen of suddenly withering his arm, at that time? If he actually *did* have a withered arm, he had surely had it since birth, and everybody in the room would have known it."

I nodded. "I cannot see Richard saying it, either. I can, however, see Morton or somebody making it up, and passing it on to More."

Baker continued. "More also has Richard saying that Jane Shore conspired with the queen in the witchcraft. Jane Shore was Edward the Fourth's favourite mistress, sir, and then became the paramour of Lord Hastings, after Edward's death."

I nodded. "Mr. Gairdner says that it is obvious that Morton was the source of the version related by More and Shakespeare." (I could not immediately recall Gairdner's words, but looked them up later in my notes. "The colouring," declared Gairdner, "is that of a partisan, though the facts, no doubt, are those of a truthful reporter.")

"Is there any evidence of a trial for Hastings?" I inquired of Baker, and I pointed towards his pile of books.

"Well, no, sir. Not according to any of the books. They all tell much the same story. Even if you leave More out of it, *Fabyan's Chronicle*, the *Croyland Chronicle*, Polydore Virgil, all say that Hastings was accused of treason, and immediately taken out and executed."

"Just like that," I said, sadly.

"Just like that, sir."

A heavy silence descended over us. After half a minute or so, Baker broke into it, tentatively. "More says that he had a priest, sir."

211

I sighed. I confess that I had half expected to find Richard innocent of this accusation, too, but the truth seemed to be that he had simply removed an awkward and threatening adversary.

Clements Markham insisted, however, that there had been, or at least could have been, a trial.

"The point is, Doctor Watson, that Hastings almost certainly did have a trial. They all say that he was executed on the day of his arrest, Friday June 13th. But I contend that he was not executed until the 20th, a full week later. There was, therefore, sufficient time for his trial and sentence by a tribunal.

"The Lancastrians, the Tudors, the Mortons, have deliberately distorted facts and dates, to create this myth that Hastings was dragged from the council chamber and hastily executed so that Richard could get to his dinner."

"You have evidence," I suggested.

"Indeed I have. A cleric from Lincoln, one Simon Stallworthe, wrote a letter to Sir William Stonor, a gentleman of Oxfordshire, on Saturday, June 21st, 1483. Hear what he has to say:–

"'As on Friday last was the Lord Chamberlain beheaded soon after noon'.

"'Friday last' was therefore Friday, June 20th," said Markham, firmly.

I paused, searching for diplomatic words. After all, if Stallworthe was talking about yesterday, why did he not say "yesterday"?

"I am a little casual myself with such expressions, Markham. I wonder if he could not actually have meant Friday the 13th, as the others have it?"

"Not a chance," replied Markham, with a confidently cheery smile, reaching for a pile of papers on the sideboard. "Why, Stallworthe's letter goes on to make that clear:–

"'On Monday last was at Westminster great plenty of harnessed men; there was the deliverance of the Duke of York to my lord Cardinal, my lord Chancellor, and many other lords temporal; and with him met my lord of Buckingham in the midst of the hall of Westminster; my lord Protector receiving him at the Star Chamber door with many loving words, and so departed with my lord Cardinal to the Tower, where is he, blessed be Jesus, merry'.

"The younger of the Two Little Princes was indeed sent forth from sanctuary at Westminster on Monday June 16th. The *Croyland Chronicle* confirms that date. So when Stallworthe wrote 'Monday last' that is exactly what he meant, Monday last, June 16th."

I finished Markham's sentence for him. "And if he meant 'Monday last' to signify the 16th, he meant 'Friday last' to indicate the 20th," I said.

"Exactly," replied Markham, performing a theatrical drum roll on his plate with his knife and fork.

"Now, we do have certainty about some dates here," he continued. "Hastings was arrested on Friday June 13th; no doubt about it. It is also certain that Richard's accession to the throne was on Thursday June 26th. Lest there be any doubt about that, Richard confirms the date himself in a letter to Ireland. So now let us start to fill in some dates between those two poles."

"Hang on," I interrupted. "I thought Richard's coronation was in July, on July 6th."

"His coronation, yes," replied Markham. "But his official accession to the throne, his formal acceptance of it in the Great Hall at Westminster, was on June 26th. It is of that event that I speak.

"Doctor Shaw's sermon about bastard slips was preached on the Sunday before the accession. That is, therefore, on Sunday June 22nd. Stallworthe and Fabyan tell us that Hastings's execution was on the Friday preceding that; the 20th, therefore."

I broke in. "So Fabyan also gives the date of Hastings's death as the 20th, rather than the 13th?"

213

"Fabyan is deceptive," replied Markham. "He does state that the execution was on the Friday preceding Shaw's address. But to make it appear that Hastings was executed on the 13th, Fabyan moves the sermon to June 15th, and Richard's accession to Thursday the 20th. But, first, the accession was certainly on Thursday the 26th. That is well documented. Second, the 20th was not a Thursday, of course, but a Sunday, so Fabyan's clumsy fiction collapses."

I shook my head in honest puzzlement. "Why would Fabyan change the dates?"

"To support the myth about Hastings's death being rushed. Morton – I suppose that you would prefer me to say More – also alters the date of the accession. It is the only date that he gives, and he falsifies it. He says that the accession was on June 19th; a Thursday, all right, but the wrong Thursday. Richard's own official letter gives the date quite clearly and explicitly as the 26th. And so says *Croyland*, too."

"But why alter these dates?" I persisted.

"To create the slanderous myth that Hastings was murdered, executed on the spot without trial, all done at racehorse speed so that the heartless Richard could go and enjoy his dinner. For one thing, in his normal practice, Richard would *already* have dined. And, indeed, the *Great Chronicle of London* says he *had* dined before the meeting – with Hastings, no less.

"The so-called More account seeks to exaggerate the myth even further. It claims that Richard had Earl Rivers, Sir Richard Grey, Sir Thomas Vaughan and Sir Richard Haute executed in Pontefract on the same day, the 13th. They were not, in fact, executed until June 25th, and they too had a trial. Thomas More misleads us again."

I scratched my head. "Markham, you say that there was sufficient time between the 13th and the 20th for Hastings to have had a proper trial. Is a trial on record?"

A leaden pause followed.

"It is not," Markham said, slowly. "The Tudors must have destroyed the records, as they sought to do with *Titulus Regius*, the Act of Parliament that formally confirmed Richard as rightful king. You remember that Richard put out a proclamation accusing Hastings of plotting with the Woodvilles? That document has vanished from the archives, too. All destroyed by the Tudors, I contend. But since there was no indecent haste, no rushed execution, I think we can take it that there was a tribunal and that all was properly done."

I looked down at the table, silently. It was Hastings who was "properly done", I thought.

Markham signalled that he had detected my doubts.

"Doctor Watson, Hastings and his fellow conspirators were caught red-handed. There was a plot, treason, against Richard the Protector. He had to act. Hastings's execution was both necessary and justifiable by the standards of the era. Richard mourned Hastings. He ensured that Hastings's wife and children were well looked after. He was generous to Hastings's brother, as well."

My subsequent dinner at Gairdner's house was more subdued; just the two of us were present, but the lightly curried fish was heavenly.

"Oh dear," said Gairdner, with a patiently reproving smile. "Poor Markham does pick and choose his authorities to suit his argument. The truth is that there is very great confusion over some of these dates."

"As I have found with the death of Henry the Sixth," I noted. "Four different writers cite four different dates."

"Just so," returned Gairdner. "Take the date of Richard's accession. The *Croyland Chronicle* gives it as June 26th, indeed. More, Grafton and Hall, however, give it as the 19th. In the last century, Paul Rapin de Thoyras, a French historian, gave the date as June 22nd, and the Scottish historian, Malcolm Laing, gave it as June 27th."

"According to Markham," I began, "Richard himself gave the date as the 26th, in a letter to Ireland."

"So he did," said Gairdner, "There seems to have been some confusion in Ireland over the date, and Richard wrote to clear it up: It was the 26th, he said. But the argument, surely, is whether Hastings was summarily executed on the 13th, or was subjected to trial and executed on the 20th. And on that point, Doctor Watson, all the evidence is entirely in favour of the 13th, and there is simply no report whatsoever, from any source, of any delay in his execution, or of any trial."

"You dismiss the Stallworthe letter?"

"I dismiss the theory that by 'Friday last' Stallworthe meant 'yesterday'," replied Gairdner, echoing my own question. "If Stallworthe meant yesterday, why did he not say so? Today is Friday. If I asked you what you did 'last Thursday', would you take it that I was referring to yesterday?"

I shook my head to acknowledge his point. Indeed, I am still shaking my head, over Gairdner's question and my own. After much reading, and silent reflection, I wrote my judgment.

"Death of William Lord Hastings: No report of a trial. There seems little doubt but that Richard arbitrarily removed a powerful opponent, without a hearing. Even by the standards of 1483 this must have been of doubtful legality. Verdict on Richard: Guilty."

Baker also brought up the execution of William Collingbourne in 1484. A popular account that I remember from school had it that Collingbourne was savagely butchered by Richard merely for a famous piece of doggerel:–

"The Ratte, the Catte and Lovell our dogge
Rule all England under an Hogge."

The Ratte and the Catte were Richard's acolytes, Sir Richard Ratcliffe and Sir William Catesby. The dogge was Francis Lord Lovell, Richard's chamberlain and friend of Richard since childhood, whose emblem was a wolf. The Hogge was Richard himself, from his insignia of the white boar.

Baker's books, however, established that Collingbourne, a Wiltshire landowner, was not executed for his impertinent poetry, but for treasonable correspondence with Henry Tudor. He had promised to cause an uprising, had recruited men to Tudor's cause, and with others, had invited Tudor to land invasion forces at Poole.

"Verdict on Richard: Not guilty."

Chapter Twelve

Following the hasty and tragic death of Hastings in the chronology of Richard's alleged crimes came the executions of Rivers, Grey, Vaughan and Haute. They were arrested by Richard at Northampton, on April 29th, 1483, as they were taking the young and uncrowned Edward the Fifth to London.

The Earl of Rivers was by name Anthony Woodville, brother of Edward the Fourth's Woodville queen. He was the governor and guardian of Prince Edward as well as his uncle. Rivers was, by all accounts, a luminary man of letters and culture, a well-spoken writer and a poet, a noble gentleman of piety and chivalry, and a champion jouster. He translated and prepared a book that was the first printed in England by Caxton. He was a classic example of Horace's 'accomplished man to his fingertips'. As I learned about his many strengths, I much regretted that he and Richard could not see eye to eye. Richard badly needed Rivers on the stage with him, loyally reciting the lines written by Richard, and not in the audience throwing rotten vegetables. Their differences, however, were ever too deep and fundamental to reconcile.

Richard Grey was the boy prince's half-brother. Sir Richard Haute was a cousin of Queen Elizabeth Woodville. Sir Thomas Vaughan was the young prince's chamberlain, and had been his servant for all of the boy's life. They were held prisoner in the North, Grey being captive at Richard's Middleham Castle.

They were all haled to Pontefract, and publicly beheaded there, according to one independent account, on June 25th, 1483.

As Markham noted, Thomas More said in his tale that they were executed on June 13th, the same day as was Hastings. However, that obviously could not be, as Rivers made out his will, at Sheriff Hutton castle in Yorkshire, on June 23rd. I shall return to that document, and its significant contents, in a moment.

Richard the Third has often been accused of murdering the four without cause or trial.

Markham insisted that there had been cause. "The bearer of Richard's appeal to York for armed men was Sir Richard Ratcliffe. And it was he who also carried the warrants for the execution of Rivers, Grey, Vaughn and Haute. I must take it, then, that there was a plot, that they were part of it, and that the royal council authorised the executions by warrant."

As for their trial, of course, trials as we know them today, in 1883, are not like those of 1483; and the summary execution of rebellious nobles without proper hearing or appeal was then by no means an uncommon practice.

Sir Thomas More insisted that there was no trial, and that Ratcliffe executed the four, at the behest of Richard:–

"Now was it so arranged by the Protector and his council that ... there were, not without his assent, beheaded at Pomfret the foreremembered lords and knights that were taken from the King at Northampton and Stony Stratford. Which thing was done in the presence and by the order of Sir Richard Ratcliff, knight, whose service the Protector especially used in the plotting and in the execution of such lawless enterprises, as a man that had long been secret with him, having experience of the world and a shrewd wit, short and rude in speech, rough and boisterous of behaviour, bold in mischief, as far from pity as from all fear of God. This knight, bringing them out of the prison to the scaffold and showing to the people about that they were traitors, not suffering them to speak and declare their innocence lest their words might have inclined men to pity them and to hate the Protector and his party, caused them hastily, without judgement, process, or manner of order, to be beheaded, and without any other guilt but only that they were good men, too true to the King and too close to the Queen."

Yet, I noted, More did at least confirm that the decision to execute them was endorsed by the royal council.

The *Croyland Chronicle* also reported that there was no trial for Rivers and his colleagues:–

"A multitude of people were moving from the North to the South under their principal leader and organiser, Richard Ratcliffe, knight, and when they reached the town of Pontefract, on the command of Richard Ratcliffe, and without any form of trial, Anthony Earl Rivers, Richard Grey his nephew, and Thomas Vaughan, the elderly knight, were beheaded before these same people."

No mention of Haute, I noted. Perhaps he in fact survived?

Another account, however, does suggest a trial or tribunal of some kind. The inimical John Rous, while inevitably vilifying Richard in no uncertain terms, named the Earl of Northumberland as their "chief judge". Wrote Rous:–

"Shortly after, the lords previously described were cruelly put to death at Pontefract, lamented by almost everyone and innocent of the deed charged against them, and the Earl of Northumberland, their chief judge, then proceeded to London."

The words "chief judge" jumped out at me. So there was more than one judge, was there? A proper tribunal, then?

Gairdner made a cogent argument, however, that, even if there had been such a tribunal, it was not constitutional.

"As an earl, Rivers, for one, ought to have been tried in Parliament, or before the Lord High Steward and a jury of peers. Just as Hastings should have been. Whatever hearing was held, if indeed there was one, was not legal. The execution was simply a violation of the law."

It was Gairdner, however, who first told me of Rivers's will.

"You may think this extraordinary, Doctor Watson, but in his will Rivers actually asked that Richard be a trustee on his behalf."

I almost spilled my wine into my lap as Gairdner made this disclosure.

"A trustee?" I queried, amazed. Gairdner laughed politely at my astonishment.

"True. Quite remarkable, it seems to us these four hundred years later, but Rivers apparently had some faith in Richard. This is what he said:–

"'I beseech humbly my Lord of Gloucester in the worship of Christ's passion, and for the merit and weal of his soul, to comfort, help, and assist as supervisor (for very trust) of this testament, that mine executors may, with his pleasure, fulfil this my last will'."

I sat in stunned silence. Was this some devious ploy on the part of Rivers? Was he trying to embarrass Richard into co-operating with his executors? Or was he truly expressing faith in Richard and thus, in effect, accepting that his impending execution was legal?

"I think, rather, that it reflects resignation," suggested Gairdner. "We know that Rivers wrote a poem, a ballad, in his death cell. There is no hint of recrimination or attack on Richard. I shall read part of it to you:–

"'Willing to die,
methinks truly
bounden am I.
And that greatly
to be content,

222

seeing plainly
fortune doth wry
all contrary from
mine intent.
It is nigh spent;
Welcome fortune.'

"He was resigned to his death, you see."

Markham, however, made much of Rivers's testamentary appeal to Richard.

"The point is, that the senior and most treasonous Woodville noble, arrested and condemned for outright treachery, had faith in the integrity and honesty of Richard. Rivers gambled and lost, yet he trusted Richard to play fair. Surely it shows that Rivers accepted his fate as proper as well as inevitable, and Richard as honest. More is both wrong and slanderous to say that the executions were a 'lawless enterprise' and 'without judgement, process, or manner of order'."

I subsequently recorded my own verdict:

"Deaths of Rivers, Grey, Vaughan (and possibly Haute): Some evidence, from a source hostile to Richard, that there was at least one judge, and therefore some form of tribunal if not a full trial. Whether it was legal is a good question. By today's standards, Richard overstepped his authority. By the standards of 1483, however, he would not have been convicted. Verdict on Richard: Not guilty."

But I do entertain doubts about the legality of Richard's actions, and certainly about his wisdom, in this sad case.

I turn now to the death of Henry Stafford, Duke of Buckingham.

He had been Richard's most important ally. It was Buckingham who warned Richard of the Woodville plot to maintain control of Prince Edward on the death of Edward the Fourth. It was Buckingham who hastened then to join Richard at Northampton, to crush the plot and to bring young Edward to London. It was Buckingham who publicly pressed Richard's claim to the throne.

Richard had most generously rewarded Buckingham. Yet this mighty magnate was soon to rise against his king.

I recalled that Gairdner had listed several theories. That Richard had slighted Buckingham, and had failed to deliver to Buckingham the Bohun estates of the Earl of Hereford. That Buckingham had his own eyes on the throne. That Buckingham wanted to marry a daughter to Richard's son, but had been rebuffed by Richard. That the wily Morton persuaded, or perhaps tricked, Buckingham into abandoning Richard. That Buckingham had cause to know of, or suspect, or might himself have carried out, the murders of the Two Little Princes.

Or perhaps, I speculated, the double-dealing Buckingham had simply been another Warwick, an ambitious king-maker who found to his chagrin that his king refused to be an obedient puppet.

In the event, Buckingham turned his coat and threw his support behind his cousin Henry Tudor, the future Henry the Seventh. Buckingham, as we know, led an armed rebellion against Richard that broke out in October 1483. I wondered if Buckingham supported Tudor only in the hopes of subsequently dethroning him, and taking the throne for himself. I could find no documentary evidence for or against this theory.

Tudor, who had long been in exile on the continent, was supposed to land with a force of mercenaries and followers, but had to withdraw. Buckingham was abandoned by his own men, and fled for his life. A follower turned him in, and Richard had him beheaded.

But was this execution a crime? A murder that could be charged to Richard?

"Not a chance, sir," insisted Yeoman Warder Baker. "Richard was the king, the anointed and crowned king. He declared the Duke of Buckingham to be a traitor, in proper legal form. He offered a reward of one thousand pounds, or land worth one hundred pounds a year in revenue, for whoever turned Buckingham in. Buckingham was on the run, in disguise, sir, after his troops gave up on him. He went for help to one Banaster. I have seen Banaster's name given both as Humphrey and Ralph, and with more than one spelling of Banaster. Some say Banaster was a servant, sir, but he seems to have had an estate near Shrewsbury, so he must have been a retainer or friend of Buckingham, rather than a mere servant. Robert Fabyan told the story in his *Chronicle*, sir:–

> "'The foresaid Banastre, were it for need of the same reward, or fear of losing his life and goods, discovered the duke unto the sheriffs of the shire, and caused him to be taken, and so brought unto Salisbury, where the king then laid.'

"That was on November 2nd. Buckingham asked to see Richard, but Richard refused. Good thing, too; Buckingham's son confessed many years later that his father had somehow concealed a knife under his clothes, and had planned to assassinate Richard. Richard would not see him, sir, and Buckingham was executed the very same day."

Banaster was rewarded with a manor and lordship in Kent, that had been owned by Buckingham. But Richard gave a pension to Buckingham's widow, just as he did with Hastings's widow, and paid off Buckingham's debts.

"Executed the very same day?" I inquired. "Did Buckingham not have a trial?"

"Thought you would ask that, sir. Now, Edward Hall wrote much later that he did not:–

> "'Without arraignment or judgement, he was, in the open market place, on a new scaffold, beheaded and put to death.'

"On the other hand, Master More does speak of an examination:–

> "'The Duke, being diligently examined, uttered, without any manner of refusal or sticking, all such things as he knew, trusting that for his plain confession he should have liberty to speak to the King, which he made most

instant and humble petition that he might do. But as soon as he had confessed his offence towards King Richard, he was out of hand beheaded.'

"You see, sir, when Buckingham rebelled, King Richard appointed Sir Ralph Ashton as vice-constable of England, and commissioned him to judge and execute traitors. Buckingham was constable for life, you see, so Ashton had to be named vice-constable. I would take it that Buckingham was examined and condemned by Ashton, sir. So there was some form of hearing, if with no appeal."

"Yes," I mused. "Of course, I keep thinking of a trial as being what *we* would call a trial today. I keep forgetting that in Richard's time the king's powers were immeasurably more sweeping than those of our own good queen."

And so Henry Stafford, proud Duke of Buckingham, went to his death. In a later age, a skeleton was found beneath a yard in Salisbury. There was no skull. It was proposed that these were Buckingham's bones. Some say that Buckingham's ghost still walks in Salisbury each November 2nd.

I reached my verdict: "Execution of Buckingham: Legal execution of proclaimed and confessed traitor, in keeping with the times. Verdict on Richard: Not guilty."

I therefore recorded the same verdict in the case of the executions of other rebel leaders. While most fled, a dozen or so were taken. They included Richard's own brother-in-law Sir Thomas St. Leger, who had been married to Richard's eldest sister Anne. Not even this connection could save him from execution. Also executed were a few opportunists from Richard's own establishment, who had been identified in Buckingham's confession as co-conspirators.

Richard's wife, of course, was another Anne, Anne Nevill, and her premature death gave rise to yet one more charge of murder against Richard the Third; and to that charge was attached another explosive allegation.

It was said that Richard had planned after Anne's death to marry his own niece, Elizabeth, eldest daughter of his brother King Edward the Fourth.

Markham dismissed the proposition as simply absurd.

"However, Doctor Watson, I can certainly understand why the rumour circulated. Her mother, Elizabeth Woodville, was in favour of it. Indeed, I suspect that she came up with the idea. Failing that, I contend that it was Richard's councillors and advisers who came up with it. But there is evidence that she and her daughter both supported it."

I shook my head vigorously as surprise piled upon surprise.

"Elizabeth Woodville? The great arch-enemy of Richard? Wait a minute, Markham. Richard has supposedly seized and murdered her young sons, the Two Little Princes. He has proclaimed her surviving children as bastards. He has executed her brother, Earl Rivers, and her son Lord Grey. Yet now she is proposing that her daughter should marry Richard. You must be joking. Further, was not Elizabeth supposed to marry Henry Tudor?"

The explorer laughed, then shook his head sadly.

"It is, I am afraid, all a sad commentary on the fate of royal daughters in the fifteenth century. If you go back to 1475, back when Elizabeth was nine years of age, she was promised to the Dauphin, the little son of Louis the Eleventh of France. The Dauphin was five. Louis eventually backed away from that pact. Now let us go again to the autumn of 1483. You are correct; Elizabeth of York is now seventeen years of age, and it is a facet of Buckingham's rebellion that she is to marry Henry Tudor, if he succeeds in ousting Richard and becoming king himself.

"Then, according to Thomas More, at least, Richard gets to hear of this little plot, and comes up with a novel plan to foil it. Supposedly, he decides to wed Elizabeth himself.

"Now, some sort of *rapprochement* undoubtedly did develop between Richard and Elizabeth Woodville. In the spring of 1484, she sends her daughters – she had four surviving daughters in addition to Elizabeth of York – out of sanctuary, and to Richard. He agrees to look after them well, and to find them husbands of rank.

"But the idea of Richard himself marrying Elizabeth is clearly absurd.

"Shakespeare has Richard saying:–

"'I must be married to my brother's daughter, or else my kingdom stands on brittle glass.'

"But that is entirely ludicrous. Richard had nothing to gain by such a marriage, and everything to lose. The marriage would certainly scuttle Henry's plans to marry Elizabeth, true, but Richard's claim to the throne is based upon, and was approved upon, the finding that Edward's children are bastards. Any monkey business with Elizabeth, any marriage, would have been nothing short of an act of self-impeachment. Richard could have married her and legitimated her, but that would have legitimated the Two Little Princes as well. The young Prince Edward would then have been king.

"Marrying Elizabeth would have been, at best, an admission that Richard's claim to the throne was flawed; at worst, a confession that the boys were dead. Either way, it would have been an incredibly stupid act of self-impeachment, and rebellion would have broken out again. No, marriage was out of the question, even if Richard really had thought of it in the first place.

"Still, tongues really start to wag after an incident at court. Elizabeth of York appears at a Christmas dance in 1484, wearing a gown that is either identical to one of Queen Anne Nevill's gowns, or actually is one of the queen's gowns. The Latin of the *Croyland Chronicle* leaves me confused as to whether they merely exchanged gowns, or whether Richard had given identical gowns to both. I suppose, too, that it is possible that Anne Nevill gave Elizabeth the gown, or had a copy made for her. Regardless, the tongues flap, in full force. Here is what the *Croyland Chronicle* says:–

"'The people spoke out against this and the nobles and prelates were thoroughly astonished, and it was said by many that the king was putting his mind in every way to arranging a marriage with Elizabeth, either on the expected death of the queen or by way of a divorce, for which he believed he had sufficient cause. He saw no other way of confirming his reign or destroying the hopes of his rival.'"

"How old was Elizabeth, did you say?" I asked.

"In her eighteenth year, at this point, and Richard was two and thirty."

Markham's eyes shone. "To go with that, I think that I have another surprise for you, Doctor Watson. Some of the Tudor writers seize upon the tale, and say that young Elizabeth abhorred the idea of being married to Richard. But there is a strong report to the contrary by Sir George Buck, who wrote a defence of Richard in the seventeenth century.

"Buck cites a letter from Elizabeth to the Duke of Norfolk, in February 1485, in which she asks Norfolk to sound out Richard on the idea of marriage to her. According to Buck, she wrote that Richard was 'her only joy and maker in this world, and that she was in his heart and in his thoughts, in body and in all'. She certainly sounds infatuated with Richard.

"Further, according to Buck's manuscript, Elizabeth had previously asked Queen Anne's doctors how long Anne was expected to live. Supposedly, Anne would not last until April. In the letter to Norfolk, Elizabeth expresses her concern that it is now late in February, and the queen will never die.

"Thus it is clear that Anne is already ill and under the care of doctors. And, further, that Elizabeth seems to have been serious about the idea of marrying Richard. Why else make inquiries about Anne's health, and express the concern that she is not dying quickly enough?

"This letter no longer exists, so we can not confirm its details, and Buck was admittedly a leader in the public defence of Richard. Yet while he did not reproduce the actual text, he gave persuasive detail in his summary of it, and I understand that he saw the letter himself.

"If so, then young Elizabeth of York was apparently taking the idea seriously. As for her mother, Buck says that she was so delighted with the prospect of Elizabeth marrying Richard that she wrote to her son the Marquis of Dorset. He was with Henry Tudor in Brittany on the Continent, but she proposed that he abandon Tudor, and come back to England under Richard's favour.

"Sir Thomas More tells that story, too, saying that Richard had first sent envoys to persuade Queen Elizabeth Woodville to send her daughters out of sanctuary, and to him:–

"'These messengers, being men of gravity, handled the Queen so craftily that soon she began to be allured and to hearken unto them favourably, so that in conclusion she promised to be obedient to the King in his request, forgetting the injuries he had done her before, and on the other hand not remembering the promise she had made to Margaret, Henry's mother. And first she delivered both her daughters into the hands of King Richard. Then, after, she sent secretly for the Lord Marquess her son, being then at Paris with Henry (as you have so heard), willing him to forsake Henry, with whom he was, and speedily return to England, for all things were pardoned and forgiven, and she was again in the favour and friendship of the King, and it should be highly for her son's advancement and honour.'"

I shook my head with vigour. "That is still very hard to swallow – if Richard were as guilty as he has been painted. I can accept that Elizabeth Woodville was perfectly capable of playing two or more games of chess simultaneously. And I can even see her wondering if Richard might not be a better bet than Tudor. After all, Richard was on the throne; Henry would have had to take it by force. As well, she had no guarantee that Henry would live up to his commitment to marry her daughter. But when three of her sons, and her brother, have supposedly been slain by Richard, Elizabeth Woodville simply approves of one daughter's marriage to Richard, and hands her other daughters over to him? And then she urges another son to come home from France and put himself into Richard's hands? Hard to believe."

"She *did* hand her daughters over to Richard," observed Markham. "As I say, Richard swore to protect the lasses, and to find them good husbands, and to give them dowries. And so he did. And Elizabeth Woodville did so appeal to her son. He never made it to England, though; Tudor prevented him from leaving France."

I was about to suggest that the appeal to her son must show that Elizabeth Woodville had good cause to trust Richard, when another thought struck me.

"Surely this all lends weight to the theory that the Two Little Princes were dead," said I, gravely.

"If neither of them could ever come to the throne, then at least Elizabeth Woodville could have the hope that her daughter could become queen. Either as Richard's queen or as Henry's, come to that."

Markham laughed, his eyes twinkling.

"Or the Princes were in fact alive, and Elizabeth Woodville was carefully placing her bets on all the horses in the race. If the Two Little Princes were able to re-establish their legitimacy, the Crown would go to the elder. If they remained legally as bastards, at least her daughter could become the queen, even if a bastard herself. Bastardy might have been a bar to the crown, but not to marriage. Further, if Henry successfully took the throne, he could then be deposed in favour of the 'rightful' heir, young Prince Edward. Or, similarly, Richard could be deposed."

In the end, Henry's first Parliament, in November 1485, confirmed his kingship, and legitimated Elizabeth. That also reversed the bastardy of the Two Little Princes. "That, too, would suggest they were dead at that time," I pointed out.

Markham's face became wreathed in smiles. "Let me posit yet another theory: Elizabeth Woodville knew in 1483 that the boys were dead, but was satisfied that *Richard* was not responsible. Indeed, the writer Richard Grafton insists that she *did* know they were dead; that she was so informed by a doctor named Lewis, and that she was distraught and hysterical. But she clearly did not believe that Richard was the villain. She soon released her daughters to Richard, and urged her son to come home to join Richard. She knew that she could indeed trust Richard with her daughters and her son."

"Who, then, was the murderer of the Two Little Princes?" I asked.

Markham smiled. "The Duke of Buckingham is sometimes named as a suspect, but I shall hope yet to demonstrate to you that – no matter what Elizabeth Woodville knew or believed – the Two Little Princes were not only alive, but lived into Henry the Seventh's reign before meeting their end, and at his hands."

"In the event," I noted, "Richard and Elizabeth did not marry."

"Of course not," rejoined Markham. "But the rumours did reach such a pitch that Richard had to deny them. The Croyland chronicler heard the stories, and insists that Richard's councillors forced him to make a public denial:–

"'Eventually the King's plan and his intention to marry Elizabeth, his close blood-relation, was related to some who were opposed to it, and, after the council had been summoned, the King was forced to make his excuses, at length, and said that such an idea had never entered his mind. There were some at the council who had knowledge to the contrary. Those who were most strongly opposed to this marriage were Richard Ratcliffe, knight, and William Catesby, squire of the body. These men told the King, to his face, that if he did not deny such a purpose and did not counter it with a public declaration before the mayor and common people of the city of London, the people of the North, in whom he had the greatest trust, would rise as one against him, and would accuse him of bringing about the death of the Queen, the daughter and one of the heiresses of Warwick, and through whom he had obtained his first honour, in order to complete his incestuous association with his close kinswoman, to the insult of God. In addition, they brought more than a dozen doctors of theology who insisted that the Pope had no power of

232

dispensation over such a degree of consanguinity ... Shortly before Easter, therefore, the King took his place in the great hall of St. John's, in the presence of the mayor and citizens of London and in a distinct, loud voice carried out fully that advice to make such a denial, as many people believed more by the desire of the councillors than his own.'"

"If they had to bring in a dozen theologians to persuade him," I observed, "it looks as if Richard did entertain the idea."

Markham simply shrugged. "On the contrary, since Richard's wife was dying, he was already beginning to exploring the possibility of a marriage with a princess from Portugal, or a princess from Spain. England needed an heir, and a foreign alliance would be of benefit, too.

"A marriage to Elizabeth would have been political suicide. Richard could not have been so stupid. Note that he was not accused of *committing* incest; it is merely stated that if he went ahead and married her he *would* be accused of it.

"Now, it would not surprise me at all if *some* of his council had argued for such a marriage, preferring an English marriage. I would take it, then, that the theologians were summoned to persuade *them*, rather than Richard."

That I could see, too.

"Given Anne's ill health," I replied, "I imagine the council would indeed be considering a number candidates to succeed her. With Anne seriously ill, the council would naturally address the question of who would make a suitable queen if she died, and who might produce another heir."

"Quite so," rejoined Markham. "The rumours of marrying Elizabeth of York would then have been based on one or more members of the council thinking aloud, and not on *Richard* talking about it or planning it. Richard's public rejection of the idea would have been natural and politic, and not a forced denial as the *Croyland Chronicle* proposes.

"By the way, Polydore Virgil reported that Tudor was 'pinched to the very stomach' by the thought that Elizabeth might be married to Richard. It would wreck his plans."

"Hum. Why did not Richard simply marry her off to somebody else, then?" I asked. "That would have scuppered Henry."

"Obviously he should have," replied Markham. "Perhaps he was too chivalrous.

"I suppose I should add that a French chronicler, Jean Molinet, declared that Richard had a child by young Elizabeth. However, he is the only writer to make this claim, and I do not think that anybody has ever taken him seriously."

Anne Nevill, wife of Richard the Third and daughter of the unfortunate Warwick, died on March 16th, 1485.

The *Croyland Chronicle* said that her final illness began after the Christmas dance and the episode of the dresses:–

> "A few days after this, the Queen began to be seriously ill, and her sickness was believed to have got worse and worse because the King himself was entirely spurning his consort's bed, stating that it was by the advice of doctors that he did so. What else is there to report? About the middle of the following month, on the day when a great eclipse of the sun occurred, the before-named Queen Anne died and was buried at Westminster, with honours no less than befitted the burial of a queen."

John Rous, always anxious under Henry the Seventh to stick a knife into Richard (although he had apparently never heard of the rumours of Richard plotting to marry Elizabeth), accused Richard of murdering her:–

> "And Lady Anne, his Queen, daughter of the Earl of Warwick, he poisoned."

Thomas More positively revelled in the matter:–

"King Richard, when Queen Elizabeth was thus brought into the fool's paradise, after he had received all his brother's daughters from sanctuary into his palace, thought there now remained nothing to be done but only the casting away and destroying of his wife, which thing he had wholly purposed and decreed within himself. ... And first of all he abstained from bedding or living with her and also found himself grieved with the barrenness of his wife, that she was not fruitful and brought forth to him no children, and he complained thereof most grievously to the nobles of his realm and, above others, to Thomas Rotherham, then the Archbishop of York, whom he had freed a little before from prison. The Bishop gathered from this that the Queen would be out of the way before long (such experience did he have of King Richard's disposition, for he had accomplished many similar things not long before), and at the same time he made some of his privy friends secretly aware of his intentions.

"After this the King caused a rumour to run amongst the common people, though he would not have the author known, that the Queen was already dead, with the intent that, hearing of this marvellous rumour, she would take so grievous a shock as to become seriously ill soon after. But when the Queen heard that so terrible a report of her death had gone abroad amongst the common people, she suspected the matter, and supposed the end of the world to be upon her; and hastily she went to the King with a countenance of lamentation, and with tears and weeping she asked him whether she had done anything that would judge her worthy of death. The King made answer with a smiling and deceitful countenance, and with flattering words bade her to be of good cheer, and to pluck up her heart for there was no such matter towards her that he knew.

But howsoever it came about, either by sorrow or by poisoning, within a few days after, the Queen was dead, and afterwards was buried in the Abbey of Westminster."

I looked hard at Markham. "Well, Markham, if she was suffering from some fatal disease, such as advanced consumption, I would certainly hope that Richard *did* avoid her bed, *per Croyland*. The doctors would have ordered him to stay away from her. More appears to have placed the blackest possible interpretation on that point."

Markham nodded, and continued. "The Tudor writers spread still further the charge that Richard poisoned Anne; Polydore Virgil for one:–

"'But the Queen, whether she was despatched with sorrowfulness or with poison, died within a few days and was buried at Westminster.'

"Edward Hall, in Henry the Eighth's time, circulates the same slander:–

"'Some think that she went at her own pace to her grave, while others suspect that a substance was given to her to quicken her in her journey to her eternal home.'

"Grafton suggests that she was probably poisoned, and our continental friend, De Comines, declares that some people said that Richard had her killed.

"But it is surely significant that Bernard André, Henry Tudor's own biographer, makes no mention of Anne's death by poison."

Markham looked serious. "It is hardly surprising, given Anne's illness and death, and the fable of Richard planning to marry Elizabeth, that rumours of poison would circulate. Those with vicious tongues will always find cause to exercise them. And it would certainly have been in Henry Tudor's interest to have Richard seen as having poisoned his wife so that he could marry his young niece.

"What I say is that, when you examine the record, there is no evidence of Richard's marriage to Anne being anything but successful and happy. Their son Edward's death clearly struck both of them hard. The *Croyland Chronicle* says that they were 'almost out of their minds for a long time.' I do not think it too fanciful to guess that Edward died of consumption, and that his mother caught the same disease, and so died a natural death."

I reached the same conclusion as I rendered my private judgement.

"Death of Anne: No evidence of any crime in her death; full stop. Verdict on Richard: Not guilty."

Now, at last, I was free to turn my attention to the horrible charge of double murder that has rung out for four hundred years, the deaths of the Two Little Princes, and then to take my results and report to Masterman-Pugh and the men of Magdalen.

Chapter Thirteen

As the time came for our second journey to Oxford, where I was to make my report to the dreaded Masterman-Pugh and his academic colleagues, the myriad butterflies in my stomach turned into wheeling vultures. I was both nervous and queasy, and my confidence was at an abysmally low ebb.

"I think I should be more comfortable facing Marwood, the hangman," said I to Holmes, in a weak voice.

"The 'Nine O'Clock Walk' to the gallows?" laughed Holmes. "Nonsense, Watson," he continued, firmly. "You have done a very professional job so far, and you will acquit yourself well.

"By the way: William Marwood is not at all well. Some affliction of the lungs, they say. Perhaps it is the wages of gin after so many judicial executions. He is getting on for one hundred and eighty, I think; one of them being the notorious Charlie Peace in '79."

I intoned the doggerel verse oft heard when Marwood was conducting one of his "long-drop" hangings, designed and mathematically calculated to ensure a speedy death.

"'If Pa
"Killed Ma,
"Who'd kill Pa?
"Marwood'".

Holmes chuckled. "Let me see, Watson, you must weigh fourteen stone these days, and you have a rugby player's neck. Knot under the left ear and jaw, and a drop of some six and a half feet according to Marwood's science, I think. The Nine O'Clock Walk in London, and Eight O'Clock in the country."

I grimaced. "They say that Marwood tells the condemned man, 'Come with me; I shall not hurt you.' I hope that the men of Magdalen will be so considerate towards me.

"I have had no time to rehearse before you my findings in the matter of the murder of the Two Little Princes," I continued, my voice quivering and my internal vultures flapping violently once more. "I shall make my entry unprepared."

"Then let us devote the train journey to that," replied Holmes, lightly.

"Tumbril journey," I replied, gloomily.

"Oh, Watson, please do stop fretting," returned Holmes. "I shall be there. Baker will be there. You will not be alone."

With Masterman-Pugh's permission, I had invited an excited Yeoman Warder Baker to accompany us to Oxford. General Milman enthusiastically gave his approval. I had invited Miss Rivas, too. I had written to her at length after my first visits to Markham and Gairdner, relating some of what I had learned from them, and recalling with much pleasure our interesting tour of the Tower. I was delighted to receive in return a warm reply, with the freely reiterated promise of assistance should I require it from York. Indeed, she advised me that she had already begun to read about Richard the Third, starting with Caroline Halsted's *Richard III as Duke of Gloucester and King of England*.

"Miss Halsted finds Richard to have been a very good, humane, fair and popular king [wrote Miss Rivas]. This is not the common story, and, as you know, I am curiously attracted to the uncommon story. I shall therefore devote my initial research to the question of

Richard's character, if you will be gracious enough so to permit."

I accepted with alacrity, and we exchanged a number of letters. And so, as I made plans to go to Oxford, I asked my new friend if she would be free to join us there.

"I regret that the headmistress cannot spare me to go to Oxford [I read, with disappointment]. I hope that you will find it some compensation that I have begun to take my summer girls, on our daily walks, to those places in York associated with Richard. 'My fair City of York', he did call it. It was the Northern capital when he was, *de facto* if not *de jure*, Edward's vice-regent in the North, and it remained as the home of Richard's Northern Council after he took the throne.

"My summer girls are those who cannot return to their homes for their holidays. Some have parents who are travelling abroad. Some, sadly, have no home to go to; they are supported here all year through the generosity of church or charitable bequest. We do our best to make life jolly and interesting for them. We are studying the history of York, and of England during Richard's time. The girls have adopted medieval titles such as duchess or countess, and play their roles well. We have visited the wonderful Minster, where, we believe, Richard intended to be buried. Some say that his son Edward was buried in his place, in front of the main altar, but this is open to question. The tomb of a boy at St. Helen's Church in Sheriff Hutton, nine miles from here, is popularly said to be that of young Edward, although a number of authorities doubt it. The Minster was nearing completion in Richard's time, and he gave to it enormously generous gifts of gold and silver ornaments for the altar, a large jewelled cross, and costly vestments.

"We have also visited the garden and ruins of the Archbishop of York's Palace, where Richard stayed on his royal progress, where he invested little Edward as

241

Prince of Wales, and where he knighted his illegitimate son John.

"We have been to the Chapter House, where Richard met the City Fathers in 1483, and to the Guild Hall, where he dined with them. We have visited the city gate of Monk Bar, to which the upper floor was added during Richard's reign. We have been to Toft Green, also known as Pageant Green, where were housed the waggons that served as stages for the actors in the famous Mystery Plays of Corpus Christi. Richard saw in person these plays, which moved from station to station throughout the city for the entire day.

"We have been to Micklegate Bar, the chief city gate upon which the heads of enemies of the state were displayed upon pikes to discourage further rebellion. The head of Richard's father was one so treated, as you have mentioned in your letters. In 1572, the head of the Earl of Northumberland was placed there at the behest of Queen Elizabeth; and they say that his ghost walks the grounds of Holy Trinity Church, searching still for its missing head. I note, for your interest, that the last heads so savagely displayed were those of some Scottish Jacobites in 1746. I was happy to hear from a learned friend, Mr. Bird, that, much to the consternation of the authorities, these last heads mysteriously came down and disappeared one night in 1754, thanks to a brave and loyal Jacobite.

"The Augustinian Priory where Richard often stayed has long gone, thanks to Henry the Eighth, but we can visit the site, and hope to spot some of its stones. I understand that many were used to strengthen the river bank. We shall also seek traces of the old royal palace on the River Ouse.

"We shall repeat these visits when all the girls have returned for the new term. I can thus, in good conscience, at the same time conduct my historical research, and broaden the knowledge of my pupils.

"The summer girls are of quick intelligence and wit. Being of the age they are, however, one of their most pressing questions is as to whether King Richard was really a hunchback. I can hear their squeals still as they relished the question, all the while professing to be most disgusted at the very thought."

Mr. Holmes and I took an early train down to Oxford, then went out for a walk, shortly after our arrival, from our small hotel off the High Street. "Just 'The High'," explained my friend, "is the customary name. Why St. Aldate's over there is known as 'St. Old's' is perhaps less obvious." We had passed the old castle mound and castle tower, the huge castellated prison, the neighbouring stations of the Great Western Railway and the London and North-Western Railway, and the Old Gate House Inn, when I noticed the nearby stables. I made the suggestion, half joking, that we take two horses and, to my considerable surprise, Holmes agreed without a murmur. "Certainly, Watson; it is your holiday, after all."

If I were a vindictive man, and had wanted to repay Mr. Sherlock Holmes for those occasions upon which he had subjected me to marked embarrassment, I could have had no better revenge than by taking Holmes riding. I am no natural equestrian myself, but learned enough in the army to take my seat competently enough, particularly on a docile and oft-rented horse from a public stable. Holmes, however, was so ill at ease and clumsy on horseback that I almost laughed aloud. To his credit, however, he stuck it out bravely.

He suffered his first tumble, fortunately at a slow walk, before we had even crossed the little bridge over Potts Stream. By the time we approached the stone-flagged Perch Inn at the hamlet of Binsey, he was a touch less awkward, and a shade more confident. Still, upon more than one occasion, the commanding language he directed at his hollow-backed mare was regrettably akin to that used by our London cabbies when they believe that customers are safely out of earshot.

I knew from the strained look upon his face, as he fell off his horse once more at the tiny church of St. Margaret near

Binsey, that he was very glad to be on foot again. We poked around the church, looked down at the sunken St. Margaret's Well, and even, following an ancient local tradition that Holmes related to me, touched a little of the so-called healing waters on our eyelids. St. Frideswide had fled here, seeking to escape marriage to a king of ancient Mercia. He furiously pursued her, and was struck blind. Her saintly forgiveness and her prayers gave rise to the well, whose waters cured him. The place became a place of pilgrimage, attracting visitors who once included Henry the Eighth.

We walked our stolid mounts slowly back to the Perch, and there I offered to cut short the expedition and to return at once to Oxford. My friend bravely declined. "No, Watson, I thank you, but in for a penny, in for a pound."

We rode on, in contented and companionable silence for the most part, beside the sparkling river, passing narrow Godstow Lock and making a brief detour to circle the grey-walled remains of historic Godstow nunnery. By the time we stopped at the picturesque stone-roofed Trout Inn, Holmes was in much better command both of his horse and himself, and, indeed, insisted to me over a good and welcome, if rather late, luncheon that he had so far enjoyed the experience immensely.

After our rest and repast by the roaring weir, we rode away from the river to Wytham, a pretty and secluded stone and thatch village, close by a fine, turreted manor house that, said Holmes, was often mis-named as 'the abbey'. Wood pigeons cooed softly, and doves echoed them from the dovecote behind the White Hart inn. I watched the carefree swallows for minutes on end as they darted and dived and swooped. This, I thought, is the true and gentle rural England, an ageless and serene England that London knows not of. I rejoiced inwardly that Londoners did not, and so had not despoiled it with their noise and litter and their squabbling children.

By the time we returned our patient horses to the stables in the late afternoon, we must have covered a good twelve miles and more, and Holmes winced as he descended carefully from the saddle and attempted to stretch himself to his normal full height.

"Well, Watson, I appear to have muscles in places previously unsuspected. Every single one of them is woefully sore, or soon will be, I suspect."

At dinner, I was seated between Baker and Thomas Terry, the former Cambridge mathematician and home bursar of Magdalen. Terry discovered in Baker a fellow enthusiast of cricket. I had been a fair wicket-keeper while in school, and much loved the sport. But now I was distracted and withdrawn, and the pair talked across me all through the dinner, chatting of Tinley and Tarrant, of Southerton and Shaw, and of Grace's season of '76.

Baker spoke with reverence of his Yorkshire cricket heroes, "Happy Jack" Ulyet, the great all-rounder; Louis Hall, and Billy Bates, "The Duke", the man who bowled England's first hat-trick in a Test.

Above all, Baker bemoaned the Test match of last August, when the merciless Australian bowler, Fred Spofforth, "The Demon", visited chaos upon our English side at The Oval. Spurred by insulting banter from English spectators in the pavilion, and by an unsportsmanlike runout committed by Grace, an angry Spofforth took fourteen wickets for only ninety runs, and delivered twelve maiden overs in a row. We lost by seven runs, in our first defeat at home. The *Sporting Times* ran the following item:– 'In Affectionate Remembrance of ENGLISH CRICKET, which died at The Oval on 29th August, 1882. Deeply lamented by a large circle of Sorrowing Friends and Acquaintances. R.I.P. N.B. – The body will be cremated and the Ashes taken to Australia.'"

My mouth was dry as, after dinner, I finally took my place nervously behind an oak lectern in the State Room. As I opened my leather case of carefully indexed note books, I saw and felt the professional academic eyes of Magdalen fixed expectantly on me. I had not felt such terror since that bloody day three years ago when the brave Murray had hurled me inert atop a packhorse, like a sack of coals, and had conducted me so heroically to safety at Maiwand. But I had learned in the army that assumed confidence is oft taken for the real thing. I was able to keep a deceptively steady hand as I sipped from my glass of water, and I began with a deceptively strong and confident voice. I led my learned audience at a gallop through Richard's early life and his accession to the throne. I was able successfully to answer a number of penetrating questions as I led my listeners through my Newgate Calendar, and up to the deaths of the Two Little Princes. By now feeling more confident, I suggested a short break to recharge glasses. "After all, I have been speaking for well over an hour, and my throat needs a rest. So do my poor feet."

President Bulley nodded in kindly manner. "Indeed, Doctor Watson, you must not exhaust yourself upon our account. If you are game to carry on with your most fascinating address tonight, please do so; but we would all, I am sure, oblige you by adjourning until tomorrow."

As my hearers arose and stretched, Masterman-Pugh broke in loudly.

"I am most impressed, Doctor Watson. It has more than once been made clear to me by my colleagues here that I have trespassed most severely upon your good will in this enterprise. I would wish, before them, fully and publicly to apologise to you for my ill manners, and to congratulate you upon the quality of scholarship that you have demonstrated so far. My own studies of the Middle Ages have extended little beyond Littleton's *Tenures* and Fortescue's *De Laudibus Legum Angliae*. I am now, I confess, almost desperate to hear your story of the deaths of the two young princes."

He hastened forward to shake my hand energetically. The Magdalen men buzzed with pleasure, and, visibly moved, President Bulley himself then seized Masterman-Pugh's hand and shook it warmly. It was thus, happily, in a comforting atmosphere of cordiality that I resumed my lecture.

"You mention Chief Justice Fortescue, Masterman-Pugh. A loyal Lancastrian, he. The treatise that you name was drawn from his lectures to Prince Edward, the son of Margaret of Anjou and Henry the Sixth. Fortescue was Edward's tutor.

"But let me return to our investigation. My friend Mr. Holmes has a rule that he applies ardently in his investigations. 'Assume nothing; verify everything.' In that vein, we must first verify: Did the Two Little Princes die? Undoubtedly.

"But when and where and how did they die? We simply do not know. Did they die in Richard's reign? That is open to question. Did they die at Richard's hand? That is most definitely open to question. Were they murdered, or did they die of natural causes? We truly do not know. The best I can do is to lay before you what evidence I have gathered, and what historical assumptions, and to ask you to rid yourself of any pre-conceptions."

"And to send me the blessed account," interjected Masterman-Pugh, generating a hearty burst of good-natured laughter.

"Let me list for you the prime possibilities," I continued.

"One: The boys died natural deaths during Richard's reign, at the Tower or elsewhere; but, for reasons entirely inexplicable, Richard did not make this known. If this happened, his silence was a gross error.

"Two: The boys were indeed murdered at the Tower, on Richard's command or with his knowledge, as his many enemies aver.

"Three: The boys were murdered at the Tower, but not on Richard's command or with his knowledge. Those who hew to this theory generally point the finger of accusation at Henry Stafford, the Duke of Buckingham. Some accuse Henry the Seventh.

"Four: Richard secretly removed the boys from the Tower, and *then* murdered them.

"Five: Richard secretly removed the boys from the Tower, but sent them away for safekeeping. Perhaps in the North, as Clements Markham proposes, but more probably with Richard's sister Margaret, dowager duchess of Burgundy, in Burgundy.

"Six: Richard secretly removed the boys from the Tower, but they were lost in a shipwreck on their way to Margaret in Burgundy.

"Seven: Someone other than Richard took the princes from the Tower, and without his knowledge. Perhaps the Woodvilles, perhaps agents of Henry Tudor, or even agents of the French.

"Eight: The boys lived into Henry' Tudor's reign, then died natural deaths but *Henry* did not make this known.

"Nine: The boys were murdered, at the Tower or elsewhere, during Henry's reign, on the command of Henry the Seventh or with his knowledge.

"Ten: The boys were murdered during Henry's reign, but not on the command of, or with the knowledge of, Henry the Seventh."

I surveyed my audience and saw several heads nodding as their owners followed my list. They sat rapt, beneath a thick cloud of tobacco smoke.

"I shall not address all ten possibilities one by one, but shall cover the essential ground.

"Let me say again: We truly do not know when, where or how the boys died," I continued. "But let us start with the seminal story told by Thomas More. Yeoman Warder Baker will assist me by reading to you More's account." This Baker did with enviable confidence. He began his recital with those significant words of More's: "I shall rehearse you the dolorous end of those babes, not after every way that I have heard, but after that way I have heard by such men and by such means as methinks it were hard but it should be true.*"

"Yet for all that," I pointed out, as Baker sat down, "Master More also wrote that 'Some remain yet in doubt whether they were in his days destroyed or no'."

"Let us assume nothing and verify everything," I repeated.

"First, were the Two Little Princes ever in the Tower? Can we verify that? We can verify that young Edward, the uncrowned Edward the Fifth, was moved to the Tower at some point between May 9th and May 19th, 1483. We can verify that his younger brother Richard was taken to the Tower on

June 16th. Following which, if you believe the words of *Fabyan's Chronicle*, 'They never came abroad after.' That, however, we can not verify.

"Second, were they murdered, there or elsewhere? As I say, we truly do not know. Mr. Gairdner insists that all the evidence points to their having been slain in August 1483. According to More's story, read so dramatically to you just now by Yeoman Warder Baker, they were smothered by assassins acting for Richard the Third. Yet at the same time More says that there were *other* stories about their fate, and that there were doubts that the boys were really killed during Richard's reign.

"Bernard André, Henry the Seventh's blind biographer and poet laureate, declared that Richard 'ordered the princes put to the sword.' Yet Polydore Virgil, the commissioned Italian historian working for Henry, reported a belief that 'the sons of Edward the Fourth were still alive, having been conveyed secretly away, and obscurely concealed in some distant region'. That, I repeat, is from Henry the Seventh's own historian. He does not, however, suggest *who* took them away and concealed them.

"Lord Chancellor Bacon also wrote in 1622 that reports circulated during the first two years of Henry's reign that one or both of the children were still alive.

"Why would these reports circulate if all were so sure that the boys had been killed in August 1483?

"It is true that, at some point or points, there circulated rumours of their deaths. As *Fabyan's Chronicle* recounts:– 'The common fame went that King Richard put to secret death the two sons of his brother.'

"The *Croyland Chronicle* is often quoted as saying that rumours of the boys' end arose in the summer of 1483. That, in fact, is not quite what *Croyland* says. It says that such a rumour arose *after* it had become known that Buckingham had broken with Richard. And the evidence indicates that this break was not generally known until October 1483, rather than in the summer. I believe that Richard himself did not learn of the extent of Buckingham's betrayal until the second week of October.

"Further, the fact that there were rumours of the boys' deaths does not mean that the boys truly *were* dead. Were those rumours in fact spread, falsely, by Buckingham and Morton and their agents, to win support for this rebellion? The Latin of the *Croyland Chronicle* is unfortunately not precise, but it can fairly be read, in the context, as suggesting that the rumours were false, and were spread to further the rebellion.

"Allow me to make a very important point here: The *Croyland* chronicler, who was often inimical towards Richard, *never accuses Richard of their murder*. He says only that there were rumours that they were dead. Entirely free to accuse Richard after Richard's death, the chronicler significantly does *not* accuse him.

"Now, I agree that he included a poem in Latin, by 'a certain poet', that some have translated as saying Richard 'destroyed' the princes. However, the Latin word the poet used was 'opprimeret', which can in fact be translated as 'overpowered', 'suppressed', 'blocked' or, to use a chess term, 'checkmated'. It does *not* have to mean murdered or destroyed." I saw heads nodding from the Magdalen men who understood Latin.

"Rumours of the boy's deaths arose also in Europe. The Chancellor of France said that the boys had been slain and that their assassin had been crowned; but his remarks were not made until January 1484 and France, of course, had no love for Richard.

"It has even been suggested that Richard spread the rumour of their deaths himself, to make it clear that he was the only male Yorkist heir alive, to confuse his enemies and also to extinguish any spark of rebellion.

"Mr. Gairdner will tell you that 'The belief in this murder appears to have been general'. He simply does not establish that generality of scope as fact, however.

"And, indeed, some years after the disappearance of the Two Little Princes, a pretender named Perkin Warbeck appeared, claiming to be the younger prince. This Warbeck may, or may not, have been a horse trained and entered by Margaret of Burgundy, sister of Richard the Third and Edward the Fourth.

"Warbeck may or may not have been the surviving younger prince, Richard. We do not know. He may or may not have been an illegitimate son of Edward the Fourth. We do not know. Whoever he was, posing as the young Prince Richard, he gave out that his elder brother Edward had been murdered. He later confessed – or was forced to confess by Henry the Seventh – that he was not Prince Richard, but a commoner, and a foreign commoner, to boot. While most historians these days do believe that he was indeed an impostor that, in fact, has never been proven.

"We must note that at the time, however, this Warbeck did attract some well placed believers. That in itself suggests that Gairdner speaks too confidently, and that the demise of the princes was *not* so generally believed, even in higher circles.

"In turn, Markham will tell you that the rumours and reports of assassination mentioned by *Croyland* and the French chancellor were generated by Morton. But Markham does not establish that case, either. Morton may indeed have taken initial refuge at Ely, which is not far from Croyland, but that does not prove that Morton was the informant for the *Croyland Chronicle*. Indeed, since the *Chronicle* does *not* accuse Richard of killing the boys, it is surely unlikely that Morton was its source.

"The French chancellor, Guillaume de Rochefort, said in an official speech in January, 1484, that the boys had been murdered and that the crown had been 'transferred to their murderer.' Those remarks may in truth have followed Morton's arrival on the continent; but that coincidence does not establish that Morton was the fount of the statements.

"Let me return, then, to the realm of facts, to try to determine when the boys supposedly met their end.

"John Rous says that the boys were killed three months after April 30th, 1483; another vote for August, therefore. De Comines first puts the boys' deaths before Richard's

251

coronation on July 6th, but then goes on to place the deaths after that event. The unreliable Frenchman Jean Molinet says that the boys died in July. Unreliable? He gives Prince Edward's age incorrectly, and says the younger prince, Richard, was called George. I have also heard an argument for June, close to Richard's accession. However, Sir Robert Brackenbury, named by More as the Constable of the Tower at the time, was not appointed until well into July 1483. If More's chronology is to be believed, the boys were killed in the second or third week of August. It is thus commonly said that the boys were assassinated in August 1483.

"Even so, the *Croyland Chronicle* may in fact suggest a later date. The chronicle refers to a 'second coronation' for Richard the Third, in York. We now know that there was no second coronation, and that the ceremony in question was in fact the investiture of King Richard's own son, Edward, as Prince of Wales. We know that this took place on September 8th, 1483. And what *Croyland* goes on to say is this:–

> "'Meanwhile, and while these things were going on, the two sons of King Edward were under an especially appointed guard in the Tower of London.'

"That seems to indicate that the boys were still alive, then, if in prison, on September 8th. *Croyland* also reports that the rationale for Buckingham's rebellion was to liberate the boys from the Tower. They were alive at that point, then.

"According to Richard Grafton, the later Tudor writer, Richard confessed the murder of the Two Little Princes to Buckingham, in Gloucester.

"I mention Grafton because of the dates. We know that Richard was in Gloucester on August 2nd or 3rd. Therefore, according to Grafton, the princes were already dead at that time. According to More and those who follow More, it was not until Richard was in Warwick, beginning on August 8th, that he dispatched his assassins to London for the second time, the first attempt having been rebuffed by Brackenbury. Polydore Virgil, however, says that Tyrrel rode to London from York, and we know that Richard was not in York until

August 29th. So we have quite a span of dates proposed for 1483.

"Clements Markham offers an interesting document that, he argues, proves that the princes were still alive much, much later, in 1485.

"He cites a warrant dated March 9th, 1485, directing that some clothes be delivered to 'John Goddstande, footman unto the Lord Bastard.' It may be argued that this does not refer to Prince Edward, but to John of Gloucester, illegitimate son of Richard the Third. But John of Gloucester was not a lord. Edward *was* a lord, and is so referred to in other documents. Markham thus holds that there was only one 'Lord Bastard', Prince Edward, and that he was therefore alive in 1485. This thesis is clearly not proven, however, and is most furiously challenged by James Gairdner.

"Markham cites a second document that, he insists, shows that the Two Little Princes were at one of Richard's estates in the North. However, while the document does speak of children there, and makes it obvious that they were of very high rank, it does not explicitly say *who* these children were. Markham's theory could conceivably be true, though. Richard accommodated his brother George's son at Sheriff Hutton castle in Yorkshire. As the threat of a Tudor invasion from France mounted, he also sent his niece Elizabeth of York there for safety. Perhaps the Two Little Princes had been similarly sent north. Or perhaps they were sent abroad, to Richard's sister in Burgundy. But for these theories, we have no evidence and, if they were sent away, we do not know what happened to them, or why they were never found there.

"Let us, however, put aside all these points of doubt. Let us say that the charge against Richard tonight, in our Magdalen court of historical justice, is the murder of both boys in August 1483; and we shall examine the evidence in that case.

"Where was Richard in August 1483? We know that on July 23rd he began his royal progress from Windsor. On July 24th and 25th, of course, he was here at Magdalen. He went on to Woodstock and Minster Lovell, and by August 2nd he was at Gloucester. It was from Gloucester, supposedly, that he

253

dispatched John Green to Sir Robert Brackenbury, with a letter from Richard, and a command to put the two princes to death. According to More's story, Brackenbury refused, and Green rode off to report this to Richard at Warwick. Our best information is that Richard was at Warwick from August 8th to August 13th.

"Again, according to More, Sir James Tyrrel was thereupon sent to get the keys of the Tower from Brackenbury, and on the following night the boys were murdered. We can say, then, if More's story is true in some degree, that this was in the second or third week of August. Richard, meanwhile, went on from Warwick to Coventry, and then on to Leicester, Nottingham, Pontefract and York. He did not leave York until September 20th. He stopped here at Oxford again, on October 28th, and was not back in London again until November 25th."

The heads of my Magdalen audience bobbed in concentration, comprehension and obviously genuine interest as they intently followed my dates. Holmes favoured me with a supportive wink, and Masterman-Pugh with an open and friendly smile. Baker's round and honest face, too, beamed approval.

"The second or third week of August, *if* More's tale is true.

"Let us now examine that tale, as read to you just now by Yeoman Warder Baker. It is detailed. It is elaborate. Markham declares that it is *too* elaborate. Even Mr. Gairdner, while accepting the thrust of More's story, concedes that it contains 'certain details which it does seem difficult to accept as credible'. And we must all of us wonder how and why some of the supposed details, which could have been known only to the secret assassins themselves, reached Thomas More, who wrote about it some thirty years later.

"Let me begin with More's *dramatis personae*. There is John Green, who is supposedly sent with heinous orders to Sir Robert Brackenbury. According to More, Green is a 'trusty follower' and yeoman of Richard. We do know that one John Green was comptroller of the customs at Boston, before August 1483, and had supplied the royal stables. We are told in one report, of unknown authority, that after the murder he received two lordships, the receivership of the Isle of Wight, and the castle of Portchester. It seems to be assumed that these were his rewards for the double assassination, but I cannot find evidence of this, nor can I find proof that we are even talking about the same John Green. It would have been a common enough name.

"Sir Robert Brackenbury? He is well known to history; there are no doubts there. Constable of the Tower, keeper of the royal mint there, and keeper of the king's lions. A loyal supporter of Richard, steadfast to the end. He died fighting for Richard at the final Battle of Bosworth. Now, he supposedly first refused this dreadful criminal commission from John Green, and Green immediately ran back to Richard. One wonders why, if Richard was *really* behind some plot to murder the two boys, he did not carefully sound out Brackenbury before leaving London. Later writers, we should note, paint Brackenbury as a true gentleman, and do not accuse him of the least complicity in any such crime.

"We are then asked to believe that another player, a page, heard the king's frustrated annoyance – while Richard was sitting in the privy, for heaven's sake – and drew to the king's attention Sir James Tyrrel as a suitable candidate for a royal assassin. We know no more of this page, if he ever existed.

"Sitting in the privy. A suitably indelicate piece of information; but it is surely a significant question as to how such a precise piece of very private intelligence, presumably known only to Richard and the page, later reached Thomas More to be cited as an historical fact. Certainly Thomas More never spoke to the page.

"And how likely is it that Richard the king, in the privy or elsewhere, would declare to a mere *page* that he was offering a situation for a murderer?

"Now then, who was Sir James Tyrrel, who would supposedly be nominated by this page as a royal murderer?

"Tyrrel was, as one author puts it, of 'ancient and high family', and held various offices. Edward the Fourth chose him as a commissioner for the office of High Constable. He was Master of the Horse for Edward, and he attended

Richard's coronation in that office. He was Master of the Pages for Richard, and a member of Richard's royal body guard. He and his qualities were, as you can therefore see, well known to Richard, and no mere page would have needed to introduce or to recommend him.

"And let us note here another significant point. Thomas More says that Tyrrel was knighted as a reward for murdering the two princes in the summer of 1483, but that, gentlemen, is demonstrably untrue. Tyrrel was, in fact, knighted by Edward the Fourth in 1471, and in 1482 Richard created him a knight banneret, for his merits in the Scottish campaign. One more egregious mistruth to Master More's discredit.

"I shall return to Sir James Tyrrel, but allow me first to continue with my cast of other characters from More.

"There is William Slaughter, Black Will, one of the princes' guards or servants. We know nothing more about him than the name.

"One of the accused murderers was one Miles Forest, who supposedly had killed before. We know nothing of that, or of his past, or of his past victim or victims. He appears, according to More, to have been one of the princes' gaolers.

"According to some authors, one Miles Forest is also recorded as keeper of the wardrobe for Richard's mother at Baynard's Castle, at her home on the Thames in London. They suggest that this situation was Forest's reward for murdering her grandsons in cold blood.

"Markham has seen the relevant document himself, however, and it quite clearly says that Miles Forest was a servant at *Barnard* Castle, one of Richard's properties in County Durham, not at *Baynard's* Castle. Gairdner agrees that this is so.

"And I must further note that, as with Green, we do not know if this was the same Miles Forest named in More's tale, or whether there were two Miles Forests.

"The other assassin named by More was one John Dighton. He supposedly was Tyrrel's groom or horsekeeper. There is no known record to support that. We do know that Richard appointed a John Dighton as bailiff of Aiton, in Staffordshire.

Once more, however, we do not know if this was the same John Dighton, or another with the same name.

"Who else could or would have known details of the murder of the princes? The page who told Richard of Sir James Tyrrel? We hear no more of him in More's *History*, or in any other. The priest who supposedly reburied the bodies, and then conveniently died? We hear no more of him, either. The other attendants and Tower *employés* who were sent from the scene before the assassination? We know nothing of them. And while they may have had the darkest suspicions about the subsequent disappearance of the princes, they obviously had no inside knowledge of the slayings.

"In all, I think, we have eight men who, at least in More's tale, knew directly of the supposed murder. Leaving aside the royal page, whose name and extent of knowledge are unknown to us, our eight are Richard the Third himself, Green, Tyrrel, Brackenbury, Slaughter, Forest, Dighton, and the Tower priest. Now, what became of them?

"Richard was killed at Bosworth Field. So was Brackenbury. The priest, if he ever existed, vanished from history, and died before he could say where the boys were buried. Of the fates of Black Will Slaughter and John Green, too, we know nothing further. We are left with three remaining suspects: Tyrrel, Forest and Dighton."

My audience was still engrossed in my unfolding story. My voice, however, was beginning to rasp and fade. My jaw ached, and my brain and body were weary. With a glance at my watch, I decided to end the night's meeting on a suitably dramatic note.

"With your permission, gentlemen, we shall, as President Bulley so generously suggested, resume tomorrow morning.

"At which time I shall tell you about the extraordinary confession, by an honoured knight of England, to this supposed murder."

Chapter Fourteen

It seemed that the affairs of Magdalen had been set aside for me after breakfast the next day. The State Room was full, and I was both proud and a little shaken. Even more surprising was a new face, that of Miss Rivas.

"How on earth did you get here?" I asked.

"Mr. Holmes can keep a secret, I see," said she, with a warm smile. "He and President Bulley kindly prevailed upon my headmistress. Miss Black was deeply impressed by receiving a telegram yesterday from the President of Magdalen himself, and moved heaven and earth to have me on the next train. I arrived last night, and have three days of leave. I am expected to reciprocate, mind you, by addressing on my return a local historical society in which Miss Black is prominent."

With happily renewed spirit, I faced my audience.

"Let me start with Henry Tudor's capture of the crown," I began. "In June 1485, Richard proclaims Henry a traitor who has plotted with France. Richard sends instructions to officials in every county to have soldiers equipped and ready. Henry, meanwhile, assembles an army of mercenaries from France and Brittany. He sails from Harfleur on July 26th, 1485, and lands in Wales, at Milford Haven, on August 1st. He calls himself Earl of Richmond, although that is not legally his title. It had been his father's, true, but had been taken back by Edward the Fourth. At one point, indeed, it was *Richard* who was the Earl of Richmond.

"Henry recruits more men in Wales, and marches into England by way of Shrewsbury. Now we come to August 22nd, 1485, and the Battle of Bosworth.

"The opportunist Stanleys – Lord Stanley, who is Tudor's step-father, and Stanley's brother William – abandon Richard and go over to Henry. Hah! The Stanley motto was *Sans Changer*; it should have been *Toujours Changer*. Then Henry Percy, Earl of Northumberland, holds back Richard's rearguard, perhaps through a mis-understanding or from an excess of caution, but probably by design.

"The battle is lost. Fighting bravely, and trying to force his way through the ranks to cut down Henry himself, Richard is felled, the last English king to die on the battlefield. He is hacked savagely to death.

"Then his body is stripped, perhaps by some of Henry's men as a mark of contempt, or perhaps by battlefield looters. His corpse is thrown over a horse and taken to Leicester. By all accounts, he was buried there, in the church of the Grey Friars, and Henry the Seventh later provided some sort of monument.

"In the time of Henry the Eighth, however, the church was plundered and demolished. Tradition says Richard's grave was desecrated, and a much later tale proposes that his bones were thrown into the River Soar. However, it is more likely that they are still somewhere, now unmarked, beneath the site of the old Franciscan church.

"At Bosworth, we begin to learn something of Henry's devious character. He starts by dating the beginning of his reign from August 21st, the day *before* Bosworth. A crafty device, by which he could later attaint Richard and a number of his followers.

"Henry goes to London. The Tower falls into his possession; the Tower where, we are told, the Two Little Princes have been cruelly murdered and have disappeared.

"And what does Henry do?"

I paused for effect.

"*Nothing,*" I declared, my voice ringing.

"He does nothing. He says nothing. Nothing at all. It would surely well suit Henry to proclaim throughout the land that Richard had foully murdered his two sweet, innocent little nephews. It would surely strengthen Henry's case; it would surely destroy the last trace of any sympathy and support for Richard. But Henry does and says *nothing*.

I paused, and surveyed my audience intently. "Think of it this way: Henry takes over the Tower. If he finds the boys are missing, does he not ask what has happened to them? And if Richard has assassinated them, surely at least *one* person would speak up. 'Well, your Majesty, they *were* here, yes, but one day Sir James Tyrrel came and got the keys, and we have not seen hide nor hair of the little lads since then.'

"It is simply not conceivable that nothing was found or said. But Henry did and said *nothing*. There is no record of a hue and cry. Does he arrest Tyrrel? No, he leaves him in his post over in Calais, gives him government commissions, and pays him well.

"Later, Henry's Act of Parliament attainting Richard did not accuse Richard of murdering the princes. It charged Richard explicitly with numerous crimes, among them the 'shedding of infants blood.' But it did not say that by this was meant the murder of the princes."

"What else could it mean?" interrupted Masterman-Pugh, sharply.

"That I cannot say," I replied. "But if it meant the assassination of the Two Little Princes, why on earth would Henry not say so? Surely this would have been a fundamental point on which Henry could immeasurably strengthen his case, and ruin Richard's. That is so obvious I think it unanswerable."

"Where was the apostrophe in the Act of Parliament?" interjected Holmes. "Infant's blood, singular; or infants' blood, plural?"

"The same question crossed my mind," I replied. "There was no apostrophe in either position."

Here, Henry Wilson, the junior bursar and librarian, broke in. "I am afraid that one can conclude nothing from the punctuation of a medieval document. There was simply no agreement then on the rules of punctuation, nor were there any conventions on spelling or the use of capital letters. Punctuation of that era cannot be relied upon to tell us anything."

Masterman-Pugh sniffed. "If the Act did *not* mean our two princes, then to whom else did it refer? You have no answer, I see, Doctor Watson."

"I have this answer: If Henry *did* mean the Two Little Princes, then why in heaven's name did he not say so? He did not. He did nothing and he said nothing. Henry had been up to his ears in plots before the rumours arose of the deaths of the princes. Whether or not the rumours were true, why on earth did Henry not seize upon the reports as a foundation for his invasion? At Bosworth, did Henry bolster his army's spirit with a ringing declaration that they were fighting this battle to avenge two innocent little children who had been murdered by their wicked uncle Richard? No, he did not; there is no contemporary report of any such speech.

"Oh, it is true that the writer Edward Hall *claims* that Henry made a speech that included this:–

"'Behold your Richard is both Tarquin and Nero; yea, a tyrant more than Nero, for he hath not only murdered his nephew being his king and sovereign lord, bastarded his noble brethren and defamed the womb of his virtuous and womanly mother, but also compassed all the means and ways that he could invent how to stup'rate and carnally know his own niece under the pretence of cloaked matrimony, which lady I have sworn and promised to take to my mate and wife."

"But historians accept that Hall, who was writing in the mid-1500s, simply made up this speech. After all, Hall also quotes Richard as admitting in *his* pre-battle speech that he killed the Two Little Princes:–

"'I, being seduced and provoked by sinister counsel and diabolical temptation, did commit a facinorous and detestable act ... I have with strait penance and salt tears (as I trust) expiated and clearly purged the same offence, which abominable crime I require you of friendship as clearly to forget, as I daily remember to deplore and lament.'

"Good heavens above. Can you really envisage an experienced military leader, going into battle, trying to whip up morale and courage in his men by making a ridiculous appeal such as that? No, Hall obviously invented these speeches himself. And Hall, you know, is the fellow who called Henry 'more like an angelical creature than a terrestrial personage.'

"When Henry took the Crown, did he seek to justify it by *then* accusing Richard, throughout the realm, of the foul murder of two little boys? No, he did not.

"Let me sum it all up: Henry did not cite the murder of the Two Little Princes as the *raison d'être*, or even as one reason, for his invasion and war. He produced no bodies. He did not proclaim the death or even the disappearance of the boys. He did not accuse Richard.

"The answer must be that the princes were *still alive* when Henry took the Crown. That they disappeared, therefore, during his reign. And surely that can only mean at his behest."

Masterman-Pugh looked hard at me. "But if they were still alive in Richard's time, why did Richard simply not produce them when rumours held that they were dead? Why did he not clear the air?"

"I trust that you are not suggesting that Richard must be guilty, on the grounds that he failed to prove his innocence," I replied, carefully.

Miss Rivas caught my eye, and smiled at this *riposte*.

"One theory as to why he did not speak out, or produce the boys," I continued, "is that he had good reason not to. At a superficial glance, your question is a telling one. But if Richard did show that they were still alive, then their allies in the nobility would have a more concrete and visible reason to rally, the Scots would come to their aid, and the French would inevitably have joined the campaign, or even have started it. By continuing to conceal the boys and their fate, Richard could keep his enemies off-balance and guessing. Silence was the best policy. Indeed, if you believe Polydore Virgil, Richard himself allowed rumours of the boys' deaths to circulate, to reinforce acceptance of his kingship. Frankly, I cannot see why silence under such circumstances would help Richard.

"But there could be quite another explanation: Richard did not know where the boys were, or what had happened to them. Picture this: The Tudor rebels or the French sneak one or two men into the Tower, with the connivance of insiders. They remove the boys, telling them that they are being rescued from their evil uncle. They take them somewhere secret, and then, or later, kill and bury them. Or tie weights to them and drop them into the Thames. Their disappearance is quickly noticed at the Tower, but neither Brackenbury nor Richard has a clue about what happened, where the boys are, or whether they are still alive. If Richard cannot *prove* what happened, he will obviously be the prime suspect. He will certainly be convicted in the Court of Public Opinion. So, wise or unwisely, he stays silent. And thus becomes convicted in the Court of Public Opinion anyway."

Masterman-Pugh shook his head heavily, with doubt branded deeply across his face. "I remain hard to persuade on all this. But did you not say last night that a knight confessed? Who was that?"

"Oh, yes. Years later, in 1491, the foreign pretender Perkin Warbeck came to the surface. Warbeck claimed to be the young Prince Richard, and began to gain remarkable support. It all took time, but by 1495 even William Stanley, of all people, was somehow involved in the Warbeck plot. Naturally, the Scots and the French backed the plot. Henry arrested and executed Stanley. In 1497, Henry managed to capture Warbeck in England, got him to confess that he was an impostor, and executed him in 1498.

"But Henry had *still* not proclaimed the deaths of the Two Little Princes, and his silence threatened him. If people believed that one or both of the boys was still alive, would not rebellion find a foundation? Could not yet another pretender emerge, posing as one of the princes, and win support? In 1502, Henry eventually arrested Sir James Tyrrel and John Dighton. And, according to the account of Richard Grafton, Henry subsequently announced that the pair had confessed under examination to the assassination of the two princes.

"Let me re-introduce Richard Grafton. Thomas More never completed or published his little book. Why, we do not know. Some of those who defend Richard propose that it was because More had come to see that what he had been told about Richard, by Morton and the others, was simply not true. Whatever the reason, More's account did not appear in print until 1543. The publisher was Richard Grafton.

"But More's own story simply breaks off in 1483. Grafton went on to provide a 'continuation' of More. It picks up from More in, as it were, mid-conversation between Morton and Buckingham. Grafton's account is so detailed that some claim he obviously got his information from Morton. That we cannot confirm. But in the case of Tyrrel's supposed confession, we can say that it was certainly *not* Morton. Morton died in 1500, and we speak here of events in 1502.

"Gairdner insists that Grafton obviously had some reliable authority. But Lord Bacon says that Tyrrel's confession was as Henry the Seventh himself gave out. Perhaps, then, Henry himself was the fount and authority. If so, his value as a source is patently tainted.

"Regardless, something very peculiar happened, or, rather, did not happen. Inexplicably, Henry did not publish and circulate Tyrrel's confession.

"Henry's son Arthur had just died. It would have served Henry well to prove that there were no Yorkist heirs alive, and to prove that Perkin Warbeck could not have been Prince Richard. Thomas More says that Tyrrel's confession was 'well known'. But was it? Lord Bacon wrote that Henry, supposedly armed with confessions from Tyrrel and Dighton, 'made no use of them in any of his declarations.'

"There is no record of such a confession or confessions; none was given to Parliament; there is not even a mention of one. If there had been such a confession, surely Polydore Virgil would have known of it, as Henry's official historian, with full access to the records; but, writing well after Tyrrel's execution, Virgil does not speak of it at all. Nor does Bernard André, Henry's official biographer. Nor does Robert Fabyan, the London chronicler. No mention of it at all; full stop."

"As I have just said, if you read Lord Chancellor Bacon's account, you will find that the story of Tyrrel's confession was, in Bacon's words, 'as the king gave out.' Let me underline that: nothing in writing, no record, but merely a story that 'the king gave out.'

"Further, Dighton was set free. Bacon suggests that this was so that he would go and spread the story. A most peculiar way to treat the murderer of two little boys who were heirs to the throne, would you not say? Would a king simply free a regicide like that? Further, there is no evidence that Dighton ever *did* spread the story. And if he really was at large, why on earth did not Thomas More seek him out and get the story first-hand?

"There is an even more peculiar thing to note: The crime for which Tyrrel was eventually executed was *not* the murder of the Two Little Princes. If there *was* such a confession, why on earth not?

"If Tyrrel really had confessed, why did not Thomas More simply relate the story of Tyrrel's villainous deed as incontrovertible fact, and forego the mention of *other* stories? After all, it is only More – in Grafton's version – who says that there ever was such a confession. If Tyrrel had confessed, how could Polydore Virgil write just two years later that 'with what kind of death these innocent children were executed, it is certainly not known'? And why did nobody know where they had been buried?

"There were no public accusations of Tyrrel. And what did Henry do to punish Tyrrel and Dighton in connection with the murders of the Two Little Princes? He did nothing. And there is no record of Miles Forest ever being arrested or accused at all, or John Green, or Will Slaughter.

"If Henry had suspected Tyrrel and Dighton of murdering the boys on Richard's behalf, why did he not arrest and examine them earlier, before Warbeck appeared, or when Warbeck was under arrest?

"It was not until 1502 – that is, some seventeen years after Henry seized the crown – that he finally threw Tyrrel in the Tower. And I repeat: It was *not* for the murder of the princes.

"Tyrrel was accused, rather, of aiding in the escape from England of the Two Little Princes' Yorkist cousin, Edmund de la Pole, Duke of Suffolk, in 1501. And it was for *this* that Tyrrel was executed, not for the murder of the princes.

"James Gairdner proposes that Tyrrel perhaps confessed to the murder of the Two Little Princes to ease his conscience, as he faced the block for his support of De la Pole; and Gairdner further suggests that this was the first Henry learned of Tyrrel's involvement in the murder. But even Gairdner finds that the purported confession looks 'exceedingly suspicious'.

President Bulley elegantly shook his majestic head. "How do you explain all this, Doctor Watson? It does strike me as quite extraordinary that Henry did not firmly seize the occasion, at and after Bosworth, publicly to accuse Richard. If the bodies of the children had been moved and somehow lost, well, why did not Henry raise a storm against Richard, regardless?

"And why wait until 1502 – some seventeen years later, as you observe – to clear up the matter? And if Henry was indeed trying to clear up the matter, why did he not make public Tyrrel's confession?"

I smiled heavily. "You invite me to speculate, President. And there are some possibilities that could explain it.

"Possibility the first: It was not Richard but Henry who disposed of the two youngsters.

"Let me propose a case against him. The boys were still alive when Henry took the crown. It was he who had them killed. I have never denied that Richard had opportunity, means, and perhaps motive. But Henry, too, definitely had motive, opportunity and means. More motive than Richard, one can argue. Richard was an anointed king. The princes were illegitimate, and but a modest threat to him, if any threat at all. They were a great deal more of a threat to Henry, because of his flawed and spurious claim to the throne; a claim that now relied on military conquest and not on heritage.

"Perhaps, therefore, More's story about Tyrrel and Dighton and Forest and the others is generally true, although it was not *Richard* who commissioned them to commit the murder, but *Henry*.

"After all, Tyrrel was a prominent Yorkist and agent of Richard, and Henry had him by the nose. What if Henry threatened to execute Tyrrel for treason? Henry had dated his reign from the day before Bosworth, and could accuse Tyrrel on that ground alone. Why did Henry spare and reward Tyrrel, when Henry executed or attainted some other prominent supporters of Richard? He quickly executed Sir William Catesby, for example. Catesby was initially Hastings's man, but betrayed him to Richard; he then rose in Richard's service, becoming Chancellor of the Exchequer and Speaker of Parliament. Henry quickly had *him* killed after Bosworth.

"But, somehow, Tyrrel continued very comfortably in public office under Henry. He was captain of the castle of Guisnes, guarding Calais. Richard had given him that post, before Bosworth, and Henry kept him in that situation, and then employed him on royal missions in Europe such as negotiating a treaty with the French.

"How is it that Tyrell escaped execution like Catesby? Suppose that Henry had told Tyrrel that the only way he could survive, and prosper, was to do Henry the favour of killing the boys? And then to stay out of the country.

"This, remember, is the Henry who was called a 'dark prince' by Sir Francis Bacon, a later chancellor of England and no friend of Richard the Third. Henry who brought us the infamous Star Chamber; Henry the secretive, Henry the manipulator, Henry the avaricious, Henry the extortionist."

I paused for effect, waiting until all eyes were riveted upon me.

"It would also explain something else. Back on June 16th, 1486, Tyrrel was granted a general pardon by Henry for unspecified offences. One month later, on July 16th, he was granted a *second* general pardon. One such pardon, for offences unspecified, was certainly not unusual in those days; a second – within a month – was, as far as I can determine, unique.

"The first pardon was presumably for so-called 'crimes' committed while Tyrrel was a Yorkist employed by Richard. The second, then, surely suggests Tyrrel had committed some further offence or offences while subsequently in the service of Henry. Does that mean that *this* was when the Two Little Princes died, between June 16th and July 16th, 1486, at Tyrrel's hands, on behalf of Henry?

"Then suppose that Henry came to believe in 1502 that Tyrrel was going to disclose the secret; or that Tyrrel threatened to do so. And so Henry had him executed.

"Further, I invite you to wonder why Henry in 1487 stripped the boys' mother, Elizabeth Woodville, of her estate, and confined her in the Abbey of Bermondsey. Henry said that it was because she broke a promise to him when she sent her daughters from sanctuary to Richard's court in 1484. But Henry did nothing about this supposed offence when he took the throne in 1485, and he did nothing about it in 1486, either. Why suddenly punish her now, in 1487? Was it because Elizabeth had accused *him* of murdering the Two Little Princes? She had found him out?

"To be fair, I have heard another explanation. In that year, 1487, another pretender, an English commoner called Lambert Simnel, led a rebellion. Pretending to be the son of Richard's late brother, George of Clarence, he won support from Ireland. Henry vanquished him and his troops at the Battle of Stoke. It is said that Elizabeth Woodville was involved in some way in the Simnel plot, and that is why Henry punished her. We cannot be certain.

"Let me return to the princes' bodies for a moment. Henry did not produce them. Was Thomas More right? Had the bodies been moved, in Richard's time, re-buried by the unknown priest who held a position at the Tower? Or did Henry know full well where they were, and how they had got there, because he had had them killed? Or had they been killed after Henry took the throne, but without Henry's knowledge or command?

"Now, there was a report that Henry searched the Tower for bodies. Lord Bacon says that Henry paid agents to investigate. But was this a genuine search for the bodies of the two princes? Because he need to confirm their deaths to secure his crown? Or was it a sham search, to make Henry *appear* innocent and Richard guilty? Was it a search that Henry *knew* would not succeed?

"And was there, in fact, such a search? None was reported by More, Virgil, or Bernard André.

"According to a man called John Rastell, Henry had 'all places open and digged' without success. That was written in 1529, and, I am afraid, raises immediate problems.

"We have no idea of *when* this supposed search took place, or how many places, if any, were 'digged'. Second, Rastell was Thomas More's brother-in-law. Third, Rastell, although a lawyer and publisher, was known to be an erratic character. He gave two entirely different versions of how the boys supposedly died. Either he had somehow, inexplicably, not read More's account in full, or he simply did not believe it. All in all, Rastell's credibility must be in doubt.

"Strange, is it not? A point against Richard is that he failed to prove that the boys were alive; the telling point against Henry is that he failed to prove that they were dead, and at Richard's hand."

Dean Rigaud threw back his head and laughed heartily. "Yes, I see. Richard needed to show the boys alive, and Henry to show that they were dead. But it seems that we will never know, in either man's case, whether it was a matter of 'He would not' or 'He could not'."

Masterman-Pugh interrupted. "This is all mere speculation, Doctor Watson. If Henry *had* quickly killed the boys, or if Tyrrel had done it for him, why would Henry need to dig? Why not promptly produce their bodies, attach the blame retrospectively to Richard, and hold a great public funeral so as to play upon the sympathies of the people?"

"Your question is fair," I returned. "One can only guess at Henry's actions and intentions. But suppose that Tyrrel, or other agents of Henry who killed the boys, had misunderstood Henry's intent, or had panicked, and tossed the boys' bodies into the Thames? There *were* also reports that they were thrown into the river or the sea, rather than buried. There were then no corpses for Henry to produce. His later hunt for them, if there was one, *was* a blind."

"But if Tyrrel *had* killed the boys at Henry's behest," asked Masterman-Pugh, "why would he have turned Yorkist again, and supported De la Pole?"

"Fear of Henry?" I suggested. "Promise of profit? There is no answer upon record."

I looked at each face in turn. All were paying close attention.

"Possibility the second: The boys were killed on Henry's behalf, but without his explicit direction. Perhaps his own mother, Margaret Beaufort, Countess of Richmond, had commissioned the murders; an accomplished plotter, she, and quite capable of it. Indeed, Sir George Buck, as an amateur historian, wrote that, according to some old manuscript he had seen, Morton and an un-named countess had poisoned the boys. Could that countess have been Margaret Beaufort?

"What about Henry's step-father, the time-server Lord Stanley? If the boys were out of the way, his step-son would be safe as king. Or perhaps French agents were sent by King Louis to aid Henry's cause. Or perhaps there was a repetition of the earlier historical instance of 'Who will rid me of this troublesome priest?' Who would rid Henry of these troublesome princes? Somebody did. Was it the French? Or was it Tyrrel, seeking to stay alive and to maintain his situation? Again, there were then no bodies for Henry to produce. Perhaps silence was the safest policy.

"Possibility the third: Henry did not kill the boys, but did remove them from the Tower and secrete them somewhere, perhaps overseas. He could keep them prisoner for as long as it suited him, or could produce them and make use of them if it suited him. Perhaps he sent the boys overseas, but their ship was wrecked and they were lost; it is a theory that I have heard also applied to Richard's time. In *that* theory, Tyrrel got the keys to the Tower not to kill the Two Little Princes but to smuggle them out of the Tower to safe-keeping, on behalf of Richard, who was sending them to his sister Margaret in Burgundy. They disappeared in a shipwreck, and that explains Richard's silence; he did not *know* what was their fate.

"Perhaps Henry smuggled the boys out of the Tower and sent them alive to France, but there the treacherous French killed them. This could certainly explain Henry's lack of public condemnation and action. The French were his especial friends. I remind you once more that Polydore Virgil, Henry the Seventh's own historian, reported a belief that the boys had been conveyed secretly away, and concealed. He does not suggest by whom, or to where."

I paused, to secure the full attention of my audience.

"Possibility the fourth: It was not Richard or Henry who killed the princes, but Buckingham."

President Bulley's voice called out. "I think I know my lines now, Doctor Watson. Did Buckingham have 'motive, opportunity and means'?" The Magdalen men laughed as Bulley thus continued the questioning but friendly approach of my academic audience.

"Indeed he had, President," I responded. "He had all three. For motive, one may lean upon the several theories as to why Buckingham rebelled against Richard. Whether for his own ends or for Henry's, whether he was seeking the throne for himself or for Henry, the boys had to be removed.

"As for means, he was Lord High Constable. That position would give him access to the Tower and authority there. He

272

undoubtedly out-ranked Brackenbury, the lieutenant of the Tower. Buckingham or his men could certainly have made their way into the princes' quarters. As for opportunity, Buckingham had plenty. Polydore Virgil says that Buckingham accompanied Richard on his progress, as far as Gloucester. But Buckingham's name is *not* on the list of dignitaries who attended here at Magdalen. His name would hardly have been omitted if he truly had been here. That means that Buckingham presumably stayed in London as Richard set off on the royal progress. He could have killed or abducted the boys then.

"We know that Buckingham was with Richard in Gloucester on August the 2nd or 3rd. We believe that Buckingham then went directly to his castle at Brecknock, where his so-called prisoner, Morton, suborned him. We know that Buckingham was in Wales, with an army, in early October. Between August and early October, however, we do not know all of his movements. He could again have had much opportunity to go to the Tower himself. Even if not, he could most certainly have dispatched agents at any time, under his authority as Constable.

"So, yes, President," I said with a nod to Bulley, "Buckingham also had motive, opportunity and means. But whether Buckingham did kill the boys is quite another, and unproven, question.

"The Flemish historian, De Comines, says explicitly at one point that Buckingham was the one who killed the Two Little Princes. However, De Comines elsewhere says that Richard killed them, or had them killed. The French writer Jean Molinet also says that Buckingham was believed to have been the murderer, although Molinet challenges the belief, and points his finger at Richard."

Masterman-Pugh rapped on the wooden arm of his chair. "You suggest that Buckingham had motive, opportunity and means to act on his own behalf, or that of Henry. However, could not Buckingham have indeed murdered the princes, but on the explicit orders of Richard?"

I nodded. "I have heard the proposition, of course, and it is an obvious one. Shakespeare in his play has Richard instructing Buckingham that 'I want the bastards dead.' But there is no evidence to support it. Again, Shakespeare strikes a blow for dramatic fancy, rather than fact.

"I suppose it is conceivable that Buckingham killed the boys not on Richard's behalf, or on his own behalf, but in Henry Tudor's interest. We know that Buckingham had been in touch with Henry in September, 1483. Perhaps the two were plotting together in August; but we have no evidence of that.

"However, let me offer you another possibility. What if Buckingham had *presumed* that Richard wanted the princes dead?"

"Hum!" mused Hopkins, the estates bursar and rowing enthusiast. "You mean that Buckingham, to please Richard, assassinated them without explicit orders from Richard? That is the theory? It is Becket again?"

"It is a popular theory," I replied. "And it is one that would explain why Richard remained silent to the end regarding the fate of the boys. You might expect that if Buckingham had killed the boys, Richard would publicly accuse him of it. In the circumstances, however, perhaps Richard could not expect people to believe that Buckingham had acted on his own, or that unknown assassins had managed to get into the boys' quarters, kill them, and remove the corpses.

"Perhaps Richard could not prove that Buckingham had done it. Worse, Buckingham could very well have threatened to accuse *Richard* of being the author of the crime. 'Oh, I would never have harmed the poor little boys myself, but the king told me to do it for the good of the country, and threatened to execute *me* if I did not obey'. Richard had to remain silent."

As the saying goes, you could have heard a pin drop in the room. I nodded at my audience.

"Grafton's edition of More's history declares that Richard disclosed to Buckingham, in Gloucester, that he had killed the princes. Let me find the words that Grafton attributes to Buckingham:–

> "'When I was credibly informed of the death of the two young innocents, his own natural nephews, contrary to his faith and promise (to the which, God be my judge, I never agreed nor condescended) O Lord, how my veins panted, how my body trembled, and how my heart inwardly grudged; insomuch that I so abhorred the sight, and much more the company of him, that I could no longer abide in his court, except I should be openly revenged.'

"Whereupon, we are told, Buckingham went off to his castle of Brecknock, where he was holding Morton as a state prisoner, and was soon persuaded by Morton to stage an armed rebellion against Richard.

"Grafton relates, in considerable detail, as if from an eye-witness, a long conversation between Morton and Buckingham. One is tempted to assume that some archival document of Morton's must have been Grafton's source; however, we have no certain knowledge either way. Regardless, Morton's honeyed words won Buckingham over to Henry's cause. Soon, Buckingham raised his revolt against Richard. Our foxy friend Morton, however, did not stand with his new ally; Morton instead fled from Brecknock to the fen country, and then to the Continent, where he joined Henry."

Holmes picked up the ball. "I wonder if Buckingham and Richard might have fallen out in Gloucester over *whether* the boys should be killed. Could it be that Richard disclosed his *intentions* to Buckingham on August 2nd or 3rd, then Buckingham broke with him in disagreement, and went to Brecknock?

"On the other hand, perhaps *Buckingham* was the one who proposed on the 2nd or 3rd that the boys be dispatched; Richard refused, and Buckingham stormed off to Brecknock, sending his own assassins to the Tower, in defiance of Richard. At that point, Brackenbury would not have known that Buckingham and Richard had fallen out. He would have obeyed orders from Buckingham that he thought had Richard's royal approval.

"But I have an important question: If Richard had so confessed to Buckingham, or had plotted with Buckingham, and that was all known to Morton and thence to More and Henry Tudor, then why would More and the others, years later, make note of the several reports that the boys were still alive? Why does there remain a mystery now in 1883?"

I nodded, and I could see Miss Rivas nodding with me.

"Precisely, Holmes, precisely. If Tyrrel and Dighton had really confessed to Henry, or if Richard had really confessed to Buckingham, why is there still a mystery? Why are we here today? Even if Tyrrel's confession itself had disappeared, surely at least the *date* of the murders would be remembered.

"But suppose that it really *was* Buckingham who disposed of the princes, in the hopes of pleasing Richard. He comes to Richard in Gloucester. 'I have done you an enormous service,' he tells the king, 'I have removed those wretched little boys for you. See, you have no better friend than me in all of England. Now reward me suitably.'

"In retrospect, it might have been wise for Richard promptly to arrest Buckingham for murder and execute him, of course. But Buckingham was a powerful man to tackle. And even if Richard had so challenged him, would England really have believed that Buckingham truly acted on his own? Richard's enemies would definitely not have believed it. Richard would inevitably have come under suspicion. Indeed, to defend himself, Buckingham might very well accuse *Richard* of being the real murderer or author of the murder. Perhaps, as I say, Buckingham threatened to do just that.

"I can see, therefore, that Richard might well have decided, simply if unwisely, to keep silent, to conceal the deaths, to act as if nothing happened, to keep Buckingham in office, and to pack him quietly off to Brecknock, and continue making State payments to him, all to gain some breathing room. 'Go to your castle, my friend. I will discuss your reward with you later.'

"In the event, as you know, the silver-tongued Morton seized Buckingham as a prize, before Richard could settle accounts with him. Richard could have accused Buckingham *after* executing him, but that would inevitably have been seen as altogether too convenient in timing. And perhaps it *was* better to keep Richard's enemies guessing as to whether the boys were alive or dead.

"Further, if Buckingham told Morton anything of value at Brecknock, it obviously did not include the details of the boys' deaths or of their burial; otherwise Morton would undoubtedly have passed the information on to Henry Tudor. Either Buckingham did not know, which is unlikely if Richard had in fact confessed to him; or Buckingham had good cause not to reveal the details to Morton; because he, Buckingham, was the murderer.

"I have suggested that perhaps More had the *manner* of the assassination right, but that it was Henry, not Richard, who commissioned Tyrrel to commit the murders. That construction could fit Buckingham, too. It could have been *Buckingham* who sent Tyrrel to do the job, citing royal authority from Richard.

"Another alternative is that Buckingham indeed had the boys killed, but did *not* admit that to Richard. What if he simply told Richard that the boys had vanished, taken from the Tower by agents unknown? Perhaps he blamed the Woodvilles? This would explain Richard's silence; he had no idea where the boys were, and would hardly be believed if he announced that they had simply vanished. He would *have* to keep quiet.

"So, to sum up: In the matter of the assassination of the Two Little Princes, Buckingham indeed had motive, opportunity and means.

"However, it is surely significant that when Buckingham went to the scaffold in November 1483, he said not a word about the deaths of the princes. Not a word to admit or to deny his own guilt or complicity, and not a word to accuse or acquit Richard. In the same vein, Richard did not accuse Buckingham of infanticide. Does not this suggest that both men were innocent of this crime, and that the boys were still alive?

"Until now, we have assumed that the boys were dead, and dead in August of 1483. We do not *know* that they were dead.

"And if they were not, we enter upon another possibility: That Richard did not kill the boys, but merely concealed them; shipped them to one of his Northern castles, or sent them overseas after becoming aware of people plotting to free them. Markham, as I have mentioned, is sure that the boys were in the North. Others suggest Richard might have sent the boys to his sister Margaret in Burgundy.

"Polydore Virgil, Henry's official historian, reported a belief that the boys had been taken away and hidden. After Buckingham's rebellion, Richard was well aware of the plotting of Morton, Tudor and the Lancastrians. The rumours about the deaths of the boys would quickly suggest to Richard that there was, or could be, a plot not to free them but to kill them and blame him. It would make sense for him to move them and to conceal them, to put them out of harm's way. Indeed, perhaps *that* was what the supposed letter to Sir Robert Brackenbury concerned: instructions to *move* the boys, not to kill them. A command that Sir Robert did not have to disobey.

"The disappearance of the boys would badly unsettle Henry; particularly if Richard maintained his silence. Henry might fear that, even if he did defeat Richard, a very live heir to the throne could turn up, with Yorkist support and Woodville support, and a legally stronger claim to the throne than Henry."

Yeoman Warder Baker politely raised his hand. "Or perhaps the *Woodvilles* smuggled the princes out of the Tower and took them to one of their strongholds. Useful tools they would be, for the Woodvilles. And if they had taken the boys secretly from the Tower, what was Richard to do and say? He would have to remain silent, at least until he found the Princes, or their bodies."

"If either were the case," interjected Masterman-Pugh, "then where in heaven's name *were* the boys? Why were they not produced or found? Why did they not turn up after the Battle of Bosworth?"

"Because Henry found them first and killed them," shot back Dean Warren. "Buckingham's silence upon the scaffold must suggest that neither he nor Richard had killed the boys, and that the youngsters were still alive. Henry's claim to the throne was very weak. If the Two Little Princes were alive, it was weaker still. It was in his interest to dispose of them."

Within seconds, the room was in unruly chaos. Arguments and counter-arguments flew among the Magdalen men. The debaters quickly formed three camps, accusing Richard of the murders, accusing Henry, or accusing Buckingham. I was surprised and stunned by this impact of my words.

I heard Masterman-Pugh snap at Warren:– "A cut-and-dried case, is it not? The princes were a threat; Richard had to remove them."

Warren replied heatedly:– "The same could be said for Henry; the princes were a threat to *him* and *he* had to remove them."

Dean Rigaud tossed in a new point. "If Richard *had* been bent on disposing of the princes, why did he not simply have a tame doctor issue reports of their declining health from a mortal illness; then smother the boys, and attribute their deaths to the illness? Nobody could have proved otherwise."

"Exactly," I broke in. "Killing the boys and remaining mysteriously silent would have been the stupidest thing Richard could do, and he was not a stupid man. He could have smothered them and told a convincing story about illness, as you suggest, but killing them and remaining silent would have been lunacy."

"But Richard did remain silent," said Masterman-Pugh, heavily.

"Because," returned Warren, "they were still alive. He had nothing to explain."

Henry Wilson spoke up. "If the boys were indeed dead in the summer of 1483, and Morton knew it, then Henry knew it too. So why didn't Henry immediately accuse Richard and use the murders and the accusation to reinforce his *coup*? Henry could thus quash any doubts as to whether they were alive or dead, and could attach the opprobrium for their deaths to Richard."

"What I don't understand," said Thomas Terry, almost shouting to be heard above the exchanges, "is the business of the princes' bodies. If they had been killed at the Tower as More says, then Tyrrel knew where the bodies were. If he confessed, why did not Henry exhume the bodies and give them a proper burial?"

"Because their bodies had been moved by the priest, sir," interjected Yeoman Warder Baker with a sarcastic smile. "A kindly priest who *could* have buried them in consecrated ground in the Church of St. Peter ad Vincula, a stone's throw away, but –"

"– who chose instead to dig a great big hole ten feet deep under a staircase, all by himself," broke in Terry. "And then he threw in a heavy wooden chest containing two bodies? And then covered it all up again? All by himself again? Unseen and unheard? And then he conveniently *died*? Oh, that is too fantastic."

"*Most* of Thomas More's account is fantastic," threw in Warren, derisively.

President Bulley struggled to restore order and decorum. "Doctor Watson, it appears that your jury is divided. But are we not premature in discussing the evidence? We act as if you have closed your case, but the court-room is still yours."

I bowed my head in appreciation.

"There is one more corner of the field that we must explore. To this point, we have concentrated upon the Two Little Princes. If they were threats to Richard's security upon the throne, they were not the only ones. So, how did Richard deal with these others? More foul murders.

"On the contrary, he was clearly above board.

"I give you the example of another of Richard's nephews, the son of his brother George, Duke of Clarence. Attainted, yes, but attainders could be, and were, reversed. One such had been reversed against Richard himself. This boy, another Edward, could also have been the rallying standard for rebellion. Even if, as some say, he was something of a simpleton, he was legitimate, and could have been a most useful tool for rebels. A tool who, they would obviously say, had a stronger legal right to the throne than Richard. Did Richard murder him to get him out of the way? No, he did not. Richard knighted him, placed him in a high position, and made him a member of his council.

"Does it make sense that Richard would murder two of his nephews – nephews who *might* have some claim to his crown – but leave alive the third nephew who *would* have a claim if his attainder were reversed?

"John Rous says that, after the death of his own son, Richard named George's boy as his heir. Rous is the only writer to say this, and I do not have to remind you of Rous's proven unreliability. Would Richard really have named a ten-year-old attainted simpleton as heir to the throne? I wonder.

"We do know that, after the death of Richard's boy, Richard's nephew, his sister's son, John de la Pole, was the nearest adult male heir. Richard named him Lieutenant of Ireland, and some historians say that this, in effect, confirmed him publicly as heir to the throne; just as Richard had named his own son as Lieutenant of Ireland, and just as Edward the Fourth had so named Clarence, then the ranking prince of the blood royal. Richard also named De la Pole as president of the Council of the North.

"What of George's daughter? Did Richard murder her? No, he treated her well and protected her. Arguably, she was a potential heir to the throne, although no woman had worn the crown of England; unless you count the unfortunate Matilda back in 1135, and Matilda's disputed claim to the crown was behind a long civil war.

"What about Edward the Fourth's five daughters? They, too, could have been regarded as heiresses to the crown, and used as rallying points for rebellion. In the summer of 1483, indeed, there were reports of a plot to get one or more of them out of England so that one of them could perhaps take the throne if anything happened to the boys. Did Richard murder them? No, he did not. He protected them and saw to their well-being."

The room was hushed again. Sipping from my glass of water, I picked up my skein once more.

"In contrast, what did Henry the Seventh do? He imprisoned George's boy for some fifteen years, and at length judicially murdered him. At the same time, he executed Perkin Warbeck. He gave a pension to Richard's bastard son John, but then threw him in gaol, and John died there. Henry married Edward the Fourth's eldest daughter Elizabeth, and that silenced her. One of the first things that Henry did after Bosworth was to arrest and imprison Bishop Stillington. Henry released him, then imprisoned him again without charging him with any offence. Henry further executed at least four other prominent Yorkists.

"Given that bloody record, if the Two Little Princes were still alive, what do *you* think happened to them under Henry?"

Into the ensuing buzz of conversation, President Bulley interjected a call to luncheon.

Holmes rose quickly to his feet. "If I may have a moment before luncheon, Miss Rivas, gentlemen? You have heard me speak of 'motive, opportunity and means'. Doctor Watson has ably addressed these issues in regard to each of the suspects. There is, however, another factor. The fuller expression that I use is, in fact, 'motive, opportunity, means and bent.' In other words, does the suspect – or in this case, do the suspects – have the bent to commit the crime, the inclination, the pre-disposition, the character."

This brought Masterman-Pugh to his feet as well.

"Thank you, Holmes; once more, you successfully read my mind. Doctor Watson, you are not merely an adept teacher of history, but an excellent *raconteur*. We must thank you, too, for the objectivity of your research. As soon as I begin to make up my mind in one direction, you undermine my case and send me off in another direction. I find myself not ready to reach a reasoned verdict without more subjective information.

Mr. Holmes has put it very well. Did Richard have the bent to commit such a murder?

"In short: What kind of a man was Richard?"

Chapter Fifteen

The question of Richard's character was well addressed in three letters that I had received from Miss Rivas. To give my voice a rest, I asked her to read them aloud herself to the men of Magdalen after our luncheon.

"Allow me first [she read] to deal with the question of whether Richard had a hunchback, or was physically deformed in some other way.

"My summer pupils think that this is a subject of rare fascination. Combining the supposed hunchback with Shakespeare's colourful description of Richard as a bottled spider, they have taken to attempting to scare the wits out of each other by portraying Richard as a macabre scuttling arachnid, twisted and hunched, limping on bent and halting legs, with a fiendishly contorted face and speaking with a wildly exaggerated and sinister lisp. As their drama teacher, I find this imaginative interpretation one that the Bard of Avon would no doubt hail as entirely authentic; as their history teacher, however, I must challenge the accuracy of their grotesque portrayal.

"Shakespeare indeed paints a monstrous picture of Richard:–

'Why, love foreswore me in my mother's womb;
And, for I should not deal in her soft laws,
She did corrupt frail nature with some bribe,
To shrink mine arm up like a wither'd shrub;

To make an envious mountain on my back,
Where sits deformity to mock my body;
To shape my legs of unequal size;
To disproportion me in every part.'

"The fact of the matter, however, is that not one contemporary account, other than that of the unreliable John Rous, mentions any deformity whatsoever.

"The *Fleetwood* chronicler saw Richard in person. The annalist William of Worcester saw him in person. So did the abbot of St. Alban's. So did the chronicler Robert Fabyan. Sir John Paston, of the *Paston Letters,* saw him in person, and knew him and his family well. The chronicler of Croyland must have seen Richard in person. Philippe De Comines saw him in person, in France. Yet not one of them speaks of any deformity at all.

"Rous saw Richard in person, at Warwick. Later, after Richard's death, he described Richard as 'small of stature, having a short face and uneven shoulders, the left being lower than the right.' (Rous, of course, was the ardent Lancastrian who also maintained that Richard was two years in his mother's womb.)

"Thomas More wrote precisely the opposite, that Richard's left shoulder was higher than his right. In full, More described Richard as 'little of stature, ill-featured of limbs, crook-backed, his left shoulder much higher than his right.'

"The great Erasmus, More's friend, recorded that Thomas More himself had a habit of carriage in which 'the right shoulder is a little higher than the left, especially when he walks.' Is that a strange coincidence? Or is More's description of Richard but literary symbolism, perhaps the author's proposal that the best of us contain a little bad, and the worst of us a little good?

"Polydore Virgil mentions the supposed inequality of Richard's shoulders, but fails to say which was the higher and which the lower.

"More, of course, also proposed, later on in his book, that Richard had in addition a withered arm.

"Given the circumstance and context of More's report – that Richard was claiming that his arm had newly become withered by witchcraft – we can simply dismiss this tale out of hand. If Richard had indeed had a withered arm, he would have had it for many years, and presumably since his birth, thirty years earlier. Obviously everybody around him would have known full well of it. Further, of course, Richard would have been well aware that they knew. It would have been ludicrous for him to act as More says that he did. Not one source other than More (and thence Shakespeare) mentions a withered arm. And is it likely that Richard could have been such an accomplished soldier with 'an envious mountain' on his back and one arm distorted like a 'wither'd shrub'?

"Later, Sir George Buck could find no evidence of deformity; and John Stow, the famous London antiquary and author, spoke in person with aged men who had seen Richard, and they, too, told of no deformity.

"Richard was stripped to the waist for anointment at his coronation; there is no mention of any deformity. Finally, his body was stripped naked at Bosworth, and seen by many; yet there is no report either of a hunchback or of a withered arm.

"Still, I suppose it is possible that he perhaps suffered from some slight curvature of the spine. This might explain the reports of one shoulder bring higher than another, and be exaggerated by his ill-wishers into a hunchback.

"Interestingly, by 1643, Richard's supposed deformities have somehow miraculously increased!

"By then, Sir Richard Baker's *Chronicles of the Kings of England* described Richard not only as crook-backed but also as 'hook-shouldered, splay-footed and goggle-eyed', and with a withered left arm. In 1665, another writer (a bishop, no less) invented 'a prominent gobber-tooth'. I can only suggest that these authors were, if you will pardon a play on words that I can not resist, entirely myth-taken.

"A number of surviving portraits of Richard, although clearly painted in later times, show no deformity.

"Indeed, the paintings show a man of serious but gentle mien, rather than that of Shakespeare's 'elvish-marked and abortive rooting hog'. Richard most certainly has no goggle-eyes or gobber-tooth. John Rous's own simple drawings of Richard show no physical defect. We should especially note that not even the drawing in Rous's revision of his work for the Tudors shows or suggests any deformity.

"An interesting story here, from the Records of the City of York, notes than in 1491, one William Burton (a school master, indeed) was accused before the Lord Mayor of describing Richard as 'crookback' who was 'buried in a ditch like a dog'. Burton's opponent in an unseemly squabble called him a liar and hit him with a stick. Of course, this being six years after Richard's death, Burton could well have been merely repeating Tudor propaganda.

"Caroline Halsted, whose rather fanciful and impassioned volumes of *Richard III as Duke of Gloucester and King of England* are beside me as I write, suggests that the shoulder of Richard's sword-arm (presumably his right) may indeed have been larger than the other, as a result of the exercise of his military training.

"This last suggestion I can neither confirm nor challenge, but clearly the Shakespearean portrayal of Richard as a horribly deformed hunchback is entirely out of court. It is a calumny heaped upon Richard by his enemies, their writers, and the egregious William Shakespeare."

Miss Rivas's second letter from York was long and fascinating:–

"I shall commence with an encomium of King Richard from Bishop Thomas Langton, who accompanied Richard on his royal progress; to wit:–

"'He contents the people where he goes better than ever did any prince, for many a poor man that hath suffered wrong many days has been relieved and helped by him and his orders in his progress. And in many great cities and towns were great sums of money given him which he hath refused. On my faith, I never liked the qualities of

288

any prince so well as his. God hath sent him to us for the weal of us all.'

"Is this the same man as the 'poisonous bunch-backed toad' of Shakespeare? Is the hideous, malignant, and depraved child-murderer, the corrupt and perverted monster portrayed by the Tudors?

"There are those who dismiss Langton as prejudiced. After all, he was a Northerner who had just been promoted to the bishopric of St. David's, and who was in 1485 to be given the greater See of Salisbury. Yet hear the words of Lord Chancellor Bacon:–

" '… a prince in military virtue approved, jealous of the honour of the English nation; and likewise a good law-maker for the ease and solace of the common people'.

"And Bacon was most certainly *not* an admirer of Richard, admitting these virtues but insisting that they were 'feigned'."

Miss Rivas looked up from her letter, and addressed directly the men of Magdalen. "Bishop Langton was here at Magdalen on Richard's royal progress. Your archives note his presence. Richard later sent him to Rome, to pay Richard's formal respects and homage to the Pope."

She resumed the reading of her letter. "Let me examine now, briefly, Richard's public record both before and after he became king. Unfortunately, few documents survive that attest to the personalities and politics of that era. I wonder how many Polydore Virgil *did* burn?

"There remain, however, documents that attest to many hundreds of Richard's grants, appointments and of items of the business of the state. Few shed much light to assist your investigation, but some do help in mine; and I think that from these it is clear that his government can be well summed up in one word: enlightened.

"Even your Mr. Gairdner writes this of Richard:–

"'As king he seems really to have studied his country's welfare, passed good laws, endeavoured to put an end to extortion, declined the free gifts offered to him by many towns, and declared he would rather have the hearts of his subjects than their money'.

"*Item:* Edward the Fourth exacted enormous sums of money from the wealthy. While these were called 'benevolences', they were in truth brute exactions extorted by royal pressure. Richard ended this disgraceful business. And it is important to recognise that what Richard did in this regard was to establish the vital principle and precedent that taxation is the prerogative of Parliament, not that of the king.

"Thomas More suggested that the gathering of money is 'the only thing that withdraws the hearts of Englishmen from a prince.' If, by ending these exactions, Richard won the hearts of Englishmen, surely he deserved them. It is true that, towards the end of his reign, Richard borrowed money from his nobles and from the church, but the chronicler Fabyan establishes that he gave 'good and sufficient pledges' for repayment, which his brother Edward most certainly had not done. Richard's need for money is hardly surprising, by the way, since the Woodvilles had looted a good part of Edward the Fourth's treasury from the Tower.

"*Item:* Richard's interest in the welfare of the common man and his attention to the complaints of ordinary people were well known and well recorded. Although your Mr. Gairdner cynically proposes that Richard did good deeds to buy friends, Richard gave freedom to many bondsmen. He compensated ordinary people who had lost property to fires. As Bishop Langton noted, Richard declined gifts from a number of cities, among them London, Worcester, Canterbury and Gloucester. He reversed Edward the Fourth's confiscation for royal use of large amounts of land in the area of Woodstock, where Edward had maintained a hunting lodge. Richard thus restored the land to its owners and users. He restored to the Priory of Pontefract land that Edward had taken. He gave to York a new and valuable charter. He granted to the city of Gloucester freedom from various fees and taxes, and created its own shire. He even made

Scarborough into a shire incorporate. These are but a few examples.

"*Item*: He had a keen interest in justice, and corrected a number of abuses.

"As Lord Chief Justice Campbell wrote in 1845:–

"'We have no difficulty in pronouncing Richard's parliament the most meritorious national assembly for protecting the liberty of the subject and putting down abuses in the administration of justice that had sat in England since the reign of Henry III.'

"Richard commanded England's judges to be impartial and just. He improved the jury system by requiring jurors to meet certain qualifications of property. He took steps to protect jurors from harassment and intimidation. He allowed Justices of the Peace to bail people who had been arrested on suspicion alone. He brought to an end deceptive and dishonest practices in the selling of properties. He prohibited the seizure of property from those who had been accused of felonies, but not yet convicted. He improved the 'pie-poudre' courts that regulated buyers and sellers at the fairs, and that dealt with their cheating, petty offences, and drunken disorders. He showed interest in, and acted upon, the complaints of the poor and the down-trodden. He provided assistance for penniless litigants, and this became, under the Tudors, the famous Court of Requests. He fought corruption in the public service and in the jury system. He improved the system of recording and accounting for royal expenditures. His Parliament's Acts were the first published in English, so that they could be read by more than just the *elite*. He passed edicts against gambling. He ended a number of abuses in property laws."

At this, Miss Rivas nodded, with a friendly and respectful smile, at Masterman-Pugh, himself a noted expert in the law of property.

"Even James Gairdner is forced to conclude:– 'The public acts of this Parliament have always been noted as wise and beneficial.'

"*Item:* Richard's regulation of trade and business was universally praised. While he protected English artisans, he also opened doors to foreign traders. He expanded the wool trade, and encouraged maritime commerce and the Northern fisheries. Here in the area of York, he had the river cleared of illegal private fish-traps that were obstructing mercantile vessels and robbing the ordinary folk of fish.

"*Item:* Richard was a benefactor of the university at Cambridge, as even John Rous noted. He gave most generously to King's College, although Henry the Sixth founded it. Richard endowed Queen's College with a grant of 500 marks a year, and established four Fellowships at Queen's – although Queen's had been founded by Margaret of Anjou and completed by Queen Elizabeth Woodville! He further gave to Queen's College and to the university 'great rents' from a number of properties and fairs in England. Much of this was done in Queen Anne's name. Your friends at Magdalen" – she looked up, with a quick smile – "will perhaps be disappointed that, while a patron of Oxford as well, Richard was less generous to that university. He did, however, give to Magdalen itself some land forfeited by the traitor Buckingham, and relieved Oxford of certain fees due to the king.

"*Item:* Richard generously supported the arts. He was a patron of composers, he made numerous grants to musicians and minstrels, and he established a royal band and choir. He gave birth to an Act that allowed printed books to be brought into England. We have some record of his own books and good literary taste. He was the patron of Caxton the printer, who dedicated to him his book *The Order of Chivalry.* In truth, Richard was in many ways a Renaissance king before that time.

"*Item:* He founded the College of Heralds, who still exist today as the College of Arms. He named the first Kings at Arms, granted their officers freedom from tolls, and provided them, at his expense, with a mansion in London as their quarters, and their own chaplain. By the way, Henry the Seventh then seized their building.

"*Item:* Reports and records are legion of his support of, and his donations to, the Church. At Middleham, for example, he founded and endowed a collegiate church with a dean and twelve priests. At Barnard's Castle, in County Durham, he founded another collegiate church, with a dean, twelve priests, ten chaplains and six choristers. He commissioned a chantry of one hundred chaplains at York Minster. This was still being established when he died, and was soon halted by the Tudors. He commissioned a college of priests at Barking in London. He gave rich ornaments and vestments to York Minster, as I have mentioned in a previous letter. He was a benefactor of many, many other churches, chapels, abbeys or monasteries, among them Tewkesbury Abbey, where were buried his brother George, and Edward the son of Henry the Sixth. He gave also to churches at Pontefract, Cambridge, Carlisle, Coverham and Skipton, and to St. George's Chapel at Windsor. He gave to the church a charter confirming clerical rights and immunities.

"He was widely hailed, therefore, as a generous benefactor of the Church, yet his opportunistic detractors quickly claimed that he had been so only because of a guilty conscience, either concerning his brother George's death or the deaths of the Two Little Princes. His critics' dice are *always* loaded against him.

"Richard's myriad titles, honours and dignities are too numerous to list and discuss. Before he became king, he was, among other things, Warden of the Northern Marches, Warden of the West Marches, Lord High Admiral, Great Chamberlain of England, Lord High Constable of England, High Sheriff of Cumberland and Cornwall, and Chief Steward of the Duchy of Lancaster. He held the earldoms of Dorset and Somerset, and scores of lordships, manorships, castles and estates.

"The mere holding of a title or estate was, and is, no guarantee of good character. However, we do know that, acting as King Edward's loyal viceroy of the North, Richard ruled with a fair and even hand. He ably preserved the peace, checked the forays of Scottish raiders, maintained the king's troops, and repaired the fortresses. As king himself, Richard made new alliances with Scotland and Spain. He also made a treaty with Brittany, although it failed in its prime purpose. That was to secure Henry Tudor, or at least to place him in checkmate. Tudor had been living in exile in Brittany but escaped to France after hearing of Richard's negotiations with Brittany.

"Richard dispensed firm justice without favour. In York, for example, he executed a number of his own soldiers who had committed crimes and outrages on their march back from London.

"He was a builder of some note. The public records list many buildings throughout the kingdom that he commissioned or had completed or restored. The castle here in York, the Tower of London, and the castles of Nottingham, Sandal (one of his father's old strongholds), Sudely, Windsor, Carlisle, Penrith, Tutbury, Kenilworth, Warwick and Baynard's Castle are among those places where building or re-building was done during his reign. He built the huge Great Hall at Middleham and a tower at Westminster.

"I am not in the least qualified to assess Richard's military prowess and career, any more than I may assess his well known passion for hunting and hawking. Nevertheless, whether fighting in Wales, or at Barnet, or at Tewkesbury, or in his Scottish campaign of 1482, his record is unarguably one of valour and good generalship, even at the young age of eighteen. In his Scottish campaign, after King James breached his treaty with Edward the Fourth, Richard captured Edinburgh. I must say that this was hardly a singular victory. The Scottish leaders were largely absent and there was apparently little resistance from the disorganised people of Edinburgh. Richard did not hold onto the city, presumably on orders from Edward the Fourth, but he negotiated a new treaty, and took back our city and castle of Berwick from the Scots. Margaret of Anjou had turned these over in 1460."

Miss Rivas looked up at me, with a quick grin. "I say 'our' city and castle, Doctor Watson; but perhaps your Scottish ancestors had a different view of their rightful ownership."

We all laughed with her, and she addressed the men of Magdalen directly and with grace once more.

"Richard's bravery at Bosworth was noted even by his enemies; among them his severe critics, John Rous and Polydore Virgil. His bravery strikes me as being, in truth, impetuous, rash and foolhardy. Surely he should have withdrawn, raised more men from his loyal North, and lived to fight another day. But the *men* of history have their own way of looking at military valour, and Richard's bravery is oft mentioned to his credit.

"He rebuilt and strengthened Edward the Fourth's navy. And I note in my letter to Doctor Watson one more accomplishment with a military connection: For military and government purposes, Richard re-established Edward's briefly used system of mounted couriers, stationed every twenty miles, on the main roads. Thanks to these relays, a letter could travel a good one hundred miles in a day. It was, gentlemen, the precursor of our post."

Miss Rivas nodded solemnly, and returned to her letter.

"These many good deeds and policies may not all have been Richard's own ideas; this we do not know, yeah or nay. But as the world would surely vilify him for bad and oppressive laws, surely the world should praise him for the many good laws and regulations that his Parliament passed. Some of his laws remain in effect today, four hundred years later.

"Sadly, it seems that all this was to rebound upon Richard. Such improvements in law and justice did not sit well with many in the entrenched nobility. Every small advance for the common man was a threat to their power and wealth. Small wonder that, when Richard needed them at Bosworth Field, so many stayed home. One could argue that by signing popular laws, he signed his own death warrant."

In a third letter, Miss Rivas explored Richard's moral character and probity.

"I find little upon record that will help us to determine at this lengthy remove if Richard was a moral or immoral man.

"His brother King Edward publicly credited him with 'innate probity and other virtues'. And Richard certainly wrote to the bishops of the kingdom that 'our principal intent and fervent desire is to see virtue and cleanness of living to be advanced, increased and multiplied, and vices and all other things repugnant to virtue, provoking the high indignation and fearful displeasure of God, to be repressed and annulled'.

"Richard had two illegitimate children (a daughter named Katherine and a son named John) before he married Anne Nevill and fathered little Edward. Today, we might take these illegitimate children as a stain upon his character, but I do not think that this was so in his era. Medieval men were not judged by the same standards as were women. Incredibly, that is still the case today; but I must not argue that cause now! There is clear evidence that Richard fully and willingly accepted his paternal responsibility for these children, and ensured that they and their futures were well supported. I find that redounds to his credit.

"There is a story or tradition to the effect that Richard had another illegitimate son, also named Richard, who became a stone-mason in Kent. The passage of centuries has robbed us of fair opportunity to confirm or refute this story, but the parish register at Eastwell does contain an entry recording the burial of one 'Rychard Plantagenet'.

"Of Richard's marriage, we know truly too little. His detractors see his marriage to Anne as a devious way of acquiring for himself her Warwick properties, and then to deprive Anne's mother of her rightful estates. Ardent supporters such as Miss Halsted propose that it was a romantic love-match; that Anne was 'the playmate of his childhood, the companion of his boyish days, the object of his youthful affections'. And she adds that they went on to enjoy 'halcyon days of peace' together. Perhaps all this is true, but at this remove we really can not say how happy or romantic was their marriage. What we *can* say, and say with confidence, is that there is absolutely no evidence from any writer, coeval or later, that there was any shadow on their relationship. There are no later references to mistresses after the marriage. And certainly the *Croyland Chronicle* says that, when their son died, both parents *together* were stricken 'almost mad with grief'.

"(I must note in passing that Miss Halstead notes in her book some speculation that Richard and Anne had, but lost, another son or sons. She writes of an official document that described little Edward as 'the eldest son' of Richard, and another in which Richard himself called Edward his 'first-begotten son'. I know no more than that, and I see no such references anywhere else.)

"Sir John Paston wrote of Richard that 'his genius is enterprising, and his temper liberal'. Richard undoubtedly displayed liberality and clemency to the widows of the traitors Buckingham and Hastings. To Buckingham's widow, he granted a pension, even though she was a Woodville. Richard also paid Buckingham's debts. To the widow of Hastings, Katherine Neville, sister of Warwick the King-maker, Richard gave Hastings's own estates, and the profitable wardship of Hastings's son, with his castles and revenues. In the same way, Richard treated Rivers's widow generously after her husband's execution. Richard gave a good pension to the wife of the great Lancastrian general, the Earl of Oxford, who had been imprisoned abroad. When Henry Tudor's mother, Margaret Beaufort, plotted against Richard, Richard's punishment was merely to hand over custody of her and her property to her husband, Lord Stanley. Richard gave pensions and money to the wives and families of other plotters who had been outlawed and fled abroad.

"These are simply not the characteristics of the vindictive and vicious scorpion that the Tudors and Shakespeare have portrayed.

"And surely no other king would have spared such persistent back-stabbers and traitors as Bishop Morton (whom Richard pardoned after the Buckingham Rebellion) and Lord Stanley.

"I must confess, however, that I am disappointed by Richard's alleged punishment of Jane Shore, the paramour of Edward the Fourth and, later, of Lord Hastings. Richard supposedly forced her to walk barefoot through London, clad in a long white under-garment and carrying a lighted candle, in an humiliating form of public penance normally exacted upon harlots from the stews of Southwark. A courtesan she may have been; a common prostitute she was not. Perhaps, as some suggest, Richard was at heart a puritan; witness his circular to the bishops deploring the state of public morals. In the end, Richard redeemed himself somewhat in this case by giving, if reluctantly, permission for Jane Shore to marry his own royal solicitor, Thomas Lynom, and Jane was released from Ludgate Prison. Still, I suppose that one can argue that her punishment was, in a purely legalistic sense, lenient. She supposedly had been an agent in the plotting against Richard and, therefore, could have been executed for treason.

"I have questions, too, about the manner in which Richard took control of the estates of the Countess of Warwick and the Countess of Oxford. If the reports that I have read are true, he showed little respect for their legal rights; but the reports themselves are clearly very much open to charges of bias, and came years after Richard's death. Further, in the case of the Countess of Warwick, Edward the Fourth must bear much of the blame for relieving her of her assets. As you know, he had her property assigned to her daughters by Parliament, as if she were 'naturally dead'; and that put her riches into the hands of her daughters' husbands, George and Richard.

"There is some argument, as well, about Richard's disposition of the lands of some traitors and rebels. He supposedly gave some of it to friends and supporters *before* the formal attainders against the previous owners had passed into law. In other cases, he did await the attainders. I suspect here that the complaint is more one about Richard transferring the estates of Southern rebels to Northerners, than about the legal process itself.

"In the end, when considering Richard's moral character, I must naturally place considerable reliance upon the action of Earl Rivers, in asking Richard to oversee the execution of the terms of Rivers's will.

"Surely there can hardly be a higher testament to Richard's personal probity and virtue than this ultimate expression of confidence in him by an unrelenting foe who lay under sentence of imminent death. And to this day there has never been any suggestion from anybody that Richard betrayed this trust of Rivers.

"As well, in March 1484, something happened that perhaps *was* a higher testament. Elizabeth Woodville, once Richard's greatest enemy, released her daughters from sanctuary into Richard's care and custody. And she urged her son to return from France and to go in safety to Richard's court. Clearly, she now saw Richard in a different light, and trusted him with her own daughters. And, as he had promised, Richard did look after them and their futures. That is indeed a testament to his probity and character.

"I began my last letter with an outpouring of praise from Bishop Langton. Perhaps the good bishop was a little enthusiastic, having just been named to the See of St. David's. But when news of Richard's death reached York, this grieving entry was made in the City records:–

"'... King Richard, late mercifully reigning upon us, was thrugh grete treason of the Duc of Northfolk, with many othyr that turned ayenst him, with many othyr lords and nobilles of thes North Partes, was piteously slane and murderd, to the grete hevyness of this citie.'

"Norfolk is named in error, Doctor Watson. The writer certainly meant the Duke of Northumberland, who was widely held up here to be a traitor to Richard for his failure to engage the Tudor enemy at Bosworth. In 1489, Northumberland was seized near Thirsk, while on a mission for Henry the Seventh, and was hanged, like a common criminal, from an oak tree.

"As Lord Chancellor Bacon observed:–

"'The Northern parts were not only affectionate to the House of York, but particularly had been devoted to King Richard III.'

"I think at this point of Herrick, who wrote:– 'Twixt kings and tyrants there's this difference known; kings seek their subjects' good, tyrants their own'. So let me close this letter by reproducing the words of Rous in his *first* testament to Richard:–

"'The most mighty prince Richard, ... all avarice set aside, ruled his subjects in his realm full commendably, punishing offenders of his laws, especially extortioners and oppressors of his commons, and cherishing those that were virtuous; by the which discreet guiding he got great thanks of God and love of all his subjects, rich and poor, and great laud of the people of all other lands about him'."

She turned directly to Masterman-Pugh. "Your question, sir, was 'What kind of a man was Richard?' There, from even his enemies, you have your answer."

Miss Rivas bowed (yes, bowed, rather than curtsied) as she concluded her lecture, then blushed deeply as the men of Magdalen broke into resounding applause, in which Holmes and Baker and I most heartily joined, clapping until our hands smarted.

Still standing at the lectern, she once more won the rapt attention of her audience.

"President Bulley, this forum is indeed akin to a court, the Criminal Court of Magdalen. If you are ready, then, I suggest it is time for us to present our closing arguments to your jury in the matter of the deaths of the Two Little Princes."

Bulley looked inquiringly at me, and I nodded back. "Yes, President, I think that we can say that the evidence is all in."

The president smiled. "Then, if this is to be a criminal court, who will act for the Crown? And who for the defence?"

Masterman-Pugh held up his hand politely. "I for the Crown, if you please, President."

"And I for the defence," said Miss Rivas, with determination and pride.

Bulley looked startled, and there was a low murmur from the men of Magdalen.

"Perhaps you all expected Doctor Watson to present Richard's case," said Miss Rivas. "But the role of the doctor has been that of our agent, to gather the evidence and to present it in a fair and neutral fashion. Doctor Watson and I have discussed this, and I will, if you gentlemen will accept my standing, present the case for Richard's defence. "

The president inclined his head. "The university may be a man's world, Miss Rivas, but you have indeed earned your standing today, and our respect.

"Then, if I have my order of procedure correct, Masterman-Pugh will first address us for the prosecution, and Miss Rivas will reply for the defence. Masterman-Pugh, the court is yours."

301

Chapter Sixteen

Masterman-Pugh locked his fingers into his gown, at the level of his chest, and began to promenade slowly and regally up and down the State Room. He spoke dispassionately and clearly.

"I shall be brief and decisive, as usual. The long and short of the case is simply this: The overwhelming weight of the evidence points clearly to the disappearance, for good, of the Two Little Princes under Richard the Third.

"They were certainly in the Tower as he began his reign. And – hear me – they were never seen alive again. They were never seen again, alive *or* dead.

"If they were alive, why did Richard not produce and parade them when it was in his interest to do so? Prior to the reports of their deaths at his hands, perhaps he had no reason to. After those reports circulated, he had *every* reason to. His failure to do so, his silence, must speak volumes.

"Doctor Watson has argued that, seen alive, they would have provided a focus for rebellion at a time when Richard's hold upon the Crown was somewhat precarious.

"Surely that very precariousness stands as an obvious and compelling motive for Richard to remove them, both as a rallying point for revolt and as an obstacle to his future security.

"Richard may have been moderately popular in the North, but it is clear that he had a powerful phalanx of enemies in the

South. The remaining Woodvilles, and other dissatisfied magnates, inevitably would continue to plot against him and inevitably would use the boys as tools.

"And where would Richard have been if the Woodvilles had returned to power? He would not have lived to see another dawn. That we all know.

"Gentlemen of the jury: If the boys were *not* a threat, why did Richard lock them up as prisoners in the Tower?

"The boys *were* a threat; and we know full well what Richard did when Lord Hastings emerged as a threat. He killed him, without a trial, in deliberate and knowing violation of the law."

Masterman-Pugh was a compelling master of oration. He paused to let his perfectly paced words sink in, and then began again in a more silky tone.

"If the little boys were not secretly murdered during Richard's reign, then why were they secretly buried?

"If they had died naturally, why did Richard not disclose and demonstrate that?

"If the princes had been murdered by somebody else, by Buckingham, for example, why in the name of heaven above did not Richard publicly proclaim that, and publicly prosecute him? If Richard was reluctant to accuse Buckingham while he was alive, why on earth did he not do so after Buckingham's death?

"Doctor Watson even suggested, to my amusement, that French assassins may have made their way into the Tower and killed them. We must find it hard to believe that foreign murderers could simply walk into England's most secure fortress, kill England's most celebrated royal prisoners, and then simply disappear again. And if they had, would not Richard have made political hay of it? He of all people had no love for the French.

"I remind you of the Act of Parliament that declared Richard guilty of shedding infants' blood.

"Whose blood could that possibly be, other than that of the Two Little Princes? There was no need to name them;

everybody knew. Reports of their murder had circulated in England and abroad.

"Henry legitimated his wife-to-be, Elizabeth of York, reversing her bastardy. If the boys had been alive, they would have been made legitimate at the same time, and restored to their position as legal Yorkist heirs. They would thus indeed have been a clear threat to Henry. They were obviously dead, then.

"Miss Rivas will no doubt attempt to argue that the actions of Elizabeth Woodville, in releasing her daughters to Richard, were consistent with the boys still being alive. I contend, however, that her actions in supporting Henry Tudor's cause, and his marriage to Elizabeth of York, are far more persuasively consistent with the boys being already dead.

"She had a vitriolic hatred of Richard, and for good reason. He had foully murdered her sons. They were dead, and she knew it. Why else would she leap to the support of Henry Tudor?

"Why else would she support so ardently this plot to have Henry invade England, dethrone Richard, take the crown, and marry her daughter Elizabeth of York?

"Plain and simple: Elizabeth Woodville would not have backed Henry Tudor unless her boys, the *real* heirs to the throne, were dead.

"And Elizabeth of York would not have agreed to marry Henry unless her little brothers had been killed. By accepting Henry's hand, she acknowledged that they were dead.

"Yes, the Woodville queen eventually released her daughters to Richard. But if she had not, he would no doubt have simply seized them from sanctuary, just as he had, in effect, seized her son Richard from sanctuary. At least upon this occasion Elizabeth Woodville was able to exact a high price: a solemn and public oath that Richard would care for her daughters. I point out that the agreement did not mention the Two Little Princes and guarantee *them* safety and good marriages. It was too late, of course; they were both dead.

"Richard had the motive, the opportunity, the means and, with all respect to Miss Rivas's extremely well presented case for 'Richard the Good', he had the bent. A bent of the bloody times, if you like; but a bent clearly demonstrated in the planned murder of Lord Hastings. And then in the illegal executions, the murders, of Rivers and Grey and Vaughan and Haute.

"While others in the case of the Two Little Princes may arguably have had motive, opportunity, means and bent, the cases against them as presented by Doctor Watson are remarkably tenuous. A little opportune smoke; but no fire; and no evidence.

"I need not waste my time or yours pursuing fanciful cases against Henry Tudor's mother, his step-father, imaginary Frenchmen, or mythical shipwrecks. Buckingham is simply a convenient scapegoat, as is Henry the Seventh himself.

"Doctor Watson's authorities ask us to believe that Richard would never have slain Henry the Sixth unless acting upon orders from Edward the Fourth. May we not accept, then, that Buckingham would never have assassinated the Two Little Princes unless acting upon orders from Richard the Third?"

"What about Becket?" threw in Warren. "Henry the Second's knights murdered him without orders from the king." Masterman-Pugh ignored him.

"As for Henry Tudor," he continued, "if *he* had murdered the princes, he would surely have blamed Richard, and produced an unassailable if posthumous case against him. If he was clever enough to assassinate the boys and keep that a secret from all, then he was clever enough to concoct a solid case against Richard. It was 1485; he could easily, for example, have had a minion murder two unwanted orphans, and then passed their bones off as those of the princes.

"Speaking of bones, the human bones found in the Tower in 1647 were accepted as those of the princes, and their location coincides with that given by Thomas More.

"But I do not reply on those bones. The central argument for the prosecution is this: Richard undoubtedly packed off the Two Little Princes to the Tower. Reports soon arose of their death. It was, as Fabyan said, the 'common fame' that they were dead. And, as Mr. Gairdner observed, all this was not the invention of later writers under the Tudors. Richard was suspected *at the time.*

"Richard never even attempted to disprove those reports. The two little boys were never seen alive again. Never.

"They were under Richard's protection, and he was in law responsible for their deaths.

"Their own mother and sister acted as if they were dead, and they knew it.

"And Henry Tudor won not only the support of Queen Elizabeth Woodville. He won also the support of many English nobles, despite the supposed weakness of his claim to the crown. Why would these men have backed him unless they knew the boys were dead? Doctor Watson talks of untrue and malicious 'rumours' that the boys were dead. Would cynical and pragmatic medieval magnates have lined up behind Tudor on the strength of mere rumours? No, the boys must have been dead, and these nobles knew it.

"It was, we know, an era of political assassination and regal murder. But not of little children, not of innocent little babes. Gentlemen, Richard the Third assumed not merely the crown of England, but also the bloody mantle of Herod.

"I need say no more, and I know that I can count on you all, as if we were in the Criminal Court, for a reasoned verdict of guilty as charged."

Miss Rivas smiled at me sympathetically as Masterman-Pugh briskly resumed his seat.

She took his place, her blue eyes flashing as she spoke with clarity and determination.

"Gentlemen, we have no proof at all that the Two Little Princes *were* murdered. That is the first of Doctor Masterman-Pugh's sweeping assumptions – and far from his last."

Masterman-Pugh looked, by turns, startled, angry, and then grudgingly accepting. He smiled wryly, and half-bowed, as if granting that Miss Rivas had scored a court-room point.

"I am happy to hear the Crown, if I may so describe Doctor Masterman-Pugh, conceding that the bones are of no value as evidence. They may have been 'accepted' by Charles the Second, but as Doctor Watson has established, all we can say is that those bones were of two people of small stature, genders unknown, ages unknown, identities unknown, who died of causes unknown at a time unknown.

"I am less happy to hear the Crown insist that the boys were locked up in the Tower as prisoners. That is another assumption. The Tower of London served as the metropolitan royal residence, not simply as a prison.

"But let us, for the sake of argument," she continued, "say that the boys perhaps were murdered, by a party or parties unknown. To look at opportunity and means, however, is somewhat futile, as all the suspects had such. Motive is therefore perhaps of more promising importance to us.

"Gentlemen, Richard simply had no *need* to kill the princes.

"He was the legal king, chosen by the estates of Parliament, which had every legal right to choose the king, just as they had chosen his brother Edward. Richard was anointed, and that had a special meaning and significance then. The princes were proven in law to be illegitimate, and thus had no legitimate claim to the throne. So why would Richard kill them? To do so would be an open admission that his right to the throne was spurious.

"The prosecution have made much of the fact that Richard remained silent as to their fate, and did not put them on show to prove that rumours of their deaths were groundless.

"From the vantage point of hindsight, we may naturally ask today why Richard did not parade them publicly to show they still lived. But kings and queens of our time do not publicly react to rumours from the gutter, and kings did not then. Richard was under no obligation to *prove* they still lived, and why should he?

"The prosecution have suggested that Richard needed to eliminate the boys as a rallying point for revolt. I propose that, rather, that is why he did *not* produce them alive. Their public appearance would have further fanned the flames of rebellion among those self-interested southerners who hated Richard.

"Think upon this: The boys could or would have been focal points for rebellion whether alive or dead. Dead, though, they would have been more trouble for Richard than if alive and illegitimate. Dead, they made Henry's dubious claim to the throne stronger, and he was thus of far more danger to Richard and his crown. It was *Henry* who needed them dead, not Richard."

Miss Rivas now paused for effect herself. Masterman-Pugh half bowed in his chair in acknowledgment of this skill, and served her with a quizzical but half-admiring smile. With her bright eyes directly engaging those of the men of Magdalen, man by man, one by one, she continued her argument.

"If Richard were intent upon removing the boys because they were potential threats to his crown, what of the other threats?

"Did Richard secretly assassinate the son of George of Clarence? On the contrary, Richard made him a member of his regal council, and knighted him.

"Did Richard secretly murder Edward the Fourth's daughters, or George's daughter? On the contrary, he protected them and treated them well. And why kill the princes, and leave the princesses alive? While the right of a woman to the crown was untested, Edward's daughters *were* in the line of succession. If rebels could rally around the sons, they could just as well rally around the daughters. There was, indeed, a plot to seize them with just that in mind.

Miss Rivas again paused, until her audience was fidgeting with anticipation.

"If Richard the Third did not murder the Two Little Princes, then who did?"

Once more, like a seasoned barrister, she paused again.

"Henry the Seventh had an overwhelming motive, gentlemen," she resumed. "As Doctor Masterman-Pugh has reasoned, if Henry reversed the bastardy of Edward the Fourth's children, in order to make legitimate Elizabeth of York as his wife, then the boys would also be legitimate. They would be once more the legal heirs to the throne, and Henry's pretentious claim to the crown would be fatally flawed. If they were still alive, that is.

'Doctor Masterman-Pugh says that they were 'obviously dead'. I agree; but not at Richard's hands.

"To sum up: Richard had no need to kill the Two Little Princes. *But Henry did.*

"Did Henry have the bent?

"Look at how he imprisoned Clarence's son and executed him. Look at how he threw Richard's illegitimate son John into prison, and kept him there until he died. Look at how, as soon as he had taken the throne, he promptly imprisoned the doomed Bishop Stillington. Look at how Henry seized and executed the other leading Yorkists as well.

"As Doctor Watson observed: Given Henry's record, what do *you* think happened to the Two Little Princes under Henry?"

Masterman-Pugh interrupted testily. "They were assassinated by then."

"Prove it," shot back Miss Rivas. "Prove that they were dead by then. Prove that they were *ever* assassinated. You merely *assume* that they were killed during Richard's reign, and then tailor your supposed facts to fit that thesis.

"If they were dead when Henry came to the throne, then why all the open doubts about it? Why did Thomas More report such doubts? Why did Lord Bacon speak of the belief that they were still alive in Henry's reign? Why did Polydore Virgil, Henry's very own tame historian, with access to Henry and to all of his records, record the belief that the boys has been taken secretly away and hidden? As Mr. Holmes has asked, why is there still a mystery today?

"If indeed they were killed in Richard's time, why did Henry do nothing? Why did he not cite the murder of the Two Little Princes as the *raison d'être* for his invasion? Why did he not immediately proclaim the death or disappearance of the boys? Why did he not trumpet up and down the land an accusation against Richard? Why did Henry not produce their bodies? Why was there no investigation? Where was his hue and cry?

"Why his silence, his clamorous, screaming silence?"

Again, Miss Rivas paused. Her audience sat motionless and attentive.

"Henry went from Bosworth to London. Once there, as Doctor Watson noted, Henry said nothing about the princes. Let me now expand on this theme:

"Henry arrived in London and said nothing of the fate of the Two Little Princes. He was crowned on October 30th. He still said nothing. Parliament met on September 7th. Still he is silent. Henry was married to Elizabeth of York on January 18th, 1486. Still he is silent. He left London a few weeks later and went on a progress that included Richard's strongholds of Nottingham and York. Still he is silent. His son Prince Arthur was born on September 20th. Still he is silent. Parliament meet again on November 9th. Still he is silent. His queen is crowned on November 25th. Still he is silent.

"Sixteen months have passed since Bosworth and Henry is still silent on the fate of the princes. Later, but still, I think, in Henry's time, an official epitaph for Richard is written. Again, there is no mention of this supposed crime.

"Once more, I ask: If the Two Little Princes really were dead, and at Richard's hand, why Henry's screaming silence?"

Once again, Miss Rivas paused for effect, and slowly swept her audience, face by face, with her confident blue eyes.

"And when Henry conveniently got around to accusing Tyrrel and Dighton, *seventeen years later*, why did he not publish their confessions and execute them?

"He did neither. He set Dighton free, and executed Tyrrel for some *other* crime. There were no charges against Forest or Slaughter or the others. Why not? If Tyrrel had confessed, why not?

"If Tyrrel had *really* confessed, why did Henry not publish the confession? He was quick enough to print and circulate Perkin Warbeck's confession throughout the country.

"To use your own words, Doctor Masterman-Pugh, Henry's silences must speak volumes.

"If Tyrrel had really confessed, why did not More reproduce the confession? Why did not Virgil or Fabyan mention the confession at all? Virgil had full access to Henry's records. Why did he not disclose this confession? If Dighton was running free, why did not More and Virgil speak to this perfect witness, and settle the guilt firmly and finally upon Richard? Doctor Masterman-Pugh spoke of mythical Frenchmen; here we have a mythical confession. A trumped-up confession that Henry 'gave out'.

"And why *two* pardons for Tyrrel?

"Doctor Masterman-Pugh is right on *one* point: I shall indeed cite the action of Elizabeth Woodville in releasing her daughters to Richard.

"Richard has supposedly cruelly slain three of her sons, and her brother, yet we see that she willingly turns over her daughters to the custody of this vicious, depraved monster. She promotes the marriage of her daughter Elizabeth to this hunchbacked assassin, and she appeals to her eldest son to return home from France, to abandon Henry Tudor's cause and to go in complete safety to this bloody child-murderer.

"No matter how you view medieval morality – and the fate of medieval daughters, who married whom they were told to marry – these are *not* the actions of a mother who believes that Richard has murdered her two little boys.

"Markham declares that the boys were not dead. Grafton says that they were, and that Elizabeth Woodville was so informed by the Welsh doctor, Lewis.

"Mr. Gairdner, however, told Doctor Watson that Lewis was an agent of Henry the Seventh's mother, Margaret Beaufort. If that was so, perhaps Lewis simply lied to Elizabeth Woodville about the princes, to secure her support.

"If she *did* believe that the boys were dead, she clearly did *not* believe that Richard was to blame. She trusted him. And she did not misjudge Richard. Edward Hall called her daughters 'lambs ... committed to the custody of the ravenous wolf', but Richard *did* treat the daughters very well.

"The Crown sought to score a point by noting that Richard's public oath to protect the daughters did not extend to the Two Little Princes. Of course not; they were *already* under his good care and protection. No oath was needed; no oath was asked for.

"The oath did not explicitly cover Elizabeth Woodville's traitorous son the Marquis of Dorset, either. He thus had no protection, no guarantees, and no written promises. Yet Elizabeth urged him to abandon Henry Tudor, urged him to give up on the idea of the marriage of Henry and Elizabeth of York, and urged him to return to England and join Richard.

"Again, these are not the actions of a mother who believes that Richard has murdered her two little boys."

Miss Rivas took a sip of water from the glass on the lectern.

"The prosecution contend that Elizabeth Woodville had displayed vitriolic hatred of Richard. Surely it was, if anything, vitriolic *jealousy*, because she knew that, thanks to her own philandering husband, her sons were not the rightful heirs, and Richard was."

Masterman-Pugh interrupted once more. "Richard had without doubt killed her brother, Rivers, and one of her sons, Grey. Argue that away, Miss Rivas."

"I do not need to," she countered, with spirit. "They were guilty of treason, and no one knew that better than Elizabeth Woodville, their co-conspirator. They had prepared, under arms, to oppose the legal Protector. That, simply, was rebellion and treason. The penalty was death, and all of the plotters knew it. They gambled, and lost."

"If she urged her son Dorset to abandon Henry Tudor," asked Masterman-Pugh, "why did she go on to support Henry?"

Miss Rivas laughed, unabashed. "As Clements Markham suggests, Elizabeth Woodville was placing her bets on all the horses in the race. Even as a woman, I must concede that could have been typical of her. Think of her as Henry the Eighth's grandmother, and that may help you determine her character.

"Even while the boys were alive, it takes no stretch of the imagination to see Elizabeth Woodville concluding that Henry stood a good chance of overthrowing Richard, with support from Southern and Welsh magnates. That done, her own supporters, many of them these same magnates, could then rise on behalf of the young Edward the Fifth, and overthrow Henry. Thus the plan to support Henry.

"I will even grant you that she might have feared, no matter how wrongly, that Richard might dispose of young Edward later, as he grew up. If so, supporting Henry Tudor, with the idea of overthrowing him next, would be an obvious option for her."

Miss Rivas took another tactical sip from her glass of water.

"Let me start you down another road. As I have proposed, if Elizabeth Woodville knew or believed that the Two Little Princes were dead, she clearly did *not* believe that they were dead at Richard's hands. She must have accepted and known that Richard was innocent.

"And, if they were indeed dead at that time, which, I remind you, is not proven, that would be because she knew that someone else had killed them, and had done so without Richard's knowledge or approval. Buckingham, for example?"

"But Morton and Buckingham were supporters of the plan to have Henry take the throne and marry the daughter," countered Masterman-Pugh. "Does that not prove that the boys were dead at Richard's hands in the late summer of 1483? How do you explain that away?"

"I am not entirely sure that the prosecutor should be cross-examining the barrister for the defence," laughed Miss Rivas, comfortably.

"But my answer would be this: Casting about for potential candidates to replace Richard on the throne, they knew that no Woodville child could legally be in the race, and that Buckingham himself was simply too much of a long shot. The convenient solution was Henry Tudor, and I am sure that they secured guarantees from him of very generous rewards for their support. Certainly, we know that Morton was well rewarded. He became Archbishop of Canterbury, Lord Chancellor, and, with the assistance of Henry the Seventh, a cardinal. Whether the Tudor solution would be permanent,

314

whether they intended to allow Henry to keep the crown once he had it, is quite another question."

Masterman-Pugh subsided with a shrug, and a crisp mutter of "far-fetched."

"Even if the Two Little Princes were indeed killed in Richard's time," Miss Rivas continued, "then Buckingham is seen by some as a plausible murderer.

"I accept that if Buckingham was aiming for the throne himself, he faced an uphill fight. But he may have indeed *begun* that fight. He was clearly blinded enough by pride and ambition to have begun it. He could well have killed the boys for that reason, the theory runs.

"And Buckingham could equally well have killed the Two Little Princes without Richard's authority, in the hopes of gaining Richard's approval and reward.

"However, if Buckingham had murdered the boys, or knew that Richard had done it, why did not Buckingham speak up when he was being led to the block in Salisbury? He confessed under examination to his rebellion, and named a number of his co-conspirators. Why did he not also confess to murdering the princes, if he had done so?

"And if Buckingham was innocent, but knew or believed that Richard had killed the boys, why did Buckingham not accuse Richard? He could at least have had the twisted satisfaction of taking Richard down with him.

"Does not Buckingham's silence upon the matter of the Two Little Princes suggest, then, that they were still *alive* at this time, in November 1483?

"And then there is the question of why Richard did not publicly accuse Buckingham. As Doctor Watson argues, surely the two silences show that both men were innocent, and that the boys were indeed still alive.

"Let me return to something Doctor Masterman-Pugh said a few moments ago. He observed that Henry legitimated Elizabeth of York, and said that if the boys had been alive, they would have been made legitimate at the same time, and restored to their position as heirs. So, he argued, the boys were obviously dead at that time.

"That time, however, was months after Henry seized the crown. Months in which he plenty of time, as well as motive, opportunity, means and bent, to dispose of the princes. Henry is clearly, as I say, a leading suspect.

"I remind you that the *Croyland* chronicler suggests that the boys were still alive on September 8th, 1483. We know that Buckingham had been in secret correspondence with Henry Tudor in that month, and that word spread that the boys were dead. Perhaps, then, Buckingham had the boys killed on *Henry's* behalf.

"Henry or Buckingham. In either case, gentlemen, then Richard was *not* the murderer."

"Your so-called evidence is all circumstantial," volleyed Masterman-Pugh.

"As is yours, sir, and that does not reduce the burden of proof upon you," Miss Rivas fired back. "Indeed, gentlemen, the evidence before you, by its very nature and antiquity, is and must be circumstantial.

She spoke crisply. "The very foundation of the case against Richard is flawed. No, more than flawed; it is not a foundation at all.

"The failure of the case against Richard was very well summed up by Doctor Watson's friend Mr. Hornidge. As he pointed out, the picture that the public have and hold of Richard today is a thoroughly distorted one painted by Thomas More with the brush of prejudiced hearsay, touched up by Henry the Seventh's paid man, Polydore Virgil, then embellished with fictitious detail by Hall and Holinshed, and finally framed and put on theatrical display by Shakespeare.

"More erred or lied or showed bias many more times than once. In a court of law, that makes his entire story suspect. Would not a judge advise the jury that if a witness's testimony is shown to be false or perjured in one detail, the jury is free to consider if it is not false or perjured in all its details?

"And it is surely significant, as Doctor Watson has noted, that the *Croyland Chronicle* never accuses Richard in the boys' disappearance. Free to lay this charge after Richard's death, and with motive to do so, the chronicler simply does *not*.

"In conclusion, permit me to say it once more: With this twisted and distorted picture of Richard in front of us, we have been talking and acting here as if we were dealing with a case of murder. But we do not, in fact, know if there *was* a murder. And if there was, we most certainly do not know who committed it. We have no evidence against Richard the III – not even circumstantial evidence.

"Thus the Crown have simply failed to prove Richard's guilt beyond reasonable doubt. Richard must therefore be declared not guilty. That is what the law of England requires.

"And that is the fair and honest verdict for which I call."

She began to resume her seat, but the "jury" honoured her with another round of warm and enthusiastic applause. Miss Rivas stood again, looking a little embarrassed, and thanked them. Another quick buzz of conversation followed.

I leaned over to Miss Rivas, tears welling in my eyes. "That was marvellous," I whispered. "I hope to heaven that they agree with you, or all my work has gone for naught."

Holmes overheard me, and clapped me on the shoulder. "Come, Watson, come. Your commission was to investigate, to act as an investigator for both sides, and not to act as the barrister for one side. And you have done your job excellently, as I knew you would."

President Bulley, in a tone as solemn and ringing as that of any High Court judge, now asked the jurors to deliver their individual verdicts.

"Dean Rigaud?"

"I am certainly most suspicious as to why Richard failed to prove the boys alive when it was advantageous for him to do so. I see the merits of a case against him. But the evidence is horribly confused, contradictory, and weak. I therefore, if with some misgivings, vote for not guilty."

Warren?"

"Not guilty. There is no actual evidence against Richard, other than lack of proof of his innocence. There were recorded doubts that the boys had actually been killed. There were reports that they lived on, and had been smuggled away or taken abroad. As Miss Rivas observes, we really do not even know if we are in fact dealing with a murder. I can not find a man guilty of a crime that I do not know occurred."

"Wilson?"

"If those bones of 1674 were indeed those of the Two Little Princes, probably they *were* murdered. Why else go to such lengths as to stuff the corpses into a chest and bury it ten feet deep in the ground? But I do not know if they were the bones of the princes. I do not know if the princes were murdered, or when, or how. And, if they were, I have heard no evidence to enable me to identify convincingly the assassin or assassins. Not guilty, therefore."

"Yule?"

"I am with Masterman-Pugh. The boys were a threat to Richard's security. Word quickly spread that he had killed them; that *he* had killed them; not Buckingham or the French or the Stanleys. Richard then did and said nothing. *His* silence speaks volumes. If he had removed the boys for safe-keeping elsewhere, in the North or abroad, then why were they never found or seen again? Let us face it: They *were* never seen alive again. And the behaviour of their own mother and sister is consistent with them being dead, while in Richard's care and custody. The case against Richard is, to me, beyond reasonable doubt, at least in this informal court of ours. Perhaps if I were in a real criminal court, I might have to vote otherwise. In a Scottish court, a verdict of 'not proven' would, I am sure, meet with the approval of the Lord Justice-Clerk. Here, however, I am prepared to find Richard guilty."

"Terry?"

"On the slight and contradictory evidence presented to us, I would have to say that the Crown's case is most certainly not solid. I declare Richard not guilty."

"Hopkins?"

"I find it easier to accept the accounts of the *Croyland Chronicle* than others. Thomas More I find to be unreliable and prejudiced. With all respect to More and his memory, the best we can say is that More's sources were at second-hand and inimical to Richard. More's mentor, John Morton, obviously, had every reason to slander Richard. *Croyland* is a reasonably contemporary account. My point is this: The *Croyland* chronicler displays bias against Richard, and in favour of Henry; yet he does *not* accuse Richard of the murders of the Two Little Princes. Three years after their supposed deaths, and some time after Richard's death, as well; yet this well informed writer, despite his antipathy towards Richard, reports only *rumours* of the boys' deaths. He does not validate those rumours, nor does he accuse Richard of murder. I find that significant. Not guilty, then."

"Vice-President Bramley?"

"I began by trying, objectively, to weigh motive, means, opportunity, bent and evidence. Unfortunately, I find myself with too many suspects, too little evidence, and too much doubt. One thing that I feel bound to do is to dismiss from my mind the Tyrrel confession. Given that Henry the Seventh never produced it, and given that he let Dighton go free, I must find that there never was any such confession. That said, I am left with more than sufficient doubt as to Richard's guilt. I must vote for not guilty."

"Roberts?"

"I am quite struck by Miss Rivas's argument that Elizabeth Woodville would not have turned her daughters over to Richard if she thought that he had killed her sons. On the other hand, I have difficulty seeing why on earth she would support Henry Tudor if her boys were alive. If she hoped to dethrone Richard, why not try to do so directly? Why go to the elaborate plot of first replacing Richard with Henry, and then replacing Henry with her son? However, the Crown has not proven its case, and I would vote Richard not guilty as charged."

Bulley turned next to Baker. "Yeoman Warder Baker? I am not entirely sure whether you are a member of the jury or an official of the court. But perhaps we should hear your verdict, if you have one?"

Baker frowned solemnly. "I must say that I have never been satisfied as to Richard's guilt. With my best apologies to

319

Doctor Watson and Miss Rivas, however, I do have to say that a case against Richard can certainly be made. But I do not find it to be a very good case, and it is certainly not one on which I could send a man to the gallows. Not guilty, then, is my vote."

"Mr. Holmes?"

"The lack of data is infuriating. I hesitate to say it before Watson and Miss Rivas, but the scales of probability do seem more weighted against Richard than for him. However, his guilt is no more proven than his innocence. Was this a Scottish court I might very well, like Dean Yule, vote for 'not proven'. The so-called 'Scottish verdict' is, in effect, a finding that if the guilt of the accused has not been clearly established, neither has his innocence been clearly established. There may thus *be* a case against the accused, but it is not a compelling one. But Yule and I are not in a Scottish court. So, here and now, and in the absence of more data, I have no choice but to deliver a verdict of not guilty."

"Ogle?"

"The boys were indeed a threat to Richard's security, for a number of reasons. They did disappear and, as far as we know, they were never seen alive again. But when and how they disappeared seem to me to be in doubt. I have grave suspicions to direct against Richard, but as Dean Rigaud says, the evidence is horribly confused and contradictory. It has been very well presented, however. Reasonable doubt having been raised, I find Richard not guilty."

"Bordon-Sanderson?"

"It all boils down, you know, to us being asked to judge a man on the word of Thomas More. Yet More's word is clearly fraught with inaccuracies, and clouded by cavils. Above all, it is all clearly fed by prejudiced sources who were hostile towards Richard. It is unarguably clear that More knew of Richard and his reign only what he was told by Morton and others in the Tudor era: hearsay and prejudiced court gossip. Yet the world seems for centuries simply to have taken More's story as the true gospel. A martyr More may have been, a witness he was not.

"If you will excuse the levity, I must label myself as Doubting Thomas! I return a verdict of not guilty."

The poll went on, with President Bulley taking the verdicts of all of us present. In all, there were four and twenty of us in the State Room, and the outcome was two and twenty votes for not guilty, and two for guilty.

"A very well deserved victory for you and Miss Rivas, Doctor," concluded President Bulley.

Masterman-Pugh swiftly rose and commanded silence.

"Doctor, after your magnificent work and presentation, I must seek your pardon for what I am about to do. I am undoubtedly about to cause you horrible embarrassment. Please forgive me."

With that, in ringing tones, he called for "Three cheers for Doctor Watson."

And to my shock and tearful delight, all the men of Magdalen, and Miss Rivas, leaped to their feet to cheer me.

Miss Rivas passed me a most necessary handkerchief, and the men of Magdalen stood, smiling and beaming, as, without shame, I applied it.

Then, with perfect dramatic timing, Masterman-Pugh broke in.

"When shall I call for my bill, Doctor?"

Chapter Seventeen

Mr. Holmes, Miss Rivas, Baker and I returned to London on a late train. We spoke little, and I was glad to get to my bed. The following morning, I found that Holmes had disappeared during the night, and had left no note. I thus found myself alone, and, for some minutes, was happy so to be, musing on my moving experience of the last weeks.

Soon, our landlady knocked and brought in not only a generous breakfast for two, but also Miss Rivas, who had stayed in her spare room for the night. The young teacher and I were enjoying a companionable meal, much laughter, and a deepening friendship, when I heard Holmes's tread literally bounding up the stairs. He flung himself into our room, grinning broadly and jigged up and down like an excited schoolboy, rubbing his hands together in glee.

"Your case –" I began.

"– is solved," replied Holmes, glowing. "Solved. I have sufficient proof. I have the elusive Somerset in my net."

"How –" I began again.

"The search of rubbish that you so intelligently recommended," said Holmes. "Wiggins found a discarded paper that caused him to place observation upon the house of a pawnbroker and money-lender in Lambeth. The money-lender is a man by name Butters, who is well known to me. His ill works occupy two very full pages in my index. Last night, Wiggins followed Somerset himself to that house, and dispatched a messenger to summon me. I then dragged Butters from his bed. I was able – eloquently, I assure you – to persuade him that he had a most reasonable choice: He could co-operate with me, or he could confidently expect me to deliver to the authorities sufficient evidence of his nefarious dealings with certain figures in the underworld that he could count upon some inconvenient interruption to his business. In short, he could inform upon Somerset, or he could prepare for a lengthy holiday in a private room at one of Her Majesty's high-walled hotels."

Holmes laughed aloud at his own wit, and grinned at us as we caught on.

"You blackmailed him, Holmes," I protested with mock severity.

"I merely pointed out to him the obvious advantages of assisting me," replied Holmes, with a satisfied chuckle. "It took him no time at all to see it my way, and he gave me what I needed.

"Somerset had initially taken money from the company to pay gambling debts. Intending to repay the firm, he then borrowed from this villain in Lambeth. But instead of repaying the company, Somerset stupidly placed further wagers with Butters's money, hoping to win handsomely and to retire both debts. He lost, of course, and found himself trapped, owing considerable sums both to the company and to Butters. Butters craftily persuaded him to 'borrow' more money from the firm, to begin to repay his loan. The money-lender is a much more experienced and artful trickster than is Somerset. When it appeared that his company might at last uncover Somerset's actions, he panicked, and turned again to Butters. Butters advised him to remove the records. Butters even offered to hold, 'for safety', the stolen documents. The money-lender then planned further to milk Somerset, by threatening to expose him.

"But the evidence is in my hands, and it and I will be at the company before another hour is up. Somerset's fate will be up to his partners, and my commission will be complete. Their cheque can come none too soon. The Michaelmas quarter-day will be upon us before we know it, and our landlady will be happy to see our own cheque."

Miss Rivas and I congratulated him, though from Miss Rivas's frowns I deduced that she was less than comfortable with Holmes's forceful tactics with the moneylender. The moment passed, however, and Holmes was so full of pride in his success that he did not notice her discomfort. I had to reassure her later that Mr. Holmes would, somehow, see that Butters did not in the end escape punishment.

"But if I have had some slight success in my case," continued Holmes, "you had a veritable triumph in yours yesterday, Watson. I must congratulate you again, with all my heart. You uncovered, produced and presented the evidence in a most professional and masterful way. You too, Miss Rivas. Only two of the four and twenty voted for a verdict of guilty, and one of those was qualified. Very well done, both of you."

He beamed benediction upon us, and pretended solemnly to draw a sword, and to touch with it my shoulder, and then Miss Rivas's shoulder.

"At the very least, you have both most certainly earned your spurs as historians, detectives and orators. You have established that no court could or would convict Richard today on the evidence against him. And you have clearly shown that the picture we and others have of Richard today is very largely distorted and twisted.

"Richard would be a free man, thanks to you both. *Fiat justitia.*"

"Let justice be done," I echoed.

"Although," I added, "I do not think that Miss Rivas is actually permitted to wear a knight's spurs, even if she well deserves the honour."

As we laughed, we heard our landlady answer the front door. "Masterman-Pugh was to take an early train," said I. "That may be he."

I was proved right. The lanky professor joined us at the table.

"I promised to call this morning for my accounting," said he, solemnly.

With a gentle flourish, I extracted it from my desk and presented it to him. Without more than a glance at it, he wrote out a cheque for the full amount in his meticulous script.

"Doctor Watson," said he, "I must say that I have rarely felt my money better spent. I forced you into your mission with a cynical and most impolite lack of faith in you, for which I once more heartily apologise. You have more than shown me how insulting and demeaning I was. If you were one of my academic colleagues, I would be no less loud in my praise of your work. In my own school, too, history was the endless regurgitation of dates. You have well proven the validity of the remark of Clements Markham, that history is not dates, but what happened between the dates.

"On the train up, I wondered if we should have treated the case under a different standard of proof. We looked at it as a criminal case, with the onus being upon the prosecution to prove 'guilt beyond reasonable doubt'. I asked myself if we should have approached it with the lesser legal standard of 'balance of probability'. However, the greater onus was my own idea, since Richard was charged with murder. And our jury quite rightly found him not guilty under it.

"Further, if we were to apply the lower standard of probability, I now believe, upon much reflection, that we would have had to acquit Richard of virtually all of the crimes for which historians and the public hold him to blame."

Miss Rivas broke in. "The deaths of the Two Little Princes?"

Masterman-Pugh frowned. "On the balance of probability? That we may have to debate for a further four hundred years. It is hard to shake off the argument that the boys went into the Tower under Richard's *aegis*, and were never seen again. I am myself prepared to give Richard the benefit of the doubt, for now, but can certainly understand those who do not.

"The one crime for which I find him unarguably guilty is the execution of Hastings. That was clearly illegal; a planned murder. As well, the executions of Rivers, Grey and Vaughan were of at least doubtful legality. By today's standards, anyway; although perhaps the rules *were* different four hundred years ago.

"However, all in all, I am forced to agree that, in so many of the charges against Richard, the so-called evidence, as amassed by our historians and writers, really comprises very little 'evidence' at all. It is clear that the entire legend of Richard is rife with speculation, interpretation, propaganda, bias, and wishful thinking; and very little 'evidence'."

Masterman-Pugh nodded to me.

"Two fundamental points that you have made ring true, Doctor Watson. The first is when you spoke of history under the Tudors starting with innuendo, innuendo becoming accepted as truth, this so-called truth becoming embellished with fictitious detail; and finally, as you put it, historical fable thus becoming accepted fact.

"The second is the finding that you attributed, I recall, to your Mr. Hornidge. The world has of Richard a distorted picture, painted by More with the brushes of prejudice and hearsay, touched up by Henry the Seventh's agent Polydore Virgil, spuriously embellished by Hall and Holinshed, and finally re-cast and put on show as pure entertainment by Shakespeare. Most unsatisfactory.

"So the verdict rightly stands: King Richard the Third is not guilty."

I am sure that I looked as proud and embarrassed as I felt, particularly when Miss Rivas and Holmes spontaneously began to clap. Masterman-Pugh glanced at Holmes.

"Holmes has told me that you intend to offer at least one of his cases as light reading for the masses. If so, I shall make every effort to join your audience. I trust that you will take this promise as intended, as a compliment to you. Will you now turn this little foray into history into such a popular tale?"

"I had not thought of it," I replied, "but perhaps I will set pen to paper. I certainly have voluminous notes to assist me. First, however, I intend to take the well earned holiday that I have so far been denied."

Holmes looked at Miss Rivas and me with a kindly and knowing twinkle in his eyes.

"Oxford, Watson?"

"York, Holmes. York. *Fiat justitia.*

Postscript

As Chapter 14 notes, after his death at the Battle of Bosworth, Richard III was reported buried in Leicester, in the priory church of the Grey Friars.

The church was later demolished. Richard's gravesite thus became unmarked and unknown. A story spread that his grave had been desecrated, and that his bones had been thrown into the River Soar.

Historians did not endorse that tale, however. And in 2009, British screenwriter Philippa Langley, a longtime member of the UK's Richard III Society, sparked and spearheaded a three-year drive to search for Richard's remains. Funds were raised from Ricardians around the world, and in August 2012 a team of archaeologists and experts from the University of Leicester began a professional excavation and scientific investigation.

Langley was instinctively sure that Richard was buried beneath what is now a parking lot in Leicester, above which the Grey Friars church had once stood. On August 25th, 2012, in the archaeologists' first trench in that parking lot, skeletal remains were found. Later, DNA samples were taken from it.

And in February 2013, that DNA proved to match with DNA samples from two current descendants of Richard III's family. The skeleton was indeed that of Richard III.

The skeleton showed Richard suffered from spinal curvature, characteristic of scoliosis. This could have affected his stance – and thus no doubt gave rise to the popular but unproven belief that he had a hunchback.

A forensic reconstruction based on his skull produced a face that could have been recognizable to Richard's contemporaries.

Read about the exploration and investigation (and see Richard III's 'new face') on the website (www.richardiii.net) of the Richard III Society of the U.K.

Author's Afterword

Oddly, this book was *not* sparked by Josephine Tey's *The Daughter of Time*, in which a fictional modern detective investigates the accusations against Richard III. The idea came when the late Jeremy Potter, then a very-much-alive chairman of the Richard III Society in England, invited to a society dinner a guest from the Sherlock Holmes Society of London.

Since 1951, though, Tey's entertaining book *(The MacMillan Company, New York, 1951)* has generated huge interest in Richard and his era.

Much research, writing and re-interpretation on the history of Richard III and his era was done in the last century. One important medieval document, the account of Dominic Mancini, an Italian cleric, was not discovered until 1934. It was published in 1936, and persuaded some subsequent writers to be less charitable towards Richard. It was something of a challenge, therefore, to write this book, which is set in 1883, using only historical facts, documents and interpretations that were known in 1883. I have attempted to do so with accuracy and balance.

Most of the Victorian characters in the book truly lived in 1883; only a handful are my creations. Masterman-Pugh is a fictional character whom I have inserted into a very real Magdalen College. All other Magdalen men cited were there in 1883, in the positions described. Their conversations and letters I have obviously invented. Callie Rivas of York did not exist in 1883. But Clements Markham and James Gairdner were alive indeed. While their conversations with Dr. Watson are my constructs, their arguments are theirs as reflected in their published works. Yeoman Warder Henry Baker's fictional role as an amateur historian stems from the true-life role of Yeoman Warder Brian Harrison at the Tower of London in the 1990s; but Baker certainly lived and worked at the Tower in 1883, as did Yeoman Warder Watson. So did General Milman as their commanding officer. As described, Marmaduke Hornidge lived at Milbourne House in Barnes in 1883; I have chosen to make him into a student of Shakespeare and a friend of the Watson family.

Finally: Were Sherlock Holmes and Dr. Watson "real"? That I leave to you …

Acknowledgments

Thanks are due to many people who helped me in my researches. Among them are Anthony Smith as president and a gracious host at Magdalen College, Oxford; Dr. Janie Cottis, Magdalen archivist; Yeoman Warder Brian Harrison for generous assistance and notes about the Tower as it was in 1883, and his wife Mary for a warm welcome to their home in the Middle Tower; John Paul, for a gift of research material; stalwarts Peter and Caroline Hammond of the Richard III Society in London; my former wife Barbara Sigerson, for her endless support and patience, her foot-slogging around Oxford, York and London and her enthusiastic digging in the Oxford Public Library; and to my late stepfather, Philip King, for valuable research into ancient Army records in the Public Record Office at Kew.

Spellings

I have used Victorian spellings suitable to 1883. For example, 'sergeant' (a spelling that dates only from the First World War) is given as the Victorian 'serjeant'. Similarly, I use 'gaol' and 'gaoler' rather than 'jail' and 'jailer'; 'alarum' instead of 'alarm', 'waggon' instead of 'wagon', etc. Sticking to such purist Victorian spelling, I have used 'recognise', 'apologise' and 'theorise' rather than 'recognize', 'apologize' and 'theorize', and so on; although the *The Strand Magazine*, in which so many Holmesian adventures were published, used both 's' and 'z' versions unpredictably.

In the matter of historical names, spelling was and is a remarkable challenge. Medieval documents used a creative variety of spellings; there were then few agreed spellings or conventions. The major writers consulted by Dr. Watson and Miss Rivas in 1883 often did not agree on spellings, either. Thus, for example, we typically have a surname given variously as Sha, Shaa and Shaw in assorted documents and books.

Where Victorian writers James Gairdner, Caroline Halsted and Clements Markham disagreed, I have normally gone with their majority choice of spellings. Thus the book uses Nevill, Tyrrel, Woodville, Virgil, Fabyan, Rous, and De Comines; while Nevil, Neville, Tyrrell, Wydville, Vergil, Fabian, Rows, De Commines and De Commynes were also commonly used then, and often still are today.

English

I have generally used modern punctuation, to make life easier for the reader. But I have stuck to some Victorian English rules for authenticity. For example, collective nouns are plurals, rather than the singular better known to North American readers. Thus we have 'The army are' (rather than 'is'), 'The court were' (rather than 'was'), etc. And the possessives of words ending in 'S' are given in Victorian fashion: 'Holmes's' and 'Hastings's' (rather than today's more common 'Holmes' and 'Hastings').

I have started many sentences with 'And' and 'But'; again to make life easier for the modern reader. Purists will insist that this is, and was, improper. In fact, it *was* done in some Victorian writing, but rarely, and was most certainly frowned upon by purists.

A note to devoted Holmesians

I have taken only a few and, I think, pardonable liberties with the Canon. Mr. Holmes's embezzlement case is not mentioned in any of the 60 stories, but we know that there were many unrecorded cases. Some details of Dr. Watson's school and personal background are my own creations, including his charitable work in the East End and his acquaintanceship with Robert Louis Stevenson. But I have proposed nothing ringingly un-canonical – assuming, that is, that you can accept that the good English doctor had some distant Highland ancestors. (I note that author Dorothy L. Sayers proposed that Dr. Watson had Scottish ancestors, although she declared that they were not of Highland stock.)

In the age-old Sherlockian debate as to whether Mr. Holmes attended Oxford or Cambridge, I have obviously plumped for Oxford (and there is, of course, some canonical evidence for that.)

Websites

Like to know more about Richard III online, and Richard III societies? Check out these places:

Richard III Society (UK)
www.richardiii.net

Richard III Society (UK) on Facebook
www.facebook.com/pages/RICHARD-III-
SOCIETY/114452911904874

Richard III Society (American branch)
www.r3.org

Richard III Society of Canada
home.cogeco.ca/~richardiii

Richard III Society of New South Wales (Australia)
www.richardiii-nsw.org.au

Richard III Society, New Zealand
www.richard3nz.org

What is *your* verdict?

Now that you have heard the case for and against Richard, what is *your* verdict, and why?   Please e-mail me at: donmacrichard3@gmail.com, or take part in discussion on the Facebook page listed above.

Selected Bibliography

For those interested in further reading, these are the main sources I consulted:

Peter Ackroyd, *The Life of Thomas More*, Chatto & Windus, London, 1998.

Bernard André, *Historia Regis Henrici Septimi*, James Gairdner, ed., Rolls Series, London, 1858.

John Ashdown-Hill, *The Last Days of Richard III*, The History Press, Stroud, Gloucester, 2010.

Francis Bacon, *The History of the Reign of King Henry the Seventh*, The Folio Society, London, 1971.

David Baldwin, Richard III, Amberley Publishing, Stroud, Gloucester, 2012.

John Bayley, *History and Antiquities of the Tower of London*, Jennings & Chaplin, London, 1830.

Walter G. Bell, *The Tower of London*, Duckworth, London, 1935.

B.J. Bradley, *Richard III-The Black Legend*, Winding Road Publishers, United States, 2007.

J. Bruce, ed., *Historie of the Arrivall of Edward IV in England and the Finall Recoverye of his Kingdomes from Henry VI, A.D. 1471*, Camden Society, London, 1838.

George Buck, *The History of the Life and Reigne of Richard the Third*, EP Publishing Ltd., York, 1973.

R.M. Butler, *The Bars and Walls of York*, Yorkshire Architectural and York Archaeological Society, York, 1974.

Col. E.H. Carkeet-James, *Her Majesty's Tower of London*, Staples Press Limited, London, 1950.

Annette Carson, *Richard III: the Maligned King*, The History Press, Stroud, Gloucester, 2008.

Fred H. Cate and David C. Williams, eds., *The Trial of Richard III*, Indiana University School of Law-Bloomington, Bloomington Indiana, 1997.

John Charlton, ed., *The Tower of London: its Buildings and Institutions*, Her Majesty's Stationery Office, London, 1978.

Anthony Cheetham, *The Life and Times of Richard III*, George Weidenfeld and Nicolson Limited and Book Club Associates, London, 1972.

Mary Clive, *This Sun of York*, Macmillan London Ltd., London, 1973.

Philippe de Commynes, *Memoires*, J.L.A. Calmette and G. Durville, eds., 3 vols., Classiques de l'Histoire de France au Moyen Age, Paris, 1924-5.

L. Cope Cornford, *Robert Louis Stevenson*, William Blackwood and Sons, Edinburgh and London, 1899.

Thomas Costain, *The Last Plantagenets*, Doubleday & Company Inc., New York, 1962.

Caroline Crimp and Mary Grimwade, *Milbourne House, Barnes*, Barnes & Mortlake Historical Society, London, 1978.

Robert Davies, ed., *Extracts from the Municipal Records of the City of York During the Reigns of Edward IV., Edward V., and Richard III.*, Gloucester Reprints, Dursley, 1976.

Keith Dockray, *Richard III: A Reader in History*, Alan Sutton Publishing Limited, Gloucester, 1988.

Richard Drewett and Mark Redhead, *The Trial of Richard III*, Alan Sutton Publishing Limited, Gloucester, 1984.

Rhoda Edwards, *The Itinerary of King Richard III 1483-1485*, Alan Sutton Publishing Limited, Gloucester, for The Richard III Society, 1983.

Henry Ellis, ed., *Three Books of Polydore Vergil's English History*, Camden Society, London, 1844.

Robert Fabyan, *The New Chronicles of England and France, in Two Parts*, (Henry Ellis, ed.), F.C. & J. Rivington, London, 1811.

Bertram Fields, *Royal Blood*, ReganBooks/Harper Collins, New York, 1998.

Plantagenet Somerset Fry, *The Tower of London: Cauldron of Britain's Past*, Quiller Press Ltd., London, 1990.

James Gairdner, *Life and Reign of Richard the Third*, Longmans, Green and Co., London, 1878.

James Gairdner, *Henry the Seventh*, Macmillan and Co., London, 1889.

Louise Gill, *Richard III and Buckingham's Rebellion*, Sutton Publishing, Stroud, Gloucester, 1999.

Gillingham, John, ed., *Richard III: A Medieval Kingship*, Collins and Brown, London, 1993.

Edward Hall, *The Union of the Two Noble and Illustre Families of Lancaster and York*, Henry Ellis, ed., Camden Society, London, 1812.

Elizabeth Hallam, ed., *The Chronicles of the Wars of the Roses*, Penguin Books Canada Limited, Markham Ontario, 1988.

Elizabeth Hallam, ed., *The Plantagenet Encyclopedia*, Penguin Books Canada Ltd., Markham Ontario, 1990.

Caroline A. Halsted, *Richard III as Duke of Gloucester and King of England*, 2 vols., Longman, Brown, Green and Longmans, London, 1844.

P.W. Hammond and Anne F. Sutton, *Richard III: The Road to Bosworth Field*, Constable and Company Limited, London, 1985.

P.W. Hammond, ed., *Richard III: Loyalty, Lordship and Law*, Alan Sutton Publishing Limited, Gloucester, for The Richard III and Yorkist History Trust, 1986.

Alison Hanham, *Richard III and His Early Historians*, Clarendon Press, Oxford, 1975.

Peter A. Hancock, *Richard III and the Murder in the Tower*, The History Press, Stroud, Gloucester, 2009.

Dennis Hay, ed., *The Anglica Historia A.D. 1485-1487 of Polydore Vergil*, Butler & Tanner Ltd., London, 1950.

Christopher Hibbert, *The Tower of London*, The Reader's Digest Association Limited, London, 1971.

Michael Hicks, Anne Neville: Queen to Richard III, The History Press, Stroud, Gloucester, 2006.

Michael Hicks, *Richard III: The Man Behind the Myth*, Collins and Brown Limited, London, 1991.

Michael Hicks, *Richard III and His Rivals*, Hambledon Press, London, 1991.

David Hipshon, *Richard III*, Routledge (Taylor and Francis Group), Abingdon (Oxon) and New York, 2011.

Rosemary Horrocks and P.W. Hammond, eds., *British Library Harleian Manuscript 433*, Vols. 1-4, Alan Sutton Publishing Limited, Gloucester, 1980.

Elizabeth Jenkins, *The Princes in the Tower*, Hamish Hamilton Limited, London, 1978.

Paul Murray Kendall, *Richard the Third*, W.W. Norton & Company Inc., New York, 1955.

Paul Murray Kendall, *The Yorkist Age: Daily Life during the Wars of the Roses*, W.W. Norton & Company Inc., New York, 1962.

Paul Murray Kendall, *Warwick the Kingmaker*, George Allen & Unwin Ltd., London, 1957.

Anthony Kenny, *Thomas More*, Oxford University Press, Oxford, 1983.

D. M. Kleyn, *Richard of England*, Kensal Press, Oxford, 1990.

V.B. Lamb, *The Betrayal of Richard III*, Alan Sutton Publishing Limited, Gloucester, 1990.

J.R. Lander, *The Wars of the Roses*, Alan Sutton Publishing Limited, Gloucester, 1992.

Philip Lindsay, *King Richard III*, Ivor Nicholson and Watson, London 1933.

Taylor Littleton and Robert R. Rea, eds., *To Prove a Villain: The Case of King Richard III*, The MacMillan Company, New York, 1966.

Dominic Mancini, *The Usurpation of Richard III*, C.A.J. Armstrong ed. and tr., Alan Sutton Publishing Limited, Gloucester, 1989.

Richard Marius, *Thomas More*, Vintage Books, Alfred A. Knopf Inc., New York, 1984.

Sir Clements R. Markham, *Richard III: His Life & Character*, Smith, Elder & Co. Ltd., London, 1906.

Kenneth J. Mears, *The Tower of London: 900 Years of English History*, Phaidon Press Limited, Oxford, 1988.

R. J. Minney, *The Tower of London*, Prentice Hall Inc., Englewood NJ, 1970.

Dorothy Mitchell, *Richard III and York*, Silver Boar Publishers, York, 1983.

Thomas More, *History of King Richard III*, in Paul Murray Kendall, ed., *Richard III: The Great Debate*, W. W. Norton and Company, The Folio Society, London, 1965.

Thomas More, *The History of King Richard III*, Richard S. Sylvester, ed., in *The Yale Edition of the Complete Works of St. Thomas More*, Vol. 2, Yale University Press, New Haven, 1963.

Allardyce Nicoll and Josephine Nicoll, eds., *Holinshed's Chronicle as Used in Shakespeare's Plays*, J.M. Dent & Sons Ltd., London, 1927.

John Julius Norwich, *Shakespeare's Kings*, Viking, London, 1999.

James Petre, ed., *Richard III: Crown and People*, Alan Sutton Publishing Limited, Gloucester, for The Richard III Society, 1985.

A.J. Pollard, *Richard III and The Princes in the Tower*, Alan Sutton Publishing Limited, Gloucester 1991.

Jeremy Potter, *Good King Richard?*, Constable and Company Ltd., London, 1983.

Nicholas Pronay and John Cox, eds., *The Crowland Chronicle Continuations: 1459-1486*, Alan Sutton Publishing Limited, Gloucester, for Richard III and Yorkist History Trust, 1986.

The Ricardian: Journal of The Richard III Society, numerous editions since 1979.

Charles Ross, *Richard III*, University of California Press, Berkeley and Los Angeles, 1983.

Charles Ross, *Edward IV*, University of California Press, Berkeley and Los Angeles, 1974.

H.T. Riley, ed. and tr., *Ingulph's Chronicle of the Abbey of Croyland*, Bohn's Antiquarian Library, London, 1854.

Charles Ross, *Edward IV*, University of California Press, Berkeley and Los Angeles, 1984.

Charles Ross, *The Wars of the Roses*, Thames and Hudson, London, 1986.

A.L. Rowse, *Bosworth Field*, Doubleday & Company Inc., New York, 1966.

A.L. Rowse, *The Tower of London in the History of the Nation*, Weidenfeld and Nicolson Limited, London, 1972.

Desmond Seward, *Richard III: England's Black Legend*, Franklin Watts Inc., New York, 1984.

Desmond Seward, *The Hundred Years War*, Atheneum, New York, 1978.

Giles St. Aubyn, *The Year of Three Kings 1483*, Atheneum, New York, 1983.

A.H. Thomas and I. D. Thornley, eds., *The Great Chronicle of London*, George W. Jones, London, 1938.

Pamela Tudor-Craig, Richard III, National Portrait Gallery, London,1973.

Sharon Turner, *The History of England During the Middle Ages*, 3 vols., Longman, Rees, Orme, Brown and Green, London, 1830.

Polydore Vergil, *The Anglica Historia A.D.1485-1537 of Polydore Vergil,* Denys Hay, ed., Butler & Tanner Ltd. London, 1950.

Horace Walpole, *Historic Doubts on the Life and Reign of Richard the Third*, Alan Sutton Publishing Limited, Gloucester,1987.

John Warkworth, *A Chronicle of the First Thirteen Years of the Reign of King Edward the Fourth*, J.O. Halliwell, ed., Camden Society, London, 1839.

Alison Weir, *The Princes in the Tower*, The Bodley Head, London, 1992.

Alison Weir, *Lancaster and York*, Jonathan Cape Random House, London, 1995.

Audrey Williamson, *The Mystery of the Princes*, Alan Sutton Publishing Limited, Gloucester, 1981.

Derek Wilson, *The Tower: The Tumultuous History of the Tower of London from 1078*, Charles Scribner's Sons, New York, 1979.

Maj.-Gen. Sir George Younghusband, *A Short History of the Tower of London*, Herbert Jenkins Limited, London, 1926.

Titulus Regius

And here for history buffs is the text of *Titulus Regius* ("Title of the King") the Parliamentary document that established Richard's title as king.

To the High and Myghty Prince Richard Duc of Gloucester.

"Please it youre Noble Grace to understande the consideracon, election, and petition of us the lords spiritual and temporal and commons of this reame of England, and thereunto agreably to geve your assent, to the common and public wele of this lande, to the comforts and gladnesse of all the people of the same.

"First, we considre how that heretofore in tyme passed this lande many years stode in great prosperite, honoure, and tranquillite, which was caused, foresomuch as the kings then reignyng used and followed the advice and counsaill of certaine lords speulx and temporelx, and othre personnes of approved sadnesse, prudence, policie, and experience, dreading God, and havyng tendre zele and affection to indifferent ministration of justice, and to the comon and politique wele of the land; then our Lord God was dred, luffed (loved), and honoured; then within the land was peace and tranquillite, and among neghbors concorde and charite; then the malice of outward enemyes was mightily repressed and resisted, and the land honourably defended with many grete and glorious victories; then the entrecourse of merchandizes was largely used and exercised; by ehich things above remembered, the land was greatly enriched soo that as wele the merchants and artificers as other poor people, laboryng for their lyvyng in diverse occupations, had competent gayne to the sustentation of thaym and their households, livyng without miserable and intolerable povertie. But afterward, when that such as had the rule and governaunce of this land, deliting in adulation and flattery and lede by sensuality and concupiscence, followed the counsaill of persons insolent, vicious, and of inordinate avarice, despising the counsaill of good, vertuous, and prudent personnes such as above be remembred, the prosperite of this land dailie decreased soo that felicite was turned into miserie, and prosperite into adversite, and the ordre of polecye, and of the law of God and man, confounded; whereby it is likely this reame to falle into extreme miserie and desolation, - which God defende, - without due provision of convenable remedie bee had in this behalfe in all godly hast.

"Over this, amonges other thinges, more specifially we consider howe that the tyme of the raigne of King Edward IV, late decessed, after the ungracious pretensed marriage, as all England hath cause to say, made betwitx the said King edward IV and Elizabeth, sometyme wife to Sir John Grey, Knight, late nameing herself and many years heretofore Queene of England, the ordre of all politeque rule was perverted, the laws of God and of Gode's church, and also the lawes of nature, and of England, and also the laudable customes and liberties of the same, wherein every Englishman is inheritor, broken, subverted, and contempned, against all reason and justice, so that this land was ruled by self-will and pleasure, feare and drede, all manner of equite and lawes layd apart and despised, whereof ensued many inconvenients and mischiefs, as murdres, estortions, and oppressions, namely of pooe and impotent people, so that no man was sure of his lif, land, ne lyuvelode, ne of his wif, doughter, no servannt, every good maiden and woman standing in drede to be ravished and defouled. And besides this, what discords, inward battailes, effusion of Christian men's blode, and namely, by the destruction of the noble blode of this lond, was had and comitted within the same, it is evident and notarie through all this reaume unto the grete sorrowe and heavynesse of all true Englishmen. And here also we considre howe the said pretensed marriage, betwitx the above named King Edward the Elizabeth Grey, was made of grete presumption, without the knowyng or assent of the lords of this londe, and alsoe by sorcerie and wiche-crafte, committed by the said Elizabeth and her moder, Jacquett Duchess of Bedford, as the common opinion of the peole and the publique voice, and fame is through all this land; and hereafter, if and as the case shall require, shall bee proved sufficiently intyme and place convenient. And here also we considre how that the said pretenced marriage was made privately and secretly, with edition of banns, in a private chamber, a profane place, and not openly in the face of the church, aftre the laws of Godd's churche, but contrarie thereunto, and the laudable custome of the Churche of England. And how also, that at the tyme of the contract of the same pretensed marriage, and bifore and longe tyme after, the saide King Edw was and stood marryed and troth plyght to oone Dame Elianor Butteler, doughter of the old Earl of Shrewsbury, with whom the said King Edward had made a precontracte of matronie, long tyme bifore he made the said pretensed mariage with the said Elizabeth Grey in manner and fourme aforesaid. Which premises being true, as in veray trouth they been true, it appeareth and followeth evidently, that the said King Edward duryng his lyfe and the said Elizabeth lived together sinfully and dampnably in adultery, against the lawe of God and his church; and therefore noe marvaile that the souverain lord and head of this londe, being of such ungodly disposicion, and provokyng the ire and indignation of oure Lorde God, such haynous mischiefs and inconvenients as is above remember, were used and committed in the reame amongst the subjects. Also it appeareth evidently and followeth that all th'issue and children of the said king been bastards, and unable to inherite or to clayme anything by inheritance, by the lawe and custome of England.

"Moreover we consider howe that afterward, by the thre estates of this reame assembled in a parliament holden at Westminster the 17th. yere of the regne of the said King Edward theiiijth, he than being in possession of the coroune and roiall estate, by an acte made in the same parliament, George Duc of Clarence, brother to the said King Edward now decessed, was convicted and attainted of high treason; as in the same acte is conteigned more at large. Because and by treason whereof all the issue of the said George was and is disables and barred of all right and clayme that in any wise they might have or challenge by inheritance to the crowne and roiall dignitie of this reame, by the auncien lawe and custome of this same reame.

"Over this we consider howe that ye be the undoubted sonne and heire Richard late Duke of Yorke verray enheritour to the said crowne and dignitie roiall and as in right Kyng of Englond by way to enheritaunce and that at this time the premisses duelly considered there is noon other peron lyving but ye only, that by right may clayme the said coroune and dignitie roiall, by way of enhertiaunce, and how that ye be born within this lande, by reason whereof, as we deme in our myndes, ye be more naturally enclyned to the prosperitie and comen weal of the same: and all the three estates of the land have, and may have more certain knowledge of your birth and filiation above said. Wee considre also, the greate wytte, prudence, justice, princely courage, and the memorable and laudable acts in diverse battalls which we by experience know ye heretofore have done for the salvacion and defence of this same reame, and also the great noblesse and excellence of your byrth and blode as of hym that is descended of the thre most royal houses in Christendom, that is to say, England, Fraunce, and Hispaine.

"Wherefore these premisses by us diligently considered, we desyring affectuously the peas, tranquilitie and wele publique of this lande, and the reduction of the same to the auncien honourable estate, and prosperite, and havyng in your greate prudence, justice, princely courage and excellent virtue, singular confidence, have chosen in all that is in us is and by this our wrytyng choise you, high and myghty Prynce into our Kyng and souveraine lord &c., to whom we know for certayn it appertaneth of enheritaunce so to be choosen. And hereupon we humbly desire, pray, and require your said noble grace, that accordinge to this election of us the three estates of this lande, as by your true enheritaunce ye will accept and take upon you the said crowne and royall dignitie with all things thereunto annexed and apperteyning as to you of right belongyng as well by enheritaunce as by lawful election, and in case ye do so we promitte to serve and to assist your highnesse, as true and faithfull subjietz and liegemen and to lyve and dye with you in this matter and every other just quarrel. For certainly we bee determined rather to adventure and comitte us to the perill of our lyfs and jopardye of death, than to lyve in such thraldome and bondage as we have lyved long tyme heretofore, oppressed and injured by new extorcos and imposicons, agenst the lawes of God and man, and the liberte, old polce and lawes of this reame wherein every Englishman is inherited. Our Lorde God Kyng of all Kynges by whose infynyte goodnesse and eternall providence all thyngs have been pryncypally gouverned in this worlde lighten your soule, and graunt you grace to do, as well in this matter as in all other, all that may be accordyng to his will and pleasure, and to the comen and publique wele of this land, so that after great cloudes, troubles, stormes, and tempests, the son of justice and of grace may shyne uppon us, to the comforte and gladnesse of all true Englishmen.

"Albeit that the right, title, and estate, whiche our souverain lorde the Kynge Richard III hath to and in the crown and roiall dignite of this reame of England, with all things thereunto annexed and appertynyng, have been juste and lawefull, as grounded upon the lawes of God and of nature and also upon the auncien lawes and laudable customes of this said reame, and so taken and reputeed by all such personnes as ben lerned in the above-saide laws and custumes. Yet, neverthelesse, forasmoche as it is considred that the most parte of the people of this lande is not suffisiantly lerned in the abovesaid lawes and customes whereby the trueth and right in this behalf of liklyhode may be hyd, and not clerely knowen to all the people and thereupon put in doubt and question: And over this howe that the courte of Parliament is of suche autorite, and the people of this lande of suche nature and disposicion, as experience teacheth that maifestation and declaration of any trueth or right made by the thre estats of this reame assembled in parliament, and by auctorite of the same maketh before all other thyng, moost faith and certaintie; and quietyng men's myndes, remoweth the occasion of all doubts and seditious language:

"Therefore at the request, and by the assent of the three estates of this reame, that is to say, the lords spuelx and temporalx and comens of this lande, assembled in this present parliament by auctorite of the same, bee it pronounced, decreed and declared, that our said souveraign lorde the kinge was and is veray and undoubted kyng of this reame of Englond; with all thyngs thereunto within this same reame, and without it annexed unite and apperteynyng, as well by right of consanguinite and enheritance as by lawful election, consecration and coronacion. And over this, that at the request, and by the assent and autorite abovesaide bee it ordeigned, enacted and established that the said crowne and roiall dignite of this reame, and the inheritaunce of the same, and other thyngs thereunto within the same reame or without it annexed, unite, and now apperteigning, rest and abyde in the person of our said souveraign lord the kyng during his lyfe, and after his decesse in his heires of his body begotten. And in especiall, at the request and by the assent and auctorite abovesaid, bee it ordeigned, enacted, established, pronounced, decreed and declared that the high and excellent Prince Edward, sone of our said souveraign lorde the Kyng, be heire apparent of our said souveraign lorde the kyng, to succeed hym in the abovesaid crown and roiall dignite, with all thyngs as is aforesaid thereunto unite annexed and apperteignyng, to have them after the decease of our saide souveraign lorde the kyng to hym and to his heires of his body lawfully begotten."

Lightning Source UK Ltd.
Milton Keynes UK
UKOW05f2020020514

231000UK00001B/16/P

9 781901 091595